Beyond the
Burn Line

Beyond the Burn Line

PAUL McAULEY

First published in Great Britain in 2022 by Gollancz
an imprint of The Orion Publishing Group Ltd
Carmelite House, 50 Victoria Embankment
London EC4Y 0DZ

An Hachette UK Company

1 3 5 7 9 10 8 6 4 2

A CIP catalogue record for this book is
available from the British Library.

ISBN (HB) 978 1 399 60371 3
ISBN (ETPB) 978 1 399 60848 0
ISBN (eBook) 978 1 399 60373 7
ISBN (audio) 978 1 399 60374 4

Typeset by Born Group
Printed and bound in Great Britain by Clays Ltd, Elcograf S.p.A.

www.gollancz.co.uk

'Who shall compute what effects have been produced,
and are still, and into deep Time, producing?'
Thomas Carlyle

Part One

Archaeologies of Memory

1.

Three days after Master Able's body was committed to the Mother, a notary appointed by the Office of Last Things met with the old scholar's secretary. Settlement of the estate was in hand; it was time to discuss disbursements and distributions.

'My master's kin gave me a letter setting out terms at the committal,' the secretary, Pilgrim Saltmire, said. 'Including a demand that I quit the house without delay, since my services are no longer required.'

'They should not have approached you directly,' the notary said, with a grimace of professional displeasure. 'So I told Master Able's brother after he admitted to it. As for the quit notice, I may be able to allow you a few days' grace. An inventory must be made and approved, and I can see that it will be no small task.'

They were talking in Master Able's study. A small oval room like a chamber of a stilled heart, lined with specimen cases and book racks, and lit by a single pole lantern draped with a red silk scarf. The notary, a stout, middle-aged person with a precise, patient manner, was perched on the edge of the couch where Master Able had taken his customary afternoon nap. Pilgrim stood before him like a supplicant, leaning on his cane and dressed in the long white shirt, carefully ripped in several places, that signified bereavement and mourning.

'And what about my master's work? The work that is still unfinished?' he said, gesturing towards the low table that squatted in the centre of the room, covered with stacks of books and monographs, letters and loose papers. A fossil coilshell held open the pages of a weighty volume. A saucer caked with dried green ink sat next to a half-empty box of inkstones and a translucent horn cylinder packed with drip pens. It was hard for Pilgrim to think that only he now knew the secret order and significance of this shrine and storehouse, these accoutrements and extensions of his master's marvellous mind. The magnifying lens with which he had scrutinised specimens; the case of measuring callipers; his hand abacus, its black and white stones arranged in his last calculation. A faint ghost of his musty scent haunted the air and the goatskin hassock beside the table was still indented by the weight and shape of his body. Pilgrim had found him sprawled next to it after he had been struck by the thunderbolt to his brain, his breathing harsh and irregular, his eyes open and glassy, pupils different sizes, a book splayed like a broken bird by his head.

'The terms of the settlement are quite straightforward,' the notary was saying. 'Certain books and specimens are to be gifted to the Library of All People. Perhaps you would help me to find them. The rest of his material possessions, including manuscripts, notes and other personal papers, will pass to his brother and his sisters.'

Pilgrim had anticipated this moment. He pulled a folded sheet of paper from his wallet and said, 'According to this, it may not be quite as straightforward as you think.'

'It's far too late to raise an objection to the settlement,' the notary said. 'Especially by someone not related to the deceased.'

'It's a short note my master wrote on his death bed. He was insensible for most of the time, but rallied in his last hours and was able to set down a request that I should be given everything I need to finish his work. His handwriting was affected by the injury to his brain,' Pilgrim said, his heart beating quick and high as he watched the notary unfold the sheet of paper. 'But he signed and dated it, and embossed it with his stamp.'

The notary pinched a pair of spectacles over his snout and read the note carefully, holding it close to his face in the dim red light, then sat back and studied Pilgrim for a moment. 'Its intent is clear. Unfortunately, since it lacks a countersignature by an independent witness, it has no standing in law.'

'It was my master's last wish,' Pilgrim said. 'And I will need very little to carry it out. A small allowance to support me. Travelling expenses for research. No more than a year's salary, all told. And access to the relevant books and papers, of course. I have made a list.'

'Apart from you, was anyone else present when this note was written?' the notary said.

'My master's physic visited several times. A few of his friends and colleagues paid their respects, but did not stay long. The rest of the time I cared for him as best I could, helped by his homekeeper. But she was out on an errand when my master woke, and made signs asking for pen and paper.'

The notary took off his spectacles and refolded the note and set it on top of the sheaf of papers beside him. 'Since there was no independent witness, I cannot accept this as a variation of the terms of the settlement. The best I can do is pass it to his kin and ask if they wish to honour it.'

There had been just two representatives from Master Able's family at the committal on the bare hilltop at the edge of the city. Able's eldest brother and one of his nephews, dressed in mourning shirts of much finer quality than Pilgrim's, standing

5

a little way apart from the sparse gathering of friends and colleagues, and like them holding smouldering sweetwood branches and chanting the ancient prayers while two knife-workers prepared the body for the carrion birds. Afterwards, Able's brother had watched while the nephew had given Pilgrim the notice to quit, and both had left immediately afterwards, without a word to anyone else.

'Given the circumstances, I would think that honouring the spirit of the note is more important than any law,' Pilgrim said.

'I wish I could help you,' the notary said. 'But the regulations of my office make no allowance for that kind of flexibility.'

Pilgrim knew that it was not the notary's fault, but for a moment his anger and disappointment poked through.

'The opinion of my master's kin and tribe is worthless. They were happy to bask in the glow of his reputation in earlier days, but quick to join the chorus of naysayers and jealous rivals who mocked him.'

'Because of this business of the visitors,' the notary said.

'I suppose his brother told you about it.'

'I find it helps to know a little about the deceased.'

'His kin claimed that his work on the visitors had made him a laughing stock and sullied their own standing, and when he refused to give it up they cut off his stipend, out of spite. He wanted me to have the means to finish it. To prove them wrong. To find out what the visitors are, if they are real. To consider what it says about us if they turn out to be some kind of common delusion.'

'How long did you serve as Master Able's secretary?'

Pilgrim touched the pendant that rested on the laces of his white shirt. Inside its amber teardrop a large black ant curled amongst a swirl of tiny bubbles, perfectly preserved by the resin which, seeping from a wound in the bark of a pine tree, had trapped it millions of years ago.

'He gave me this last summer's end, to commemorate five years' service.'

'You were close to him.'

'He could be difficult,' Pilgrim said. 'Obstinate, irascible, obsessed with his work. But he was also a brilliant scholar. The cleverest person I ever knew.'

The notary pressed the flat of his hand over the note. 'When I present this to his kin, I will have to explain that it has no legal standing. But I can also point out the unusual circumstances in which it was written, and ask them to take that into consideration.'

'They will be interested only in its legality.'

'Sometimes the jolt of a death prompts people to reassess their relationship with the deceased,' the notary said. 'So don't give up hope just yet.'

2.

'Able's kin refused to accept the amendment, of course,' Pilgrim told his friends Swift Singletree and Ardent Whitesand a few days later. 'And they didn't have the decency to tell me in person, or even by letter. No, they had the notary do their dirty work.'

'At least you won't be beholden to them,' Swift said.

'Even if it didn't have any legal standing, they shouldn't have disregarded a dying man's wishes,' Ardent said.

'I agree. Even though, strictly speaking, they didn't,' Pilgrim said.

'But the note— Hoy!'

Swift had cuffed Ardent around the back of the head.

'Have you forgotten how Master Able was, when we saw him last?' Swift said. He was a tall, sharp-muzzled person, dressed as usual in his black velvet surcoat, the nap worn smooth at cuffs and elbows. 'Did it look like he was going to wake up, call for pen and paper, and write down his last wishes?'

'You know that, but his kin didn't,' Pilgrim said. 'Since they failed to pay him a visit after he was struck down.'

'You wrote it?' Ardent said. 'I mean, you made it up?'

'I believe that it was what Able would have wanted,' Pilgrim said. 'Knowing him as I did.'

It was early evening. Pilgrim's last in Highwater Reach. He had written to his sister and his mother, giving them the news about Master Able's death and telling them that he was returning to the territory, and had used his meagre savings and the small amount of cash raised by selling most of his books to buy a ticket for the cross-continental train. He hoped that his mother, now a senior auntie, would support his plan to finish his master's last project, and that his grandfather, even though he was ailing and had recently moved into the Elders' Lodge, might also put in a good word.

Now, a few hours before the train was due to depart, Pilgrim had entrusted the remnants of his little library to his friends and they were sharing a bowl of mussels and drinking small beer at one of the stalls in the riverside cheap. Ardent Whitesand was assistant to a senior librarian, Swift Singletree a bookrunner who scraped a living by sourcing rare volumes for scholars and searching out misshelved books, manuscripts and hard-to-find oddities that fell outside the scope of the indexing system of the Library of All People. The three of them were united by their love of books and scholarship, by similarities in age and background (rural; hardscrabble) and because they identified as pures, those who were not affected by the urgent sexual heat which gripped men and women during the Season's carnival of attraction and desire in spring and early summer, and had no interest in what Swift called the low comedy of procreation.

'Doesn't the Library have a fund for cases like yours?' Ardent said as he cracked open the last of the mussels. Despite his bottomless appetite, he was a neat, slender person, carefully sucking up the morsel of flesh and plucking a square of cloth from the pocket of his brocade waistcoat and patting his lips.

'I looked into it,' Pilgrim said. 'And was told that only scholars are eligible.'

He had asked his master's friends and former pupils for help, too, but those few who had not criticised or condemned Able's work on the visitors had little or no funds to spare, and the rest had advised Pilgrim to move on. One, meaning it kindly, had said that the best way to honour Able was to let his last obsession die with him, and remember him for what he once was rather than what he had become. Another had told Pilgrim bluntly that a bright young fellow such as himself should not waste his time chasing ghosts and phantasms.

'What about the Sweetwater Collective?' Ardent said.

'They didn't send so much as a note of condolence after I informed them of Able's death,' Pilgrim said, with a little swell of bitterness. The Sweetwater Collective had been the only sponsor of Master Able's work on the visitors, and he'd hoped, desperately, foolishly, that they would help him, too.

'Shame on them,' Swift said.

'That's why, having tried everything else, I am reduced to asking my kin and tribe for support. There's also an idea about raising some funds of my own that I want to explore.'

'Don't be away too long,' Swift said. 'And don't you dare forget about us.'

'We'll miss you,' Ardent said, reaching across the table to grip Pilgrim's hands.

Ardent wasn't the quickest or cleverest of the three, but he was good-hearted and unstintingly generous. In some part, he'd be the first to admit, because he'd had an easier childhood than most pures, unblighted by prejudice and intolerance. Pilgrim and Swift had come of age in tribes which believed that what Pilgrim's mother had called 'the condition' was not part of the continuum of sexual orientation but a phase or a mental or physical defect, something which could be cured by trials of endurance, folk remedies, vigils at shrines and prayers and petitions to the Mother, but Ardent's tribe believed that

10

pures were especially blessed by the Mother's grace because they were unencumbered by base desires. Traditionally, they had served as seers or shrine keepers; Ardent had been sent to Highwater Reach to apprentice in the scholar trade so that he could take charge of the tribe's archives when he returned home.

Pilgrim was grateful for his friend's concern, told him that he would be back as soon as he had finished the work and written it up. 'Hopefully with enough money left over to pay for a small printing of a slender monograph.'

Ardent said, 'But who will agree to print it, if Able's kin owns the rights?'

'They own the rights to his manuscript, but the facts belong to everyone,' Pilgrim said, trying to look and sound as if he believed it. 'That's why I am going to re-interview witnesses and find as many new ones as I can.'

Swift's whiskers twitched when he smiled. 'A sweet little revenge for their disgraceful callousness.'

'This isn't about them,' Pilgrim said.

'Really?'

'Perhaps a little bit,' Pilgrim admitted. 'But mostly, I'm doing this for Able. He was trying to discover the truth about the visitors, and I want to finish what he began. Set it against the nonsense peddled by lunatics and charlatans. Speaking of which, Intrepid Windrush paid me a visit yesterday.'

Intrepid Windrush, a plausible opportunist who claimed to be the foremost expert in the matter of the visitors, had published a series of pamphlets promoting a former bear trapper turned preacher, Foeless Landwalker, who claimed to have communicated with the visitors in dreams and visions. He had arrived at Master Able's house uninvited and unannounced, expressing his sympathy for the great loss to what he called the community of the elect and offering to help

11

Pilgrim make the best use of the invaluable material Able had accumulated.

'I hope you told him exactly why you didn't need his help,' Swift said.

'I didn't say anything,' Pilgrim said. 'Just shut the door on him. Not quite fast enough – he managed to pitch a copy of his latest pamphlet through the gap.'

'If you haven't thrown it away, I wouldn't mind adding it to my small collection,' Ardent said.

'If you read too many of those things their crazy ideas will poison your mind,' Swift said.

'Their pathology is interesting,' Ardent said.

'It's banal,' Pilgrim said. 'Promises of empowerment and secret revelations peddled by pseudo-scholars who stitch stray facts into grand theories of everything. I added Intrepid's offering to the papers the notary will pass to Able's kin. Wrote on the cover that my master had been trying to make the world a better place by disproving this kind of foolishness.'

'Here's to him, and to you,' Swift said.

The three of them drank to that. For the tenth or twelfth time, Pilgrim looked at the coloured glass jars of the water clock that stood at the centre of the cheap's crossway.

Ardent said, 'I still don't understand this settlement business.'

'Why Able left everything to his kin? It was a condition of his stipend,' Pilgrim said. 'Even though they took it away from him, the condition still applied.'

'I mean the principle of it,' Ardent said. 'Why someone would gift their property and possessions to their immediate family, instead of allowing everyone in their tribe to benefit.'

'Do you still feel that you belong to your tribe?' Swift said.

'Of course.'

'Well I don't. And plenty of people who move from hearth and home to the cities don't either. Especially if they make their fortunes there.'

'It's a violation of the great harmony,' Ardent said.

'The rich believe they contribute to the great harmony by passing their wealth to their children, so that they can make even more,' Swift said.

'Able's kin want to suppress his work because they believe it taints his reputation, and theirs. I'm going to do my best to prove them wrong,' Pilgrim said, and drained his glass of small beer to the suds and banged it down on the table.

It was time to move on.

3.

Pilgrim Saltmire had arrived in Highwater Reach six years ago, with a trunk of clothes and books, and a case of fossils carefully packed in straw. It was the first time he had travelled outside the territory of his tribe. Thanks to his grandfather's recommendation, the celebrated scholar Master Able had hired him as his personal secretary, and he'd been brimming with giddy anticipation and foolish optimism.

Master Able had first won fame while he had still been a pupil of Master Hopestart, the natural philosopher who advanced the theory of selective change, which explained that the vast variety of plants and animals had developed from simpler organisms by the slow, cumulative acquisition of new characteristics. It had been denounced as heresy by priests and philosophers who claimed that because the form of every species was a perfect realisation of the Mother's will, no change was possible unless She desired it, and those changes were always accompanied by global catastrophe. The great flood which had destroyed the terror lizards; the cleansing fire which had put an end to the wickedness of ogres and left the narrow line of char found in sites all across the Union and United Territories; the plague which had turned bears into crazed beasts after they strayed from the right path. Master

Able had been at the forefront of debates which had over-turned those old beliefs, explaining the principles of selective change with devasting clarity, mocking the chop-logic of its detractors and famously saying that just as natural philosophy should not seek an explanation for the Mother, so religion had no business measuring the world. He had reinforced his status with his work on comparative anatomy, including studies of selective change in bears and the ancestors of people, but by the time Pilgrim became his secretary his reputation was greatly diminished, his health was failing and he had fallen out with many of his colleagues because of his interest in sightings of the visitors.

Pilgrim hired a homekeeper to cook meals and clean the burrow, regularised his master's financial affairs and sorted through stacks of neglected correspondence. He soon became a familiar figure in the halls and reading rooms of the Library of All People and the terraced streets of Highwater Reach, the town in the Library's shadow. Impeccably dressed, leaning on his ironwood cane with every other step as he visited book-shops and printers, or collected packages, letters and tapcode messages from the ferry terminal. He discovered that he had a talent for editing and proofreading Master Able's articles and essays, and for extracting and summarising useful data from books and articles which Able did not have the time or inclination to read. And in addition to his usual duties, he nursed the old scholar whenever he was incapacitated by the polymorphous symptoms of an illness which had afflicted him ever since the excavation of the burial ground of a ruined bear city more than forty years ago – violent headaches, bone-chilling fevers, fluxions of the bowel and flare-ups of the arthritis which had so bent and stiffened his fingers that even on his best days he had to write with a pen slotted into the gnarled knot of his fist, and increasingly relied on Pilgrim to take down his scattershot dictation and turn his digressions and half-finished thoughts into clean prose.

Master Able's worsening health changed their relationship: they were no longer scholar and secretary but dependent and carer. Yet although Pilgrim was often impatient with Able's stubbornness and vagaries, and had no scruples about bullying him into eating and bathing at regular intervals, he was still in awe of the deep powers of concentration and forensic analysis and flashes of the old brilliance that his master applied to his last obsession.

And now Pilgrim was setting out to finish the research which had consumed the final years of Master Able's life, with little more than a case of clothes and fair copies of the incomplete draft of Able's monograph and the relevant notes, correspondence with witnesses and transcripts of interviews. He was driven by loyalty to his dead master and a stubborn belief in the importance of the work, but he had lost his living and after paying for the train journey back to his childhood home was very nearly destitute. As he stood at the rail of the river ferry and watched the pale flank of the Library of All People and the small lights of Highwater Reach recede into the night he felt a deep pluck of sorrow and a quailing of his resolve. It seemed more like a retreat from a disastrous rout than the chance to save his master's reputation and establish his own scholarly credentials.

After the ferry sidled into its berth in the docks of Concord, the capital of the Union of Civilised Territories, Pilgrim caught a tram that rattled towards the Central Terminus through wide tree-lined greenways lit by the moonglow of incandescent lamps. The underground temple of the railway station was mostly empty at this late hour, as was the cross-continental train. It was drawn by a pair of electric locomotives that were, along with the streetlamps, trams and much else, a product of

Master Able's sponsors, the Sweetwater Collective. Like the wealthy dynastic families which were reshaping the economy and politics of the Union, the collective was a new kind of tribe: an association of like-minded people who pooled their skills to reverse engineer artefacts excavated from the fossilised remains of ogre cities, and shared the profits amongst themselves rather than with their kin. As he climbed aboard one of the passenger wagons Pilgrim thought with grim amusement that although the collective had refused to sponsor him, their powerful new locomotives would at least shorten the journey he must make to beg for scraps from his tribe's table.

He rented cushions and a spongy mat, slept as best he could as the train rattled out of the city and sped through the night, and was woken early the next morning when a pair of train hands rolled back the tarpaulin that had covered the wagon during the night. He spent the next three days rereading Master Able's manuscript and making extensive notes and rehearsing the case he needed to make to his mother, or simply watching the scenery flow past the sides of the wagon. Motion was good. It gave him purpose and direction.

Forested hills and broad river valleys patchworked with fields and orchards gave way to the grass plains of the heartland. Pilgrim purchased food from the train hands or from platform vendors when the train stopped at stations to take on or offload passengers and freight and swap out the locomotives' batteries, and early on the morning of the fourth day of his journey, in a cloud forest high on the flanks of the mountain range that curved down the spine of the Union, he disembarked at the station, no more than a low platform and a couple of sheds, beside the saw mill of the little town of Tall Trees.

He was met by Righteous Redvine, one of the animal collectors who had supplied Master Able with specimens for his studies on comparative anatomy and three moonspans ago had sent a note about a sighting in the ruins of a bear city. Pilgrim had conducted an interview with the witness by mail, and wanted to follow it up with his first field interview and examine the place where the sighting had occurred. After leaving his luggage in the care of the station master, he and Righteous Redvine set off in a trotcart drawn by a bowbacked mara to meet the witness, passing the grassy mound of a workers' lodge and a stretch of strip fields.

Righteous, a stocky, forthright person dressed in a waxed longcoat, told Pilgrim how sorry he was to hear of Master Able's death, said that he would miss the man's letters.

'He didn't write often, but it was always a treat when he did. His mind had some interesting corners.'

'It certainly did,' Pilgrim said, with a pluck at his heart.

The forest edge rose up abruptly beyond the far side of the strip fields and the road drove straight into it. Big cedars, yellowwood pines and stands of giant bamboo stood along either side, with glimpses of gaps here and there where trees had been felled. The air was close and warm and windless; the strip of sky between the treetops dull white with low cloud.

Righteous explained that trees were harvested singly or in small groups, what was known as patch cutting.

'Bears clear-felled most of it when this was their territory. Apart from a few isolated valleys, the forest is what we call second growth, but we try our best to enrich the Mother's bounty. To heal the land. So we take great care in what we select to cut and let the clearings which are left regenerate naturally.'

The witness Pilgrim had come to meet, Mercy Redvine, a distant cousin of Righteous, was a scout who spent his days hiking through remote parts of the forest, searching out trees suitable for felling and staking likely routes to bring the timber out.

'They're independent fellows, scouts,' Righteous said. 'Wilfully solitary, with a wildness in their blood. But old Mercy is reliable enough. Straight talking, not prone to exaggeration or tale spinning. And knows more about the forest than anyone else hereabouts. Remember the ring-tailed imps I sent to Master Able?'

'I think that must have been before my time,' Pilgrim said.

'Well, they're rare, hard to spot, even harder to track, and clever, too. You set a trap, they'll use a stick to spring it, and eat the bait. But old Mercy caught two alive and sold them to me, and I sent them off to Master Able. Helped him prove that they were not related to something similar that died out at the Burn Line, but had developed from rats in some kind of parallel fashion.'

'Master Able called it functional selection,' Pilgrim said. 'Two species that live in the same way can come to look somewhat alike, and possess similar features and habits, even though they are descended from different stock.'

'I suppose you must have picked up a fair bit of his schooling.'

'Not nearly enough,' Pilgrim said.

The road narrowed and grew ever more rutted, winding up a steep slope in long, lazy curves. The trees thinned and the trotcart turned onto a track that followed the crest of a bare ridge, meandering past outcrops of rock and runouts of loose stones, stands of ferns and clumps of gnarled junipers. A range of mountains lay off to the west, peaks lost in cloud. At last, Righteous pointed to a thread of smoke rising beyond a distant patch of trees, told Pilgrim that was where Mercy had pitched his camp.

It was little more than a slant of canvas in a space pinched between rugged boulders. Mercy Redvine was waiting for them by the campfire. A spry weatherbeaten person with a grey muzzle and tattered ears, barefoot and bare-chested in canvas trews held up by a rope belt knotted under the swag of his belly, he gave Pilgrim a searching look as Righteous introduced him.

'Righteous told me your boss died. Said you were carrying on his work.'

'I'm going to try my best.'

'I see you walk with a cane and haven't changed out of your city clothes, but it's no matter. The place where I saw the ghost lights is just along the ridge, and we can ride most of the way in Righteous's trotcart.'

'I'd like to hear the story of your encounter,' Pilgrim said. 'If you don't mind telling it again.'

'To judge if I told it straight the first time?'

'Talking it through may help you to recall fresh details,' Pilgrim said.

No point explaining that the real reason was to get around any claim Master Able's kin might make on the original interview.

'I know it sounds far-fetched,' Mercy said. 'But I also know that what I saw was as real as the three of us standing here. If you want to hear it, let's make ourselves comfortable. I don't have much, but I'm happy to share it.'

They sat around the fire, Mercy pouring a pale tea made from pine sap into bark cups, searing skewers of meat over the flames, saying that he hoped they were partial to rock rat, it was all he'd been able to catch that morning. Pilgrim dutifully sipped astringent tea and nibbled stringy meat, and pulled out the little wire recorder he had purloined from Master Able's study. The sleek battery-operated machine was one of the gifts from the Sweetwater Collective, the curves of its bamboo casing fitting snugly into his hand, plastic reels spinning smoothly as he demonstrated how it could catch and play back Mercy's voice.

'We live in an age of miracles,' the scout said.

'When you're ready, tell me what you saw, and where you saw it.'

'Best if I start from the beginning,' Mercy said, leaning close to the recorder's soundcatcher. 'It was three moonspans ago, not far from where we're sitting. I'd come up here because young Righteous had a customer in need of a catamount hide.'

'And you were in need of the bounty,' Righteous said.

Mercy ignored him, telling Pilgrim and the wire recorder, 'I was three days on the trail of a young male, and he knew I was tracking him and had quit the forest proper, reckoning it would make it harder for me to follow. What he didn't know was that I can mark and follow a single raindrop through a thunderstorm, and even though fog was covering the ridge I tracked him all the way to the old bear city at the northern end. And that's where I saw what I saw.'

'The ghost lights, as you called them,' Pilgrim said.

'Ay-ya. The fog was thick, but I could see the shadows of the pyramids, and the ghost lights flickering around them. Little patches of green lines, sharp and bright. Never less than ten or twelve of them, sometimes double that number. Flickering off in one place, flickering on in another. That went on for no small while, with the cold and damp settling in my bones while I sat as still as I could, not wanting to draw the attention of whoever or whatever was making them. Scavengers visit those ruins sometimes, looking for carvings. The kind bears made before they went mad and started to killing each other and tearing down their cities. I hear rich folk buy 'em to decorate their houses. Not something I'd recommend. Those stones may be old, but they are still cursed. Steeped in the suffering of our ancestors, as the saying goes. Point being, people who trespass in those ruins aren't the kind you want to cross.'

21

'And did you see anyone?'

'Not a one. Only the ghost lights moving about. At last they started going out one by one, but even when none were left I kept still, because whoever was responsible for 'em might still be poking about. Just as well I did, because all of a sudden there was a noise like a screech or a whistle, so loud I clapped my hands over my ears, and a flame shot up into the fog and was gone in an eye blink.'

'Did you see what made it?'

'Just the flame, rising straight up. White it was, like the coals in a smithy's forge, and bright enough to cast shadows through the fog before it disappeared.'

'Tell him about the fire you found afterwards,' Righteous said.

'It wasn't a fire as such. More a kind of scorching,' Mercy said. 'A patch of stones blackened and still hot. Smouldering tufts of grass.'

Pilgrim asked the usual questions Master Able had asked those witnesses he had been able to question in person, but Mercy was adamant that he had not seen any figures, only the nets of green light and the white flame which had flung itself into the sky.

'How did I do?' he said, after Pilgrim had run out of questions and checked that the wire recorder had captured the interview.

'I'm grateful that you told it so well. I believe that I explained in my last letter that the lights are a new thing.'

'Reckoned they might be, given how you came all this way to ask me about them.'

'Just one other thing – you said that you didn't see any footprints, but do you recall seeing any fresh markings? Something like this, perhaps, scratched in stone or on the ground,' Pilgrim said, opening his jotter to the first page, where he had copied the marking that several witnesses had found after sightings of visitors.

22

'Looks like a bird,' Righteous said, squinting at it.

It was drawn with a single continuous line: a long narrow beak and small round head, a spar on either side of the body for wings, and three more spars, the one in the middle longer than the other two, representing a tail.

'We think it might be a flowersipper,' Pilgrim said.

Mercy shook his head. 'All I found was the remains of that fire.'

'Perhaps we will learn something new when we visit the place,' Righteous said.

The three of them rode in the trotcart, following the track along the ridge. They hadn't gone far, five stades or so, when blocks of worked stone began to appear, sunk in the ground and thatched with moss or dry grass, scattered singly, roughly stacked in low heaps. The track slanted into a cutting between tall stone walls and the cutting opened out and Righteous reined in the mara. The end of the ridge lay below, a blunt prow of flat ground raised above the confluence of two river valleys and occupied by a cluster of circular stair-stepped pyramids. Five, six, seven of them, standing amongst trees and scrub. One of the so-called new cities, built by a philosopher sect which had flowered just before the collapse of bear civilisation and the emancipation of their slaves, the many-times-great-grandfathers and -grandmothers of everyone now alive. Master Able owned – had owned – one of the sect's books, a tall heavy volume with ragged pages of maraskin parchment bound between wooden boards that set out a cosmology based on concentric celestial spheres in which the Daughter Moon, planets and secondary spheres were embedded.

Sitting between Righteous and Mercy, Pilgrim leaned forward eagerly, taking in the view. He had heard stories about the ruins of bear cities from Grandfather Bearbane and Master Able, and had read about them in books, but this was the first he had

23

visited. The pyramids were all the same size, around a hundred ells across and fifty ells high, constructed from big stone blocks with tightly fitted mortarless joints, rising in diminishing tiers. The flat top of one pyramid had collapsed in a dish of jumbled blocks, the side of another slumped in a great gash, but the rest were more or less intact. Massive, monumental, indifferent to the passage of time. Old stories claimed that because the philosopher bears refused to own slaves, they had instead enhanced their strength with potions, enabling them to shift those enormous blocks of stone as easily as a juggler flipped balls through the air. Pilgrim knew that the blocks had most likely been hauled up temporary earth ramps by a system of winches and levers, but even so the amount of energy and organisation it must have required was dauntingly impressive. He tried to imagine what the city might have looked like when it had been inhabited, tried to imagine the ruins cloaked in fog, with sharp green lights moving inside it.

Master Able had always maintained that unless and until it could be proven that the visitors were something other than phantoms or delusions, any attempt to speculate about their nature and motives would be no more than an amusing but futile intellectual game, for theories that lacked a firm foundation of fact were no better than the fantasies spun by self-important pseudo-scholars like Intrepid Windrush. But as he studied the ruins Pilgrim couldn't help hoping that Mercy's account was real and true, couldn't help wondering why the visitors had come here and what they might have been trawling for with their nets of ghost light.

He asked Mercy where he had taken refuge, and the scout pointed to a spot a little way down the track that descended towards the ruins, said that he'd crawled under a clump of thorn bushes and hadn't moved until the lights went out and the white flame shot up.

24

'You had a good view.'

'Ay-ya. Even with the fog.'

'We should show our guest that patch of burnt ground, cousin,' Righteous said.

The trotcart rattled down the track, cut around blocks of stone that littered the space between the brooding hulks of two pyramids. A thin scrub of dry grass and dwarf juniper had colonised their tiers, overtopped by tall risers decorated with carved panels and pierced with the square mouths of shafts that piped sunlight to the chambers inside. Righteous pointed out a long scar on one riser where panels had been prised away by scavengers, saying that scenes of battle and the like seemed to be the most popular prizes.

The track gave out at a square filled edge to edge with thorn bushes, and the sepulchral silence of the ruins was briefly broken when a flock of small green birds whirled up, screeching indignantly at the trotcart and each other before fleeing around the flank of one of the pyramids. Pilgrim, Righteous and Mercy climbed down from the trotcart and followed a narrow path tunnelled through the thorns to the narrow point of the city's prow, where a lone pyramid stood against the hot blank sky.

The scar left by the white flame was in the shadow of the pyramid's footing. It was much bigger than Pilgrim had expected, an oval of charcoal and ash ten ells across at its widest point, perhaps twice that in length. He took out his dip pen and bottle of ink, turned through his jotter to one of the pages of smooth vellum he'd had bound in the back and made a quick sketch, telling Mercy and Righteous that two other witnesses had mentioned seeing something fly off into the sky after their encounters with the visitors.

'One said it was shaped something like the pip of a sourapple; the other described a blunt cylinder, and found a burnt patch much like this.'

'I didn't see anything but the fire,' Mercy said.

'No footprints or any other tracks?'

'If there were footprints I would have found them. And there weren't. No sign of any scratchings like you showed me, either, but you're welcome to look.'

Pilgrim stuffed his jotter and pen into his wallet, thanked Mercy and Righteous for bringing him here and told them that he had learned some new things today.

'But not yet what my ghost lights signified, or who disturbed these old stones, and frightened an old man,' Mercy said.

'Back home, we have little rockets that youngsters set off during the midsummer festival,' Righteous said. 'Maybe your intruders had a bigger one.'

'I told you it wasn't like no rocket I ever saw,' Mercy said. 'And even if it was, it don't explain the lights.'

'Solving a mystery is like building a house. There are many small steps on the path to completion,' Pilgrim said, quoting a favourite saying of Master Able's.

'I know one thing,' Mercy said. 'I've spent most of my life in the forests and mountains. I thought I knew them as well as anyone can, but now it's as if I don't know them at all.'

4.

Pilgrim caught the late-afternoon train to Red Rock Junction, spent the night in the strangers' lodge and in the morning sent a tapcode message to his tribe's Hearth before boarding the local service. Hauled by an old wood-fired potbelly locomotive, it took most of the day to wind north and west out of the cloud forest, passing through high meadows and crossing canyons and arriving more than an hour late, in the last light of the day, at the station which served the territory of the Saltmire tribe.

A hand from the lodge captained by one of Pilgrim's uncles was waiting with a wagon hauled by a matched pair of maras. They rattled up the slant of a narrow valley to the plateau beyond, everything that Pilgrim had forgotten about his home since he had last seen it immediately and thrillingly familiar. The scrub of sawgrass and dwarf bloodbark trees. The lake that stretched down the centre of the valley, Lake Spearpoint, gleaming in the distance. The knife-edged peaks of the Little Hatchet Mountains etched against long bands of orange light stretched either side of the setting sun.

The sharp cries of mountain foxes sounded here and there and the cool air was scented with the medicinal odour of the bloodbark trees. A small flock of blueleg fowl moved

27

off through the scrub like clockwork toys as the wagon passed by in its caul of dust; a little further on the hand hauled on the reins and snapped the peg brake as an armadillo the size of a jitney lumbered across the road. At last, a cluster of lights in the distance resolved into the lamps of the lodge where Pilgrim had spent his adolescence after outgrowing the care of the Hearth. His bad leg and slight build unsuited him for most ranch and farm work, but he had made himself useful by assisting the lodge's cook and keeping the ranch's accounts and taking charge of its storeroom, and that might have been the course of his life if Grandfather Bearbane hadn't found out that Master Able was looking for a secretary.

Pilgrim's uncle, Blessed Sandhill, was waiting for him on the long porch that fronted a string of rooms dug into a low ridge with a cluster of wood-frame windmills (they were new) turning on its crest. Blessed's fringe of jaw hair had turned grey, but otherwise he didn't seem much changed: a sturdy pragmatic person dressed in the high-waisted trews and canvas work vest of a drover, a stub of chewbone hung on a loop of string around his neck. After Pilgrim had washed up and changed his clothes, Blessed insisted on opening the flask of vintage vinewater Pilgrim had brought as a gift. They sat on the porch in the gathering dusk, sipping from thimblecups. Pilgrim told his uncle about his plans to finish Master Able's work on sightings of the visitors, and Blessed told Pilgrim about the plan to run a railway stub up through the valley and north across the plateau to the Hearth.

'The aunties want to build a big new strangers' lodge, too, so rich city folk can pay to hunt and fish by day and carouse at night. In short, we're getting civilised around here. Can't say I much like the idea, but as long as it doesn't interfere with lodge work I'll keep my peace.'

28

Lodge hands were heading into the canteen for supper. The soft green stars of glowbugs were adrift in the darkening air and insects batted at the bare incandescent bulbs strung along the edge of the porch's slant roof. Pilgrim thought with a pang that Master Able would have wanted him to collect a few choice specimens. The old scholar had possessed a particular fondness for beetles, which exhibited extravagantly plentiful and various examples of selective adaptation. Pollen eaters, wood borers, placid leaf grazers, lumbering carnivores that stalked their prey through miniature forests of moss . . . On warm, rainless summer nights Master Able and Pilgrim had sometimes strung up a sheet on top of the burrow and set a light behind it and examined the insects that flocked there. Once, they had discovered a new species of beetle and had written a short article describing it − their second collaboration, following a brief account of one of the fossils Pilgrim had found in a disused quarry in his tribe's territory.

Blessed refreshed their thimblecups and told Pilgrim that talking about the aunties' plans reminded him that Thorn, Pilgrim's mother, expected to see him the next day.

'I look forward to it,' Pilgrim said. 'And also to seeing Willow, and my new nephew. And Bearbane, of course. I have to tell him about Master Able, and want to thank him for the last six years.'

'Don't expect too much of him,' Blessed said. 'He has suffered a grievous decline recently.'

'Willow told me that he had moved to the Elders' Lodge,' Pilgrim said, with a little plunge of apprehension.

'We had him here, for a fair while,' Blessed said. 'Looked after him as best we could. I'd take him up to the pastures while he could still ride, and after that became too difficult for him he liked to sit in the smithy, or out by the pens, watching the animals. But he took to wandering off, and the

29

last time we were three days searching for him before he was found, suffering grievously from cold and thirst. That's when we knew he needed better care than we could provide.'

'How is he now?'

'Stubborn as ever. Our family's strength and curse. Stubborn, but frail and almost blind. And very forgetful.'

'I'm sorry to hear it,' Pilgrim said, thinking of the last time he had seen his grandfather. Bearbane had taken him to the station when he had left for Highwater Reach, giving him a purse of Union coins and enveloping him in a crushing embrace before he boarded the train. His grandfather had been old then, bent-backed and big bellied, but he had still been strong, had still been a significant power in the tribe.

'It comes to us all, one way or another,' Blessed said. 'But I don't doubt that he'll enjoy seeing you again.'

Pilgrim said that he would visit his grandfather as soon as he could, and asked after his mother's health, thinking that without Bearbane to speak for his cause it would be much harder to win her over.

Blessed reached for the flask. 'Let's just say that becoming a grandmother hasn't softened her. One more round to celebrate your return, and then we'll find out what's being dished for supper.'

When he set out the next day, mounted on one of the sturdy piebald maras bred for the territory, Pilgrim reckoned that he had time to visit the Elders' Lodge before heading towards the Hearth and the meeting with his mother. Find out how bad things were with Bearbane. Whether his worst fears were justified.

He followed a road above the long reach of the lake and cut north and west, riding up through a scant forest of stunted yellowwoods, passing the haven where newly handfasted couples spent their first Season together, the traditional grassy mounds of the burrows scattered amongst trees and stands of fern and bamboo, their chimneys smokeless and windows shuttered. Pilgrim rode on, the paws of his mara, shod in wood-soled boots, padding soundlessly over soft layers of fallen needles. Small birds winged through sunlight and shadow between the trees or sang from unseen perches. High in the blank blue sky an ossifrage hung on outspread wings, turning in slow circles as it scried the land below. Everything he had run away from. Everything he missed.

The Elders' Lodge was a cluster of log-walled, turf-roofed cabins set on a broad apron near the treeline. A hot spring burbled amongst white rocks, feeding a stream that dropped away in a series of pools and small waterfalls; paths wandered amongst clumps of birch and gardens of rock and raked gravel. Pilgrim sat on a bench, shivering a little in the cool air, while one of the carers fetched Bearbane. His grandfather was somewhat shrunken, dressed like the other residents in a blue shift and padded woollen trews and his good eye (the other had been lost when he'd faced down a berserker that had torn free of its trap) was frosted by a cataract, but he seemed amiable and alert. Caressing Pilgrim's face and hands with his fingertips, saying that it had been far too long since his last visit.

'I've been living in Highwater Reach, Grandfather. Working for your old friend Master Able.'

Able hadn't been much older than Pilgrim was now when, with Bearbane as his guide, he had led a small expedition to an ancient city mound in the high western desert of the New Territories and disinterred the remains of bears from the city's burial ground. Layers of bones packed one on top of another. More than twenty thousand years of history set out in an orderly sequence. Able's detailed measurements of bones from different layers revealed that bears had already been smaller and more slightly built than their feral ancestors when they had begun to construct their first cities, and had changed very little throughout the city-building epoch. Contrariwise, similar measurements of bones from contemporary specimens showed that, a mere six centuries years after the fall of their civilisation, bears had become larger and more robust. The findings had given Able a famous example of two extremes of selective adaptation in a single species. Bear civilisation had been stable and unchanging for more than thirty thousand years, so any selective pressures would have been stable and unchanging too. But after it had collapsed, changes in the habit and diet of surviving bears, and competition for scarce resources and suitable mates, meant that only the strongest individuals were likely to survive and reproduce.

In some of the oldest layers the skeletons of people had been found next to those of bears. The remains of favoured slaves, killed when their masters had died, and buried with them. Measurements of those bones confirmed the findings from so-called slaughter pits where the bones of thousands of slaves were jumbled together in no especial order: people enslaved by bears, even those who had lived and died twenty thousand years ago, were anatomically indistinguishable from contemporary people. Most likely they had not endured the lash as dumb brutes, but had suffered as any ordinary person might suffer.

Bearbane was smiling as a memory surfaced. 'I haven't seen Able in a long while, but he still writes to me.'

'I have some news about him. And I am afraid that it is not good,' Pilgrim said.

Bearbane didn't appear to have heard him, saying, 'Such interesting letters about his work. I should write back . . .'

'He has returned to the Mother, Grandfather.'

'Who has?'

'Your friend. Able. It was mercifully quick. He was felled by a thunderbolt to the brain and passed the next day.'

'Are you sure? I know he wrote to me last year. I think it was last year . . .'

'I was with him when he died. I was his secretary. You wrote the letter of recommendation that convinced him to hire me.'

'I did?'

Pilgrim felt a pang of sorrow, watching the old man try to puzzle it out.

'Well, never mind,' Bearbane said at last. 'We'll walk in the garden, and you can tell me what you have been doing.'

Pilgrim took his grandfather's arm and they shuffled down a path to the mossy bank of the stream and sat on a square stone. Bearbane tilted his face to the sunlight and said that he had always liked the sound of running water, and the smell of it too. Although he had trouble understanding where Pilgrim had been, he liked the stories about sightings of the visitors, and Pilgrim's account of the visit to the ruined city where strange lights had been seen. They prompted him to tell a tall tale about phantoms which haunted bear ruins in the tribe's old territory in the south, and then the story about how, when camping out in the boggy forests of the far north, he had heard three bears singing, one after the other, and knew that he had stumbled into the meeting point of their territories and doused his fire and crept away in the night. He had earned the right to adopt a new name after spending thirty years in the New Territories, driving the last of the bears ever northward, and he admired and respected their resilience and resourcefulness, and believed that they had not entirely lost their powers of reasoning.

Although Pilgrim had heard those tales many times before, he was happy to hear them again: they were good stories and his grandfather scarcely stumbled as he told them. But

33

when they returned to the lodge and shared a small lunch of pickled vegetables and steamed mudfish in the sunny commons Bearbane had to be reminded again who Pilgrim was and why he was there, and when Pilgrim told him that he had to leave because he had business to discuss with his mother, Bearbane took his hands, his grip trembling but still strong, and said, 'You're as stubborn and steadfast as me, Boundless. Stick to what you need to do and you'll most likely get it done.'

Boundless was the name of Pilgrim's father, who had died when Pilgrim had been a pup. He didn't have the heart to correct his grandfather, and took those few words of encouragement as a blessing.

It was late in the afternoon by the time he had retraced his path and headed east, crossing a wooden bridge that arched over the river fed by the lake, passing through a belt of wild olive and black gum and emerging at the edge of the rough pasture where shag-pelted coneys grazed, little bells around their necks tinkling out a fitful music. The rammed-earth outer wall of the Hearth loomed beyond. The gate stood open. Pilgrim rode under its arch and told the guard who he was and whom he had come to see.

'I know who you are, young Pilgrim,' the woman said. 'Welcome back. But you'll have to wait for an escort, like any other visitor.'

She ducked inside an office built into the slant of the wall's inner side to send a tapcode message to the bastion, and Pilgrim climbed down from his mara and hitched it to a post and brushed road dust from his clothes and leaned on his cane and waited for his escort. Presently, a mara and rider came up the straight white road that cut through the strip fields and stands of fruit trees beyond the gate. Pilgrim's sister, Willow, come to meet her errant brother.

5.

After Willow alighted from her mara she and Pilgrim moved together and clasped forearms and swayed in the slow, blissful comity of blood on blood, immersed in each other's scent and touch. His sister wore plain work clothes and there were blue dot tattoos under her eyes and in the stripe shaved into her pelt from her forehead to the nape of her neck – tribal signifiers of her status. She had barely been a stripling when Pilgrim had left, was grown into a woman now. Handfasted, with a son. Amazing to think of it.

'Look at you,' she said, stepping back. 'Got up in your finery.'

Pilgrim had dressed carefully to meet his mother. The white mourning shirt, short-legged grey felt trews, their cuffs fastened by horn buttons just below his knees, his good yellow stockings for a touch of colour, long-toed side-laced pike boots.

'It's nothing out of the ordinary in Highwater Reach,' he said. 'Apart from the shirt, of course.'

Willow told him how sorry she was for his loss. 'Your letters made it clear how much you admired and respected your master.'

Pilgrim had a clear sharp picture of the old scholar bent over his desk, studying a document through his magnifying glass while his left hand, like an independent animal, scratched notes on a scrap of paper.

35

He swallowed something hard and said, 'He was the finest, cleverest person I have ever known.'

'And you haven't yet finished serving him.'

'That isn't the only reason why I came back. I wanted to see you, and to meet my new nephew.'

'And ask Thorn for help. You had better see her straight away. She let me know that she expected you to arrive much earlier.'

'I paid a visit to Bearbane before I came here.'

'I hope that was not too much of a shock.'

'He mistook me for our father,' Pilgrim said. 'It was as if I had been erased from his mind.'

'He is often confused now,' Willow said. 'You mustn't take it personally.'

'I wrote to him faithfully, but he hardly ever replied.'

'He was never much good with letters. Do you remember the story about how, when he was trapping bears in the far north, Thorn didn't hear from him for five years? Didn't know if he was dead or alive until one of his cousins ran into him in a frontier camp.'

'He can still tell a good story.'

'The past is realer to him than the present,' Willow said. 'The only comfort is that he no longer remembers that he is ailing.'

They rode side by side along the road towards the walled mound of the Hearth's bastion, passing strips of sweetroot and starchroot, beans, fat grass and thread grass. Rows of custard-apple trees, peermelon trees, grapevines. Pilgrim gave Willow a brief account of his interview with Mercy Redvine and the visit to the ruins of the bear city, and she asked him if he had told Thorn about his plans.

'I thought it would be better to explain the details in person rather than in a letter.'

'If you want to know the truth, this business with the visitors has always sounded crazy to me. It still does.'

'I am going to explain why it is important to define the nature of that craziness. Blessed told me that she has not much changed.'

'She is what she is,' Willow said. 'But I know that she is looking forward to seeing you.'

They rode past barns and storage tanks, past the stinking tannery and the sheds where the rugs for which the territory had some small fame were woven. Past the pups' compound, with its red-painted cabins and neat flower and vegetable gardens, where Pilgrim had spent the first years of his life, and through the gate in the mud wall of the bastion. They left their maras in the courtyard and Willow led Pilgrim through the maze of passageways under the central mound, his cane rapping on the woodblock floor, anticipation parching his mouth.

He'd always had a difficult relationship with his mother. She was a strong-willed and decisive person with a clear vision of what needed to be done and how to achieve it, and had never allowed him to make excuses or avoid challenges because of his lameness or, when it became evident, his 'condition'. If he had to work harder than others to overcome his handicaps, she had told him, it would instil resilience and self-control that would serve him well later in life. And if he failed after trying his best, then at least it would be an honourable failure. Better that than never trying at all. At the time, he had often resented her unrelenting discipline, but now he was grateful that she had trained him to be focused and conscientious. Qualities that had served him well as Master Able's secretary; qualities that he hoped would help him make good his ambition to finish his master's work. And although Thorn was more admired than

37

well-liked, for she was not concerned with pleasing others and was very particular about choosing whom she could trust, she had become a leading voice in the tribe's community, an important and energetic mover and shaker. Pilgrim didn't doubt that the innovations Blessed had mentioned were largely due to her, and knew that if he could convince her about the importance of his plans the rest of the aunties would fall into line behind her.

She was waiting for him in her office, dressed like Willow in work clothes – a tan vest, high-waisted trews, reedstem sandals. No adornments except for the usual tattoos of a woman of her age and standing, and the bracelet of braided goat hair that she wore on her left wrist in remembrance of her long-dead partner, Pilgrim's father. She greeted him briskly, as if he had been away for six days rather than six years. There was no embrace. Overt displays of affection had never been her style. Instead, they settled on hassocks on either side of a low table, and Thorn poured tea, one of Willow's blends, into thimble cups, and thanked him for his letter and expressed sympathy for Master Able's death.

'You know that I did not approve of Bearbane making arrangements behind my back, but you seem to have served his scholar friend well enough. I understand that he had been unwell for a long time, but the end must have been a shock, even so.'

Pilgrim told her that it had been, and still was, but she was already pressing on.

'You mentioned that you had plans to finish a monograph. If you came here looking for a place where you can work undisturbed, I'm sure we can accommodate you. And if you are uncertain about what to do with yourself once you have finished, I have a few suggestions. We can discuss them when you are ready.'

Pilgrim thanked her, asked if she remembered what he had told her about Master Able's work in his letters to her. What his master had been working on when he died.

It was still hard, saying that. *When he died*. Openly acknowledging his death. Confirming its reality.

'Something to do with ghosts or visions, I believe,' Thorn said. 'One of those silly popular manias.'

'Master Able was trying to find out if there was something more to it than that,' Pilgrim said.

He explained that in the course of his usual work Master Able's interest in sightings of so-called visitors had been sparked by a letter sent by a trapper who worked in the forests of the west coast of the New Territories, describing a brief glimpse, at night, of tall figures that moved in the darkness under the trees and shone like the Daughter Moon. Master Able had recently done some work on the bones of a dwarf species of ogre which had lived on one of the Spice Islands for tens of thousands of years beyond the Burn Line, and wondered if the trapper might have encountered members of a similar species which had survived until the present day. He had written to his contacts, seeking evidence of similar encounters, and had tasked Pilgrim with sifting through local wallsheets, and they had compiled a short list of reliable sightings and had interviewed the witnesses by mail or in person. The sightings had been scattered across the Union and the New Territories and none of the witnesses appeared to have any connection with each other, yet their accounts shared a number of striking similarities. All of the encounters had been in remote areas and mostly in the last light of dusk, or at night: distant glimpses of two or three slim, tall figures clad in white, disappearing amongst trees or behind rocks or ridges, dissolving into darkness. Two witnesses had said that the figures had been blank-faced.

Another had claimed that they had worn helmets with visors of black glass.

'In several cases ridged footprints were found. In others, markings scratched in the dirt or on a rock,' Pilgrim said, and showed Thorn his drawing of the flowersipper sigil, explained that rumours about the sightings had inspired all kinds of outlandish theories, from claims that they were avatars of the Mother to Foeless Landwalker's assertion that they hailed from Morningstar, the second planet of the sun, where they had built a paradise of peace and universal enlightenment. Critics and naysayers had questioned Master Able's motives and attacked his reputation, but he had persisted in his quest for the truth, painstakingly analysing the veracity of new sightings, including descriptions of what might have been flying machines and a report of strange lights in the ruins of a bear city.

'I investigated that last on my way here,' Pilgrim said, and related the account of Mercy Redvine's encounter. He had it by heart after transcribing the recording of Mercy's story in the stranger's lodge where he had overnighted.

Thorn said, 'What did your master think these visitors were? You mentioned dwarf ogres. Or did he believe in ghosts?'

'Despite the footprints and the gravings and so on, my master believed that more evidence was required before he could come to a conclusion,' Pilgrim said. 'And even if the sightings turned out to be nothing more than mistaken observations of natural phenomena or outright hoaxes, he thought it important to discover why they were so popular, and why rumour of them spread so quickly. Perhaps they are a symptom of people's fears about changes driven by new techne. Changes which they can neither control nor understand. Fantasies of powerful beings who promise a paradise of universal peace, where all are equal and none are in want, may be a way of regaining control of the future and direction of their lives.'

'They would do better to have faith in the mercy and grace of the Mother.'

'It may be that too many have lost faith in Her. Or fear that She has lost faith in them.'

'And what do you believe?'

'Like my master, I believe that more research is needed. That's why, when he lay on his death bed, I promised him that I would finish his work.'

Master Able had been insensible when Pilgrim had made that vow, but he believed that it was no less binding for that.

'I need only a small stipend to pay for travel and other expenses, and a place to collate my findings and complete my master's monograph. I set out the estimates here,' he said, sliding the sheet of paper across the table.

Thorn did not even glance at the estimated expenses he had worked and reworked. She said, with a look he remembered all too well from the many times when he'd been chastised for daydreaming when he should have been paying attention to his teachers and instructors, or for failing to give every challenge or chore anything but his best, 'You brought this to me because you thought that I would look at this favourably, and persuade the other aunties to approve a disbursement.'

As usual, she had seen clean through him.

'I think of it as an investment,' Pilgrim said, knowing that everything hinged on this moment. His words. Her judgement. 'It may be that the visitors are no more than phantoms. But if they are real, if we share the Mother with an undiscovered tribe of people or another race of intelligent beings, it will change everything.'

6.

Pilgrim's nephew, Amity, was a sturdy pup a little over two years old, pleasingly bold and curious. Asking if the ant inside Pilgrim's amber pendant was real, wanting to know if Pilgrim walked with a stick because he had hurt his leg.

'I was born with one leg weaker than the other,' Pilgrim said. 'And I've grown so used to it that I hardly notice it anymore.'

'He doesn't mean anything by it,' Willow said, smiling at Pilgrim over her son's sleek head.

'I'm pleased to see that he's as inquisitive as I was, at his age.'

'Do you really live in the capital?' Amity said.

'In a little town called Highwater Reach, on the other side of the river. Have your teachers ever told you about the Library of All People?'

Amity shook his head.

'It is a collection of books and many other things from all over the Union. Scholars who study in it mostly live in Highwater Reach. I was the secretary to one of those scholars.'

'We learnt about the capital in geography,' Amity said. 'It's called Concord. It's smaller than the territory but lots more people live in it.'

'The very definition of a city.'

'And it's a long long long *long* way away.'

'On the other side of the Union. I came here by train. Do you know what a train is?'

'Of course!' Amity said scornfully. 'Did you come to see me?'

'And your mother, and my mother – your grandmother Thorn. I brought you a gift,' Pilgrim said. 'It's in my wallet. Why don't you look for it?'

It was a bestiary more than a hundred years old, its entries organised by a quaintly outdated phylogeny and illustrated with hand-tinted plates. Amity paged through it with rising excitement, pointing to animals and birds he recognised, asking about others he didn't.

'It's almost bedtime,' Willow told him. 'Why don't I help you get ready, and then your uncle can tell you about some of those beasts.'

The dormitory of the pups' compound was unchanged, with rows of sleeping niches down either side, dusty columns of reddish light slanting through the painted glass of the clerestory, the homely chatter of pups being prepared for sleep by their carers or visiting parents. After he had shown his collections of bird feathers and snail shells to his uncle, Amity settled in his sleeping niche and Pilgrim perched on a small stool beside him and they studied the bestiary. Here was a picture of a tiny tree rat from the Spice Islands which made its home in the hulls of a certain kind of nut. Here was the agile hopping rat from the hot dusty central grasslands, with its springy hind legs and the large naked shells of its ears, which it used to catch the warmth of the early-morning sunlight after the cold nights and radiate away excess body heat during the hottest part of the day. And here was a fierce lean mountain hob, and a tree glider from the cloud forests, with membranes of skin stretched between its fore and hind limbs, and a queen army rat and her attendant workers. Pilgrim asked Amity what they had in common, and explained, after

43

the boy had made several guesses, that they shared a common ancestor which had looked something like the little spiny-tailed rats which had to be kept from the root stores, and lived in the long-ago time before the world had caught fire.

'Two hundred thousand years ago, before there were people like us.'

'Because there were ogres instead.'

'That's right. After the fire, the ogres were gone, or almost all of them, and so were most of the animals. But our little rat and her friends and relations survived, and her children and her children's children found new places to live and new kinds of food to eat, because the animals which had once lived in those places and eaten that food were no longer around. And slowly, bit by bit, the rat's children were changed by where they lived and how they made their living, and became different kinds of new animals.'

'Is that a story, or is it true?'

'It's a true story. The best kind. My master discovered it by comparing the shapes of their bones and teeth.'

They studied more pictures, leaning together over the little book. A river dolphin, several kinds of seal and an animal Amity recognised – a water buffalo with a pink, hairless hide, a stiff dark crest crowning its head and a pair of tusks curling to the left and right of its snout. It was a relative of the forest hogs, Pilgrim told Amity, and one of the fiercest and most dangerous animals known, even though it ate nothing but grass and water hyacinths. Amity nodding, saying that water buffalos lived in the lake and you had to keep well away from them, asking if it was true that they could fight off spotted cats.

'They are so fierce that their children sometimes chew on a crocodile's tail for practice,' Pilgrim said. 'And the crocodile lets them, because if it objected that would be the end of it.'

'Are crocodiles the little rat's children too?'

'No, they are very old and wise animals who knew how to hide from the worst of the fire.'

At last Amity fell asleep, and Pilgrim tucked the book into the straw at the bottom of his sleeping niche. Willow said that it was an overgenerous present; Pilgrim told her that one of the things that had surprised him most, living in Highwater Reach in the shadow of the Library, was how cheap books could be. There was a narrow street in the old quarter where shops sold books authorised by the Library, self-published tracts, theses and pamphlets produced by the so-called bootleg print shops, and the contents of the personal libraries of scholars who had died or moved away. He had spent many happy hours browsing there.

'I had to sell most of my little collection to pay for my train ticket, and put what was left in the care of my friends. But I kept the bestiary for Amity because your letters mentioned that he is keen on natural history.'

Pilgrim and Willow were sitting under one of the Hearth's grandmother trees, looking out across the fields towards the slow sunset. Willow said, 'I'm not sure if it's a phase or something more serious, but he loves to collect bird feathers and snail shells.'

'As I saw.'

'You had your fossils, and the animal skeletons you wired together,' Willow said. 'And that ant farm you kept between two sheets of glass.'

'I employed the ants to strip the flesh from the bones of dead mice and birds,' Pilgrim said. 'A very useful arrangement.'

'Until one of our teachers made you throw it out because of the stink.'

'And with no better place to live the ants made nests under the classroom, and got everywhere.'

They smiled at the shared memory.

Willow said, 'The teachers couldn't bring themselves to punish you, because you told such good stories about ants and fossils and all the rest. The big coilshell you found in the old quarry is still on display in the pups' classroom.'

'That's good to know.'

'Perhaps you could tell Amity and the other pups about how you found it and what it means, the next time you visit.'

'Why not? It looks like I'll be here for a while.'

Pilgrim had already explained how things had fallen out with Thorn. She had told him that his project had nothing to do with the aunties and the Hearth, said that if he wanted to try to win support from the tribe he was wasting his time with her, and must petition the men's council instead. It was not an outright rejection, but it was a major setback.

Willow said now that she had been thinking about how he could best make his case: that he should present his work as a commercial proposition. Tell the council what kind of profit he hoped to make from publishing his book, and so on.

'The tribe has never been rich, and we are struggling more than ever. The world is changing more quickly than we reckoned, we still rely too much on export of food and cloth, and the price of both has dropped considerably in the past two years. If you want the council to invest in your work, you will have to show how the tribe can profit from it.'

'Is that how you convinced them to sell new kinds of tea?'

'After spending a great deal of time working up a detailed budget. And selling tea is something they can understand,' Willow said. 'A book about mysterious visitors, not so much.'

'I hope that it will prove my master was right to take the visitors seriously, and that it will convince others to take them seriously too.'

'If you want to convince the men's council you will need something more than that,' Willow said. 'Think about how the old stories are structured. The way their heroes over-come difficulties, grow in skill and stature, and win what was thought to be an impossible prize. It isn't too different from your situation. You could tell the council how your master's kin refused to support his work and tried to stop you carrying out his dying wish. Explain that everyone else thinks his ideas are crazy, that only you think that he could be right. Give them a story that excites them. Tell them how your work could change the world, and that when it is done you will write a book that will sell so many copies that it will make back far more than your expenses, and embellish the tribe's reputation.'

'It doesn't sound much like the monograph I hope to finish.'

'A bloodless account of interest only to scholars will be hard to sell to the council. You need to catch their interest.'

Pilgrim thought about that. 'If I draft a proposal, I'd be forever in your debt if you could look at it and suggest improvements. But I can't promise that it will be as exciting as one of those old stories. The truth rarely is.'

Willow smiled. 'You are as stubborn as Thorn.'

'If you mean that I know what I need to do, I'm not going to disagree. And if the men's council is unwilling or unable to give up a little money, there is something else I could put to them.'

'Is this other thing more likely to turn a profit?'

'First, we should concentrate on the work I need to do. Not on the work I might have to do to support it.'

'You brought it up. The least you can do is give me a hint.'

'Let's just say that it involves finding bigger and better coilshells.'

7.

It was too late to make the journey back to Blessed's lodge, so when the Hearth's curfew bell tolled Pilgrim rode out through the gate to the strangers' lodge close by and ate at one of the communal tables in the noisy crowded commons. Despite the pleasure of seeing his sister and meeting his nephew for the first time, he was weary and dispirited. The shock of Grandfather Bearbane's malaise lingered still, and although he had known from the outset that there was only a small chance that his mother would volunteer unconditional help, her swift dismissal still stung.

Most of the men in the commons were rovers, migratory workers with no tribal affiliations who laboured in the Hearth's fields, workshops and tannery for a year or two before moving on, but Pilgrim spotted a distant cousin, Creed, at a neighbouring table. Creed was sharing a bowl of sweetroot beer with two friends, looking up and making a comment to his companions as Pilgrim limped past after he had finished his meal, all three of them snickering.

Pilgrim stopped, leaning on his cane, waited for Creed to look at him and asked him if he could hear the joke he had just made.

Creed stared back, insolent and half drunk. He was dressed in patched and dirty workclothes and there was beer froth on his muzzle.

'I have to wonder what someone like you is doing here,' he said. 'Son of one of the aunties, slumming it amongst hard-working folk. Are you spying for her? Or are you looking for a strong man to take care of you?'

'Is that meant to be a joke? It needs some work.'

'The joke is you,' Creed said. 'Got up in that fancy costume, reckoning it makes you better than ordinary folk.'

'If that's what you think, you are either stupid or very lucky,' Pilgrim said.

'You think I'm stupid because I work for a living?'

'Because you don't recognise a mourning shirt,' Pilgrim said and turned his back on Creed before he could think of a reply.

'That unfortunate fellow quit the territory five years ago,' Blessed told Pilgrim the next day. 'Went west, over the mountains to Finfoot territory on the coast. Found work on a boat in one of the fishing towns there. And got into trouble when he hurt a man badly in some stupid drunken fight. They went at each other with gutting knives and Creed cut the other fellow badly. Blinded him in one eye.'

There was a quiet moment as Pilgrim and his uncle contemplated this uncommon act of violence.

Blessed said, 'Creed claimed he was the one who was attacked, and did no more than defend himself. The Finfoots didn't believe him, put him to a year's hard labour. And when he had done his time he came home, begging for forgiveness. The council set him to work as an ordinary labourer, so he could atone for what he did and prove he is willing to improve himself.'

'I remember him as the kind of person who reckons everything that goes wrong for him is always someone else's fault,' Pilgrim said. 'I doubt that he believes he has anything to answer for.'

'It certainly doesn't sound like he has lost any of his temper,' Blessed said. 'And he won't like that you called him out in

49

front of his friends. Probably best to take a long path around him in future.'

'I don't plan on looking for trouble, Uncle,' Pilgrim said. 'I have some improving of my own to do.'

He found a quiet corner in the commons of the lodge and spent two days working on a summary of what he wanted to do and why it was important, using plain language and cutting out everything that seemed extraneous. At last, when he was satisfied that he had made his case as simply and directly as he could, he showed the draft to his sister.

'It's not bad,' Willow said, after she'd read it through. 'You make a strong argument about the importance of the work, there's a sensible explanation of what you want to do and how you expect to achieve it, and your costings are reasonable. There's just one thing missing – you haven't explained how the tribe will recoup its outlay.'

'This isn't about making money; that's the purview of charlatans like Intrepid Windrush. What Master Able set out to do, the task I want to take up and complete, is to discover the facts of the matter. It may not turn a profit, but it should win some small fame and honour.'

'And how will you complete your task if the council decides that it cannot afford to subsidise it?'

'Are you upset because I rejected your idea about adding an overwrought account of my struggle to the proposal?'

'I'm disappointed that I can't make you understand how thinly stretched things are, here.'

'But I do understand. That's why, if the council can't or won't support me, I'll ask it to take up my idea of selling fossils.'

'You mean coilshells? I thought you were joking when you told me about that,' Willow said.

'It's a serious idea,' Pilgrim said. 'And one that could turn the kind of profit you're so keen on.'

50

They were sitting in Willow's tea-packing workshop. She had given Pilgrim a short tour, showing him where bark, leaves and flowers from plants picked in the wild or grown in the Hearth's strip fields were sorted and cleaned, the racks where the material was dried, the tables where it was weighed and packaged, and the neat little handpress that printed the colourful labels. Pilgrim told his sister that he was impressed, and meant it. Now, as they lounged on cushions and sipped redbark tea, he explained about the old quarry where he had once hunted for fossils, and the shops in Concord that specialised in the sale of fossils and the relics of ogres and bears.

'Is this what you did with the fossils you took with you, when you left?' Willow said.

'Those were a gift for Master Able. One was a small fish that turned out to be unknown to naturalists. He wrote an article about it, naming me as co-author, and donated the fossil to the Library. The rest he kept.'

They had been the best specimens from Pilgrim's child-hood collection. The fish, the mostly intact shell of a young sea turtle, a slab bearing some particularly fine sea flowers, a coilshell and a coneshell. The fish was in a drawer in the Library's Hall of Stones and Bones; the rest, hard to think about it, were now in the possession of Able's kin.

Willow said, 'So you hope to dig up more, and sell them to the Library.'

'The Library accepts donations, and by law has to be given two copies of every book, monograph and pamphlet published in the Union. It doesn't have to pay for anything. But there's a fashion amongst wealthy people in Concord to use fossils as decorations in their homes. Fossils of fish and sea flowers and coilshells in washrooms, and so on. And there are some serious collectors, too. One merchant built a special chamber to house his collection, including the articulated skeletons of two thunder lizards.'

Pilgrim had visited it with Master Able, who had advised the merchant about his purchases. It was as large as one of the bays of the Library's Hall of Stones and Bones, with a marble floor in which fossil imprints of shells were inlaid, and adjustable skylights that could direct beams of sunlight on different specimens.

'If the quarry could give up the bones of a thunder lizard, it would subsidise a life's work,' Pilgrim said. 'But its fossils are marine, and from an earlier epoch. It would take no small amount of work to make money from them, but I think it's possible.'

Willow had a hard time understanding why anyone would spend so much on a collection of creatures from the deep past. It seemed like flirting with the displeasure of the Mother, given that She was the author of the catastrophe which had destroyed them.

'I don't question why people want to collect them,' Pilgrim said, suppressing the impulse to correct his sister's misapprehension about the extinction of the thunder lizards. 'But they do. If the men's council won't support my research, I'll tell them how to make money from stones the quarrymen discarded out of superstition, and use my cut of the profits to subsidise my real work.'

'Scholars may not be as unworldly as I thought,' Willow said.

'Master Able was the scholar; I was his secretary. I spent six years trying to balance his accounts and placating his creditors. After his family cut his stipend I did a little book-running on the side to make ends meet. Finding books scholars lusted after, buying them as cheaply as possible, selling them on. It did not make much, but helped to put food on the table, and paid for my master's physics and salves.'

'It would be better if you told them about the fossil trade, and left the research into the visitors out of it. Offer it up as a gift, and don't mention why you want to take some of the profits. Explain that you want to give something back to the tribe. That you want to satisfy the great harmony.'

'Setting up the fossil business would delay the research by many moonspans, which is why it is a last resort.'

'But it's the kind of thing the council is more likely to support,' Willow said. 'It would be a good idea to have a proposal to hand, setting out costs and likely profits. I'll be happy to look it over. And you should have some examples to show the council, too.'

'There's the coilshell in the pups' classroom.'

'It might be better if you can show them some freshly collected material. The kind of things you want to sell.'

'I hope there'll be no need for it.'

'You should not count on being given what you want,' Willow said. 'Most likely you will have to work for it, like everyone else.'

She made a fresh cruse of tea and asked Pilgrim what he planned to do after he had written his monograph.

'I haven't thought that far ahead. Go back to Highwater Reach, I suppose. Arrange publication of the monograph. Find a scholar who needs a secretary, take up bookrunning again . . .'

'Or you could stay here. Supervise this fossil business. And I think you'd make a good teacher.'

'Thorn made the same suggestion, after she told me that the aunties wouldn't fund my work,' Pilgrim said. 'Said that I could do my research in my spare time. She also said that I should think of settling down, and suggested that I could be matched with an older woman. A widow for whom the Season has lost its spell. Who is more in need of company than sex.'

Willow poured tea with a steady hand. 'She means well, even when she is somewhat careless of your feelings.'

'It's disappointing that she still can't see me for what I am, rather than what she hoped I would be.'

'You mentioned in your letters that some of your friends in Highwater Reach were handfasted. How are things with you? Is there anyone special I should know about?'

'They handfasted for love, not to satisfy social custom and expectation. I haven't found the right person yet,' Pilgrim said. 'Or perhaps there is no right person for me, or I have no need of one. It may be that I am destined to be bound to my work.'

'A life without someone you love, someone who loves you in return, sounds more than a little sad,' Willow said.

'I love you. And Thorn, difficult though she sometimes makes it. And Amity, too, of course. And don't you love your work?'

'Work is one thing. Finding someone you can share your life with is something else.'

'I have found a community of men and women like me, and made some good friends. Unlike Thorn, we accept each other for who we are, and celebrate our multitudinous variety.'

'I remember you telling me, in your letters, how wonderful it was to have found others like you. And you do seem happier,' Willow said. 'Happier, and calmer.'

'Happier, certainly,' Pilgrim said, and changed the subject and told Willow that it was time he met Perseverance Blackwater, the husband he had been told so much about.

'He's working in one of his tribe's sawmills, just two days' ride away,' Willow said. 'I know he would make you welcome if you care to visit.'

'Do you miss him?'

'You told me about the scandalous out-of-Season associations between men and women in the capital. I can't ever imagine that happening here. I have Amity, and my work. And the old saying is true – separation does make the heart ever fonder. The Season comes around faster every year, it seems, and we see each other at high days, too.'

'The world is changing, Willow. New techne. New ideas. It may not be changing here quite as fast as in Concord, but it will change nonetheless. We didn't have tapcode links when we were growing up. Or electricity, either. And here you are, handfasted, yet still living and working here, instead of in the Blackwater Hearth.'

'Only because I had already started the tea business when I handfasted. Perseverance has been very understanding. His family and tribe, too. And between you and me, now that making and selling tea is doing rather better than I hoped, we have been talking about having him move here. Our tribe lacks people skilled in the forestry trade, and Perseverance has surveyed some of our woods and thinks that with the right management they could yield a useful profit.'

'And I thought I was the radical in the family.'

'Times are changing, as you said. We must change with them, or be left behind.' Willow paused, then added, 'I haven't told Thorn yet, so this is between ourselves. Now that the tea business is established, we're going to try for another child.'

'I'm sure Amity would love a brother. Or a sister.'

'Will you have time to see Amity before you leave? He has been reading your book. Well, mostly looking at the pictures. It's all he talks about.'

'Of course. It's the main reason why I came here. But first, I should visit Thorn. Make peace with her.'

'And perhaps,' Willow said, 'you could get her opinion about this fossil business, too.'

8.

As Pilgrim rode through the Hearth's gate someone stepped into the road and caught hold of the bridle of his mara. It was Creed, looking up at him with a grimace that might have been meant as a smile. 'I've revised my opinion of you since I heard you were planning to set out for the New Territories,' he said, 'and am here to offer my services as a guide.'

'Who told you about my plans?'

'Maybe you've forgotten, having spent so long in the capital, where everyone is a stranger to everyone else, that we know each other's business here,' Creed said. 'As is right, seeing as we all share blood to some degree or other. When I learned you were heading out to hunt bears in wild places, I thought to myself that I would be the man to help you. I've seen my share of such places, and know how to handle myself in a tight spot.'

'It isn't bears I want to find. And I don't need a guide, either.'

'There are places where trouble can find you, even if you don't go looking for it,' Creed said. The stale-sweet reek of beer was on his breath and his ungroomed pelt was spiky with grease. 'Especially when you don't know what it looks like or how to deal with it.'

Pilgrim said, wanting to end the conversation as quickly as possible, 'I heard the men's council gave you a second chance when you came home. Won't you need their permission to leave the territory?'

Creed's gaze sharpened. 'When I was sent into their care, that passel of old fools told me that they were going to see to it that I learned my lesson and paid my debt. Said that I could work as a foreman, and because I owed compensation to my victim, my pay would go to him. I said the man attacked me, if there was any victim it was me, but they wouldn't listen. Said maybe I could just leave, save everyone the trouble, but no. I was told if I didn't like the offer I could do another year of hard labour instead. As if I hadn't already paid the Finfoots with my blood and sweat.'

'I assume that's a long way of saying that you need permission,' Pilgrim said.

'I need to get out, is the beginning and end to it,' Creed said. 'Having had enough of working for no pay and bunking with rovers. You're planning to leave. I figure I could go with you. You do me a favour, I do you one back. Because, let's face it, where you're planning to go, someone like you is you're going to need someone like me.'

'Someone like me?'

'A cripple and a, you know, a pure. Not that it's anything to be ashamed of. And I respect you found a way of getting on, using your learning and all. But all the learning in the world counts for nothing in a tight spot, which is why you'll need me riding alongside. I won't even ask for pay in advance. Just a fair split of the proceeds.'

'You have been listening to the wrong kind of gossip. This isn't about money. And I'm not about to run off with a brawler like you,' Pilgrim said, and nudged the mara into a trot.

Creed had to let go of the bridle or be pulled off his feet, but he tried to keep up, telling Pilgrim that he was making a big mistake, that he shouldn't rely on the help of strangers, he'd be sorry if he did, tripping and falling to his hands and knees as the mara got into its stride.

'I knew it the first time I saw you!' he shouted. 'Knew you are no kind of man!'

Pilgrim rode on without looking back. The upset of the encounter quickly bled away and he discovered a little sympathy for Creed's desperation. Pilgrim loved Willow and his new nephew, loved Thorn and Bearbane and Blessed and all the rest, and felt an unconditional loyalty to his tribe and a deep cellular connection with its territory, but like Creed he knew that it was no longer where he wanted to live. He had moved on, had found a new home and new friends in Highwater Reach. The community of pures, and the people who shared his love of knowledge and books and of exploring and explaining the hidden machineries of the world. He had returned to his tribe only because he hoped it would give him what he needed to finish Master Able's work, and find a way back to the life he had made for himself.

The last of the sunset was fading above the mountains to the west and dusk was deepening across the marshes and water meadows on either side of the road. The flat dark countryside and the cries and shrieks of night birds, the croaks and whistles of frogs, the secretive rustling of unseen creatures, made him nervous. The muffled footsteps of his mara seemed overloud. Every pocket of deep shadow under the trees alongside the road harboured a potential ambush. At last he sighted a distant glimmer of lights, and urged the mara into an ambling trot and was relieved when the gateway of the Lodge of the Eastern Shore appeared, a lantern hung from the apex of its arch.

The lodge was strung along a rise above a long arm of the lake. When Pilgrim woke early the next morning men were already setting out in flat-bottomed skiffs to trawl for shrimp or fish for perch, striped eels, toothfish and the big mudfish that lurked in the lake bottom. He broke his fast alone in the commons and the cook made up a packed lunch for him and he rode on towards the old quarry in the low hills at the southern end of the lake, following a track that switchbacked up stony slopes to a half-circle of steeply terraced limestone cliffs where stone had been quarried for the construction of the Hearth's inner wall, and watchtowers and animal pens built when bears still prowled the territory.

He had decided to inspect the quarry after his conversation with Willow, and was relieved to see that it was little changed from the time when he had hunted for fossils as a precocious stripling. Conical spoil heaps piled along the north side of the cliffs. Tough thorn bushes growing amongst tumbled boulders; half-shaped blocks of stone lying alongside an open-walled shed with a broken roof of sunbleached planks. A splitting maul half as tall as a person leaned against one of the shed's supports. A tiny, gem-green lizard, perched alertly on a stone, flicked away when his shadow passed across it.

The limestone quarried there had once been part of the floor of a warm shallow sea, built layer upon layer by the chalk shells of tiny animals and plants snowing down from the sunlit surface. Larger animals had fallen to the sea floor, too. Some had been covered in silt before scavengers could devour them, and their shells and bones had mineralised, turned into stony replicas. Coilshells, jaguar toenails and clams, sea flowers, fish, turtles and a single specimen of a big marine reptile, commonly called a snakefish, that quarry workers had uncovered and now stood in the men's lodge. People had once believed that these creatures, along with thunder lizards and

59

other monsters, had been made by ogres to spite the Mother, and were destroyed in the same catastrophe which had burned and flooded the world when the Mother had put an end to the ogres' blasphemous tenure. But those floods could never have washed as high as the Saltmire tribe's mountain territory, and it was generally agreed now that the thunder lizards had been destroyed in an earlier catastrophe; that they and creatures like the snakefish and all the rest had lived in an age long before the Mother had quickened the ogres, and in the millennia since then Her restless surface had wrinkled and creased and raised what had once been the floor of a sea to its present elevation.

Pilgrim tethered his mara in a shaded spot under a clump of saw palmettos and limped about piles of broken slabs and thorn bushes and pipe cacti on the quarry floor, the sun's heat beating on his back, his head sheltered by a conical straw hat. Ever mindful of snakes and scorpions, he levered up stones with his stick and used the brick hammer he had borrowed from the Hearth's workshop to crack promising specimens along fault lines. The smell of dust and broken stone kindled vivid memories of earlier expeditions. A clandestine chorus of crickets sent up a metallic buzz that came and went in waves. The motionless air trapped inside the quarry's cirque shimmered with heat, and time seemed motionless too. An eternal now in which past and present dissolved and mingled.

Pilgrim worked until noon, but found far less than he had hoped. A handful of shark teeth, their enamel transformed into lustrous mother of pearl, several square segments from the armoured shells of sea turtles, a hand-sized slab bearing a small cluster of the stalked feather dusters of sea flowers, and a small coilshell, its tight spiral ridged with annual growth rings. Still, he could tell the men's council that there were many more specimens like these to be found in the spoil heaps,

60

that larger fossils like the snakefish and the big coilshell he had given to the tribe could be cut out of the terraces, and with Willow's help he could explain how much the trade might earn.

As he sat in the shade of the old shed and ate the lunch of smoked eel, beans and honeyed cactus flower that the lodge's cook had prepared for him, he pictured a work gang picking through rocks in the spoil heaps or wedging out slabs on the terraces, cleaning finds in the refurbished shed, packing them in cases filled with straw and loading them onto maras. The first step on a long journey to Concord. He still hoped that the men's council would grant his request for a modest stipend, so that he could begin the work on sightings of the visitors as soon as possible, but felt a little more optimistic about the fossil business. It might be worthwhile setting it up even if he was given the stipend. It wouldn't take too long to train people; he could do that after he had completed Master Able's research, and then he could return to Highwater Reach. Act as an agent overseeing the sale of fossils sent from the territory and take a modest cut of the profits, and when he had written the monograph on the sightings he could publish it in a good edition. Tooled leather boards, the best reed paper, creamy and pleasingly heavy, hand-tinted illustrations laid in . . .

He entertained himself with these daydreams as he rode out of the foothills towards Blessed's lodge. He was sunburnt, sore in every muscle and his bad leg ached from hip to ankle, but for the first time since Master Able's death he was afloat on a balmy tide of unqualified happiness.

9.

Pilgrim rewrote his request for a stipend, sketched a proposal for the fossil trade and amended it after consulting with Willow, and handed both documents to Blessed, who agreed to tender them at the next meeting of the men's council.

'You should expect some close questioning,' Blessed warned him. 'We know little about fossils and less about these visitors.'

'I look forward to it,' Pilgrim said, and meant it. He believed that he had made his submissions as tight and plausible as possible, and relished the opportunity of using everything Master Able had taught him about the art of oratory to persuade the council to support his work.

The meeting was half a moonspan away. Pilgrim visited Grandfather Bearbane again, and they shared a bath in one of the wooden tubs set outside the lodge and filled with sulphur-scented water from the hot spring. Bearbane bent over his knees, humming happily as Pilgrim scrubbed the threadbare pelt of his humped back, but afterwards, as they bonelessly relaxed in the warm water, he asked after people whose names Pilgrim either didn't recognise or knew were dead, and repeated the story about how he had earned the right to adopt a new name. Pilgrim tried his best to sound cheerful and engaged, but was reminded again of how much he had lost. His master, his comfortable life in Highwater Reach, and now the person who had been such a strong and vital presence when he had been growing up.

He gave Amity a fossil shark tooth and told the story of how it had ended up in a quarry far from the ocean, and went riding with two of his cousins, answering their questions about life in the capital as best he could, rediscovering old haunts and places which had once seemed to him more important than anywhere else in the world, and hunting for rock conies. Although he had been lent one of the brand-new windup crossbows that could fire half a dozen bolts before reloading, he missed with every shot, and took to practising his marksmanship in the yard of the lodge, using an old straw target he'd found in one of the barns. When Blessed commented that he might better improve his skill by trying to reduce the numbers of coneys that infested the western pasture, Pilgrim promised that he would, once he could hit the target regularly.

Blessed pushed up his broad-brimmed straw hat and scratched his forehead. The hat band was sweat-stained and his clothes were dusty from a long day's work and his rawhide gloves were tucked in his belt. 'Are you planning to take down these visitors?'

'Some of the places I intend to visit are fairly remote. I want to be sure that I can live off the land should I need to.'

'Running out of supplies might be the least of your problems. You ought maybe to think of hiring a guide. Even the best rover can get into trouble if he's riding on his own.'

'I have to keep expenses to the minimum,' Pilgrim said, thinking of Creed, knowing that he been right to refuse that desperate and dubious offer. Travelling with someone convicted of a violent offence against the great harmony would most likely be more dangerous than riding alone.

'Then maybe I'll find you a better crossbow,' Blessed said. 'That one is fine for coneys but wouldn't be much use against spotted cats or reavers wanting to rob you. I have one that swaps out wheels, so reloading is much faster. Carried it when I used to spend time up in the summer ranges. I'm too old for that now, so you're welcome to make use of it.'

'That's a generous gift, Uncle.'

'It isn't a gift. I expect you to bring it back when you're done.'

One day, while Pilgrim was unsaddling his mara after a ride along the lakeshore, a lodge hand came up and told him that he should hurry on over to the commons. It seemed that he had a couple of visitors. The hand shrugged when Pilgrim asked who they were. 'Strangers. Didn't catch their names.'

The visitors were sitting with Blessed on goat-hide cushions by the big stone fireplace in the commons. One was Intrepid Windrush, sleek and composed in a brightly patterned waistcoat and whipcord riding trews; the other a person Pilgrim didn't recognise.

'I've been learning about your friends' work in the New Territories,' Blessed said cheerfully. 'Dash was telling me how he was a scout one time in the borderlands. We were trying to figure out if he ever met Bearbane.'

'Stories grow large in the telling,' the second visitor, Dash, said. 'Even so, your grandfather sounds quite the character.' He was a compact muscular blunt-muzzled person, a white stripe in his pelt running from his forehead across his scalp, dressed in canvas trews and a patchwork vest with rawhide lacing. He gazed at Pilgrim with calm self-possession.

'I know Intrepid Windrush slightly, but this fellow I haven't yet met,' Pilgrim said, looking at his uncle.

'Dash Crow,' Intrepid Windrush said. 'An invaluable companion and guide whenever I make a visit to the New Territories.'

'At your service,' Dash Crow said to Pilgrim with a lazy smile.

'Your guide seems to have led you somewhat south of your destination,' Pilgrim said to Intrepid.

'We thought we'd break our journey to bring you the latest good news.'

'They've been telling me about the preacher who's stirring things up on the west coast,' Blessed said.

A tray of tea and small eats was set on the floor by the cushions. Blessed clearly believed that Intrepid and this smiling stranger, Dash Crow, were friends and colleagues of his nephew, and was treating them to the appropriate degree of hospitality.

'I should talk to Intrepid alone for a moment,' Pilgrim told his uncle, and once outside, on the porch, he let his anger show. Aiming his cane at the charlatan, telling him that he might admire his persistence if it wasn't so pointlessly intrusive.

'I've already made it clear that I neither need nor want your help. And how did you know where to find me? I hope you haven't been troubling my friends.'

'Oh, there was no need for that, since you lodged a forwarding request with the postal service,' Intrepid Windrush said. 'As to why I came here, I have news that I know will be of great interest to you.'

'If this is about your so-called prophet, you've wasted your journey.'

'I have news about him, too. But first, I thought you should know that the Sweetwater Collective purchased Master Able's manuscript from his family, and gave it to Master Mindwell. Along with a donation to help him to continue the work.'

Pilgrim tried to hide his shock, knew from Intrepid's sly smile that he had not been successful. Master Mindwell had been one of Master Able's closest and oldest friends. One of the few who had not fallen out with Able after he had taken up his work on the sightings of the visitors, although Mindwell made it clear that he thought it at best an amusing whimsy.

'I'm glad someone else is taking it seriously,' Pilgrim said. 'But Master Mindwell is a little late to the game, and it's nothing like his usual studies.'

'He put up an advertisement several days ago, seeking an assistant who would be willing to travel out to the New Territories,' Intrepid said. 'That's how I found out about it. I'm surprised that your friends haven't alerted you.'

'Why did you rush out here to tell me this?'

Pilgrim was wondering how much Intrepid knew about his plans. How much Blessed had innocently let slip.

'The other reason I stopped by,' Intrepid said, 'is that Foeless has had another visitation.'

'And how are things on Morningstar?'

Intrepid ignored the jibe. 'I'm on my way to talk to him about his latest encounter. To hear every marvellous detail, and his interpretation of what he was shown. You could come with me. Meet Foeless, walk with him in the places he has walked with visitors. See the site where he ascended with them in their vehicle. Think of what you might learn!'

'I have research of my own,' Pilgrim said.

'And no funds to support it. I heard about that business with Master Able's family. Very unfair of them. The kind of closed-mindedness we both wish to combat.'

'My business is no business of yours,' Pilgrim said.

'Foeless's followers grow in number day by day. As do their contributions. I could persuade him to use a small fraction of that money to pay for the publication of your master's work. Annotated and organised by you, in any way you see fit. I won't change or add a single word.'

'And what would you gain?'

'Foeless is devoted to fulfilling his mission of spreading enlightenment, but there are some, scholars especially, that refuse to listen to him. Your master's work might make them take the matter of the visitors more seriously.'

There it was. A chance to beat Mindwell to publication, but only by linking Master Able's work to the very nonsense it was meant to challenge, and irrevocably damaging his reputation. And Pilgrim's too, such as it was. It wasn't much of a choice. In fact, it was no choice at all.

Pilgrim said, 'I'll be very happy to share my master's work with you. But like everyone else you'll have to wait until it is finished.'

10.

He couldn't settle after Intrepid Windrush and his companion had left, and saddled his mara and went for a ride around the boundaries of the lodge's pastures. The animal knew the way, and Pilgrim let it amble along at its own pace while he tried to work things through.

There was no possibility of collaboration with Master Mindwell, an established scholar who would take little notice of the opinions of a lowly secretary. And the Sweetwater Collective's intervention deepened the resentment and hurt that had stung him when they had refused his request for help, and strengthened his resolve to prove himself capable of completing his master's work. He told himself that if this was now a race, he had the advantage. The manuscript which had passed into Mindwell's hands was partial and incomplete, and did not mention every sighting – the ghost lights in the ruined bear city that Pilgrim had visited, for instance, and several others which had not been confirmed when Master Able had died. And because of Able's scruples about privacy, the sightings described in his manuscript did not mention any witnesses by name, and Pilgrim had taken the precaution of excising their contact details from his master's notes. So even if Mindwell contrived to get a version of that unfinished manuscript into print, it would not necessarily duplicate everything that Pilgrim hoped to publish, and might even boost interest in it.

Even so, he knew he had to press on as quickly as possible, but there were six more days before his proposal would be presented to the council meeting. He reread his submission and spotted several embarrassing flaws he might have to defend, and his small collection of fossils seemed dismally unimpressive. At least there was something he could do about that, and he returned to the quarry and clambered about the lower terraces as best he could, used a wedge and hammer to split off thin slabs of limestone. He quickly found a nice coilshell two handspans across, and soon afterwards the imprint of the tail of a fish, but after those small successes he spent several hours cracking rock and found nothing but the usual gravel of shelly matter, passing from futile anticipation to a kind of stubborn bemusement before at last giving up and clambering to the floor of the quarry and gathering a handful of commonplace sharks' teeth and turtle-shell fragments from the spoil heaps.

He told himself that it was just a dry spell, that finding good fossils was as much a matter of luck as persistence, and thought of a passage in one of Master Able's monographs about the partiality of the preservation of ogre artefacts.

For the most part only commonplace artefacts, produced in teeming multitudes and discarded in places where they were quickly buried, have been discovered. Some of the ogres' coastal cities are memorialised in thin layers of wreckage crushed into narrow strata, but their cities of the plains and deserts, if they ever existed, are entirely gone. We have discovered a few of the statues that the ogres sculpted from enduring stone, but if their most valued artforms were made from substances as ephemeral as light or cobwebs or clouds we shall never know. Most things are lost to time. In almost every case, where there should be something, there is nothing.

69

He had the good coilshell, the fish tail, the smaller fossils. He would come back tomorrow and try again. Meanwhile, it was late in the day and he wanted to reach the lodge by the lake, where he planned to stay overnight, before darkness fell.

The road out of the hills passed one of the old watch-towers, a flat-topped stump built of dressed stone blocks and standing close to a crossroads, looking out across tawny grassland towards the lake. A relic from the time, not so long ago, when bears from the forests to the north had raided the territory, slaughtering livestock and people in crazed sprees of bloodlust that ended only when they had been trapped and killed. As Pilgrim approached, weary and dusty, the low sunlight in his eyes, two men rode out of its shadows. It took him a few moments to realise who they were: Creed and one of the rovers who had shared the bowl of sweetroot beer with him in the strangers' lodge. They were perched on the broad shoulders of dray maras, riding them saddleless with rope halters, urging them forward before Pilgrim could turn his own mount, pulling up on either side of him.

The rover, a large, lumpen older fellow with a pure white pelt and pink eyes, cradled a stout length of wood. Creed held a knife down by his thigh, its blade chipped from black obsidian and wickedly hooked. He smiled at Pilgrim and said, 'Do you believe in fate? Because at this moment I surely do.'

'I'm still not minded to hire you,' Pilgrim said. 'I'm sorry, but there it is.'

'Oh, we're past that,' Creed said. 'It wasn't nice, the way you turned me down and rode off all haughty and proud. Like I was nothing and you were everything. I was angry, and rightly so, but after a while I got over it and thought, why not go anyway? Head out on my own. So I made my plans and gathered up some supplies, and I persuaded Gentle here, who works in the stables, to part out a ride for me. And he

70

decided to come along, having had enough of this place too. And here we are, and here you are, riding by where me and Gentle were resting up.'

'Waiting for cover of darkness,' Gentle said.

His voice was slow and deep. A scar pulled one eye half-closed, made him look sleepy, but Pilgrim reckoned that he was at least as dangerous as Creed.

'You can't tell me the Mother didn't intend this meeting,' Creed said. 'One way or another, you are going to help me after all.'

Pilgrim ignored him and addressed Gentle. 'I know fine well what it is to be different. That some think people like you are bad luck, cursed by the Mother, simply because you lack pigment in your pelt and your eyes. My tribe took you in and gave you work because we don't hold with that kind of cruel superstition. And this is how you repay our kindness?'

The big man shrugged. 'There are better things than working in someone else's stables.'

'If you think that it would be better to work for my cousin instead, I'm afraid that you will come to regret it.'

'No one is working for anyone,' Creed said sharply. 'Gentle and me, we're partners.'

'If you return to the Hearth with those stolen maras, I can put in a word for you,' Pilgrim told Gentle. 'Explain that there was a misunderstanding. Make sure you don't get into any trouble.'

Creed looked across at his companion and said, 'Didn't I tell you he had a smart mouth?'

'I'm trying to help you fix this before it gets out of hand,' Pilgrim said.

He had a hollow feeling in his stomach, realised that he wouldn't be allowed to ride away unscathed because Creed knew that he would raise the alarm. At best, he'd be tied up and left in the old watchtower while Creed and Gentle made

71

their escape. At worst . . . But he didn't want to think about that. He didn't want to think about Creed's worst, given what he had done to the fellow he'd fought.

'How you're going to help us,' Creed said, 'you're going to give up that fine mara you're riding, and your fancy clothes and anything else we can use or sell.'

He edged his own mara closer, warning Pilgrim to raise his hands, keep them away from his weapon.

Pilgrim realised that he meant the crossbow hung from a loop over the horn of his saddle. 'It's for hunting coneys,' he said, feeling angry and foolish. It had not occurred to him to draw the crossbow and put it on Creed and Gentle. It would not have occurred to any right-thinking person.

Creed leaned across the withers of his mara and lifted the crossbow's loop from the saddle horn. He swung it to and fro for a few moments, as if judging its usefulness, then slung it over his shoulder. 'You can rid yourself of your cane, too,' he said. 'And that hammer hung behind your saddle.'

The cane was tucked slantwise in Pilgrim's belt. He pulled it free and dropped it on the ground, dropped the brick hammer beside it, and froze when Creed raised his knife, tried not to flinch as the hooked point of its blade touched his chest, dragging upward and catching the pendant's fine chain and lifting it.

'I won't hurt you,' Creed said, 'as long as you do as I ask. You can start by handing over this bauble.'

'It was a gift from my dead master,' Pilgrim said.

'And now you can gift it to me.'

Creed's smile showed most of his small sharp teeth. He was having fun.

'Are you going to let him rob me, Gentle?' Pilgrim said. 'If you are, I won't be able to help you when my people catch up with you.'

The hollowness in his stomach was still there, but he also felt an electric recklessness tingling in his blood, lifting the hairs of his pelt.

'I know the territory as well as they do,' Creed said. 'We'll be far away before the night is out. Hand over that bauble or I'll cut it off, and won't be too careful doing it neither.'

'Better do as he says,' Gentle said.

'I have something more valuable,' Pilgrim said, and reached behind himself and unhooked one of the sacks of fossils, shook it so it dryly rattled, let it fall to the ground.

'What's in it?' Creed said.

'Rare and ancient fossils. Collectors in Concord and elsewhere will pay good money for them.'

'Take a look,' Creed told Gentle.

'Why don't you?' Gentle said. 'Since we are equal partners, neither one telling the other what to do.'

The two of them stared at each other. Creed was the first to break, telling Pilgrim this better not be another trick, swinging one leg over his mara's withers, sliding neatly to the ground. He toed the sack and looked up at Pilgrim and said, 'If there's a snake in here I'll make you eat it.'

'Does it feel like a snake?'

'Or a scorpion. I hate those little monsters. On the coast I put my boot on one time and got stung on my big toe.'

'You have to remember to shake out your boots,' Gentle said, slow and serious and patient.

'Like you done everything right your entire life,' Creed said.

'No snakes, no scorpions,' Pilgrim said. 'Just fossils, as I told you.'

Creed picked up the sack and loosened the string tied around its neck and tipped a clutch of sharks' teeth into his palm. He poked amongst them, held up the biggest. 'How much would I get for these?'

73

'Let me see it,' Gentle said, and as Creed turned to him Pilgrim snatched another sack and swung it as hard as he could, feeling the slab of rock — the one printed with the fish tail — crack in two as it smacked into the rump of Gentle's mara. As the animal bucked and bolted Pilgrim kneed his own mount, but Creed caught its bridle and yanked its head around, stepping with it as it turned in a half-circle and halted.

Still holding the bridle, Creed glared up at Pilgrim, shouting at him, telling him to get down, raising his knife. 'Get down right now or I'll cut you bad.'

Pilgrim knew, in a freezing moment, that the man was going to hurt him no matter what he did. He was still holding the sack with the broken slab inside, and swung it hard and fast, catching Creed under the chin. The blow shivered up Pilgrim's arm and Creed fell backwards and his head struck one of the rocks that lined the verge of the road. There was a sound, distinct and terrible, like a hammer striking a hollow gourd, and Creed shivered like a clubbed fish and lay still.

Gentle had halted his mara's headlong flight and turned it around. Now he urged it forward, looking down at Creed, looking at Pilgrim, his pink gaze level and serious. 'Reckon you might have killed him.'

Creed lay on his back, the knife lying beyond his outflung arm. His eyes were open and rolled back sightlessly. Blood ran from one ear, dripping into a little puddle on the baked dirt of the road.

'Help me,' Pilgrim said to Gentle, and with a sick feeling slid off his mara and knelt by Creed and felt his throat, seeking a pulse. 'Help me help him.'

'I want no part in any of this,' Gentle said, and sawed his mara around and kicked it into a lumbering trot, heading out across the dry grass, leaving Pilgrim alone with his victim.

11.

Creed had suffered a broken jaw and several smashed teeth, and a swelling to the brain that the tribe's chief physic treated with trepanation. He lay unconscious in the Hearth's sanatorium for three days and when he woke he was entirely blind, and claimed to have no memory of stealing a mara and attempting to rob Pilgrim Saltmire.

Blessed told Pilgrim that it was as if the Mother had interceded and punished the man with the loss of his sight after he had failed to show proper repentance for half-blinding another person. It was no comfort to Pilgrim. He believed that he alone was responsible for what had happened. He should have followed the code of great harmony, given up the pendant and anything else that Creed demanded. Instead, he had lashed out in fear and unthinking anger, and now the would-be robber was the victim and he was the villain, indelibly stained with shame and guilt.

He replayed the moment over and again in his mind, reliving the flare of anger and the aftermath of shock and mortification, yearning for a different outcome. He could have surrendered peacefully. Or the weighted bag could have missed Creed, or Creed could have flinched out of its path before robbing and beating him and making his escape. Pilgrim would have deserved that — the robbing, the beating. And afterwards he could have stood before the men's council, could have presented his request for their support with a clear conscience . . .

But not even the Mother could unpick that thread. It was what it was. He had badly hurt a person. Blinded him. Crippled him. It was now up to the aunties, rather than the men's council, to decide his fate, and when he gave them his account of what had happened he did not ask for clemency. Said that he did not want or expect that Creed's intentions or his own actions afterwards, tending the man as best he could before riding to the nearest lodge to ask for help, should be taken into account. He expected to be punished and knew that he deserved it.

He was exiled to a hut in the high pastures while the aunties discussed how he could make amends. No one guarded or watched over him; his promise to stay there until the verdict was delivered was deemed to be sufficient. Silence, solitude, day after day of fine sunny weather. It should have been a perfect opportunity to reread Master Able's notes and think about how to complete the monograph, but Pilgrim was unable to concentrate on any of that, and besides, there was no point. He had lost what little chance he had of winning his tribe's support, and it seemed that he had lost any advantage he might have over Master Mindwell, too. After sending a tapcode message to Swift and Ardent, he'd received a reply confirming Intrepid Windrush's story about the Sweetwater Collective's purchase of Master Able's papers and the grant given to Master Mindwell. For all of their talk of honour, the Collective's money had persuaded Able's kin to set aside their scruples, his friends had written, adding that Mindwell had appointed an assistant who had set out for the New Territories to interview witnesses old and new and visit the locations of sightings, just as Pilgrim had planned to do before his disgrace.

The assistant is someone you might know. Earnest Smallhill, one of the bookrunner tribe. Not the brightest of fellows, but methodical.

So there it was. The race was lost before it had fairly begun. Worse than knowing that he had failed himself was knowing that he had failed his dead master.

At last, Blessed rode out to the hut and told Pilgrim that the aunties had made their judgement, and when Pilgrim appeared before them for the second time it went quickly. He was told that Thorn had suggested where he should be sent and the work he must do, and the rest of the aunties had agreed to act on her recommendation. After a year he would stand before them again, and would be freed if he could show that he had fulfilled the terms of his sentence and exhibited the proper degree of humility and contrition.

'I don't deserve it,' Pilgrim told Willow the next day.

'You've been given a chance to redeem yourself,' his sister said. 'Work on that. Don't waste time wallowing in self-pity.'

'Will you thank Thorn for me? Tell her that I do not deserve her kindness, and that I understand why she doesn't want to see me.'

'Sending you away has nothing to do with sympathy or kindness,' Willow said. 'Creed isn't the first in his immediate family to get into trouble. They're a chancy crew, scraping a living by trapping and hunting on the northern edge of the territory, and hiring out as caravanners. Thorn suggested you should be sent south because she is worried that they might cause further disharmony by trying to take revenge. She reckons that they won't be able to reach you where you're going, and hopes tempers will have cooled by the time you return.'

'It might be better for everyone if I was sent into permanent exile.'

'What did I say about self-pity? While I was bound to the Hearth, like every other woman in the tribe, you were able to leave for the capital, to make a new and better life for yourself. And now you've been given the chance to restore your honour and start afresh. Don't throw that away.'

'You should take up my idea about the fossil-selling business,' Pilgrim said. 'It really could make a profit. Anything you want or need to know about it, write to me. I'll help as best I can. Tell you how to clean fossils, give you my contacts in Highwater Reach and Concord . . . Who knows? You might even get to travel there.'

'I hoped making and selling new kinds of teas might allow me to do that one day.'

'Why not do both?'

Willow said that she would think about it, told him that he had already made a good start on the path to redemption by volunteering to look after Creed's accomplice.

'That's more for my own self-interest. Considering where I am going.'

'It shows that you are capable of forgiveness and contrition. Continue to follow that path, and it will lead you back home soon enough.'

12.

The albino, Gentle, had been caught hiding in a covert up in the foothills, two days after the failed robbery attempt. His brief testimony confirmed Pilgrim's account of the attempted robbery, and Pilgrim, impressed by the man's honesty, asked the aunties if he could make use of him.

When Gentle was brought to Blessed's lodge, Pilgrim took him for a walk across one of the pastures and explained about his sentence and exile. 'I would like it very much if you would come with me,' he said.

'I thought your people were aiming to send me off to a Union camp and a spell of hard labour,' Gentle said.

'That's the alternative.'

'Aren't you worried that I might turn on you?'

'You're the one who should be worried,' Pilgrim said. 'Considering what happened. What I did.'

'What it's worth, I reckon Creed had it coming. He underestimated you and paid the price.'

'You and I must pay a price too. I think it might benefit both of us to do that together.'

Gentle stopped and turned to survey the sandy pastures. Maras resting under a clump of shade trees. Nothing moving but the blades of the windmills on the ridge of the lodge, turning slowly in the hot breeze. He was wearing a long-sleeved tunic and a wide-brimmed straw hat fastened under his jaw by a length of string. Lacking pigment in his pelt and skin, he was always at serious risk of sunburn.

'They don't have you under guard, it looks like,' he said. 'I were you, I'd be giving some serious thought about clearing out.'

'I promised that I would abide by the decision of the aunties.'

'Creed made the same promise, after he was sent back by the fishing folk. Didn't stop him trying to run away.'

'How did you fall in with him? Was it an objection to your work, or to the people you had to work with?'

'I didn't mind the work. It was mostly tending maras, and I like working with animals. Prefer them to the company of people.'

'Because animals accept you for who you are,' Pilgrim said.

'I remember you told me you understood how people judge by appearances. You being a cripple and all. But despite how it went down between you and Creed, you still have your family and your tribe,' Gentle said, without any trace of animosity or bitterness. 'While I had to walk away from all of that because they couldn't abide someone who looks like I do.'

'I'm sorry to hear that.'

Gentle shrugged. 'My tribe is poorer than yours. Scattered along the desert coast in what was disputed territory until a few years ago. Fisherfolk, mostly. Hard way to make a living. And dangerous too, going out in small boats on the big water, which is why fisherfolk cleave to all kinds of superstitions. They have tattoos they think will save them from drowning, always step on a boat right foot first, never look back to shore after they leave port, and if a wind wanderer flies too close they'll pour a libation of heart of wine into the sea to ward off the bad luck it brings. Born looking as I was, I was thought to be as much bad luck as any wind wanderer. Couldn't go anywhere near boats, had other striplings pick fights with me when I was growing up, was locked up during the Season in case I frightened off suitors come to the festival . . . I got out of all that soon as I could. Renounced my tribe before they could renounce me, don't even go by its name or the forename my mother gave me, been on walkabout ever since. Your tribe ain't as bad as some that employ rovers, but I've been here long enough. Occurs to me now that I could make a run for it right now and get a pretty good head start before you raise the alarm. If you want to do me a favour, you could maybe sit out here a while before you do it. I could even rough you up a little, so they won't think you helped me.'

'How did it work out, the last time you tried to make a run for it?'

'I know better than to lay up again,' Gentle said. 'I'll just keep going 'til this place isn't even a speck on the horizon.'

It was hard to tell if he was being serious or not, this big placid person who was cleverer than he let on.

Pilgrim said, 'The place I'm being sent to should satisfy that desire. It used to be my tribe's territory before we moved here. Far to the south and hard to reach, except by sea. The people who live there are distant relatives of my tribe, but we have little to do with each other. And to be frank, I'm not sure how they will take to me, given what I am, and what I did. It would be good to have a companion.'

'Especially one as big and strange as me.'

'Big and strange as you are, I suppose that people tend to think you must be stupid, too. I don't think you are. You just play up to prejudices because it's easier than pushing back all the time.'

'I was stupid enough to fall in with Creed.'

'I'm not Creed.'

'No, you ain't.'

'And people who are strange – people like us – should stick together. I can't promise much in the way of payment, but it will be a lot better than breaking rocks in a Union camp,' Pilgrim said.

'Tell me some more about this place they're sending you,' Gentle said. 'Tell me everything you know.'

13.

The original territory claimed by Pilgrim's tribe was on the ragged, perilous west coast of the far south. Always a marginal land, it had become even more so as the climate cooled and changes in ocean currents brought freezing water from the icelands beyond the continent's crooked tip. Summers grew wetter and cooler; winter snows came ever earlier; catches from fishing, the principal source of income, fell drastically. At last, a little over a hundred years ago, most of the tribe moved north, to land they had been granted at the edge of the great mountain range that ran down the western side of the Union, but a small number of holdout families remained, and the tribe still possessed title to its old Hearth and the land around it.

Pilgrim and Gentle, escorted by Blessed, took more than half a moonspan to reach the place. A series of train journeys took them west and south through desert pinched between sea and sere mountains. Desert at last gave way to grassland and grassland to forest, and at the little city of Fortunate Valley they embarked on a trading ship that hugged the rocky coast as it travelled south, delivering food and goods to settlements, taking on animal hides and salt meat, salt-cured fish and tanks of live crabs and lobsters, and at last slouching into the harbour of the little town of Stonehaven near the end of a dim cold day, flurries of sleet blowing across the black water and revealing and obscuring a scatter of houses along the shore. After the ship docked, Blessed hugged Pilgrim and pressed his hands together and bowed to Gentle, who was so pale he was almost transparent, having been seasick the entire voyage. 'I'll see you in a year,' Blessed promised them, and they picked up their scant belongings and walked down the gangplank to the bleak shore of their exile.

The clannish people who clung to the coastal fringe had more or less abandoned the territory's Hearth, five stone towers standing inside the circle of a wall of packed clay breached in too many places to serve as any kind of defence against the depredations of bears and wild animals. Grace Wren Saltmire, a testy, raggedy-whiskered old person who made it clear that she was greatly inconvenienced by their arrival, showed Pilgrim and Gentle to their rooms in the smallest tower, which was braced from its footings to its flat top by ancient wooden scaffolding. Pilgrim's room had once been a chapel used by the senior auntie of the Hearth for private contemplation; Gentle's, on the floor above, was smaller and plainer, but had a better view from its slit window, looking out at dense forest that rolled away towards the flanks of saw-toothed mountains. There was a small kitchen and a draughty drop easement, no electricity, no running water.

'You can buy a ration of good dry wood from the store I keep in the main tower, or you can collect it yourself,' Grace Wren Saltmire said. 'There's any amount of dead wood in the forest, and sea coal washes up along the shore of Windy Cove, along with an abundance of driftwood. As for food, you'll have to fend for yourselves. There having been nothing in the letter I was sent about providing for you.'

Small and hunchbacked, dressed in a greasy brocade tunic and a skirt of leather plates, she was the caretaker of the

Hearth, and also tended to the old men and women, maze-minded like Grandfather Bearbane or terminally ill, who were living out their final days in a warren of cells in the central tower.

'You'll need to buy candles,' she said. 'Likewise lamp oil. There's a chandler in town can supply you with necessaries. Don't let him try to cheat you because you are outsiders. Tell him I'll be asking after what he charges.'

Pilgrim thanked her, and said that they had purchased some supplies before boarding the trading ship.

'Not nearly enough, judging by your luggage,' Grace Wren Saltmire said. 'Winter's coming, so you'd best think about getting some proper clothing too. You're free to go anywhere you want, but I'd advise you to keep out of the mountains. Even in summer the weather up there can change in a moment, and there's an abundance of bears, and they're getting bolder with every passing year. And keep away from any boats. Folk see either of you so much as look cross-eyed at one, they'll not put out to sea on it until it's been purged and blessed, and they won't thank you for the trouble you've caused.'

'I come from fisherfolk stock,' Gentle said. 'I know all about ignorant prejudices and superstitions towards people who are a little different.'

'It isn't what you are,' Grace Wren Saltmire said, with a sharp look, 'but what you did. Library's in the east tower. I won't be troubling you there. It's your business to see to it. And I'll thank you for not troubling me unless you have exhausted every other course. I have enough work already.'

'And what am I expected to do,' Gentle said to Pilgrim after the old woman had left, 'while you are rummaging through old books?'

'Our little stock of food won't last long. How are your hunting skills?'

85

'No one would ever have me on a boat, but I know how to fish from the shore. Spare some of that money you were given, I'll buy hooks and line for fishing, and the makings of snares and traps. Maybe some birdlime, if they have it.'

'First we need to find some wood and get a fire going,' Pilgrim said. 'These rooms haven't seen a guest in a long time.'

He was cleaning dust and mouse droppings from the kitchen cupboards and Gentle was poking a stick up a blocked flue when Noble Seatree arrived, barging up the stairs without warning or invitation. A swag-bellied broad-shouldered person dressed in a raggedy fur coat and leather trews, accompanied by a brindled cur on a chain leash, he told them that he was the town constable and had been tasked with making sure that the terms of exile were followed to the letter. He turned to Gentle and asked which tribe had grown such a big fellow. The cur looked at Gentle too, its eyes yellow as lamps.

'My people were fisherfolk,' Gentle said. 'Like yours.'

'You're in the south now, lad. Our roaring seas are nothing like the gentle waters of where you come from. And don't think that because you have a couple of spans on me that I can't improve you should you need improving,' Noble Seatree said, pulling his fur coat aside to show the sap hung from his belt. 'This here is made of cured seatree stipe. Hard but flexible, just like me. Am I understood?'

'I have had some experience of people like you,' Gentle said, with a sleepy look.

'I'm not one of your soft northern lawkeepers,' Noble Seatree said. 'So don't try to backtalk me. If you want smooth sailing it's yessir and nosir. Simple and straightforward.'

'Yessir,' Gentle said.

'Don't forget it,' Noble Seatree said, and turned to Pilgrim. His eyes were set close together under a heavy brow; his gaze was cold and contemptuous. 'You look like you'd have to stand up twice to make a shadow, but I know why you're here and I'll be keeping a sharp watch. I'm told you've been tasked with cleaning up the old library. That right?'

'I look forward to putting it in good order,' Pilgrim said.

The cur had turned its attention to him, too. Its stout canines indented its black lips and a coarse mane crested its sloping back. Pilgrim disliked and feared its kind, having had several run-ins with free-roaming curs on the terraces of Highwater Reach. Twice, he'd had to use his cane to save himself. They seemed to pick him out, as spotted cats fix on a lame deer in the middle of a herd, and he knew that a bully and blowhard like Noble Seatree would likewise spot any sign of fear and use it against him.

'It's makework as far as I'm concerned, but that doesn't mean I won't be making sure it's done correctly, or that you aren't wasting your time on your dead master's foolishness,' the constable told him. 'Oh yes, lad, I've been told all about that. I'll be paying regular visits to make sure you stay on course, and if I catch you straying I'll have to improve your memory of what you can and can't do. Meanwhile, I expect to be compensated for my trouble, on account of your tribe neglecting to send me adequate remuneration. Let's make a start on that by taking a look at what you brought with you.'

He stepped over to the kitchen table and rummaged through the small store of bottles and cans, and fresh vegetables and fruit, choosing a bunch of green plantains and a bottle of peppercorns, shoving his booty into a capacious inside pocket of his fur coat and saying, 'I suppose you were given a fund for necessaries.'

'We were given very little,' Pilgrim said. 'And that's what it's for – necessaries. Things that we need so I can do my work.'

'I'll let that slide this once, but don't think of backtalking me again,' Noble Seatree said. 'Open your treasury and spill it on the table.'

As the constable pawed through the litter of coins and promissory notes, the familiar, unwelcome heat of shame and helplessness suffused Pilgrim's face. He and Gentle shared a look, and he knew that Gentle felt as he did.

'I'll take these,' Noble Seatree said, pocketing three notes. 'And I'll expect the same when I visit you again.'

He stared at Pilgrim and Gentle, smiled when they said nothing.

'You have your makework,' he said to Pilgrim, 'but big lad there doesn't look like he's the book-loving kind. There's plenty of useful work someone like him can do, and if he can't find any I'll help him out. Better if he sorts it for himself though, because my help will come at a price. Is everything clear?'

'As ice,' Pilgrim said.

Noble Seatree studied him for a moment, a single crease bisecting his heavy brow as he tried to work out if he should feel insulted. 'Don't cause waves, hand over my fee whenever I ask for it and we'll get along just fine,' he said, and swept out, the cur sidling at his heels.

Gentle stepped to the doorway and looked down the stairs and closed the door. 'So,' he said to Pilgrim, 'was that the kind of welcome you were expecting?'

14.

Pilgrim spent most of his time in the Hearth's library, surveying the damage caused by years of neglect and making a start on cataloguing what had survived. When his tribe had quit the territory, a number of books, chiefly records of tribal history, had gone with them, but the bulk had been left in the care of an order of vestals. The last member of the order had died more than thirty years ago, and the library had been locked up and scarcely disturbed since. Pilgrim had been tasked with choosing books worth sending home, discarding those too badly damaged and preserving the rest as best he could. It was makework as Noble Seatree had observed, but Pilgrim was determined to repay Thorn's kindness by doing the best he could. There were far worse punishments than restoring a neglected library.

It occupied three floors of the east tower. The upper floor was a desolation of papers and books ruined by water leaking through the broken tiles and rotting rafters of the tower's conical roof; it didn't take Pilgrim long to realise that there was nothing worth saving. But the two floors below were relatively dry and intact, and although the shelves had been plundered, and someone had made a bonfire of books in the big fireplace of the lower floor, the rest were in relatively good condition. Some were hundreds of years old, handwritten on pages of vellum or grass paper and bound in leather or wood, but most were copies of common philosophical works, or works that deserved their obscurity. Lives of forgotten eremites and saints, archaic treatises on medicine, agriculture, animal husbandry and natural lore, outdated popular histories . . . There were a few documents from the age of bears, too. Stiff scrolls of animal hide and a single book: twenty pages of ragged-edged birch bark inscribed with columns of knotty symbols and bound between wooden boards framed with iron.

Pilgrim decided to start with the second-floor chamber, and spent several days taking down drapes eaten to lace by moths and washing years of dust from the mosaic floor with limewater and scrubbing tables and chairs before turning to the books. He worked methodically along the shelves, wiping down each volume and entering its title and a note about its condition in his catalogue, putting aside those that might be of interest to the tribe or worth selling. That was where the constable, Noble Seatree, found him, a moonspan after the first visit. He arrived unannounced, as before, but this time without his cur. Walking so softly that Pilgrim, engrossed in the book he was studying, did not realise that he had company until the constable's shadow fell across the table.

'Don't tell me that's work,' Noble Seatree said.

'I have to examine every volume to find out if it is worth sending to my Hearth,' Pilgrim said, shutting the book and pushing to his feet.

'Don't get up on my account,' Noble Seatree said. 'I seen you out and about a couple of times and know how your bad leg troubles you. You walk like a drunk trying to cross a deck in a hard blow.'

Pilgrim ignored that, said that he hoped that the constable could see that he had made a start on tidying the place.

90

'Women's work that shouldn't have taken more than a day.'

'I have also begun to catalogue the books and put them into order,' Pilgrim said, watching as the constable paced along the shelves, stopping to run a finger along the edge of one, taking a book from another and blowing dust from it.

'Don't look like you've made much headway,' he told Pilgrim, and slotted the book back in place.

'The work is slow because it has to be meticulous,' Pilgrim said, and wondered if it was sensible to use a word that the constable might not know. 'It takes time and care to clean and assess each volume.'

'So they have some value, these old books?'

'Most aren't worth the cost of shipping them north.'

'Most, but not all, eh? What about these?' Noble Seatree said, pointing to the small stack on one corner of the worktable.

'I haven't yet catalogued them,' Pilgrim said, with a pang of apprehension.

The constable picked up the topmost book and carelessly riffled through it, studied the hand-tinted plates bound in the centre. 'Pretty,' he allowed.

'It's an account of the various species of birds found in this territory,' Pilgrim said, remembering the bestiary he had given to Amity. Would the young pup understand why his uncle had been exiled? Would he forgive him, when he returned?

Noble Seatree weighed the book in his hand. 'What would something like this fetch?'

'Not very much,' Pilgrim said. 'The text is outdated, the illustrations are clumsy and coarse, and there is considerable foxing on the forepages.'

'Find more like it,' Noble Seatree said, and slipped the book into the inside pocket of his black fur coat. 'And next time I want to see some real progress here.'

'He bootlegged the mushrooms I collected this morning,' Gentle said after Pilgrim had told him about the confiscation of the book. 'And that snow hare I was marinating in its own blood.'

'Did he take his fee, too?'

'What do you think?'

'I should have told him what that book was really worth, and asked for it to be set against what he claims we owe him.'

'Probably not a good idea,' Gentle said. 'Grace says he has a short way with people he suspects of trickery.'

Gentle had turned out to be more sensible and practical than Pilgrim had hoped. He foraged for firewood and edible plants and fungi in the forest and trapped small birds with birdlime streaked on branches baited with dabs of fat, was a fair cook, diligently scoured pots and washed clothes and kept a fire burning day and night in the kitchen in a futile attempt to keep out the cold and damp. He had also befriended the old caretaker by making himself useful to her, fixing loose or leaking windows and putting up storm shutters, sweeping chimneys and helping her look after her charges. In return she had taught him a good deal of local lore and introduced him to a pair of her cousins, who took him on deer hunts. He broiled some of his share of the meat with herbs he'd discovered in an abandoned garden, and sold the rest to the chandler's and bought candles and lamp oil and other necessaries. Every third or fourth day Pilgrim accompanied him to the beach at Windy Bay, the two of them riding a mara borrowed from Grace. After Gentle had set his trotlines in the surf they fossicked for mussels and limpets, and collected driftwood and stalks of giant kelp that could be dried for kindling, and coal extruded from a seam somewhere out to sea and washed up along the strandline.

The beach was more than a league long, backed by the mud flats and tidal creeks of the marsh which had given Pilgrim's family and tribe their name. Waves detonated against stumps of rock out at sea and rolled in and crashed onto the beach and withdrew in a boil of foam and tumbling pebbles. Big white seabirds sailed above the waves on winds that had bent and scalped the thorn trees strung along the back ridge of the beach and threshed the reeds that crowded the margins of the marsh's creeks.

One day, after a storm had washed the sky clear and sunlight sparkled on the grey-green sea and spun rainbows in spray lofted by waves breaking on the offshore rocks, Pilgrim saw someone ride a mara down the back slope at the far end of the beach – a woman wrapped in a red coat, small and vivid as a flower fallen on the beach's stony grey sweep.

Gentle said that she was Teal Leadwood, an exile who lived in a cabin outside the town, disowned by her tribe because she had wanted to become a scholar.

'Seen her now and again at the chandler's. She mostly keeps herself to herself, but sends and receives a fair number of letters and tapcode messages.'

'What kind of scholar does she claim to be?'

'Something to do with folk tales and suchlike,' Gentle said. 'Makes her living from selling amber, which is why she comes here.'

Pilgrim thought at once of his pendant. 'There's amber on this beach?'

'Washes up along the coast from a forest the sea long ago drowned. She sells it to the chandler, he sells it to a merchant in Fortunate Valley. She does a bit of doctoring, too. Knows it from book learning rather than training, but some of the women prefer her to the town physic, him being a man.'

'How do you know so much?'

'Everyone talks about everyone else, there being nothing more interesting around here than other people's business. Want to know what they say about you?'

'Not really.'

On the few times he had ventured into Stonehaven Pilgrim had felt that his guilt burned like a balestar on his forehead. The indelible mark of original sin.

Off in the distance, the woman, Teal Leadwood, was ambling along the strandline where the storm had heaped mounds of kelp amongst broken tree trunks. Leading her mara by its reins, stooping now and then to examine something, showing no sign that she had noticed Pilgrim and Gentle.

'Grace told me she let her into the library a few times,' Gentle said. 'You should ask if she took anything, or maybe find something she might be interested in.'

'Why would I do that?'

'Might do you some good to speak with someone like-minded,' Gentle said blandly. 'And in the same situation as yourself.'

'I think we have been exiled for very different reasons,' Pilgrim said.

If he introduced himself to Teal Leadwood, she would be bound to ask him why he was here, and he would have to tell her the truth, because anything else would compound his guilt. Even so, as he and Gentle grubbed for nuggets of sea coal he half-hoped that she might come over, and when they finally packed up and quit the beach and she didn't so much as glance in their direction, he felt a prick of disappointment that quickly turned to resentment. He told himself that he didn't need her, or anyone else. He renewed his vow to invest all of his time and energy in his penance. And then he found the map, and everything changed.

15.

It was a goatskin scroll tucked behind stacks of mouldering ledgers in one of the cupboards. When Pilgrim unrolled it on the table it released a brittle crackle of fragments and he saw, with a thrill of delight, a map or chart drawn in black and red and gold inks. It showed a portion of the east coast and the bent-neck isthmus that connected the Union and the New Territories, dotted with miniature illustrations of bear cities. The mounds of traditional cities on the mainland, and along the coasts of the isthmus the pyramids of three new cities. There were pictures of fabulous beasts and monsters too, krakens, merpeople, wyverns, winged panthers and the like scattered across mountains, marshes and the wave-dashed sea, and standing next to one of the cities was a white figure with a blank round head, wielding a spear tipped with a jagged bolt of what might be lightning.

'My first thought was that it was a visitor,' Pilgrim told Gentle. 'But the map must be hundreds of years old, and looks to be a copy of an original made by bears. There are two kinds of writing. You see? Here, and here? Early examples of our script, naming geographical features, set above bear symbols. And some of the fanciful creatures are commonly found in bear murals and carvings.'

Gentle was amused by Pilgrim's enthusiasm, but listened patiently while he explained that it might mean that the visitors had come here long ago, perhaps before the civilisation of bears had fallen.

'Looks like it was ready to do battle with them, whatever it was,' Gentle said, meaning the lightning spear.

'It might not be a literal depiction,' Pilgrim said, 'but an attempt by the artist to show something they did not fully understand. And the resemblance to visitors may be coincidental, of course. I know of no other records of sightings in centuries past. But if it is based on truth, it is immensely valuable.'

If he had been devout, he might think it a sign from the Mother that he had been too hasty in abandoning his promise to finish Master Able's work. For here was a fresh mystery, a new angle. Had the visitors haunted bears before the fall of their civilisation? Or was the figure purely symbolic, a mythic image representing the power bears had once held over people, or the power unleashed when the people had been liberated from slavery? An image so deeply imprinted in the common psyche that it re-emerged in visions and hallucinations six hundred years later . . .

Pilgrim made a copy of the map and sent it to Swift Singletree and Ardent Whitesand with a letter that explained what it was and where he had found it, and asked his friends to try to locate the city beside the figure of the visitor and to look for similar figures in bear murals and documents lodged in the archives of the Library of All People. He would have to wait a long time for any reply. While he had been working amongst the books, winter had crept across the land. It had been snowing almost every day, mostly flurries of sleet or showers of icy pellets that rattled on the panes of handblown glass in the windows of the towers of the Hearth, and shortly after the coastal trading ship carrying Pilgrim's letter to his friends left Stonehaven a sudden storm rolled in across the sea and delivered the first blizzard. It lasted three days, blanketing the Hearth in a span of soft snow that rounded every edge and corner and plastered walls that faced to windward. When the weather cleared, Gentle helped Grace Wren Saltmire dig out the paths between the towers, and had to do it over and again as succeeding blizzards blew across the coast and deepened the drifts until the paths that cut through them were sunk deeper than even Gentle's height, and the towers wore caps of snow which shed erratic flurries that sparkled in frigid sunlight as they fell.

Between storms the skies were clear and achingly cold. Pilgrim wore a ragged fur coat while he worked in the library, warming his hands on a ceramic cylinder stuffed with coals from the kitchen fire. He was less than halfway through sorting through the books in the second-floor chamber and the chamber below it was as yet still untouched, but the discovery of the map had rekindled his desire to continue and complete Master Able's research.

'The first thing I need to do is locate and visit the ruins of the bear city associated with that mysterious image,' he told Gentle. 'If the map is a copy of a map made by bears, other images might still survive in carved panels and the like. Images that may explain its context and significance.'

'If this means that you're planning to escape,' Gentle said, 'I'll happily come along. Winter's barely begun and I've already had enough of it.'

'I made a promise that I would serve the full term of my exile and complete the work I was tasked with,' Pilgrim said. 'And I will. But there's no harm in making plans for what I want to do afterwards.'

The days grew ever colder and the night sky glittered with a ridiculous number of stars and several times tall curtains of green light spanned it from horizon to horizon, shifting and writhing as if blown by an impalpable wind. The fabled auroras of the far south, called locally the Mother's Skirts: the sign that winter had truly arrived.

It was snowing again, lightly but persistently, when Noble Seatree came for his fee. Stamping into the library with snow on his boots and snow flecking his black fur coat, standing over the fireplace and warming his hands over the small fire, rubbing them briskly together as he told Pilgrim that he had made himself a cosy little nest here.

'Reckon I should raise my price, seeing as you're faring so well.'

'We're somewhat short of food,' Pilgrim said. 'There's not much hunting to be had in the forest, and no fishing at all now the sea has frozen.'

He had not stirred from his seat at the table, was watching the constable with the usual cold stone in his stomach, waiting to find out what petty humiliation would be visited on him this time.

'Winter's hard for everyone, so don't think you'll get a pass,' Noble Seatree said, and hawked up a bolus of phlegm and spat into the fire and stalked over to the table and asked Pilgrim what he had for him this time.

Pilgrim had been making entries in the catalogue; he reserved his work on the visitors for the evening. Partly because he needed more than ever to be certain of fulfilling the terms of his exile and winning freedom; partly because Noble Seatree never visited after dark.

He pointed to the books stacked on the corner of the table and said, 'See for yourself.'

The constable pawed through them. 'Slim pickings,' he said.

'Everything I have found since your last visit.'

'If you've been slacking off, I'll have to find some way of

improving your attitude. There's always work to be done in town. A spell of clearing snow or helping out in the weaving sheds will perk you up.'

'I've added more than twenty pages to the catalogue since your last visit,' Pilgrim said, 'and sorted through twelve ells of shelving. In three or four moonspans, I should be able to make a start on the first-floor chamber.'

'I'll hold you to that. And if it looks like you'll come short, you can spend some time shovelling snow. You and Big Lad. Put something into the community instead of taking it out,' Noble Seatree said, and waggled the book. 'So, what's this one about?'

'It's a collection of devotional material. Sermons, prayers and songs. Some of the songs are very old, including chants that may date from the time when our ancestors were slaves and worked in the fields around bear settlements.'

It was a small book and not especially well bound, the pages buckled, the leather poor quality, and scuffed and stained. Pilgrim had taken to hiding his best finds on the shelves and setting out the dross for the constable. The small pleasure of cheating him was worth the risk of being found out and punished. And besides, he was honouring the terms of his exile by saving the valuable volumes from the constable's predation.

Noble Seatree weighed the little book in his hand, then put it down and picked up something else. Pilgrim felt a clean cold wave of shock pass through him. It was the map. He had been poring over it last night, as he sometimes did, looking for things he might have missed, dreaming about an eager reaction to publication of a monograph about it, fame in the right circles, elevation to a mastership . . . Silly fantasies, but potent. He'd studied it for only a little while, and then carefully rolled it up and got on with his work on Master Able's manuscript, but although he'd put away the manuscript and

99

notes he had forgotten about the map, and now the constable was ripping off the string that fastened it, flakes cracking from its edges, and shaking it out, more flakes flying, and pressing it flat on the table.

'What do we have here?' he said.

'It isn't anything,' Pilgrim said, dry-mouthed. 'A copy of a copy of a copy. And badly damaged by damp, as you can see.'

Noble Seatree was leaning over it, hands pressed on either side to keep it flat, no doubt staining it with grease and sweat. Pilgrim could see a fresh crack had opened near the middle, like a little mouth, or a wound.

The constable looked sideways at Pilgrim. He was smiling. He thought that he had an excuse to improve him. To make an appointment with a snow shovel on the streets of Stonehaven.

He said, 'A copy of what, exactly?'

'A map, obviously.' Pilgrim's entire skin was tingling and he felt as if he was sliding backwards into an enormous vacancy. 'A copy of a map made by bears. That's why there are translations printed beneath the bear script. If it was an original, there would only be bear script.'

'Looks like the Union,' Noble Seatree said.

'Yes, exactly so. A map of the east coast of what is now the Union, with the major cities of the bears marked on it. If it was an original, it would be worth something, but as it's a copy of a copy . . . They are quite common. And this one is not in the best condition.'

Noble Seatree bent towards the map. It occurred to Pilgrim that he was near-sighted, but too vain to wear corrective lenses. A clear drop of mucus hung from one of his nostrils, lengthening, stretching, falling onto the map.

'Stinks,' Noble Seatree said.

'Yes, it does. I'd be careful breathing too closely to it,' Pilgrim said. 'It's goatskin, and water-damaged goatskin can grow some

100

very nasty moulds. You wouldn't want to get an infection.'

The constable reared back a little. Studied the map for a few moments, then pushed it away and picked up the book he had selected and shoved it into the pocket of his fur coat. 'Next time I stop by I want to see you working downstairs,' he said.

'There is still a great deal of unfinished work here.'

'So get it done, and move on. See if you can't find something worth my while down there. Is Big Lad about?'

'I believe so.'

Pilgrim's hands were trembling; he shoved them between his thighs.

'He better have something for me in his larder. This little book doesn't begin to satisfy what you owe.'

16.

A few nights after Noble Seatree's visit, Gentle roused Pilgrim from his nest of blankets and furs and led him to a narrow window. The shadows of the other towers reared against the luminous green streamers of an aurora, but that was not why Gentle had dragged Pilgrim from his sleep. In the courtyard directly below the window, something was picking its way across snow that faintly reflected the auroral light.

At first, Pilgrim thought it was one of Grace Wren Saltmire's charges, driven by deep-graven habit or phantasm of memory to quit their cell in search of something long lost. But then the flickering glow of the aurora brightened for a moment, and he saw that the intruder was barrel-chested and very tall, and dressed in a deer skin tied around its neck and a kind of stiff skirt of pine boughs.

It was not a person. It was a bear.

Pilgrim had regularly walked past the stuffed bear that stood at the entrance of the Hall of Natural History in the Library of All People, but this was the first time he had seen a live specimen. A monster escaped from tales told to thrill and frighten pups, creeping slowly across the snow, raising each foot high before planting it carefully, pausing often to cock its small head and look all around. Breathclouds plumed from its blunt snout. The crest of hair on its head and the thatch on the barrel of its chest were tinted pale green by aurora light.

'That there's an old one,' Gentle said softly. He had recently been on an unsuccessful hunt for bears up in the mountains with the two cousins and their friends and a pack of eager curs only a few generations removed from the mountain lobos from which they had been bred. 'Most likely it's still out and about because it lacks the fat it needs to survive its winter sleep.'

The bear looked up, small eyes overshadowed by its heavy brow. Even though it was three floors beneath the window, Pilgrim held his breath.

'Don't worry,' Gentle said. 'They're famously short-sighted.'

'Then it heard or smelt us, because it knows we are here,' Pilgrim whispered, thinking of the scaffolding that braced the tower, wondering if the creature could climb.

'It suspects that something is watching it,' Gentle whispered back, 'but doesn't know exactly what or where.'

The bear lowered its head and plodded on. Stopping again, dropping to all fours and remaining absolutely still for several seconds before plunging its arms deep, sending snow showering to either side as it dug and thrusting its face into the hole and rearing back, chewing something.

'Field mouse most likely,' Gentle said. 'Or a vole. It's hungry, like I said, and too old to bring down a deer.'

The bear wiped its mouth with the back of one of its forepaws, a delicate gesture peculiarly like a person's, and reared back on its hind legs and ploughed on through the snow, disappearing around the edge of the tower.

Pilgrim felt a taut string relax in his chest. 'We should warn Grace.'

'Why I knew to keep watch for it — she spotted it two nights ago. There's nothing much for it to eat here, so it'll move on soon enough.'

103

Despite that reassurance, Pilgrim slept badly the rest of the night, imagining the bear padding amongst the towers in the shifting glow of the Skirts of the Mother. Imagining it standing three floors below, looking up at its windows. Thinking about the flimsiness of the tower's outer door and the door of his room. Thinking of the darkness under the crowded trees of forests that spread for hundreds of leagues beyond this sliver of civilisation, and the remoteness of his exile.

He was not much reassured to see Gentle and Grace Wren Saltmire conferring at the foot of the east tower the next morning. Close by, a pair of maras were harnessed to the old woman's sled, ready for a supply run to town. Gentle and Grace stomped over the snow, following the bear's tracks around the curve of the tower, returning some minutes later and climbing onto the sled and setting off. When they came back, close to the end of the short day, Gentle had some news: the bear they had seen the night before had been caught.

'Cornered and roped while it was rooting in the town's garbage dump,' he said cheerfully. 'I told you it was desperate. Hunters are going to hold a contest in a couple of days.'

'What kind of contest?' Pilgrim said.

'Setting it against curs. They make a show of it and most everyone in town goes. Probably the most exciting thing that'll happen 'til spring breaks. Grace and me will be there. Want to come along?'

17.

The bear-baiting contest was held in an open-air pit lined with logs rammed into the earth and circled by tiers of benches. Despite the light snow slanting out of the night into the flickering glow of the pit's fish-oil lamps, it seemed that everyone in Stonehaven, some two hundred people, had turned out. They crowded the benches, women on one side, men on the other, muffled in fur coats and fur hats and blankets, talking noisily, drinking small beer and munching fried meat or fish on skewers. A gang of striplings jostled at the edge of the pit, shouting and jeering to get the bear's attention. Chained by one ankle to a tall post in the centre, it had been stripped of its rudimentary clothing and squatted on its haunches, ignoring the striplings and the rest of the spectators. Even when a chunk of rotten tuber thrown by one of the striplings splattered its shoulder it did not flinch or look up.

Seated on the top tier of the men's benches, wrapped in a smelly fur coat borrowed from Grace Wren Saltmire, warming his hands on a paper cup of berry tea that Gentle had fetched from one of the vendors, Pilgrim thought that there was something dignified about the bear's stolid resignation, wondered if it understood what was about to happen, if it was hoping for a chance to escape or for a quick merciful end.

Looking around, he spotted the woman from the beach, Teal Leadwood, on the top tier of the women's benches, muffled in her coat – he saw now that it was some kind of fur, dyed a vivid scarlet. She was about Thorn's age, with a pleasant round face and rings clipped along the edges of her ears. On the far side of the pit, under a lamp hung from a tall pole, Noble Seatree was talking with three men. He seemed to be in a good mood, laughing at something one of the men said, punching another on the shoulder, all of them turning as the bugling cries of curs sounded somewhere out in the snowy dark. A hush spread through the crowd and people leaned in their seats, looking towards the aisle between the tiers of benches. Gentle nudged Pilgrim and said, 'Here we go.'

Four men walked into the lamplight, dressed in the leather jackets, cord breeches and knee-high boots of hunters. One wore a green cap with a long feather cocked in it and carried a cornet, two more were armed with long pikes tipped with iron blades, and the fourth held the leashes of two curs that strained towards the pit, eager for battle. The two pikemen shoved the striplings aside and jumped into the pit and levelled their weapons as the bear pushed to its hind legs and faced them, its back pressed against the post.

When he had agreed to come, Pilgrim had told himself that he would watch the ritual with the detachment of a professional observer, but as people stood up around him, hooting and whistling and stamping their feet, an infectious excitement fizzed in his blood. Gentle had stood up too. There was another surge of noise as the man with the feathered cap blew a long discordant note on his cornet. He made a short speech, saying he was glad to see everyone gathered here in neighbourly concord, and hoped that he and his comrades would more than satisfy their expectations. There was hooting and whistling at that, and more hooting and whistling when he said that the man and his curs needed no introduction, and introduced them anyway.

The man holding the leashes of the curs raised a hand when his name was called out, and the curs howled into the noise of the crowd. They were big lean animals with grey pelts and ruffs of black hair, eyes blankly reflecting lamplight as they wailed their avowal.

The man with the feathered cap blew another braying note and asked the spectators to sit down. In the silence that followed the rustle of movement, the bear raised its paws and began to groan and grunt. Its stubby fingers were spread wide, tipped with stout black thorns. The crowd jeered and the bear shook its head and groaned and grunted again: the same sequence of sounds, a guttural groan, several short panting grunts, two more groans.

Pilgrim's hackles prickled. He remembered that Grandfather Bearbane had told him about the songs bears sang to make themselves known to other bears, and wondered what the doomed bear's song might mean, what thoughts were swimming in the unknowable darkness inside its skull.

There was a general flurry of movement and chatter in the audience around the pit. People were laying bets, according to Gentle.

'Surely the outcome is inevitable,' Pilgrim said. His excitement was quite gone and he felt faintly sick.

'Laying odds on how long the curs will last with it, which will draw blood first, which will come out of it best, so on.'

'Did you hear the bear's song? It seems to me that it might be pleading for its life.'

Gentle shrugged inside his big fur coat. 'They sometimes imitate speech when they are at bay. Try to distract the hunters.'

'They used to be like us,' Pilgrim said, but Gentle didn't seem to hear him.

107

The cornet brayed again. The cur handler and his charges were walking down a cleated ramp into the pit. The curs strained at their leashes and their handler was having a hard time holding them back. The bear had been watching the two pikemen; now it bent towards the curs and opened its mouth wide, showing a red tongue lolling between broken yellow fangs.

The crowd quietened, everyone watching the handler as he hauled the curs to heel and unclipped their leashes and stepped back. The curs stood foursquare, fixed on the bear, trembling, and the man clicked his tongue and they moved forward, one circling left, the other right. The bear took two ponderous steps, looking left and right, took two more. Its ankle chain lifted and snapped tight and there was a blur of motion as the curs attacked. One was thrown aside and the other backed away as the bear reared to its full height. There was blood on its forelegs and the patch of white pelt on its chest; blood sprayed when it shook its head. The curs attacked again, and again one was thrown sideways. It was slower to get to its feet this time, its flank raked with bloody gouges where one of the bear's swipes had connected.

The handler conferred with the man with the cornet, then whistled to the curs. They slunk to him with slanting gaits, their gazes fixed on the bear, and allowed themselves to be leashed and hauled up the ramp.

The bear shook another spray of blood from its muzzle and groaned and grunted, looking up at the crowd as people made good on their bets and called to attendants for more beer and food. Teal Leadwood was a still, solitary figure seated above the rest of the women. She saw Pilgrim looking at her and looked away, and a ripple ran through the crowd as the next pair of curs was brought in.

The second bout went much like the first, with one cur injured and the bear bitten badly on one foreleg, fighting for survival in a contest that it must know it could not win, standing its ground in the falling snow as the curs and their handler left the pit, ignoring the feints of the pikemen as blood dripped from its muzzle and the mangled fingers of one paw.

After the third bout it was hunched and trembling, panting heavy gouts of steam. Its pelt was slicked into little points and the ground around it was a trampled mess of mud and bloody slush. After the handler had hauled his curs out of the pit, it dropped to an ungainly crouch, holding its injured paw against its chest.

Pilgrim was shivering and sweating inside his heavy fur coat, sick and headachy from the noise of the crowd, the stink of smoke from the fish-oil lamps mixing with the sweet scent of blood. He wanted the spectacle to be over as quickly as possible, was dismayed when the bear pushed to its feet and with a quick liquid motion swiped at one of the pikemen when he came a little too close. The man fell on his back as he dodged the blow and the bear raised its head as the crowd whistled and hooted, the noise rising a notch as Noble Seatree came down the aisle behind two curs on chain leashes. One was the brindled cur which had menaced Pilgrim and Gentle when the constable had paid his first visit; the other was long and lean and grey. The constable had shucked his coat and was bare-chested in leather trews. Thick white scars hatched the ball of his left shoulder.

Gentle leaned close to Pilgrim and said over the noise, 'He comes in for the kill when others have done all the hard work.'

After the usual ceremonial flourishes Noble Seatree and his brace of curs descended to the floor of the pit. There was an expectant hush as he knelt between his curs and whispered to them; then he unclipped the leashes and stood, and people roared and stamped. A small rain of objects – cups and bottles, chunks of tuber, a shoe – arced out from the men's benches and dropped around the bear. It ignored the missiles, watching as the curs advanced. Noble Seatree whistled, a single sharp note, and the curs cut left and right and closed on the bear, dodging its frantic swipes and slamming into it and bringing it down. Tearing and biting as it kicked under them, face down, the grey cur fastened to its good foreleg, the brindled cur worrying at its neck. Pilgrim, dry-mouthed and feverish, leaned on his cane and pushed to his feet because everyone else on the men's side of the pit had stood up. Most of the women were on their feet too.

Down in the pit, the pikemen and Noble Seatree were looking at the man with the cornet. The crowd hushed when he raised his hand, and Noble Seatree and one of the pikemen stepped forward. The constable gripped the hind legs of the cur fastened to the bear's neck and lifted it up. It did not let go, but the elevated slant of its body revealed a patch of the bear's back. The pikeman raised his weapon, the crowd hooted and bayed, and as the pikeman thrust down everything around Pilgrim turned over in a flood of red and black.

18.

When he jolted awake, he was lying on his back on cold hard ground, looking up at a tier of empty benches rising to a black sky, the sharp reek of ammonia scorching his nostrils. Two people, Gentle and Teal Leadwood, were kneeling on either side of him. Gentle was cradling his head; Teal Leadwood, thumbing a cork into a vial, asked him if he knew where he was and what had happened.

He blinked away snowflakes that had settled on his eyelashes and said stupidly, 'They killed the bear.'

'And you dropped at my feet,' Gentle said.

Pilgrim said that he was perfectly fine now, but needed Gentle's help when he tried to sit up. Grace Wren Saltmire and several men, Noble Seatree amongst them, were watching this little drama. Pilgrim felt a flush of embarrassment that deepened and spread when the constable said loudly and to no one in particular, 'Looks like the silly little fool will live,' and walked off around the edge of the pit.

Teal Leadwood was asking something, realised that Pilgrim had not heard her and repeated her question. 'Have you ever passed out before, or been struck down by a fit?'

'I think the excitement was too much for me,' Pilgrim said, and thanked her for her help and attention.

Teal Leadwood looked across him at Gentle, said that if it was no more than a simple faint his friend would be fine after he had rested. 'But perhaps have him seen by the physic before you go home. Just in case.'

'Physic's still fixing up the curs,' one of the spectators said. 'Be a while before he's done.'

Pilgrim, wanting to escape the scene of the bear's execution and his own mortification, refused to wait. He sat quietly between Gentle and Grace as the sled rattled over hardpack snow towards the Hearth. He wanted to explain that the spectacle had disgusted rather than excited him, that the people hooting and whistling around the pit had seemed more feral than the bear, but knew that it would sound prissy and hypocritical. After all, he'd been exiled for violating one of the central tenets of the Mother's grace and harmony, and this was the edge of the civilised world, where bears were still a threat to lives and livelihoods and, as Gentle had once said, hard living made for hard-shelled people.

Even so, he was haunted by images of the brutal ceremony, and the troubling thought that the bear might have been trying to plead with its captors. The fall of the bears had allowed people to shake off the chains of slavery and claim rightful dominion over the Mother's bountiful creation, and it was universally agreed that it was a regrettable necessity, a pardonable sin, to trap and transport bears to the far north, or even to kill them when they were an immediate danger to people and livestock. But if people were more like bears than people supposed, or bears were more like people, then their deportation and slaughter would be little better than a systematic programme of extermination, and the customs and laws that regulated the peaceful co-operation of the ninety-three tribes might not have flowed naturally from a blessed, unfallen state, but were instead necessary constraints on bestial instincts that

112

might one day overmaster those who believed that they were the Mother's chosen children, as they had overmastered the bears six hundred years ago, and ogres before them.

Pilgrim put these thoughts in a note to Teal Leadwood, trying to explain why he had been overcome, formally thanking her for coming to his aid and assuring her of his complete recovery, and had Gentle deliver it with a book he had chosen, after some thought, from the library: a slim volume of old stories and fables, with several good plates depicting people confronted by miscreations, revenants and apparitions. If Teal Leadwood really was a serious scholar of folk tales she might already own a copy, but it was the thought that counted.

Gentle reported that she had accepted the book and the note without comment, and although he was disappointed, Pilgrim told himself that he did not deserve a reply.

Two moonspans went by. It was the dead centre of winter. Another storm swept across the coast and added a full span of snow to the snow that already blanketed the ground. The tops of the towers were fringed with icicles which grew ever longer until their weight snapped them clean off and they plunged spear-like into pillowy snowdrifts. In the mornings, frigid mists erased the division between land and sky, but the skies had usually cleared by nightfall, blazing with drifts and shoals of stars and so cold that trees in the forest sometimes shattered when sap froze and expanded in their cores.

One day, Gentle returned from a visit to the town with a note that Teal Leadwood had left at the chandlers, sealed with a blob of wax as red as her fur coat.

'She asks us to tell when we next plan to visit the beach,' Pilgrim told Gentle, after he had opened and read it. 'She would like to meet us there, and show us something that may be of interest.'

113

'We can go whenever you like, as we're always short of coal and kindling. If you can spare the time from your books, that is,' Gentle said.

'If it is something to do with her studies, it may not be of much interest to you.'

'Oh, I'm curious as to what she thinks might interest you. And I'm hoping it might have something to do with her amber trade,' Gentle said. 'Seeing as we're even shorter of money than of coal I'd definitely be willing to help her out with that, for the right consideration.'

19.

They arranged to meet with Teal Leadwood the day after the Daughter Moon next showed her full face. High tides had washed the beach at Windy Bay clean of snow up to the strand-line and Pilgrim and Gentle were scratching for sea coal amongst pebbles frozen in lacy matrices of ice when Teal arrived, somewhat later than their noon appointment. She led them across the marsh, their maras wading through snowdrifts up to their hocks and crunching across frozen lagoons and ponds, to a low rise at the margin of the forest where a slab of black rock stood, its flat face etched with horizontal lines of script on either side of a deep, vertical incision. It was one of the memory stones of the First People, Teal told Pilgrim and Gentle, its 'bent-branch' alphabet as yet still untranslated, the people or places or events it commemorated unknown. This part of the coast had been one of the last holdouts of the First People, who had survived here long after bears had begun to build their mound cities. When bear slaver parties came raiding from the north they had defaced ancient petroglyphs, broken into burial mounds and removed the remains of the dead and smashed most of the memory stones; this one was a rare survivor, and seemed to have escaped destruction because it had been buried in the marsh, either deliberately or by a storm.

'It was dug up and set in place here shortly before your family moved north,' Teal said. 'I found a description of its discovery and restoration in one of the year journals in the library. They mostly record the weather, harvests and fish catches, management of goat and mara herds, and so on. But there are also accounts of unusual events, including the discovery of this stone. There are some good drawings of it, too. I sent copies to a colleague, and she confirmed that the inscriptions are in the late style.'

Pilgrim said that he would look it up and also search for similar records.

'I looked through the rest of the year journals, but couldn't find mention of any other stones,' Teal said. 'But perhaps you will have better luck.'

Gentle said, 'Are these First People like the small folk in old Grace's stories?'

'The small folk are imaginary creatures of folk tales,' Teal said. 'Spirits of place. The First People were as real as you or I. They made tools from bones and flaked stones, and ornaments from squirrel teeth, bone beads and snail shells. They left middens of oyster and clam shells on the banks of tidal rivers along this coast, and buried their dead under mounds of stone and earth or in the deepest parts of caves, often bedding them on heaps of flowers with small pots of grain or honey. One famous burial was of a woman of high status, with a necklace of fish-eagle claws around her neck and a bone scimitar in one hand and a soot-smudged forest buffalo horn in the other. A lantern that may have been meant to light her path to the land of the dead.'

'An ancestor of mine excavated that grave,' Pilgrim said. 'Her bones and the grave goods are exhibited in the Library of All People.'

He told Teal that he had lived in Highwater Reach for six years, working as secretary for the famous scholar Master

116

Able until his recent death; Teal said that she was sorry to hear that Able had passed – she knew of his work on the anatomy of the First People, and his proof that although they were smaller and slighter than modern people, their brains were comparatively larger.

'The popular belief is that they were dim-witted savages,' Teal said. 'Your master's work, and my own studies, show that they were far more than that.'

Pilgrim took the plunge, asked her if she had heard of the sightings of so-called visitors.

'I may have heard a rumour of some kind of mass hysteria,' Teal said, after a moment.

'Master Able thought the sightings might be something more than hysteria,' Pilgrim said, and explained that his master had first become interested in the sightings because he believed that the so-called visitors might belong to a remnant population of ogres, like the dwarf species whose bones had been found in caves on one of the Spice Islands. 'But the eye-witness testimonies that he collected and collated suggested something stranger. His work was unfinished when he died, and I was trying to raise funds to complete and publish it when an unfortunate series of events led to my exile.'

Teal studied him for a moment, and he wondered how much she knew about his fall from the Mother's grace. Only her eyes were visible; her face was masked by a neckpiece and crowned by a fur hat, and she was muffled in her red fur coat and shod in knee-length felt boots, the kind with fur on the inside that everyone in the settlement wore in winter. The white landscape stretched all around, silent and still under a dead white sky. The maras stood hock-deep in snow, wreathed in the frozen smoke of their breath; a sudden gust of wind blew spumes of sparkling crystals from the snow-shawled trees.

'Talk in the town has it that you killed someone,' Teal said.

'I hurt someone badly, but not fatally,' Pilgrim said, meeting her gaze.

'Fellow was trying to rob him,' Gentle said. 'I should know, as I was the injured party's accomplice.'

'Despite the circumstances, I deserve my punishment,' Pilgrim said.

'He asked me to come with him, rather than serve a spell of hard labour. And here we are,' Gentle said.

'We should go to my cabin,' Teal said abruptly, as if she had just thought of it. 'We can get warm, and talk more about your master's work.'

It was in a hollow behind a drift of sand dunes, the cabin, a couple of stades to the north of the memory stone. Snow was banked to the sills of its windows; a short trench had been dug through drifts between its back door and the hummock of its latrine. Inside, roof beams were hung with bunches of dry herbs and grasses and last summer's flowers, the beaten-earth floor was lapped with rugs, and a truckle bed was curtained off in one corner. Teal stoked up the fire in the hearth and they perched on cushions in front of it, warming their hands on bowls of silky hot chocolate, nibbling hard cakes baked from sweetroot and wild oat seeds. A tame washcat squatted warily beneath a low table, small round eyes reflecting sparks of firelight. He was shy, Teal said, because she did not get many visitors.

She had been living on the coast for two years. She had not been exiled, as the local people supposed, but had chosen to come here to study the folklore and folk medicine of the far south, supported by a small bequest from her late mother and sales of raw amber she combed from the beach. If she had stayed in her tribe's Hearth she would no doubt have spent her life working in its lazarette, like her mother and two of her sisters, but she was too independently minded and had too much of a liking for roving. Still, she said, her training in the healing arts had given her a good grounding in pharmacology, and in the rules of analytical thinking and deduction that she applied to her work and to diagnosing her patients.

'I can see, for instance, that you are most likely a pure,' she told Pilgrim, and smiled when he started. 'Your slight build and long and slender fingers, the sharpness of your cheekbones and your narrow jaw – they are characteristics often associated with the condition.'

'Your studies do not appear to have taught you much in the way of discretion,' Pilgrim said, aware that Gentle was watching them over the rim of his bowl.

'You aren't the first to remark on that,' Teal said. 'And while I'm being frank, I admit that I was avoiding you because of gossip about the reason for your exile. But after your fainting fit, and the sympathy you expressed for the bear in your note, it seemed to me that you were an unlikely cut-throat.'

'But no less guilty of violating the great harmony,' Pilgrim said.

'In the course of being robbed, it seems.'

'I make no excuse for what I did.'

'I've told him that he's too hard on himself,' Gentle said. 'But he's too stubborn to accept it.'

'Even so, I am glad that I decided to take the risk of meeting you,' Teal said. 'Especially as it seems that we have something in common.'

'You invited me into your home because you wanted to talk about the visitors,' Pilgrim said. 'Are you also making a study of them?'

Teal shook her head. 'Shortly before you arrived in Stonehaven I received a letter from several of my colleagues, explaining their interest in the visitors and asking for my opinion. I hadn't given that any thought since then, but now

119

I discover that you and your late master have been pursuing the same line of work. And here we are.'

'Would one of these colleagues be Master Mindwell?'

'Is he a rival of Master Able's?'

'A rival of mine, perhaps.'

'I don't know him,' Teal said. 'As for my colleagues, they are, like me, members of the Invisible College.'

It was an organisation of female hobbyists who shared an amateur interest in various practical applications of natural philosophy. Gardeners and herbalists, animal breeders, beekeepers and so on. Pilgrim told Teal that Master Able had been in correspondence with one such, an auntie in the Hearth of a wealthy tribe who was breeding exotic varieties of doves, and Teal told him that she and her friends belonged to what they called the college within the college, studying areas of natural philosophy that by custom were the preserve of male scholars.

'Are there many of you?' Pilgrim said.

'More than you might think, scattered widely across the Union and the New Territories. We exchange letters and papers, and meet up where and when we can. My colleagues believe that the visitors may be some kind of contemporary folk tale. Which is why they requested my opinion, since I have some small expertise in such matters.'

'Old Grace, up in the Hearth, knows all kinds of stories, and not just about the small folk,' Gentle said. 'Children who stray into the forest and vanish, and come back years later, unchanged since they disappeared and with no memory of where they've been. Creatures half woman, half seal, who sing fisherfolk to their doom on rocks. Talking fish that bargain with the people who catch them, promising to grant wishes in exchange for being returned to the sea, cursing those who decide to keep and kill them. I already had a version of that

120

last one, being born into a fisherfolk tribe, but Grace knows plenty of others besides, including some she swears are true. Like the one about a boat driven south by storms and caught fast in ice for more than a year, its crew surviving by catching seals and broiling their meat over fires fuelled by blubber.'

'She told those stories to me, too,' Teal said. 'And the secret stories that women here pass down. Stories that men never hear concerning matters they know nothing about.'

That last was directed at Pilgrim, like a challenge.

'They do like telling stories hereabouts,' Gentle said. 'Comes from having to hunker down with little else to do during the long winters, no doubt.'

'Wild landscapes are like blank pages,' Teal said. 'People make up stories that give meaning to them. Often populating them with imaginary creatures like the small folk to make them more familiar, more comforting.'

'Master Able thought that some of the stories about sightings of visitors had similarities to certain folk tales,' Pilgrim said. 'Abductions, lost travellers stumbling into a place of refuge where a strange kind of people live, never to be found again, and so on. One of his more eccentric correspondents claimed that stories about the visitors are shadows cast by a world-changing event in the near future. The great day when they will reveal themselves to be supernatural agents come to save us from ourselves. A kind of shared race memory, but working backwards. That certainly fits the definition of a comforting fantasy.'

Teal said, 'Had Master Able ever seen one of these visitors? Have you?'

'My master was too ill to travel, and because I was looking after him I could not travel in his stead. But several witnesses reported finding footprints, and scribbles etched in stones that somewhat resemble the outline of a flowersipper. I myself have

121

seen a patch of burnt ground left by a fire that flew away into the sky,' Pilgrim said.

'And do you think that they are real?' Teal said.

'I think that I don't yet know enough to be certain one way or the other.'

Teal seemed to like that answer. 'But you hope to prove it, one way or the other,' she said.

Pilgrim hesitated only for a moment. Teal had a brisk straightforward manner that reminded him of his sister; he recognised the passion that drove her to defy convention and refuse to accept the ordinary lot of women. And it had been too long since he had enjoyed the cut and thrust of intellectual debate, and he wanted to impress this clever, formidable woman. To give her something, in the hope that she would give something back. Tell him a little more about the clique within the Invisible College. Tell him what they had discovered about the sightings, whether their investigations had turned up something new.

He said, 'I abandoned my research into the visitors when I came here. Vowed to focus all my time and energy on the task of cataloguing and reorganising the Hearth's neglected library, which I had been given as part of my penance. But in the course of that work I found evidence suggesting that this is not the first time the visitors have shown themselves. That they may have met with bears shortly before the fall of the bears' civilisation.'

Teal was not as surprised as he had hoped. She listened with quiet attention as he told her how he had found the map, explained why it was most likely a copy of an older map made by bears and described the figure that resembled witnesses' accounts of the appearance of the visitors.

'If you would care to visit the library,' he said, shedding the last of his reticence, 'I would very much like to hear your opinion about it.'

A little later, after they had climbed onto the borrowed mara and set off towards the Hearth, Pilgrim leaned into Gentle's back and asked if he was upset by Teal's revelation that he, Pilgrim, was a pure.

'I already knew,' Gentle said. 'I was with Creed in the commons when he called you out.'

Pilgrim was embarrassed to have forgotten that. He said, 'You never before mentioned it.'

Gentle shrugged. 'Neither did you. And if you're wondering if it bothers me — it don't. I've worked and lived alongside plenty of folk like you. Folk who come from backward kinds of tribes like mine, tribes that think people who are different are bad luck or worse and treat them accordingly, they quite often take to the roving life. You can't help being who you are any more than I can.'

'Thank you,' Pilgrim said, genuinely moved.

'Don't think it makes us brothers,' Gentle said. Adding, 'She likes to show off, doesn't she?'

'It's the intellectual equivalent of a feat of strength. Or,' Pilgrim said, recalling a favourite analogy of Master Able's, 'the kind of display behaviour that some animals deploy to attract a mate.'

'In my experience, people who feel they have to prove themselves aren't always as dependable as they want you to believe,' Gentle said. 'Do you reckon you should put your trust in her?'

'I believe that I already have,' Pilgrim said.

123

20.

Teal Leadwood rode through the gateway of the Hearth, unheralded and unannounced, a handful of days after Pilgrim and Gentle first met with her. Her fur coat bright as a drop of blood in the snowy courtyard as she reined in her mara and hallooed the towers, her voice echoing off the stone walls and startling a small bird into flight.

Gentle steeped a flask of teabark and fried sweet bean-cakes in coney grease, and after the small meal Pilgrim took Teal to the second floor of the library, where he had been working when she had arrived. While he revived the fire with scraps of birchbark and splits of driftwood, Teal admired the mosaic floor and walked slowly along the shelves of books. After asking Pilgrim's permission, she pulled out a slender accounts book bound in pebbled black leather and opened it and bent her head to the pages and breathed in their odour before studying one of the columns, her finger moving down it as she read.

'You could reconstruct entire lives from this,' she said.

'The parts involving making and spending money, at least,' Pilgrim said, watching as she slotted the accounts book back into its place and took out another book from the shelf above it, a record of the pedigrees of riding maras.

'Are they all like this?' she said.

'Mostly,' Pilgrim said. 'There are sheaves of receipts and bills of lading, and rolls of household accounts, too. I have boxed up the few volumes of value or historical interest, for dispatch to my tribe.'

He told her that he had found the book containing the account of the discovery of the memory stones and added it to the small collection awaiting dispatch, and she asked about the famous map he had found. Was that boxed up too?

'It is too important to be buried in the tribe's archives.'

'So you plan to keep it.'

'I plan to donate it to the Library of All People after I have completed and published Master Able's work.'

Teal smiled. 'Are you going to make me beg to see it?'

Pilgrim fetched it from its hiding place and unrolled it on the worktable and weighed down its corners with pebbles collected from the beach. Stood beside Teal as she sat in the chair and leaned over it, studying every part with fierce concentration.

'All of these are bear cities,' she said.

'I think so. If I had a contemporary map of ruins, I might be able to identify them.'

'And this must be the mysterious guest,' she said, pointing to the small white figure, with its spherical, eyeless head and lightning stick.

'It doesn't look like much,' Pilgrim said. 'Just another fanciful monster. Except that it closely resembles several descriptions of the visitors.'

He showed her sketches made by witnesses, said that if she and her colleagues shared their ideas with him, they might be able to prove what the visitors really were.

'I suppose it might also help you to complete your master's work,' Teal said.

'The contribution of your colleagues would be properly acknowledged,' Pilgrim said. 'And if the visitors aren't some kind of collective fiction, but are a lost tribe of bears, or people like us, or some other kind of people entirely, it would be world-changing. Too important for any one person to claim.'

'I suppose that I can put that to my colleagues,' Teal said. 'But you'll have to wait until the thaw – one of the storms brought down the tapcode line.'

She was reticent about how many women belonged to the college inside the Invisible College, and what their interests were, but told Pilgrim that it was relatively new, and as much a support network as a venue for sharing ideas. Women were chafing at the traditional roles of their sex, especially in the cities, and some were now independently wealthy, and willing to fund the work of those less fortunate.

'We are not obsessed about ownership of ideas, or their priority, or all the other things that men consider important – status, seniority – and will happily accept critical improvements rather than think them challenges to our self-esteem. If women were in charge of the Library of All People, it would be a place of conversation and co-operation. As it is, scholars jealously guard their work from the scrutiny of their rivals, and all is competition and compartmentalisation, and rigid hierarchies organised by seniority rather than ability.'

'That's not entirely true,' Pilgrim said. 'Scholars often share their ideas with like-minded colleagues. And when their work is published, the Library makes it available to everyone else.'

'To every male scholar, but not to us. We call ourselves the Invisible College not because we choose to work in secret, but because men refuse to believe that we are capable of discovering anything useful. We have to publish our work privately, and male scholars pay little or no attention to it. We cannot

126

debate with them, or visit the Library, or even lodge copies of our monographs and books in its stacks.'

'I hope that I understand a little about exclusion,' Pilgrim said.

'You may be a pure, but you still enjoy male status. You are not invisible. You do not lack a voice. I don't know much about this business of sightings and visitors, but my colleagues deserve more than credit for their work. They deserve to be seen. Remember that, if they agree to share their findings with you.'

Her disdain for the hegemony of male scholarship reminded Pilgrim of his friend Swift Singletree. But while Swift's scorn was rooted in hurt and anger, Teal was at ease with her rebellion against society's expectations, confident that she was more than a match for any man who shared her chosen field of research.

In another conversation, the two of them sitting in the library with a fire in the hearth and lamplight gleaming on the spines of the old books and snow falling outside the windows, they discussed the implications of the possibility that the visitors had made contact with bears. Whether the so-called new cities had benefited from gifts of advanced techne, or whether the visitors had favoured the new cities because their inhabitants – philosophers, mathematicians, engineers and artisans who kept no slaves, believed that the world was animated by spirits and made exquisite jade jewellery and glass-like ceramics that no one had been able to duplicate – had been more advanced than the rest of their species.

Or perhaps the figure on the map had nothing to do with the visitors, Teal said, but was some kind of storied demon, or a bear in ceremonial costume with a glancing resemblance to the descriptions given by witnesses. Pilgrim said that he had wondered about that too, and wanted to look for examples of

127

similar figures in the friezes and panels excavated from new cities and stored in the Library of All People.

He told Teal about his grandfather's work as a bear trapper, his belief that bears were smarter than most people thought. 'He claimed that when one bear worked out how to spring a trap, the idea quickly spread through the local population. Said that they scratched marks on the trunks of trees that other bears examined as if reading a wallsheet, and thought that the songs they sing to advertise their territories might be remnants of their ancient culture. He tried to talk to some of the bears he trapped, too. Claimed that they were either too stubborn to play along, or didn't believe that people had anything worth saying to them. But I really do think that the bear in the pit was trying to talk to us. That it was pleading for its life, or asking for mercy and a quick death.'

Teal and Pilgrim discussed that. The language of bears before their fall, and the language of bears now. What it might reveal about them, if it could be understood. Whether any person could understand what it was like to be a bear. On other visits, Teal interrogated Gentle about the folk tales of his tribe and told Pilgrim about finding common threads and themes in tales from different tribes, her use of recordings to show how lines and verses in sagas sung by balladeers changed from performance to performance, and her theory that sagas and stories had developed and elaborated from a few basic forms. She took Pilgrim to see the cave where the famous burial site of the woman of the First People had been discovered, too. It wasn't far from Stonehaven and the Hearth, high on one side of a deep narrow river valley and much visited by the local people. The snowy apron in front of its mouth was trampled by fresh footprints; the branches of a birch tree rooted in a crevice were hung with dolls twisted from plaited grass, parcels of food and pebbles inscribed with names; and the floor of the pit left by the excavation was covered by a quilt of withered flowers. Although the body of the woman had been exhumed more than two hundred years ago, the local people believed that the cave was still haunted by her spirit. They called her the Lady of the Flowers, and Teal had collected a number of stories about how she had answered prayers and petitions.

'We try to make sense of the world by telling stories about it,' Teal said. 'But those stories also reveal much about our ingrained habits of thought. Our tendency to reduce the wonderful complexity of the world and the people in it to simple fables and morality tales. The stories about miraculous visitors that your master collected may spring from the same root as stories about intercessions by the spirits of our long-dead ancestors. Stories that suggest we would rather appeal to imaginary beings, believing them capable of acting outside ordinary constraints, than accept that the world will not bend to our will.'

Pilgrim told Gentle that Teal favoured the idea that sightings of visitors were a kind of folk tale because of her professional interest in stories. 'The truth is, we don't yet have enough evidence to decide one way or another. And while she might be right when she says that we make stories to try to understand the world, that doesn't mean that everything in the world has to be part of a story.'

Gentle said that there was some sense in her argument that stories made things seem simpler than they were. 'It helps you see the world more clearly, as in the stories women tell pups.'

'What kind of stories did the women of your hearth tell you?' Pilgrim said.

Gentle shrugged, said that he reckoned that they were the sort of thing women told pups everywhere. 'Stories about Trickster Crow and his attempts to fool the Mother. How different animals come to be as they are, and so on. And they always have some kind of lesson in them.'

'What happens,' Pilgrim said, 'when you don't do what you are supposed to do?'

'I suppose that kind of story didn't take with me,' Gentle said. 'Or with you, neither.'

'I'm trying to make amends for that.'

'Even so, you haven't given up on what led you here. Ever since you found it, you've been obsessed with that map and what it might signify. Eager to throw in with that woman's friends despite knowing nothing about them.'

Gentle seemed to like Teal, but still didn't trust her. Thought that Pilgrim was naive to share so much with her so readily in exchange for nothing but promises. Pilgrim hadn't been able to disabuse him of the notion that the work on the visitors might have some monetary worth, or convince him that, at bottom, scholarship was a collaborative endeavour, but knew that Gentle was right about one thing: he'd taken a risk when he'd shown the map to Teal. He'd wanted to impress her, like a peacock fanning its tail for a peahen, wanted to prove that he had something worth sharing with her colleagues, but there was still much he hadn't shown her – all of Master Able's notes and interviews, to begin with – and he didn't think of her colleagues as serious rivals. Not because they were women, but because scholars didn't take women seriously. And because Master Able's last work hadn't been taken seriously either, he had some sympathy for the Invisible College and its cause, felt that they could help each other. Besides, there was nowhere else that might give him the resources he needed to finish his master's research. He'd made a promise to himself that only others could keep.

By now, halfway through his term of exile, he had finished with the second floor of the library and moved on to the

130

first. There was still much to do, but he had a distant view of the end of cleaning and sorting and cataloguing, and had found time to put the sprawling patchwork of Master Able's manuscript into a rough but logical order, partly guided by notes in Able's familiar untidy scrawl (his thoughts always outran his pen) and partly by his own ideas about filling in missing sections, bridging gaps in some arguments and reinforcing others. He knew that there was little point in making firm plans before he had subjected himself to the scrutiny of the aunties. Told himself that if they decided to extend his exile for another year, he would have to accept it. Even so, he couldn't help daydreaming about collaborating with the Invisible College. Winning funds from one of its wealthy members. Finding more representations of the visitors in bear artefacts stored in the Library of All People. Visiting places where visitors had been sighted, perhaps in the company of Gentle: it would be useful to have the advice and protection of someone experienced in roving . . .

There was so much to do! The monograph. A paper describing the map and discussing the implications of the depiction of what might be a visitor. Transcripts of interviews interpolated with his commentary. Perhaps even a popular account of Master Able's struggle to prove the significance of the sightings, as suggested by Willow.

Pilgrim pictured a triumphant return to Highwater Reach, the first small run of his monograph selling out and reprinting again and again, his fame spreading through scholarly circles, winning back Master Able's reputation and cementing his own . . . He knew that they were idle, self-serving fantasies that could no more change the world than petitions to the spirit of the Lady of Flowers, but they nurtured his small hope that exile would not silence him, and helped to quell the constant worry that, while he was locked down in this small and distant icebound corner of the Union, Master Mindwell or some other scholar might have rendered Master Able's work redundant by discovering hard evidence that confirmed the reality or otherwise of the visitors. Might have established their identity; might even have made contact with them.

Pilgrim knew that there was nothing he could do about that, and tried to focus on the work he'd been assigned. But then, as winter's grip began to loosen, news from the outside world arrived and everything changed again.

21.

Each day the sun rose a little higher and its arc above the horizon was a little longer. At last, after a final flurry of snowstorms, a slow thaw began. Meltwater dripped from the tip of every icicle; snow slumped and slid from roofs. Ice which had sheeted the town's harbour and most of the bay beyond broke up into jostling floes and long leads of black water, and fishing boats which had been icebound all winter ventured out to drop the first prawn pots and crab traps of the new year. One day, Gentle told Pilgrim that the tapcode line to the outside world had been repaired, and a few days later the coastal trading ship put in at the harbour.

On the evening of the ship's arrival, Pilgrim found Gentle in the small kitchen of their quarters, unpacking dry goods and fresh vegetables he had purchased at the chandler's. 'This came for you,' Gentle said casually, and handed over a letter.

Someone, either the chandler or the constable, had unsealed it, but Pilgrim was too delighted to comment or complain, unfolding the stiff paper and revealing unsteady columns of glyphs in Swift Singletree's cramped untidy hand.

After the usual salutations and a few choice items of gossip about acquaintances in the pure community, Swift explained that he and Ardent had failed to find any figure resembling a visitor in the murals and panels displayed in the Library of All People's Hall of Bears and Their Things, and nothing resembling Pilgrim's map, either. Swift had shown the copy of the map to booksellers and antiquarians he trusted, but none of them knew of anything like it. It was possible that something pertinent was filed away in the special collections, Swift wrote, but he could not access them and Ardent would require a pass under the signature of his master, who would almost certainly interrogate him about his interest – if Pilgrim wanted to risk that he should let them know. As for the bear city beside the figure, its location was uncertain. No cities had been discovered on the east coast of the Neck which linked the Union with the New Territories, but given that most of it was mangrove swamp or jungle that was not surprising.

It was a mixture of good and bad news. Mostly bad, Pilgrim thought. It seemed that he had found something unique, which meant that he had the advantage over Master Mindwell, but that uniqueness, and lack of any records of its origin and history, meant that detractors could legitimately claim that it was either a fancy of long-dead scribes, or an outright forgery. And it would take a full-scale expedition to locate the bear city, and even if it could be found there might not be any trace of the visitors.

He read on, and discovered more bad news. It seemed that Foeless Landwalker's fame had grown considerably over the winter. He was no longer a charlatan preaching from the back of his wagon to an audience of sceptical locals, like a mountebank touting a cure-all, but the leader of a fully fledged cult. He had gained more than a thousand followers while travelling through the towns and settlements of the west coast of the New Territories. When this procession reached Ogres Grave he had been arrested for disturbing the peace, but a notary appointed by a wealthy patron had won dismissal of the charge, and after he had been set free he had led his followers through the coastal mountains to the high desert beyond, and commanded the construction of what he called a landing field for the sky boats of the visitors.

Foeless Landwalker preached there every night to his ever-growing flock, claiming that once they had proven themselves worthy the visitors would descend from the sky and the task of building a new and better society would begin. Talk about it was general in the scholars' community and across the capital, Swift wrote, and Intrepid Windrush's pamphlets were so popular that printers could scarcely keep up with demand. One of the latest and most famous converts was Earnest Smallhill, the bookrunner Master Mindwell had hired to investigate sightings of the visitors in the New Territories. Smallhill's final message had been leaked to wallsheet writers, causing amusement and alarm in equal measure in the scholarly community: *Forget everything you think you know. Burn it all. I have found the truth.*

'What will you do, if he turns out to be right?' Teal said, after Pilgrim had told her about the so-called prophet and the attempt by his chief propagandist, Intrepid Windrush, to recruit him to the cause.

'If Foeless Landwalker really is in contact with the visitors, if he can persuade them to reveal themselves, I would be the first to congratulate him,' Pilgrim said. 'But I have read some of Intrepid Windrush's pamphlets, and it seems to me that the so-called wisdom Landwalker claims to have received from the visitors is nothing but superstitious nonsense and rabble-rousing fear-mongering. Promises of a grand reconciliation with the Mother and a return to an idyllic past that never was. Baseless warnings that misuse of ogre techne will lead us down the same path that eventually destroyed them.'

'As some already believe it will,' Teal said.

'Far too many, as it turns out. More than ever, I need to prove that the visitors are real. I need to find evidence that confirms that the map I found is genuine.'

Teal Leadwood studied him for a moment. They were sitting by the hearth in her cottage, drinking pinebark tea sweetened with shavings from a lump of raw sugar. Teal's washcat was curled in her lap, one of its handlike paws clutching a fold of her fustian kirtle. She said, 'If you prove that they are real, won't that help this prophet rather than hinder him?'

'If that figure really is a depiction of one of the visitors, if they really did make contact with bears, they may have had something to do with the collapse of bear civilisation,' Pilgrim said. 'Perhaps they are not peaceful and compassionate, as Foeless Landwalker claims. Perhaps they are malignant. Dangerous. If we could prove that, it would put a swift end to his utopian nonsense.'

'It seems to me that you are leaning too hard on speculation. Telling stories and hoping that you can find facts that you can bend into some kind of proof, rather than finding facts and then trying to discover the best explanation for them.'

Pilgrim was too fevered and anxious to heed her. 'I need to get back to Highwater Reach and do some research in the Library of All People. Gentle reckons that he can steal a boat. With luck, it will get us as far as Fortunate Valley, where I can sell books from the library to raise the train fare. But there might be a better way.'

'If you came here looking for your fare, I am about as hard up as you,' Teal said.

'I didn't come here to ask for money.'

'What do you want from me, then?'

'I believe that it is time for you to tell your friends in the Invisible College everything I've told you, and ask for their help.'

22.

Pilgrim was returning to the Hearth after buying paper and a new inkstone from the chandler's when Noble Seatree intercepted him. Stepping out into the muddy street, catching the bridle of Pilgrim's mara in one hand and a fistful of its coarse blond hair in the other, saying, 'I hear you've been visiting the crazy woman again.'

Pilgrim didn't answer. There was no point in denying it, and there was no point in giving the constable whatever pleasure he might garner by admitting it, either.

'I could ask what you two have been talking about,' Noble Seatree said. 'But seeing as I already know, having read your letter, there's no need.'

For a moment, Pilgrim was worried that he meant the letters sent to Teal's colleagues in the Invisible College, but she had handed them to the purser of the coastal trader, to avoid the scrutiny of the chandler. No, this was all about Swift's letter, and he should have known that the chandler would have told the constable about it, should have known that there would be a reckoning.

He said, 'Do you have the right to read private mail from my friends?'

'Rapscallions like you don't have any cause to whine about

137

rights, and shouldn't expect any privacy, neither,' Noble Seatree said. 'Especially when their tribe has asked me to keep a close watch on 'em.'

He was dressed in his usual leather trews and a short patchwork coat of the local corduroy unbuttoned over his bare chest, yet showed no sign that he felt the chilly fish-scented breeze.

'The letter contained nothing more than news from an old friend,' Pilgrim said. 'Things he thought I might be interested in.'

'There was mention of a map. Can't help but wonder if that was the same map I saw a while ago,' Noble Seatree said. 'I recall that you said it wasn't worth much, yet your friend seems to think it's a unique item. Maybe you can explain that to me.'

'It might be of some small interest to scholars who specialise in such matters, but it has no intrinsic value.'

'Dealers in books and the like would most likely know where to find those scholars, wouldn't they? And know the price they'd pay, too.'

'I plan to send it to my tribe,' Pilgrim said uneasily. 'It owns the library and everything in it, in case you had forgotten.'

'They won't know about it unless you tell them,' the constable said. He was smiling, but not with his eyes. 'And I reckon you haven't told them yet.'

'My friend knows about it,' Pilgrim said. 'And so do the people he consulted. Scholars and Library officials and booksellers – they have all seen a copy I made. Its provenance is known and established, and anyone who tried to sell it would have to answer to my tribe.'

'A lame little mouse who faints at the sight of blood shouldn't be making threats to a sworn lawkeeper. He might not like the consequences.'

'I'm simply telling you the facts of the matter.'

'Which I don't reckon you did before,' Noble Seatree said, and let go of the bridle. 'Time I paid you a visit, and took a proper look at everything you've unearthed in that library.'

'Gentle has taken up fishing again. I'll be sure to ask him to set something aside for you,' Pilgrim said, getting it out quickly and kneeing the flanks of the mara. He didn't want the constable to see his dismay.

'We aren't talking about fish!' Noble Seatree shouted. 'I want a taste of everything!'

He made good on his promise early the next morning, waking Pilgrim and Gentle when he stomped into their quarters, dragging his brindled cur on its chain. After making a mess of their rooms and the kitchen, searching for what he called contraband, he demanded that Pilgrim take him to the library and show him everything worth anything.

Pilgrim handed over the catalogue he had made, but after thumbing through its loose pages the constable threw it aside and told Pilgrim that all he needed to know and see was the books that might fetch a good price.

'I'm talking about the very best of the best. Don't try to palm me off with rubbish.'

'If you mean the books I think worth sending to my tribe, there is a separate list. The last two pages at the end of the catalogue,' Pilgrim said, as calmly as he could. He felt faintly sick, was trying his best not to meet the yellow gaze of the cur, which sat taut and alert beside its master. He knew that books weren't what the constable had come for.

Noble Seatree read out several titles from the list and demanded to see them.

'They are in the boxes under the table. Packed and ready to ship,' Pilgrim said.

'What about that map? Which I can't seem to find any mention of in this list.'

'Also packed.'

'Show me.'

Pilgrim had made a tube of layered, varnished paper to protect it. He fetched the tube from its hiding place on a high shelf behind ancient account books and carefully extracted the map, his heart jumping when Noble Seatree snatched it from him and held it by one edge and shook it until it unrolled.

'Still doesn't look valuable,' he said.

'Because it isn't,' Pilgrim said.

'If I ripped it in half would it be worth half as much or twice as much?'

That cold smile. That flat, challenging gaze. The cur was watching Pilgrim too, ragged ears pricked up.

Pilgrim said, as calmly as he could, 'It wouldn't make any difference to its value, but I would have to explain how it came to be damaged.'

'We could say that Chieftain got hold of it,' Noble Seatree said, wafting the map before the cur's snout, smiling when he saw Pilgrim's distress. 'He's famous for eating almost anything. Bones, shoes, belts . . . He ate a shark washed up on the beach one time. Only a baby shark, truth be told, but he left only the liver and the teeth. We could say he ate this map, and sell it and split the proceeds.'

'Anyone who bought it would have to explain how they came by a unique item known to have been found in the library owned by my tribe.'

'So you said before.'

'It's what would happen,' Pilgrim said, and a dizzy wave of relief washed through him when the constable dropped the map onto the table and told him to fetch out the boxes of books.

He rummaged inside them, dropping books on the table, on the floor, setting aside two, three, five, placing his hand

140

flat on top of the little stack and asking Pilgrim what they were worth.

'They are worth sending back to my tribe, which is why they are on the list. And because they are on the list, my people will notice that they are missing.'

'Rewrite the list. And when you find any more books you think might be worth something, don't put them on it straight away. From now on, I want to see everything first. Winter's over and the Season's almost on us, so I have extra expenses. And that means extra fees.'

Pilgrim waited until the constable had left, the cur close at his heels, before he collapsed into a chair. Noble Seatree was a blowhard and a bully, but he wasn't stupid. Pilgrim knew that he would have to be especially careful, but he also knew that, however things fell out, he would not have to endure the constable's petty tyranny for much longer. Copies of the letter he and Teal had drafted were on their way to her colleagues, and although she had warned him that it might be some time before she received any reply, he hoped that the Invisible College would see the sense of collaborating with him. And if it didn't, he and Gentle would take advantage of the disruption caused by the bacchanalia at the beginning of the Season, steal a boat and make their own way north. Meanwhile, he would lie low, do his best to avoid the constable's scrutiny and try to finish his work in the library. It wasn't much of a salve to his conscience, but it was better than nothing.

Warm winds blew in from the west. The willows in the marshes were suddenly in full leaf and hung with bunches of catkins. Golden drifts of pollen spun on blackwater ponds. There were still patches of snow in shadowed hollows amongst the pines that covered the slopes rising above the Hearth, but the air was full of birdsong and the old people in Grace

Wren Saltmire's care grew restless as the first intimations of the Season woke enfeebled habits of lust and longing.

In Stonehaven, banners were strung across streets, the big tent that would house the feasts and formal ceremonies was erected in the town square and every household was filled with a bustle of cooking, cleaning and costume making. Gentle confessed that he felt a stirring in his blood, and told Pilgrim that he reckoned he might have a chance with the widow woman who bought the mussels he collected from the foreshore of Windy Bay.

'I've always had a bit of luck with older women,' he said. 'They take little notice of my difference, and they're more grateful and no less passionate. And experienced, too, which counts for a lot as far as I'm concerned.'

'All I need to know is that you'll be ready when the time comes.'

'That's why I'm letting you know what's what,' Gentle said with deadpan imperturbability. 'She's slow coming to the boil, if you know what I mean, but I reckon I'll be in with her before we plan to go.'

'If the Invisible College sends help, we may have to leave before you get your chance.'

'Then I'll have to hope to strike lucky on our travels, or do without if I must. It won't be my first dry Season,' Gentle said. 'And you – you really don't feel anything?'

'I'm entirely occupied with what we need to do,' Pilgrim said.

'Don't waste too much energy fretting over it. Only way we can know it will work is when we do it,' Gentle said.

He believed that the world was as it was, and everything that happened was fore-ordained by the will of the Mother. That there was no point struggling against the inevitable: all you could do was accept what fell out and make what you could of it. Pilgrim, though, was kept awake at night by tabulating over

142

and again everything that needed to be done and everything that could go wrong. The biggest problem, if there was no help to be had from the Invisible College, was lack of money. Despite the risk of being found out by the constable, he had kept back the most valuable books, hiding them in plain sight on the crowded shelves of the second floor. But there were not very many, and if there was no other source of ready cash it was likely that he would have to sell his amber pendant. He would be sorry to lose it, but given the cause he hoped that Master Able would have approved of the sacrifice. And if the sale of the pendant wouldn't cover the price of their fares, Gentle said, they could always hitch rides on freight trains. Like most rovers, he'd had some experience in that, and told Pilgrim that train hands usually turned a blind eye. The only disadvantage was that freight trains were slow and you'd often find yourself laid up for days at a time in some remote junction, waiting for the next ride, but if you needed to get somewhere but lacked money to pay a regular fare you didn't have any cause to complain about the inconvenience.

Going on the run from the law and atonement and living like beggarly rovers was a dismal prospect. Even worse was the idea that, if all his plans failed, Pilgrim would have to find Master Mindwell and volunteer to replace the assistant he had lost to Foeless Landwalker's cult: a far worse betrayal than breaking the terms of his exile and stealing books that rightfully belonged to his tribe. So when at last Teal visited the Hearth, he was both relieved and apprehensive.

It was late in the afternoon and already growing dark when she rode into the courtyard, calling out her usual greeting. Pilgrim watched from a window, his heart bursting with impatience, as she talked to Grace Wren Saltmire, and he was standing in the doorway when at last she came up the steep winding stair.

The Invisible College had come to a decision, she said, having taken much less time than she had expected. 'Ordinarily, they would not want nor need your collaboration, or that of any other man. But these are strange times.'

'Does that mean that they have agreed to help me?' Pilgrim said. He felt a mixture of excitement and the yawning trepidation that had gripped him when he had stood before his mother and the rest of the aunties, waiting to be judged and sentenced.

'It seems that they want you to help them,' Teal said.

23.

Teal didn't know why her colleagues in the Invisible College had decided to meet Pilgrim, or what they expected from him. Following the protocol she and Pilgrim had devised to foil the scrutiny of the chandler, who owned and operated the only tapcode machine in the town, the message had been brief, disguised as a communication from one of the amber dealers Teal regularly contacted to discuss terms of sale of her latest finds. All she could say was that representatives would arrive in Stonehaven in a little under half a moonspan.

'Is that when the coastal trader is due?' Pilgrim said.

Teal shook her head. 'They have arranged their own transport.'

'And they'll take me with them. Me and Gentle.'

Pilgrim, Gentle and Teal were sitting close together in the kitchen of the short tower, like the conspirators they were.

'If they aren't planning to, I'll do my best to persuade them to change their minds.'

Gentle said, 'Can't you send 'em another message, asking for more details?'

'We'll find out soon enough who the representatives are and what they want,' Teal said. 'And besides, I don't want to catch the constable's attention. I've been living here two

145

years, but as far as he and the rest of the townspeople are concerned I'm still a stranger. Not to be trusted.'

'Especially when we've spent so much time together,' Pilgrim said, understanding her prudence. 'You've put yourself at risk by helping us. I won't forget the debt we owe.'

'I shall miss our conversations,' Teal said.

'You aren't coming?' Gentle said.

'I am not interested in adventuring,' Teal said. 'And my work here is far from finished.'

Later, after she had gone, Gentle said to Pilgrim, 'What will you do, if these women aren't the allies you're hoping for?'

'If they aren't, we'll have to find our own way.'

'We could do that now. Or as soon as the festivities start. I have my eye on a sturdy little crab boat that should get us to Fortunate Valley without too much trouble. You can sell those books you've set aside, and if that don't cover the train fare we'll ride the rails the rover way, as previously discussed. I don't see,' Gentle said, with the sleepy look that meant he believed that he had the better part of the discussion, 'why we need these women at all.'

'We'll wait to see what the Invisible College has to offer,' Pilgrim said. 'It should give you enough time to woo your widow.'

'She's already wooed. It's just a question of waiting until she's warmed up.'

People from outlying farms and villages had begun to arrive in town, pitching tents or roofing shallow trenches with scrap lumber to make temporary burrows. Rival gangs of young men in elaborate costumes got up from straw, rags and feathers were parading with drums and fifes and staging dance-offs against each other: rehearsals for the adjudicated competitions after the Season officially began. Gentle, returning from exchanging his catch from a day's fishing for rice and bottled

146

pickles at the chandler's, told Pilgrim how one dance-off had ended with the chiefs of the rival crews shaking in ecstatic trances face to face, while the rest hollered and whooped and beat every kind of percussion instrument.

'I'll be glad to quit this place,' he said. 'But I have to admit that they know how to have fun.'

Pilgrim knew about the build-up towards the opening of the Season only from Gentle's accounts. He was lying low in the Hearth, trying to keep his mind off futile speculations about everything that could go wrong, but on the night of the Season's official opening he watched the celebratory fireworks from the window where he and Gentle had seen the doomed bear stalk through snowdrifts. Showers of red and green sparks flowering small and distant in the night, the laggard sound of the explosions arriving as they fell and faded. He and his friends had not been affected by the tidal heat of the Season, but had liked to visit the open parties in the poorer quarters of Concord, enjoying the spectacle and the carnival crowds, the music and the food and drink, as much as anyone else. Now, alone in the half-ruined tower, he felt a forlorn pang of something deeper than mere loneliness. Felt as he had in those Seasons in his tribe's territory when he had been old enough to realise that he was different. He had been exiled twice over, first by Master Able's death and then by his well-deserved punishment. Even if the Invisible College agreed to everything he asked, even if he was able to find out everything he wanted to know, he could never return to his cozy little life in Highwater Reach.

Grace Wren Saltmire, dressed in a tattered finery of blood-red wormsilk, had locked up her charges and left for Stonehaven at sunset. Gentle was in town too, with his widow. She still wasn't quite willing, he told Pilgrim the next morning, but it had been a hot night all the same. He had come in while

147

Pilgrim was eating breakfast, reeking of beer and smoke, his pink eyes inflamed, saying that he didn't need anything to eat, wanted only to sleep so that he would be ready for the night ahead.

'Don't forget that we meet with the Invisible College the day after tomorrow,' Pilgrim said.

'It's why I want to look my best tonight, it being my last chance. Hers too,' Gentle said, and lumbered bedwards.

The next morning, Pilgrim found that Gentle had already returned from the carnival, sitting in the kitchen in his best clothes and eating fried oatcakes with a kind of absent-minded melancholy.

'Turned out she wasn't willing after all,' he told Pilgrim.

'I'm sorry.'

'But she swore it would be today. Said she could feel it in her blood and bones.'

'You can't,' Pilgrim said, realising what Gentle meant.

'There's time,' Gentle said, around a mouthful of oatcake. 'We don't meet with the people from the Invisible College until nightfall. And they haven't arrived yet. Or if they have, Teal hasn't left the sign. I checked on my way back, not an hour ago.'

'They'll be here,' Pilgrim said. 'And we're going with them.'

'You can talk to them without me. Find out what they want from you and what they'll give in return. Whatever it is, whatever you agree, I'll go along with it,' Gentle said, blotting fragments of oatcake with a broad thumb, licking it. 'And I'll be there in good time, I promise. But I need to do what I need to do. I know you can't understand that, but hope you realise that it's best for both of us if you don't try to stand in my way.'

'If you aren't back by nightfall I'll have to go without you. Leave you here.'

'I've been in worse places. And too often without the comfort of a woman,' Gentle said, and then he was up and out of the door and clattering down the stairs, singing a verse from a filthy ballad, gone.

To begin with, Pilgrim was not especially worried. He and Teal had agreed that she would signal the arrival of the representatives of the Invisible College by tying a length of white cloth to a branch at the turnoff for the track to Windy Bay. He had gone out to check last night, out of an excess of caution and impatience, and there had been no cloth there then, and there was no cloth there that morning, either.

He told himself that it meant Gentle should have enough time to make his conquest, and with nothing else to do, for he had already packed in anticipation of a quick departure, he spent the morning pottering in the library. Early in the afternoon he went out again to check for the signal, and again found nothing. There was no sign of Gentle either. He tried to read an account of the effects of seasonal changes in animal behaviour written by an ancestor three hundred years ago, but the print swam and swarmed before his eyes and he kept losing the thread of a discussion about the importance of song in establishing the territories of birds. At last he closed the book and slid it into its rightful place on the shelves and, for what he hoped would be the last time, doused the fire in the hearth and blew out the lamps and locked the library's door.

Dusk had fallen and still Gentle had not returned. Stonehaven's lights glimmered against a long veil of pinkish light that was fading into the sea and the chilly wind carried faint snatches of a wild drumming as Pilgrim walked down the track to the turnoff, the tip of his cane sinking in soft dirt, tapping on stones. He saw a glimmer low in the clump of trees beside the track to Windy Bay, hurried towards it.

It was there. The white cloth was there. The representatives had arrived, were waiting for him in Teal's cabin. It was time to go.

He saddled the mara and hung the bag stuffed with clothes and books on the saddle horn. The mara snorted and stamped, eager to be off, but Pilgrim climbed the stair to the apartment one last time. Everything was exactly as he'd left it; Gentle still wasn't back. Pilgrim trimmed the wick of the lamp and left it burning at the window and went out.

There were lights in several of the narrow windows of the fat silhouette of the central tower, too: Grace Wren Saltmire was not at carnival that night. Pilgrim wondered if he should say goodbye to her, knew that he could not risk it. He also knew that he should trust Gentle to return and discover the white cloth and find his way to Teal's cabin, but when he reached the place where the track divided he turned right instead of left, towards the town. Perhaps Gentle had stumbled into some kind of trouble, or in the heat and excitement of his liaison with the widow had forgotten his promise to make his way to the rendezvous in good time, and because he was responsible for dragging him to this neglected little town at the far end of civilisation, Pilgrim couldn't leave him behind. And besides, it shouldn't take long to find him. The town was small, and most people would be in its central square. If Gentle wasn't amongst them Pilgrim would discover where his widow lived and rouse him from her bed.

He let the mara find its way in the near dark, ambling past scrub pasture, past tents pitched either side of the track. People were prancing around a bale fire to the cross-rhythms of goblet drums, claves and handclaps. A couple was openly rutting against a tree.

He was riding through the outskirts of the town, the noise of the central square directly ahead, when brilliant lights kindled on either side and shadowy figures moved towards him. For a moment he thought that they were revellers, and called out, asking them to make way. One grabbed the mara's bridle and as she tossed her blunt head and halted Noble Seatree stepped forward, aiming the beam of an electric candle at Pilgrim's face and telling him that the game was up.

24.

Pilgrim and Gentle were imprisoned in a net store at the far end of the harbour. There was no room for them in town, Noble Seatree told them, the lockup being occupied for the carnival's duration by his wife's relatives from up in the hills, and this would keep them safe from any drunken fools who might be minded to have a bit of fun with them. The carnival would soon be over, and then they would stand before the town's council. Meanwhile, they should contemplate their sins and think about how they might offer to atone for them. If it was up to him, the constable said with malignant relish, they'd be improved by a couple of years, hard labour for the benefit of the community.

Pilgrim said that since the aunties of his tribe had sent him here it should be their responsibility to decide what, if any, punishment he deserved, adding that Gentle should be released at once, having done no more than follow his orders, but Noble Seatree laughed and told him that this was a local matter to be decided by locals, and their idea of justice was as good as anyone else's, no matter what outsiders with an inflated sense of importance might think.

'And while you're waiting for justice to be served,' he said, 'I advise you to think again about helping me find your accomplice Teal Leadwood. Things might go easier for you if you do, and your silence won't do her any good, because we'll track her down soon enough anyway.'

Neither Pilgrim nor Gentle said anything. The constable knew or suspected that Teal had been helping them plan their escape from Stonehaven, but so far he had not mentioned the Invisible College. Pilgrim hoped that meant he didn't know about its representatives, hoped that they and Teal had got away safely.

The net store was cold and dark, and smelled strongly of salt and stale fish. Its tarred timber walls leaned together high above; the ragged shrouds of old nets hung from cross beams. Gentle, battered and bruised after trying to resist arrest when the constable and his gang had surprised him on his way back to the Hearth, was chained by an ankle to a stake pounded deep in the dirt floor, like the bear in its pit. Pilgrim sat close to him, hunched and miserable, shivering from cold and exhaustion. The constable had taken his cane and amber pendant, the bag in which he had packed his clothes, the map in its tube and his notes and the annotated rough draft of Master Able's monograph and all his other papers, and he doubted that he would ever see them again. The disaster was universal.

Noble Seatree had told them that he had been keeping watch on them ever since Grace Wren Saltmire had warned him that they were preparing to escape, but Gentle blamed Teal Leadwood. 'Why she wasn't arrested along with us, it isn't that she got away. It's because she made a bargain with the constable.'

Pilgrim tried to convince him that Teal had wanted to help them, that if they hadn't arranged to meet the representatives of the Invisible College they would have tried to steal a boat instead and fallen into worse trouble, but Gentle refused to believe any of it.

'Most likely she didn't send those letters, or receive that tapcode message,' he said, staring at the shadowy wall beyond Pilgrim. 'Most likely that Invisible College of hers doesn't even exist. Or if it does, it neither knows nor cares about you and your work.'

Pilgrim slept fitfully, woke to find spears of grey light lancing through chinks in the plank walls. Their guards brought in a tray carrying beakers of strong tea and two bowls of gruel flecked with bits of salt fish, and they were given no other food and received no other attention for the rest of the day. There was a bucket of well water, and another bucket for their necessaries, and that was that as far as amenities were concerned.

Pilgrim was free to limp up and down, eight paces to the far wall, eight paces back; Gentle spent most of the time asleep, or pretending to be asleep, stirring when it began to grow dark and there was the crackle of fireworks and distant snatches of music as the feasting and dancing and coupling began again. He stood up, the chain between his ankle cuff and the stake rattling, and put back his head and howled long and loud, stopping as if to listen to the echoes rolling around beneath the high peak of the roof, then howling again, and again, until one of the guards banged on the door and told him to shut his noise or they'd come in and gag him. Gentle laughed, and sat down heavily, wincing in pain, saying ruefully that the constable and his gang had got him good when they'd caught him. 'One of 'em was a fellow I went hunting with. Didn't hold him back any.'

'They should not have hurt you.'

'Oh, they had the right, seeing as I was trying my best to throw them off.'

'This is a lawless place.'

'It's how life is, at the edges of the Union. Did you find any likely way out when you were prowling around earlier?'

154

'The walls are sound. No rotten or loose planks that I could discover. And even if we had something to dig with, it wouldn't be easy. The ground is still frozen from winter.'

Gentle gathered his chain in both hands and asked Pilgrim to help him loosen the stake, but although they heaved and tugged for several minutes it did not budge.

Pilgrim sat on the cold ground, sweat chilling in the small of his back. 'I'm sorry I got us into this mess,' he said.

'I was already facing hard labour,' Gentle said. 'I put it off for a while, is all. Come to think of it, I might be better off here. It's unlikely they keep prisoners as secure as they do in a Union camp. We might have a good chance of getting away once they put us to work.'

'But for now there is nothing we can do,' Pilgrim said. Defeat welled up in him again, deep and dark and bitter.

Gentle curled up and appeared to fall asleep again, seemingly immune to the cold. The fireworks reached a brief crescendo and died away and drumming started up, racing and slowing, racing and slowing. Pilgrim sat with his arms wrapped around his knees and fell into an erratic doze, starting awake when light flared outside, sketching the edges of the door. Gentle had woken too, a vague shadow sitting up as the door was wrenched back. Pilgrim squinted into the glare, saw two figures behind it. Two women. The one holding an electric candle, a young woman dressed in black, raised it high and stepped forward.

Pilgrim drew himself up and said, as calmly as he could, 'The Invisible College, I presume.'

'It's good to meet you at last,' the young woman said. 'We're huge admirers of your master's work.'

25.

The guards were old, but not immune to the urgings of the Season, the young woman, Poppy Greenleaf, told Pilgrim, as she unlocked Gentle's shackle. It had been easy to charm them, and ply them with vinewater, and oilcakes spiked with powdered snakehead fungus from Teal Leadwood's pharmakon store; combined with the vinewater, the powder had rendered them as helpless as newborns.

'They thought we were making ready for some bawdy sport when we tied them up,' the other woman, Fragrant Plainsrunner, said. 'By the time they're found and freed, we'll be over the horizon and out of sight of land.'

The two women led Gentle and Pilgrim to a skiff and in the darkness rowed quietly and expertly to a windjammer anchored near the harbour mouth. Teal Leadwood was already aboard. She tended to Gentle's cuts and bruises while Poppy and Fragrant and the windjammer's captain unfurled the sails and raised the anchor. Teal told Pilgrim that a group of men had ridden out to her cabin, no doubt to arrest her, but they'd been carrying torches and drunkenly whooping and hollering, and she and Poppy and Fragrant had been able to slip away while they were still splashing across the marsh. She'd tried to find Pilgrim and Gentle, she said, but they had already been arrested.

'I underestimated the constable,' Pilgrim said.

'Seems that Grace was spying on us,' Gentle said.

'Fortunately, he didn't know about your friends,' Pilgrim said.

After the windjammer was under way, running through the dark ahead of a stiff north-westerly breeze, Poppy had Pilgrim and Gentle swear a solemn oath of secrecy, and insisted that both were given shots that would tamp down what she called their innate arousal. Gentle submitted with weary patience; Pilgrim explained that he did not suffer from the Seasonal urge, but Teal jabbed him anyway.

'We've all had similar shots,' Poppy said.

'It's going to be a long voyage in close quarters,' Fragrant said. She was older than Teal, with a calm, severe manner and mismatched eyes, one dark brown, the other light blue. 'Best to keep everything nice and peaceful.'

They were heading north. Not to a town where Pilgrim could catch a train that would take him to Highwater Reach, as he'd hoped, but all the way to the New Territories and Ogres Grave, and then overland to Foeless Landwalker's desert encampment. According to Poppy and Fragrant, Landwalker's followers were cutting an outline of a flowersipper, a league across from wingtip to wingtip, in the level white salt pan where he claimed that the visitors' sky boats would land once they were ready to reveal themselves. He held a rally there every night, preaching to his followers and leading them in communal prayers that supposedly opened a psychic pathway to the visitors, and he had recruited many new followers by exploiting the resentments of settlers in the New Territories towards the Union, which imposed laws without representation and forced them to pay tithes to fund the construction of roads and railways, and to cover the cost of policing the New Territories and keeping the northern border secure from intrusion by bears. Many wanted to break away from the Union and establish a separate confederation of tribal territories, and a secret cabal, the Night Riders, had declared themselves to be the arbitrators of law and justice in so-called liberated zones, and had taken to tarring and feathering tithe collectors and other Union officials and burning down their offices.

'It seems that many of Foeless Landwalker's inner circle are members of the Night Riders,' Fragrant said. 'Union authorities believe that he is either being used by them or has aligned himself with their cause, and they are worried about the escalation in popular support for his crusade. Merchants are donating food and water and other supplies to his camp, and people all over the New Territories have been sending him money.'

'He is gaining support in the Union, too,' Poppy said. 'He has discovered something people want to believe in, and is using it to challenge the Mother's grace.'

'It is more important than ever to find out if he's a prophet or a charlatan,' Fragrant said. 'What the visitors' intentions are, if he really has met them. What his intentions are, if his claims are outright fabrications.'

'You told Teal that Foeless Landwalker's propagandist tried to recruit you after your master's death,' Poppy said. 'We think that you can use that connection to infiltrate Landwalker's inner circle and win an audience with him. Find out everything you can.'

'It could help us to win proper recognition as scholars,' Fragrant said. 'Access to the Library of All People. The right to publish in its journals.'

'And if you help us, we can give you the help you need to finish your late master's research,' Poppy said.

Somewhat later, Gentle said he was surprised that Pilgrim had agreed to help the Invisible College so readily, given the risks involved.

'It isn't likely that I'll get anywhere near Foeless Landwalker, given that Intrepid Windrush is no friend of mine, and I've twice turned down his invitation to join the cause,' Pilgrim said. 'But Noble Seatree took all my papers. My master's notes, my own writings, the map . . . In short, everything I need to finish my work. My last and only hope is that these women will make good on their promise to help me after I have done my best to help them.'

'I wouldn't mind helping you retrieve your stuff,' Gentle said. 'Especially if I can get the constable on his own for a minute or two.'

'I don't think we can safely show our faces in Stonehaven for a while,' Pilgrim said. 'And repaying violence with violence does no one any good. Besides, if I do manage to win an audience with Foeless Landwalker, I know something about the visitors that may help to determine if there is any truth to his ravings.'

Pilgrim let Gentle think about that, as Master Able had once given him time to work up answers to questions or logic puzzles. They were standing at the prow of the trim, white-hulled windjammer. It had been built by the Sweetwater Collective to a design reverse engineered from fossil remnants of an ogre craft, and loaned to the Invisible College by a wealthy patron. The windjammer's bow was slicing waves into foaming folds, its triangular mainsail bellying in the north-westerly wind, and the sun was shaping itself from a simmer of primeval light above the rugged coast. Gentle wore a borrowed black oilcoat; Pilgrim was wrapped in the snug embrace of his fur coat. He and the women had talked out the night, making plans and speculating about the visitors, he had eaten a good breakfast and he had put a useful distance between himself and the traps of Stonehaven. He was tired but wide awake. The cold salt air was exhilarating. It tasted of freedom. Of hope.

Gentle said, 'Is this about that map of yours?'

'Exactly so. If Landwalker really is in touch with the visitors, he should know if they made contact with bears before the fall, and what happened when they did.'

'Even if you catch him out, it most likely won't make any difference,' Gentle said. 'I've known a few folk who can't help but tell tall tales about everything, and they never admit to stretching the truth. You can show them that what they claimed to be black was really white, put it right in front of their eyes, and they'll just make up some even taller tale to excuse it.'

'I don't expect him to recant,' Pilgrim said. 'But I hope it will satisfy our new friends.'

'If he's in deep with these Night Riders, this plan might put you at hazard. Me too, since I can't allow you to walk into his camp on your own.'

'If you think it too hazardous, you can put off at the next port. You've already done enough and don't need to follow me any further.'

'I'm not sure I'm ready to go back to the roving life. And I admit to being somewhat curious about what happens next.'

'You might change your mind when your seasickness takes hold.'

'So far that tincture Teal gave me seems to be tamping it down.'

'And the injection?'

'That seems to be working too. Is this what it's like for you? Thinking about it, but not feeling the need?'

'I don't think about it very much,' Pilgrim said. 'Although I sometimes think about not thinking about it.'

'About being different. I know that feeling,' Gentle said.

There was a short silence as they watched the sun rising above the limitless ocean. At last, Pilgrim said, 'There's another reason why I want to visit with Foeless Landwalker.'

'Are you going to make me guess again?'

'I'm very interested in that landing field of his, and the outline of the flowersipper.'

'You think the visitors told him to build it?'

'He doesn't have to be in contact with them to know about the mark that's sometimes found where they have been sighted. Witnesses have described it. Wallsheets have published sketches of it. But if the visitors are real, if the mark is their mark, it's possible that Foeless Landwalker's giant replica has attracted their attention. That we might find some trace of them in the vicinity. Judging by reports of sightings, the Broken Isles is a place they favour.'

'I'm trying to picture your face if they appear,' Gentle said, 'and this Landwalker fellow steps forward to meet them.'

'I hope I would tell myself that truth is what matters, not who finds it first. And I hope that I would be able to make sure that Master Able was properly credited for believing that sightings of the visitors were of interest when few did.'

Gentle looked towards the cockpit at the stern of the wind-jammer, where its captain, Coral Seagrass, stood at the wheel. 'Our new friends will want some of that credit. Might not be much left for you.'

26.

It took a little over two moonspans to reach the Broken Isles. The three women from the Invisible College took turns at the windjammer's helm, and after a few days Coral Seagrass let Gentle try his hand. Although the college was a collective in which every member had an equal say, it was most definitely Coral's boat. A calm, taciturn woman, she had been born into a fishing family on the east coast of the Union, and was presently studying the reefs for which she was named. When she had been much younger, she told Pilgrim, she had spent two years aboard a clipper ship, masquerading as a cabin boy, sailing the triangle route from the Union eastwards across the ocean to Akeban, Akeban to the north-east coast of the New Territories, and back to the Union. It was commoner than he might suppose, she said, and some women spent their entire lives in masquerade, but after learning the tarpaulin trade and seeing more of the world than most men, she'd wanted to return to her tribe and raise a family.

'Yet here I am now, not as done with adventuring as I thought,' she said.

Gentle proved to be a useful recruit to the ship's crew. He scrubbed the deck every morning, spliced broken lines, climbed nimbly amongst the yards and ratlines to let out or take in sails, ran trotlines from the stern to augment their meals with fresh fish and served spells at the helm, although never on his own and never at night. Despite the women's fine words about mutual interest, there were limits to trust on both sides.

When they put in to shore to replenish the windjammer's tanks with water collected from freshets that tumbled from steep cliffs, Gentle and Teal fossicked in the windblown heath on the clifftops and returned with two bucketfuls of silverweed roots which Teal boiled up and mashed with fishgrease into a porridge and insisted that everyone eat a portion because it was rich with vital nutriments absent from their supply of canned and dried food. Although she was trying her best to make herself useful, had taken charge of the cooking and mixed up an ointment to protect Gentle's unpigmented hide from the brutal sunlight, she was somewhat subdued and withdrawn, having been forced to abandon her work and her home for no other reason than to escape the reckoning for giving aid to Pilgrim and Gentle. She'd had to turn her pet washcat loose, too, and fretted that it would not survive long in the wild. Pilgrim sympathised, having suffered his own losses, and although Teal insisted that her sacrifices had been necessary, he felt a heavy mix of guilt and obligation. A pressure to succeed when success, and how to measure it, were far from certain.

Unlike the others, he couldn't make much of a contribution to shipboard life. Couldn't climb the mast and help with the sail-work and rope-work, like Gentle and Poppy, lacked Fragrant's and Coral's navigational skills and Teal's ability to conjure meals in the tiny galley. Gentle had fashioned a replacement for his lost cane from the twisted stem of a thornbush from the clifftop heath, but it wasn't much use on the deck of the windjammer and Pilgrim mostly got about by hauling himself along lines and rails, his weak leg dragging behind him. In truth, he found being at sea more unnerving than being at the mercy of the women and their Invisible College. It was only his second time aboard a proper ship – the river ferry between Highwater Reach and Concord didn't count – and while the sturdy coastal trader ship had plodded as steadily as a draft mara through straits and channels, the windjammer seemed as nervous as a gazehound. It was constantly in motion. Not merely thrusting forward, but pitching up and down and from side to side. Pilgrim had only been properly seasick once, when they had been forced to spend a night anchored close to a rocky shore while a storm thrashed the sea into huge waves and lumps of flying foam, rain blew sideways and lightning danced at the horizon, but he was faintly unsettled all the time, and very much misliked it on the occasions when they cut a chord across an inflection in the coast and left all sight of land behind. The sea was intimidatingly vast and the windjammer was a slender, unstable sliver of wood and canvas seven paces across and seventy from stem to stern. A tiny island at the mercy of elemental forces utterly indifferent to the lives of its crew.

One day, they cut through a shoal of flying fish scudding above the waves and Gentle chased down and clubbed several which landed on the deck. Pilgrim studied one before Gentle filleted it, made sketches of its slim but sturdy body and the wing-like pectoral fins and smaller pelvic fins that enabled it to glide for short distances after it had thrust itself above the waves with vigorous movements of its tail. The pectoral fins were each as wide as his hand when outstretched, their elegant curved profile, resembling a bird wing, supported by bifurcate rays.

It was a pleasing example of convergent selection, he told Poppy, and she told him that engineers had borrowed the shape of flying-fish fins for the wings of sailplanes that, after being launched from hot-air balloons, could glide for thirty or forty stades, surveying the land below and using the new plate cameras to record it. She studied the behaviour of bears, said that she would love to use a sailplane to survey their territories and mating leks in the northern wilderness.

'It would make it much easier to get up accurate maps. But women aren't allowed such indulgences, of course. Not yet, anyway. But one day things will change, and I will be soaring above bear country, tracking my prey like an eagle. Meanwhile, I must be content to rummage through old ruins, trying to imagine how bears lived in them.'

Like Coral and Fragrant, she was dressed in a padded black jacket and loose black cotton trews, the clothing tradition-ally worn by men in the construction trade. She claimed that she and her friends had adopted it out of practical necessity, although Pilgrim suspected that it was a statement of intent, too. A studied defiance of convention.

Poppy did not have much time for convention, or tradi-tional roles. She was a sturdy spirited person with a quick and lively mind, born into a family of scholars who supported her work and her life choices. 'I want pups, but not just yet,' she said. 'First, I want to establish myself and help to bring about recognition for women scholars.' And, 'I never wanted to be like a man. I just want the freedom men have.'

She enjoyed Pilgrim's stories about his grandfather's adven-tures as a bear trapper, and took the idea that the visitors might have made contact with bear civilisation very seriously. She had read Master Able's book on his early work on the archaeology of bear cities and his monographs about bear culture and selective changes in their anatomy after their fall, and was amused by Pilgrim's stories about his master's eccentricities and kindnesses, his feuds and friendships with other scholars.

'It's plain to see that you miss him,' she said.

'I wish I could tell him about the map, and my visit to the ruins of the new city,' Pilgrim said. 'He would listen to my ideas, tell me that I had made a good start and then proceed to draw connections I had not thought of and point out patterns I had failed to see.'

His conversations with Poppy and Fragrant were welcome diversions. Fragrant was small and dark, slightly built but energetic and strong-willed. The pelt of her scalp was dyed bright crimson, small brass rings were sewn into the rims of her ears and a pendant fashioned from pitted meteoritic iron hung at her breastbone. She was a skywatcher who had searched the dry deserts of the west coast for fallen meteorites, and had ground up a fragment of a stony meteorite and dissolved it in heart of wine and swallowed it, so that her blood and bones would be one with the sky. She searched for new comets and calculated their orbits and periodicities, and made studies of the wandering stars, most especially Firestar. She belonged to a small group who observed and catalogued the seasonal changes in His icecaps and other features, and believed that it was evidence of some form of life. She showed Pilgrim maps based on many hours of observations: networks of parallel and intersecting lines that sprawled across the deserts of the northern hemisphere and might be irrigation canals that transported meltwater from the icecap that crowned Firestar's north pole to oases at His equator.

Fragrant explained that the canals might not be natural features, but could have been built by an intelligent species native to Firestar. Far older than the civilisation of the people and more advanced than even the ogres' civilisation at its zenith, it might have dwindled and failed as Firestar grew ever drier and colder, leaving only the wreckage of its vast engineering works behind. Or perhaps some small remnant persisted, studying the Mother through huge telescopes, marvelling at Her wealth of water and life. They may have observed traces of our civilisation, Fragrant said. The smudges of cities and patches of agriculture. Angular patterns of highways and railways resembling the patterns of their canals. The wakes of ships crossing the oceans. Tantalised by these glimpses, eager to learn more, they might have made the crossing between worlds, visiting the Mother to better study Her people, just as they might have studied bear civilisation and the vast cities of ogres before them. In short, they might be the visitors Pilgrim hoped to find.

Pilgrim told her that it was an interesting story, but seemed to be based on the assumption that two strange and unexplained phenomena were related, and she said that if it was no more than a story it was a better one than Foeless Landwalker's. Firestar was more like the Mother than Morningstar, which was hot and wet and permanently shrouded in cloud: a world of steaming oceans and jungle swamps that in no way resembled Foeless Landwalker's fanciful descriptions of a paradisiacal garden, and an unlikely home for an advanced civilisation. Even so, she knew very well that ideas about life on Firestar were controversial. She and her friends had been relentlessly criticised by other skywatchers in the Invisible College, who pointed out that every person who claimed that they had seen canals had drawn a different map, that the seasonal shrinkage of the icecap at the north pole of Firestar was much less than that required to fill a planet-spanning network of waterways, and occultations of stars passing behind Him showed that His atmosphere was much thinner than the Mother's, almost certainly too thin to support any life more complex than lichens and algae.

'Our critics don't understand that the canals are at the very limit of the resolution of our telescopes, and are also affected by fluctuations in the Mother's envelope of air,' Fragrant said. 'Also, their calculations about the size of the icecap are speculative, and Firestar's inhospitality is an important part of our theory: it explains why His inhabitants expended so much labour on building their canals. His atmosphere may be too thin to support animal life at this present time, but could have been much thicker when its inhabitants arose. They may have retreated to sealed underground cities, but certain kinds of plants should be able to grow on the surface, causing the seasonal changes that we observe. And if the original atmosphere of Firestar was different to that of the Mother, it would explain the appearance of the visitors – they may be wearing some kind of diving apparatus that contains air more suited to their physiology.

'But these arguments miss the point, which is that this kind of speculation usefully tests the limits of possibility. Your master took a brave risk when he decided that sightings of the visitors were a worthy subject of study, but tried to apply traditional principles to a problem that cannot be understood by collecting and cataloguing facts. If we are to fully embrace the world in all its glory and mystery we must find new ways of seeing and thinking. You'd do well to remember that, when you meet Foeless Landwalker. You should open your mind. Purge yourself of prejudices and preconceptions. I don't mean that you should believe everything, but you should not dismiss anything out of hand, either. No matter how strange or absurd it may seem.'

The forests and mountains along the coast gave way to grassland, and grassland yielded to the tawny desert where Fragrant had once fossicked for fallen stars. They kept well away from the few ships they sighted, and in the first half of the voyage put into port only once, anchoring at night outside the harbour breakwater of a small town. A ragboat piloted by a woman came out to meet them. As they took aboard crates of

168

food and canisters of fresh water, she told them that although Foeless Landwalker had not yet succeeded in calling down visitors, his congregation was still growing, and there were now satellite gatherings in towns across the New Territories and in the capital and several cities in the Union.

They were almost finished loading the supplies when Teal Leadwood came up from the cabin, wearing her red coat and hauling a stuffed rollbag. She was going to head off to her tribe's territory, she told Pilgrim. Hopefully, her family would take in their eccentric daughter and protect her from any repercussions from helping him flee Stonehaven and exile.

'As soon as I'm ashore I'll send a message to the Invisible College, confirming that you are on your way to Ogres Grave,' she said. 'And after I've settled with my family I will ask the College to help me recover all I've lost. I brought my notebooks, but had to leave my library behind. No doubt Noble Seatree has confiscated it, along with everything else. Hopefully, the College can buy it back.'

When Pilgrim began to apologise for the trouble he had caused, she took his hands and looked into his eyes and said, 'Find the truth.'

'I promise.'

'No more stories based on supposition and pieces from old myths. Find the truth and tell it straight.'

'I will,' Pilgrim said, and felt a soft swell of sorrow as the ragboat dwindled into the night. Teal had been the only friend he had made in Stonehaven. Clever, sensible and generous. He had counted her as an ally, and now he and Gentle were outnumbered.

The windjammer was already raising anchor and sail. Coral said that they hadn't put into the harbour and needed to move on as quickly as possible, because a boat crewed by women would attract the wrong kind of attention.

'Standing offshore also stopped us from jumping ship,' Gentle told Pilgrim, after the windjammer had got under way and the little lights of the town had dwindled into the empty darkness of the desert and the sea. 'Which is maybe why Teal didn't tell you she was leaving until the last moment.'

'Would you have gone with her, if you had the chance?'

'I know you think my word isn't worth much, given who I am and what I've done, but I promised to stick by you, and I will. And you need someone to look after your interests. You might not be turned by the Season, but I can't help thinking these women may have found another way to beguile you.'

'I don't trust their Invisible College, but I like them well enough. And we have a common purpose.'

'Maybe so, but do you think they'll come to your rescue if you get in trouble with Foeless Landwalker and his Night Riders?'

The desert coast seemed endless, but at last patches of marsh and grassland began to appear in river estuaries and deltas, and beyond the broad bay at the mouth of the Blackwater River were ranges of hills covered in tropical forest. A day later, Coral announced that they had crossed the waist of the Mother, and Pilgrim realised that they must have passed and left behind the territory of his tribe, and the territory of Gentle's coastal tribe too. There was a silly but solemn ceremony in which Pilgrim, Poppy and Fragrant, who had not crossed this imaginary dividing line before, were doused with buckets of seawater while reciting pledges to the Mother's sea aspect, and then the windjammer turned away from land and sailed north and west across open ocean. It was a shorter route than hugging the sinuous coast of the Neck that linked the Union and the New Territories, but still about as far as the distance they had already covered.

One night Fragrant, who was at the helm, called everyone up on deck, and they saw that the sea all around them was glowing with cold blue fire. The bow wave of the windjammer shimmered and sparkled, and as their eyes adapted they saw a vast pattern of flickering spokes or rays that slowly turned against each other, as if some secret mechanism of the world had risen to the surface. Coral explained that the glow was generated by myriads of tiny organisms, but that did not make the vast display any less wonderful. Gentle said that it was a good omen, and no one disagreed. Pilgrim thought that it might have little or nothing to do with their enterprise, but if it improved Gentle's morale it was a kind of blessing.

At last they sighted land again, Gentle and Poppy climbing the masts for a better look as a faint green line appeared under mountainous ranges of cloud at the horizon. Soon, other ships began to appear – traffic from the canal, completed only three years ago, which cut across the narrowest part of the Neck, so that ships no longer had to risk a long and dangerous passage through the stormy seas at the southern tip of the Union. Coral said that during the canal's construction, traces had been found of an earlier channel built by ogres. It seemed that they had taken advantage of the same route.

Two nights later, the windjammer anchored outside the harbour of a small town surrounded by tropical jungle, and a skiff rowed out and delivered supplies of fresh and dry fish, starchy tubers and tropical fruit – cluster figs, mammy apples, agave and melons like the rough-shelled eggs of terror lizards. The young woman who delivered this bounty had more news of Foeless Landwalker and his circus. Although the visitors still had not appeared, lights had been seen moving across the night sky, and new followers were arriving every day. Lawkeepers sent by the authorities to observe the gathering had been attacked and three had been injured, one seriously. More were on their way, and it seemed that some kind of confrontation was inevitable, most likely turning on an attempt to arrest Foeless Landwalker, who had refused a request to appear before a special court to explain himself.

Pilgrim, recalling the nets of green lights Mercy Redvine claimed to have seen in the ruins of the new city, wanted to know more about the lights in the sky above the gathering and its landing field, but the young woman said that she knew only what had been passed on to her. Small fugitive lights appearing here and there in the night sky with no obvious pattern; according to Foeless Landwalker, they were delivering new messages from the visitors through his special psychic connection.

'Sounds like he's trying to stretch out his grift for as long as possible,' Gentle said. 'Taking as much from his followers as he can before it falls apart.'

'We need to get there as quickly as we can,' Pilgrim said. 'I want to see those lights. And I won't be able to talk to Foeless Landwalker if he has been arrested.'

'If we don't run into bad weather, we'll be at Ogres Grave in twelve days,' Coral said.

'And it will take two more to reach Landwalker's gathering,' Poppy said. 'We had better hope that the lawkeepers are not eager to press their case.'

27.

They crossed the mouth of Salt Tongue Gulf, sailed past an inhospitable coast of scrub desert and bare mountains, and twelve days later, as Coral had predicted, put in at the harbour of Ogres Grave, the mainland port of the Broken Isles, a ramshackle town of low wooden buildings, clusters of shacks and dusty, unpaved and mostly treeless streets at the south-western side of a broad shallow bay. Everywhere around it, and on the islands strewn across the bay, were mine shafts sunk into layers of mudstone that covered the ruins of a great ogre city, the largest known.

Some of the islands were shrouded in the smoke of smelters extracting metals from iron pyrites and other salts bound to rocks or leached into layers above impermeable clays; there was also a thriving trade in ogre artefacts. There were fields of compressed and chemically altered bricks on the outskirts of the town, hills of milky glass fragments, charnel heaps of fossilised bones of ogres and the animals commonly associated with them. One excavation had revealed the massive concrete footings of buildings that archaeologists reckoned to have been several hundred spans tall; another had uncovered the remains of a maze of chambers and passages that floodwaters had filled with mud and sand, preserving their shape and the three-dimensional imprints of furniture which had rotted away long ago.

It was estimated that ogres had numbered in the billions when their civilisation had met its end, and they appeared to have colonised every corner of the world. Giants who had ravaged and despoiled the Mother's land and seas, leaving traces of huge mines and quarries where they had ripped minerals and metals from Her skin. Historiographers reckoned that their civilisation had been destroyed by fires, floods and rising sea levels, and the final spasm of a global struggle in which firestorms had melted metal, fused brick and stone and stamped curious glassy craters that could still be traced in the ruins of their great cities and deposited the Burn Line's layer of ash. Excavating and processing glass and brick and metal provided steady work for thousands of labourers, and along the shore and on every island prospectors searched for fossil artefacts, dreaming of finding something that the Sweetwater Collective could reverse engineer into a useful gadget or use to develop an entirely new kind of techne, and make them wildly rich.

After the windjammer tied up, Poppy headed off down the quay to pay the landing fee and send a tapwire message confirming their arrival. Their contact, a curt, middle-aged woman named Jasmine Deeproot who worked for the assay offices which certified genuine fossils, arrived a few hours later. She was the only member of the Invisible College on this stretch of the coast, and made it clear that she was not going to take part in what she believed to be a bootless quest. As far as she was concerned, Foeless Landwalker was a charlatan, and his claims about the visitors were clearly fantasies and fabrications. Airy nothings. You might as well, she said, try to catch a cloud. When Pilgrim told her about the lights haunting the sky above the gathering, and said that the region around Ogres Grave had been the focus of a significant number of sightings, she replied that it wasn't surprising, given that most of the prospectors and the labourers in the mines and smelters and refineries spent their rest days smoking kif and drinking vast quantities of corn beer and mescal tea, and the place was an enormous boneyard where rumours of phantasms and revenants were common currency.

'Your self-styled prophet hasn't yet succeeded in calling down his friends, but the gathering of his followers is still growing,' she said. 'Perhaps you've heard that the Night Riders have sided with him. He has gained the support of several rich and influential families, too. Either because they've fallen for his nonsense, or hope to make use of his popularity with the common people. There's even a rumour that the Sweetwater Collective has shown interest.'

'Is there any truth to that?' Pilgrim said.

'There are so many stories and rumours it's hard to know what's true and what isn't,' Jasmine Deeproot said. 'But the size of the gathering and Landwalker's indifference to his followers should make things easier for you. The lawkeepers are keeping their distance, too, and haven't set up any more checkpoints after a mob tore down the last one. You should be able to join it without any trouble; just don't do anything that will draw attention to yourselves.'

Coral volunteered to stay on board the windjammer; Jasmine led the others through a bustle of sailors and labourers, cranes and wagons, to a transit station on the far side of a row of godowns and sheds, and they rode a smart open-sided tram (one of the gifts of the Sweetwater Collective) across town. There were no burrows or large houses, only wooden shacks standing in sandy lots. Even the flat-fronted facades of shops and rooming houses on the town's main street had the impermanent air of a stage set. When Pilgrim remarked on this,

Jasmine told him that because the ground ofttimes trembled and shook buildings were mostly wood and paper. Cheap to construct and easy to replace, and few people would be hurt if they collapsed. The chief danger was fire. Much of the town had burnt to the ground three years ago, and almost everything they saw had been rebuilt since then.

Ten blocks of the main street were given over to the fossil trade, with displays of bones and artefacts in open windows or heaped on tables under canvas awnings. Slabs of mudstone printed with the shapes of ogre possessions, combs and cutlery, buttons and fragments of ceramics, sheets of plasticised paper which had been wiped clean of any print or images they might once have held. Pilgrim saw a complete, articulated ogre skeleton hung against black velvet drapes in one window, saw in another a display of mudstone slabs imprinted with the fossilised skeletons of chickens.

They left the tram at the far end of this bone market and walked two blocks to the stable where Jasmine had hired a short string of maras. An emporium a few doors down sold supplies to prospectors. While the women bought camping gear, a bundle of firewood and canned food and flagons of water, Gentle found a display of machetes and utility knives and suggested they should acquire some cutlery for purposes of insurance, seeing as how some folk in the Territories were downright uncivilised, with no regard for the Mother's precepts. But Poppy and Fragrant vetoed his suggestion, and when Pilgrim sided with them Gentle sulkily put back the filleting knife he'd selected, saying that he hoped none of them would come to regret travelling empty-handed.

After the women had settled the bill and Gentle had helped them to load their purchases, rollbags and Fragrant's plate camera onto the maras, Jasmine handed Poppy a map and traced the best route, east and south to a pass through the mountains. Beyond that, she said, they could find their destination by following the procession of fools.

'The college is grateful for your help,' Poppy told her.

'Remember me if you are successful. Forget me if you aren't,' Jasmine said, and walked off before they had mounted their maras.

They rode through the straggling outskirts of the town, past the shacks and shafts of prospectors' claims, past an excavation where labourers were loading carts with spoil that would be rendered in slag furnaces, past a huge circular lake that had flooded one of the strange craters, its placid water reflecting the blue sky, its shore fringed with palms and palmettos.

A cluster of square white buildings gleamed on a flat-topped hill beyond the lake: the enclave of the Sweetwater Collective, where ogre artefacts were reconstructed, analysed and reverse engineered, producing a steady stream of techne that was changing society at an ever-accelerating rate. Wire recorders and street lamps, windmill generators and electric trains and trams, tapwires and cameras, bicycles and clockwork calculators, carborundum and cellophane film and several kinds of plastic, stamping presses, automatic lathes, and half a hundred other miracles.

The Collective's purchase of Master Able's papers from his family, and their hiring of another scholar to discover the truth about the visitors, still stung Pilgrim. A rude dismissal of his talents. A callous betrayal. He wondered if there was any truth to Jasmine Deeproot's rumour that the Collective had lent their support to Foeless Landwalker, and what it might mean. Did they think that there might be some truth to Landwalker's claims about meeting the visitors, that his gathering was a prelude to their arrival? If so, it was possible that the Collective had something to do with the resignation of Master Mindwell's assistant, Earnest Smallhill, cutting

177

off the scholar as ruthlessly as it had cut off Pilgrim and commandeering his assistant in an attempt to infiltrate Foeless Landwalker's inner circle. And if that were the case, Pilgrim thought, it might well make the mission to win an audience with Landwalker even harder.

The road climbed in switchbacks towards the high pass, and joined another that ran across desert flats of cactus and grease-wood. There was an irregular procession of people heading south, walking alone or in small groups, riding maras and camels. They were mostly male and mostly young, and many wore orange scarfs around their necks — a sign of true belief in the visitors, Poppy told Pilgrim.

'How do you know?'

'It was in the one of Jasmine's reports,' Poppy said.

She and Pilgrim were riding a little distance behind Fragrant and Gentle. She was barelegged in an oversized blue shirt belted at her waist and seemed to be thoroughly enjoying this adventure, telling Pilgrim that Jasmine had been in the audience when Foeless Landwalker had given a speech after being released by the lawkeepers who had briefly detained him in Ogres Grave, and had interviewed several of his followers.

'She tried to talk to him, too, but she couldn't get past his cadre of attendants.'

'Do you have copies of those reports, and her interviews?' Pilgrim said. 'I'd love to read them.'

He was wondering what else these women hadn't told him.

'You'll have to ask Jasmine, when we get back to town. We aren't carrying anything that might link us to the Invisible College.'

'What about the sermon? What did Landwalker have to say after he had been set free?'

'That the authorities could fetter a man but not the truth. That it would not be long before the visitors revealed

178

themselves and everything would change. The doubters would be cast down and the righteous lifted up. According to Jasmine, it wasn't so much what he said but the way he said it. I suppose we'll see for ourselves soon enough. When we watch him preach, and when you meet him.'

'I've been thinking about those lights. If they really are some kind of manifestation of the visitors, Foeless Landwalker might not need or want to meet me.'

'It won't be easy, but I know you'll find a way,' Poppy said. 'You possess a kind of admirable stubbornness.'

'More often than not, it seems to lead me into trouble.'

'It also led you to us,' Poppy said. 'And here we are, in this thing together.'

Easy for her to say. She and the others would be observers, but Pilgrim had to offer himself up to the dubious mercy of Foeless Landwalker and his followers. He wanted to meet the man, but he feared him, too. Landwalker had been a bear trapper before he had become a prophet, was no stranger to killing, and Foeless was not his birth name. He had chosen it for himself, and not to signify that he was the kind of good-natured fellow who had no enemies. It was instead a boast about how he had vanquished everyone who had wanted to harm him, and a warning to anyone else who might think to try.

And now they were riding amongst his true believers. People who wore orange scarfs and chanted his name as they walked in a procession half a hundred strong. And there would be many more like them at their destination, all at his command.

Pilgrim knew that he had been short-tempered with Poppy because of his growing trepidation about the task that lay ahead, and tried to make amends when they stopped at an overnight camp of Foeless's followers. Gentle made flatbreads which they ate with cheese and sour apples they had bought in Ogres Grave, and afterwards Pilgrim asked Poppy if she would help him carry out a brief survey of the people in the camp, asking them why they were here and if they had ever seen the visitors or knew anyone who had.

She proved to be adept at getting people to talk, and Pilgrim let her take charge of the interviews while he scribbled notes in a borrowed jotter; his wire recorder had been confiscated by Noble Seatree, along with everything else. Although they failed to find anyone who had encountered the visitors, a surprising number claimed to have seen, or knew or had heard of people who claimed to have seen, lights in the night sky or silvery seeds flying high and fast. One man told Poppy that several of his maras had been mutilated, and there had been strange footprints on the ground around the eviscerated corpses. Another said that his recently dead grandmother had come to him in a dream, and led him to an old-fashioned burrow in the shadow of a ruined bear city, where two silver-pelted strangers were waiting for him. He had talked with them for a long time, but couldn't remember, on waking, what they had told him.

'All I know is that I had to come here, where I will see them again,' he said, smiling with the calm simplicity of a saint.

Most had come because they believed, or wanted to believe, Foeless Landwalker's claim that the visitors had come to help people like them. They were hoping for miracles, from cures for the mortal illnesses of children and kin to an end to the droughts, wildfires and swarms of locusts which had afflicted the west coast for the past five years.

'Making a living is hard at the best of times, and these times are far from the best,' one young woman said. 'People are starving themselves so they can feed their children. They're eating seed corn that should be saved for planting the next harvest. Meanwhile the authorities still demand their tithe and in return give little relief and less charity. So it isn't

180

surprising that people take what hope they can find. Hope that these visitors will bring the changes the prophet talks about. Fix the world so there's less suffering in it. Because right now there's plenty of that to go around.'

An old man sitting on a folding stool beside a covered cart, neatly dressed in a blue velvet vest and canvas trews with neatly folded cuffs, studied Poppy and Pilgrim and said, 'You're from the Union, ain't you? But you ain't authority.'

'We are scholars,' Pilgrim said.

'Trying to figure the truth of this, I'd guess.'

'Something like that,' Pilgrim admitted.

'As to that, I don't believe in the visitors, but I don't not believe in them either,' the old man said. 'You could say I'm neutral about the idea. But I got a living to make, and I brought a cartload of necessities to sell to the people gathered up ahead. Once everything's gone, I plan to return home and sit out whatever happens next. Because one thing I know is true: whether or not these visitors show themselves, things are going to change. When people are given a little hope they find it hard to let it go. So if these creatures from beyond the sky don't come, I reckon people will decide to help themselves, having discovered a common cause instead of fighting each other for scraps.'

After Pilgrim and Poppy reported their findings, Fragrant said that people were likely to be disappointed if hope was all they had, but Poppy disagreed.

'This isn't really about Foeless Landwalker, or the visitors,' she said. 'It's about a desperate need for change and an end to hard times.'

Later, as they were preparing to turn in for the night, Gentle took Pilgrim aside and asked if he was still set on collaborating with the women. Pilgrim was wearing his ratty fur coat and Gentle was shawled in a blanket; their shipboard clothes, cotton vests and canvas jackets and trews, could not keep out the piercing cold of the desert night.

'Are you still brooding over the business with the cutlery?' Pilgrim said.

'I've been thinking about what the Deeproot woman told us about rich families getting behind Foeless Landwalker,' Gentle said. 'There's a saying in my tribe. When you see gulls flocking over a patch of water, you know there's fish to be found. Only here it's power, and the money that power attracts.'

'You know that I'm not interested in any of that.'

Gentle looked over at Poppy and Fragrant in their bedrolls on the other side of the campfire, and stepped closer to Pilgrim and said quietly, 'Of course you are. The women want to use you and what you know to win recognition for themselves. And you're happy to be used because you need their money to finish your work.'

'It's the work that's important, not the money. Finding out the truth about the visitors, and proving that my master was right and his critics were wrong.'

'But you still need money to do what you need to do,' Gentle said patiently, as if to a recalcitrant child. 'And seeing as Foeless Landwalker has the support of people with more money than either of us can dream of, we'd be fools if we didn't try to take advantage of that.'

'You still haven't understood anything I've told you about scholarly work, have you?' Pilgrim said. 'That it's not about money, but the getting and sharing of knowledge.'

'I know you have principles, because you've told me often enough. You want to meet Foeless Landwalker, and believe you know something about the visitors that he doesn't. You were thinking of using that to test him, but wouldn't it be better to sell it to him instead? All you have to do is set aside those principles of yours this one time, and you'll be free of your obligations to these women. Have enough money to finish your work on your own terms.'

'And you'd want a share, of course,' Pilgrim said.

'I wouldn't take more than half, even though it's my idea, and I'd have to make the deal for you,' Gentle said.

'There'll be no deal to make, because I didn't come here to bargain with Foeless Landwalker. And I won't break the promise I made to the Invisible College.'

'Yet you're the one taking all the risk in this enterprise.'

'They rescued us and brought us here. And this is how you want to repay them?'

'I'm a rover,' Gentle said. 'When I see an opportunity, I do as I must.'

It was too dark to make out his face, but Pilgrim was certain that it was set in that familiar inscrutable expression, and realised that although he'd spent a long winter with the rover, he still didn't really know or understand him. In all that time, they'd been no more than kitchen companions, Pilgrim sequestered with his books, paying little attention to anything else, Gentle making forays into the forest with his hunter friends, gossiping with Grace Wren Saltmire, bargaining with the chandler, becoming part of the little town's social network. Two very different worlds and minds, barely intersecting.

'It's not certain that I can get an audience with Foeless Landwalker,' he said. 'And if I managed it, I would be in no position to bargain.'

'That's why you need my help to make the deal,' Gentle said imperturbably.

'No, I don't. Because it isn't going to happen.'

'You could sleep on it. See how you feel in the morning.'

'It won't make any difference. I'm going to do what I have promised to do, and share anything I find out with Poppy and

Fragrant and the rest of the Invisible College. And if you don't like that,' Pilgrim said, leaning on his stick and looking up at the shadowy sketch of Gentle's face, 'you're free to leave.'

'It was just an idea,' Gentle said.

'Just an idea.'

'I thought I'd put it out there. It's a good deal, if you ask me. But if you don't want to do it, that's that.'

'And we'll say no more about it.'

'Isn't anything left to say, is there?' Gentle said. 'We should turn in. Looks like we have a long hard time of it ahead of us.'

28.

The night was cold, the ground was hard and Pilgrim's back and weak leg ached from the ride through the mountains to the high desert, but he slept long and deeply. When Poppy shook him awake, he was disappointed but not surprised to discover that Gentle was gone and one of the maras was missing.

He told Poppy and Fragrant about his conversation with Gentle, said he thought that the matter had been settled.

'Clearly not,' Fragrant said, with an unforgiving look.

'Perhaps he decided there was nothing in this venture for him, and cut and ran,' Pilgrim said. He was disappointed by his friend's selfishness, and angry with himself for having been too trusting.

'Or perhaps he decided to sell everything he knows to Foeless Landwalker,' Fragrant said.

'That's also possible,' Pilgrim admitted.

'We shouldn't have brought him with us,' Fragrant said. 'But we did, and now we have to assume the worst. We need to get to where we are going as quickly as we can, and hope that you can talk your way into Foeless Landwalker's confidences before Gentle can.'

They ate the last of the flatbreads Gentle had made the night before, folding them over stripes of fish paste, and packed up and headed out in the cold dawn light while the rest of the camp was still waking. The road climbed through stark desert. Stones and sand and gravel. Cactus, thorn bushes, stretches of parched grass. Ridges of giant boulders. Long shadows shrinking as the sun rose, the air growing warmer. Pilgrim hoped to see a figure waiting for them up ahead. Sitting beside a tethered mara, standing up as they approached. Gentle's snowy pelt and pinkish gaze. A perfunctory excuse about scouting ahead, given with a slow smile that challenged them to disbelieve it. But they saw no one else on the road, and an acid uncertainty began to simmer in Pilgrim's stomach.

A distant haze of dust resolved into the site of an excavation of ogre ruins. A cluster of burrows close to the road, a banner strung between two of them declaring that the Sweetwater Collective was digging up the past to make a better future. A line of windmill generators, huge blades turning slowly and steadily in the hot wind. Further off, beyond the conical mounds of spoil heaps, a steam shovel was working at one corner of a huge pit, the tinny clank of its chain echoing small and clear in the profound stillness of the desert.

Pilgrim realised, with a little kick of excitement, that this was one of the places where the visitors had been seen. The site where traces of big square buildings and imprints left by winged machines had been discovered beneath fossil sand dunes. He would have liked to make a detour and inspect the place and talk to the people who were working there, but there was no time, they had to get on. The road entered a range of low hills, dipping into a winding canyon, and the canyon opened up and Pilgrim and the two women reined in their maras. Foeless's gathering was directly below. Bare paddocks walled with loose stones where maras were tethered, a row of large bell tents fashioned from animal skins or orange canvas on a ridge overlooking a crowd of cut-and-cover burrows and slant tents under a haze of smoke from campfires, and the outline of the flowersipper cut in the flat white salt pan beyond.

'It's much bigger than I thought it would be,' Poppy said.

'The camp or the pictogram?' Pilgrim said.

'Both.'

The flowersipper was sketched by trenches cut into the white salt to expose the dark mudstone that lay beneath. It was at least five stades from wing tip to wing tip. Tiny figures were working at its tail, deepening trenches which outlined three stylised feathers. Other figures were busy around the deflated envelope of a hot-air balloon that lay like a drop of blood at the end of the flowersipper's long narrow beak.

Fragrant said that despite its size, the flowersipper would not be visible from Firestar or even from what she called low orbit – the path that visitor craft, if there were any visitor craft, might trace around the Mother beyond the edge of Her atmosphere.

'It's meant for Foeless's followers, not the visitors,' she said. 'An advertisement for the credulous.'

'There must be a thousand people down there,' Poppy said. She was studying the camp through a short spyglass, slowly sweeping it back and forth. 'No sign of Gentle, though.'

'Perhaps he didn't come here after all,' Pilgrim said.

'He could be in one of those tents, telling all he knows,' Fragrant said. 'Warning Foeless Landwalker's people about us.'

'Three people are bound to stakes, near the balloon,' Poppy said. 'A woman and two men, pretty near to naked.'

'Staked out in the sun for punishment would be my guess,' Fragrant said. 'If we are caught when we go down there . . .'

'It has to be done,' Pilgrim said, 'so we'll have to do our best not to get caught.'

They agreed that their vantage point was too exposed, that it would be best to get closer and hide amongst the crowd of followers. Search for Intrepid Windrush, so that Pilgrim could make his case for a meeting with Foeless Landwalker. Find out where the prophet was holed up, who was guarding him and who was allowed to see him. Fragrant unpacked her plate camera and set it up on its tripod and took an exposure of the tents and the flowersipper and packed it away again, and they rode down towards the camp, following a track through stony slopes and tumbled boulders.

Heat baked off the ground. Crude versions of the flower-sipper had been daubed on boulders flanking the track and on the red rock of a bluff the message *Welcome Visitors!* was painted in large white glyphs. As Pilgrim and the two women passed beneath it, there was a stir of movement ahead and figures scrambled out of a clump of arthritic trees, blocking the way and levelling crossbows and blunderbusses.

They wore long orange shirts and had grim determined looks. One stepped forward and called out Pilgrim's name and said that he had been asked to make him and the women of the Invisible College welcome, and Pilgrim knew then that Gentle had beaten them to Foeless Landwalker.

29.

Pilgrim was separated from Poppy and Fragrant and taken to one of the bell tents pitched above the gathering. A guard was posted outside the flap, but the tent was surprisingly comfortable inside – overlapping rugs and nests of cushions on the floor and wicker paddles moving lazily overhead, stirring warm air scented with a pleasant musk. The young person in an orange shirt who delivered a wash bowl and tea and slices of fresh fruit and honeyed cakes either wouldn't or couldn't answer any of Pilgrim's questions. They set everything on a low table and bowed and left.

Hours passed. Feeling strangely calm now that the worst had happened, Pilgrim dozed in a nest of soft cushions, was startled awake when someone pushed through the tent flap. The paddles had stilled and the tent was full of shadows that vanished when the visitor switched on an electric candle and hung it from one of the tent poles. The intruder was Intrepid Windrush, dressed in an orange shirt that hung to his bare calves, a goatskin bag slung over one shoulder and a small leather box with a black glass eye hung from his neck and resting on his chest – a miniature version of Fragrant's plate camera, Pilgrim realised, as Intrepid aimed it at him.

There was a click, a flash of stark white light.

'For the record,' Intrepid said.

'That must be one of the Sweetwater Collective's inventions,' Pilgrim said, trying to blink away a green afterimage.

'A prototype. Not yet put on sale, but given as a generous gift.'

'I heard that the Collective might be supporting your master.'

'They are interested in him,' Intrepid said and folded himself onto a cushion. 'To get the obvious question out of the way: why have you come here?'

'Am I a prisoner?' Pilgrim said.

'If you want to walk out of here no one will try to stop you.'

'Yet there is a guard outside.'

'To keep you safe, not to keep you from leaving.'

'Safe from whom? Foeless Landwalker? His followers?'

'You know, I believe, a person called Gentle. Tall, pale.'

'Where is he? Can I see him?'

'He was captured by Foeless's Night Rider bodyguards when he tried to force his way into Foeless's presence, and put to the question. When I heard that he had mentioned your name, I arranged a welcoming party to save you from a similar fate, and here we are.'

Pilgrim was reminded of the migrant players who had once visited the Saltmire territory when he was a stripling fresh from the Hearth. They had put on a morality play at Blessed's lodge, an ogre and a bear and a person meeting in a forest, each taking turns to persuade a sprite to give up the secret locked in the heartwood of the forest's oldest tree. Afterwards, the players had shared a meal with the lodge's hands, and although they had not removed the makeup that exaggerated their eyes and mouths, or the blond and auburn tints that coloured the pelts of the two who had played bear and ogre, they had shed their roles and were clearly themselves. It was the same with Intrepid. He had not changed outwardly, but there was no trace of the brash, hectoring pamphleteer in his manner. He was like a courteous host, assured and urbane with a hint of flirtatious whimsy, as if playing a private game.

'And my friends?' Pilgrim said.

'Like you, the women are free to stay or go as they please. Did you find them, or did they find you?'

'We were thrown together by circumstance.'

Intrepid liked that answer. 'And do you share a common purpose?'

'You'll have to ask them why they are here,' Pilgrim said, suspecting that Intrepid had already interviewed Poppy and Fragrant. 'As for me, I have come to meet your master. Perhaps you could take me to him.'

'I don't recommend it. Foeless has grown mistrustful and erratic lately, and believes that Gentle is some kind of spy or saboteur. And since Gentle named you in his confession, you'd be hard put to convince Foeless that you aren't part of a plot against him. As would I.'

'I thought you were his trusted mouthpiece,' Pilgrim said, but Intrepid ignored that.

'I understand that you have lost your master's papers,' he said. 'As well as an unusual map that you found in an abandoned library. They were confiscated by the constable of the little town in the far south where you were exiled for injuring a person. For striking him around the head with a bag of rocks and blinding him. I'm surprised. You have always seemed like such an ordinary person.'

Pilgrim didn't see the point of replying, and felt a fresh plunge of disappointment. It was possible that Intrepid had learned about the map from the women, but the details about his violation of the Mother's grace could only have come from Gentle. His friend had sold him out. Given up everything he knew.

191

'We have a copy of Master Able's manuscript,' Intrepid said. 'But the map is something new. An interesting little mystery. Am I right in thinking that it appears to show contact with bears, before their fall? Do you think it genuine?'

'I believe that it is a genuine copy of something older.'

Intrepid smiled. 'That's a tricky answer. Having lost it, do you think you can get it back?'

'I intend to.'

'If you can, and if you bring it to me, I promise a suitable reward. Something you have been hoping to find out, perhaps.'

'Free Gentle first.'

'Foeless wants to make an example of him. I can't help him, but I can help you.'

'Then let me talk to Foeless. I'll tell him that the map is proof that the visitors are real, and have been coming here for a long time. That it doesn't challenge his claims to be their messenger but reinforces them. I'll even offer to help you write a pamphlet about it.'

'I'm afraid that I am no longer in the pamphlet business.'

There was that playful amusement again. The implication that Intrepid knew far more than he was revealing. Very different from the times they had met before, when Intrepid had made so much of very little, and it had been difficult to stop him explaining why he was right and everyone else was wrong. This time he was dropping hints, waiting to see if Pilgrim caught them.

Pilgrim said, 'It sounds as if you no longer believe in Foeless. If you ever did.'

'When you plant a crop, you must first prepare the ground,' Intrepid said. 'That was Foeless's role. He has persuaded his followers that the visitors are real, and spread the idea far beyond this gathering, but now he has outlived his usefulness. The rituals he devised to demonstrate his powers have

192

become a trap, and lately the little lights he claims to be messengers from the visitors have failed to appear. He blames it on everything and everyone but himself, and grows ever more desperate and capricious. I'm afraid that it will end badly, and soon. And then it will be time to move on to the next stage.'

'Further revelations.'

'If you like.'

'But you aren't going to tell me what they are.'

'You'll see, soon enough. As will everyone else.'

'It sounds as if you know more about the visitors than Foeless does. Or that you think you do.'

'If you had come with me when I asked, you could have helped to prepare the ground too, by telling the scholarly community the truth about this gathering. But you were too proud, too stubborn, and now you are too late. Master Mindwell will do that work instead – his assistant is already on his way back to Highwater Reach.'

'I heard that he defected.'

'Let's say that he has received a kind of revelation. As will you, if you bring that map to me, and if it is genuine.'

'Who are you?'

'I'm in the information business. Like you. So: the map. What will you need to get it back?'

Pilgrim decided that he had nothing to lose by taking the question seriously. 'Money, mostly. Train fares, passage on the ship that links Stonehaven with civilisation, miscellaneous expenses.'

'Including, I suppose, a bribe for this rural constable who outsmarted you.'

'Or whatever it costs to buy back the map from whoever he sold it to.'

'Why not? I'll even provide you with an escort. Someone

who can persuade the constable to give up what is rightfully yours, if he refuses to be reasonable.'

'And you'll let my friends go, too?'

'I already have. But they won't leave without you and insist on watching tonight's sermon.'

'I'd like to watch it too. It's partly why we came here, after all.'

'You're as stubborn as the women,' Intrepid said, and fetched an orange padded jacket from a rack and tossed it to Pilgrim and told him to put it on. 'If anyone asks, you're a visitor from Concord, come to study the gathering.'

'Which is more or less what I am,' Pilgrim said.

'The truth's easier to tell than a lie,' Intrepid said. 'You should be safe as long as you stick close to me – I've been tasked with looking after visitors and special guests. And when the night's entertainment is done, we'll discuss how to get you on the road to Stonehaven.'

30.

A crowd had gathered along the edge of the salt pan, and the balloon Pilgrim had seen earlier was fully inflated now. The teardrop of its envelope, lit by burners flaring under the taper of its skirt, glowed bright red in the dusk. Small fires torn ragged by the hot wind outlined the shape of the flowersipper symbol, and the salt pan stretched away under the darkening sky, palely glimmering as if releasing some of the light it had absorbed during the day.

Orange fishtail flags raised on tall poles fluttered above the heads of the crowd in the hot wind. Most people wore something orange – a shirt, a scarf, a headband. Some were dancing in a ragged circle around a group of musicians playing fife and drums; the rest were quietly watching the balloon and the salt pan and the black sky. Waiting for Foeless Landwalker to appear. Pilgrim saw with a small shock the ghost-white figure of a visitor looming in the firelit dusk, then realised that it was a costume, the globe of its head some kind of lath-and-paper construction, its featureless black face no more than paint.

Intrepid took Pilgrim's arm and led him slantwise through the press towards a roughly carpentered wooden platform. 'We built it for distinguished guests,' Intrepid said. 'Councillors, business people, scholars and the like. Hardly any outsiders come here anymore – you and your friends are the only guests for tonight's show.'

After Pilgrim had clambered up the steep steps to the platform, leaning hard on his thornbush stick, he saw with a glad rush Poppy and Fragrant on the far side, beyond a group of orange-shirts. A square orange cap was perched on top of Poppy's head; Fragrant wore an orange scarf, and her camera was set on its tripod at the edge of the platform, aimed towards the balloon. The two women assured him that they had been treated well, said that Intrepid had asked them about the Invisible College's interest in Foeless Landwalker's prophesies and the gathering, and had answered a good number of their questions.

'He asked us about you,' Poppy said. 'But we told him you could speak for yourself and he didn't press the point.'

'He wants us to spread the news about the gathering,' Fragrant said.

'And wants me to find the map and bring it to him,' Pilgrim said, and explained the terms of Intrepid's offer.

'If you return to Stonehaven, the constable will arrest you again,' Poppy said.

'Not if I pay him not to. And if I don't go, Intrepid will most likely send someone else.'

'Have you forgotten your promise to us?' Fragrant said.

'Of course not,' Pilgrim said. 'That's why I would like both of you to return to Stonehaven with me. You can examine the map and photograph it before we give it to Intrepid. And we could publish the photographs with an account of how it was found, and discussion of its significance.'

'What about your friend?' Poppy said. She was looking towards the far side of the platform, where Intrepid was talking with two orange-shirts, making shapes in the air with his hands as he explained something.

'He asked me to retrieve the map, and bring it to him,' Pilgrim said. 'He did not ask me to refrain from publishing anything about it. In fact, I think that he would be rather pleased if I did.'

'Because it would bolster Landwalker's claims that the visitors are real,' Fragrant said.

'I don't think that Intrepid is working for him,' Pilgrim said.

'Who, then?'

'Your camera is one of the Sweetwater Collective's designs, isn't it?'

'One of the latest,' Fragrant said.

'Do you see that box hung around Intrepid's neck? It's a miniature version of your camera. A prototype not yet for sale. A generous gift from the Sweetwater Collective, according to him. He also claimed to have a copy of Master Able's manuscript, which must be the one which the Collective purchased from Able's family.'

Fragrant understood at once. 'So Windrush is working for them. Relaying inside information.'

'He told me that his work here was almost done. That Foeless Landwalker had outlived his usefulness. Perhaps the Collective has its own plans to call down the visitors.'

'But why would they want the map?' Poppy said.

'I'm not sure. Intrepid said that it was an interesting little mystery. If the Collective is planning to meet the visitors, I suppose its people would want to learn everything they can.'

A man close to the platform blew a long blast on the carnyx that looped around his shoulders and flared into a broad bell above his head, and a ragged chorus of cheers got up as a strikingly tall person in an orange shirt made his way through the crowd. It was Foeless Landwalker, trailed by a small procession of burly, orange-shirted acolytes, presumably his Night Rider guards. Men and women fell to their knees or reached out to touch him as he passed by; the musicians kicked up a quick-time beat.

One of the orange-shirts on the platform stepped between Pilgrim and the two women and told them that they'd soon see why so many were gathered here. 'This is one of the nights our friends will come,' he said. 'I can feel it in my blood.'

'We very much hope that they will,' Fragrant said.

The orange-shirt turned to her and said she would need a lot of luck to capture their image. 'Better people than you have tried and failed. They are small and quick and they dance across the entire sky.'

'The sky is my business,' Fragrant said.

'What are they? And how do they dance?' Pilgrim said.

'You have to see it. And when you do, you'll know that it's all true. All of it,' the orange-shirt said, and for a moment something like a pup's innocent wonder shone from his face.

Foeless Landwalker had paused at the edge of the crowd while two of his acolytes draped an orange cape with a high collar around him. His orange shirt was slashed open over his broad chest, his skull was clean-shaven and a patch covered his left eye and most of the ropey scar that bisected it. He turned to the crowd and shook back the wings of the cloak and raised his hands, and as the crowd cheered and the carnyx madly brayed he started across the salt pan, towards the balloon.

Behind him, there was a scuffle at the edge of the crowd and four orange-shirts emerged, carrying a person wearing only a breechclout. It was Gentle, arms bound at his back, legs wrapped in chains.

'Before Foeless gives his sermon, he'll deal with those who've displeased him,' Intrepid said, suddenly standing so close his breath touched Pilgrim's ear. 'I'm afraid your friend Gentle is for the stake.'

'How long will he be left out there?' Pilgrim said.

'The longest sentence so far has been eight days. The prisoners aren't fed, but they're given water regularly, and turned loose in the desert afterwards.'

'Gentle has no pigment in his skin. Eight days in the desert sun without protection will most likely kill him,' Pilgrim said.

'The man betrayed you. Why are you concerned about him?'

'I'm responsible for him being here. If he dies, I'll be responsible for that, too. Can't you persuade Foeless Landwalker to let him go?'

'I told you: I no longer have that kind of influence.'

'We have to find a way of saving him. And then, I swear, I'll do everything I can to bring you the map and Master Able's papers.'

Across the salt pan, Foeless had reached a group of acolytes clustered in front of the balloon. The music stopped and the noise of the crowd ebbed into expectant silence as the orange-shirts carrying Gentle laid him face-down at Foeless's feet.

'You are infuriatingly stubborn,' Intrepid said to Pilgrim.

'So I've been told. Will you do it or not?'

'I have friends who might be able to help. It won't be tonight, though. Tomorrow night at the earliest.'

'And you'll bring Gentle to me.'

'You hope for a touching reunion, I suppose.'

'I don't plan to forgive him. I just want to know that he's been freed.'

'Hold out your hand and make a fist,' Intrepid said, and bumped his knuckles against Pilgrim's. 'That's what we do to seal an agreement where I come from.'

'Where do you come from?' Pilgrim said, but Intrepid had turned to watch the spectacle out on the salt pan and didn't answer.

Foeless Landwalker was inspecting the prisoners, turning briefly to one of the orange-shirts and making an open-handed gesture. A man and a woman were freed, both falling to their knees and pressing their hands over their bowed heads in postures of abject fealty. The crowd cheered and Foeless Landwalker raised a hand in acknowledgement.

'He doesn't look it, but he's three-quarters drunk,' Intrepid told Pilgrim. 'Lately, it's the only way he's been able to get through this.'

Gentle was being lashed to one of the stakes, and Foeless was stepping into the balloon's basket. Fragrant was bent over her camera, head and shoulders shrouded by black cloth. The crowd below the platform were hooting and stamping, the carnyx brayed long and hard, and as the balloon's burners flared at the base of its red teardrop and it began to rise the musicians struck up an incongruous dance tune.

The balloon rose until the cables that tethered it snapped taut. Foeless was standing in the basket hung beneath it, high above the salt pan, his orange shirt and cape glowing in the crossing beams of two searchlights. The crowd quietened when he raised his arms above his head, and he leaned towards the cone of a device that, after a brief mechanical clatter, amplified his voice.

He told his followers that they had come here for a great purpose. That these nightly gatherings were being watched and judged, and they must behave accordingly. Each night our gathering grows, he said. We focus our minds and pray for the visitors to come down, and each night they judge the virtue and power of our call. When they are satisfied, they will at last show themselves, as they showed themselves to me. Meanwhile, we must strive to be our best selves. We must pray for the Calling Down, and we must continue to send out emissaries to gather more people to amplify our message.

200

'There are new followers amongst us, as there are every night. For their benefit I shall explain how I was blessed by an encounter with the visitors. How they imparted the wisdom by which we organise ourselves here, and made the promise that they will fulfil when they decide that we are ready to receive it. I know that some of you have heard the story so many times before that you can tell it better than I,' Foeless Landwalker said, and paused while laughter and hooting briefly rolled through the crowd before going on, explaining that he had been hunting for stray bears in the forests of the far north when one night he had been visited by a tall figure dressed all in white, with a white helmet with a visor of black glass fitted over its head.

It had told him that its name was Afir and it was an emissary of the people of Morningstar, who believed that the people of the Mother were at a crossroads. One road was dark and led to the fate of the bears; the other was the road which the people of Morningstar had taken long ago, leading to a peaceful union with the guiding spirit of their world. That was the road they wanted to help the children of the Mother find, and they had chosen Foeless to be their emissary. He told the crowd that he had been humbled and awed by the invitation, and when he accepted a great light shone around him and the emissary, Afir, and he suddenly found himself amongst others of Afir's kind, aboard a kind of ship that shot up into the sky and crossed the gulf to Morningstar.

It was almost a word-for-word retelling of the story set out in Intrepid's first pamphlet. Pilgrim remembered that Master Able had read the parts that he found silliest before giving up on it and skimming it across his room, saying that it was entirely fiction, and not even the good kind.

Foeless described the rainy forest where the visitors' ship landed, and the glass room where he met with their spiritual

201

leaders and was told about the new age that would come if the children of the Mother could be persuaded to follow the right path. The oppressed would be relieved. The elite would be overthrown. Homes would be found for migrants and outcasts. The New Territories and Akeban would be raised up and the leaders of the Union brought low. Laws that benefited the few rather than the many would be replaced by natural law, and there would be a return to the values of land and blood, and true harmony with the Mother.

'You are the many. The visitors see you and your voices will be heard and your oppressors will be overthrown,' Foeless said, and began a complaint against his own oppressors. How he had been arrested; how he used his gift of oratory to set himself free. Stories about agents sent against him, always thwarted by his insight and cunning, either turned away or converted to the cause. Stories which portrayed him as both victim and victor. Stories about how his simple dream of justice for all rather than for the few was constantly undercut by jealous scholars who knew nothing about the real world and ordinary good-hearted people. Stories of how the elite had tried to end gatherings which had sprung up in the Union, and how they had spread lies about him.

It was a long and rambling speech, laced with self-pity and self-aggrandisement. His audience began to grow restless. Whispering to each other, yawning. Some at the back of the crowd had sat down, and a few appeared to have fallen asleep.

Foeless Landwalker had spun out too many threads to be able to knit them into a concluding message, so at last he simply stopped speaking. For a few moments there was no sound but the murmur of the crowd, the low hum from his speech amplifier.

'You must believe!' he said abruptly, and the orange-shirts around Pilgrim repeated the phrase.

'If you believe, they will come,' Foeless said. 'If you open your hearts and minds, they will come.'

A few people started up a chant of 'They will come!' but it died away when Foeless spread out his arms and told his followers to be still and to look inwards. To concentrate on the phrase they had been given to help them clear their minds and focus on the visitors.

'Many nights you have summoned them,' Foeless told the crowd. 'I hope that you will summon them again tonight. And perhaps – who knows – this is the night when they will at last come down from the sky and show themselves.'

'This is why he has to get his courage from a bottle every night,' Intrepid told Pilgrim. 'The little lights aren't ever coming back.'

'How can you be so sure?'

'I told you: he's outlived his usefulness.'

A bell clanged somewhere. Once, twice, three times. The crowd fell silent as the echo rang back from the cliffs and fled across the salt pan. Pilgrim looked towards the sky above the balloon and the glare of the searchlight beams and the little fires that outlined the enormous graving of the flowersipper. He was holding his breath. His heart was beating beneath his throat. Stars crowded the black sky above the salt pan's spectral glow. Nothing moved amongst their rigid patterns. The crowd stood silent and still, some with heads bowed, some with faces tilted skyward in rapturous anticipation. It was a moment both solemn and silly. When Pilgrim shared a look with Poppy he had to swallow the urge to laugh, and yet he wanted to believe. Despite Intrepid's forewarning, he wanted to see the lights of the visitors dance across the night. He had come so far and given so much for this moment and he ached for it.

Nothing happened, and nothing continued to happen. The crowd began to grow restless again. Someone shouted, 'Show us!' and someone else called for quiet. A man behind Pilgrim whispered, 'He's giving it up.'

The balloon was descending. There was a scattering of hooting and foot-stamping as its basket touched the ground. Several orange-shirts rushed towards it and helped Foeless climb out. After what appeared to be a brief consultation the amplification machine made its mechanic clatter and Foeless Landwalker's voice boomed out.

'You tried. We tried. Some nights they answer our message and some nights they don't. This is one of those nights when they didn't.'

He had lost the charge and energy he had possessed at the beginning of the ceremony. It was as if he had been defeated, but could not understand how it had happened or what it meant.

'You did your best,' he said, and then seemed to gather up a little of his vigour. 'We did our best. We should acknowledge that.'

The orange-shirts on the platform hooted and stamped, but only a few people in the crowd took it up.

'We really did,' Foeless Landwalker said. It sounded as if he was talking to himself now, not his audience. 'But do you know why the visitors did not show themselves tonight?'

A pause. If he was waiting for a response, it did not come.

'Do you know why? Maybe you don't. But I can tell you,' Foeless said, and with gathering energy talked about sabotage, and the conspiracies of the elite and their hatred for what was happening here. 'We are doing a great thing. A tremendous thing. World changing. And they hate that. Hate to see that ordinary people have power. They have done everything they can to silence and sabotage me. They arrested me in Ogres Grave. You remember how that went. They have arrested some of the people I sent out to spread the word, too. They have arrested people at gatherings like this one, in the Union and elsewhere. They have tried to use secret rays to silence us. Mind rays. Dampeners. I haven't told you about that before, because we stopped it and we didn't want to frighten you.'

From the glances the orange-shirts were exchanging, Pilgrim reckoned that this was the first they had heard of it too.

Foeless's voice pitched higher as his outrage grew. He named enemies. He spoke about attempts to shoot down the visitors' sky boats.

'Not that anyone could, but they tried,' he said. 'And they sent people to spy on me, and to plant wrong ideas in people's heads. One of them came to me today. Told me that the visitors had been here before. Long ago, when bears still lived in cities. Before they went mad.'

A cold thrill passed through Pilgrim, from the soles of his feet to the nape of his neck. The hairs of his pelt prickled as they raised up.

'He asked me if I knew about that visit, and of course I did not,' Foeless said. 'Because it isn't true. How do I know? Because I am the only one who has been granted an audience with the visitors, and they did not tell me this thing about the bears. And because they do not lie, it never happened. It is a made-up story. Another foolish attempt by the elite to undermine me. An attempt to distract me. To sabotage the Calling Down by interfering with the purity of my thoughts. But we will make it better. I promise. We will rest and we will gather and we will call them down.'

Scattered hoots from the crowd. People stamping their feet to show approval, the noise quickly dying away.

'We'll begin by dealing with the cause of tonight's trouble,' Foeless said. 'Staking him out under the cleansing gaze of the sun is not enough. He must be silenced.'

Another clatter from the voice amplifier. Foeless stepped towards the orange-shirts and took something from one of them and turned and strode towards the two prisoners tied to their posts. The crowd's noise was swelling, like streams of water flowing together into a flood. Pilgrim felt an awful void opening inside his chest.

Foeless posed beside Gentle for a moment, holding something above his head. A percussion pistol. Gentle lunged and wrenched, trying to loosen the chains that bound him to the post, shaking his head violently as Foeless stepped back. Took aim. Pilgrim screamed NO, but like the sound of the pistol shot it was lost in the roar of the crowd.

31.

'I caught an image,' Fragrant said. She had a strange fierce look. Fear and shock and a kind of gleeful excitement. 'I can't be sure until I've developed the plate, but I think I have it. The very moment. Clear enough to condemn Landwalker when he is brought to justice.'

'If he is ever brought to justice, which seems unlikely,' Poppy said. 'Most of the witnesses are his loyal followers.'

'Many of them weren't happy about what they saw,' Fragrant said.

They were crouched amongst rocks on the slope above the salt pan, catching their breath after escaping in the confusion after Foeless Landwalker had shot Gentle. Murdered him. Foeless's followers were returning to their camp. The searchlights were still lit, crossing above the deflating envelope of the balloon, and small figures were moving beyond it, snuffing the little fires that illuminated the outline of the flowersipper.

'Intrepid knew,' Pilgrim said.

'That he would kill Gentle?' Fragrant said.

'That the visitors would not appear. He told me that Foeless's time was up. That he had outlived his usefulness.'

The two women thought about that for a few moments.

Poppy said, 'Do you mean that Intrepid might be in contact with the visitors?'

'Or perhaps the lights have nothing to do with the visitors. Perhaps they are some kind of trickery,' Pilgrim said.

'Who could do such a thing?' Fragrant said.

'My guess would be the Sweetwater Collective. It would be a way to keep Foeless's followers happy. Keep them together, in case they really could call down the visitors.' Pilgrim looked all around, at the lights of the tents at the top of the slope, the lights and campfires amongst the tents and scrape burrows at the bottom. He said, 'We have to find Intrepid.'

'I was watching him while everyone else was watching Foeless,' Poppy said. 'He left when the balloon started to come down.'

'If he works for the Sweetwater Collective, he most likely has gone back to Ogres Grave,' Fragrant said. 'We need to ask them some hard questions.'

'There's a place closer than that,' Pilgrim said.

They climbed the slope to the sandy paddocks where maras were tethered. They didn't know where saddles and harnesses were kept, but Pilgrim found a coil of rope and began to tie halters, a skill Blessed had taught him long ago. His hands were shaking. The moment when Gentle had been shot was still at the front and centre of his mind. Foeless Landwalker's theatrical pose. His outstretched arm jerking up from the pistol's recoil and Gentle sagging in his bonds, a scarlet bib streaking the snowy pelt of his chest.

He had to fashion a sling strap for Fragrant's camera and tripod, too. After it was secured, Fragrant and Poppy helped him climb onto the back of one of the maras and he jammed his stick through the sash of his trews and followed the two women as they rode up the track.

It was a moonless night, but the starry sky was bright enough to cast blue shadows. They skirted the bluff where they had been intercepted, passed the place where they had stopped to survey the camp and the flowersipper, rode up the canyon into the desert beyond. When they passed a small camp of followers who had either quit the gathering or were heading towards it, Poppy asked if anyone had seen a man in an orange shirt go past, possibly riding alone, but either no one had or no one was willing to say.

'He could have gone in the other direction,' she said as they rode on.

'We have to get back to Ogres Grave,' Fragrant said. 'So this is the right way as far as I am concerned.'

At last Pilgrim saw a few small lights shimmering off in the distance, and soon afterwards they reached the excavation site. The mounds of the burrows were starkly lit by electric pole lamps. No one came out to meet the riders; no one answered when Pilgrim limped up to the door of one of the burrows and rapped on it with the gnarled head of his stick.

'Are you certain he came here?' Fragrant said.

'Let's take a look at the diggings,' Pilgrim said. 'Someone was working there when we went by earlier.'

They found and followed a stony track cut through desert scrub and scattered boulders. Riding under the immense dome of cold indifferent stars, Pilgrim wondered if anyone or anything might be hovering up there, watching their trivial and most likely hopeless quest with unsympathetic amusement.

The trenches of the diggings, when they reached them, were as deserted as the burrows. Stretching away into the night, terraced sides stepped down to fathomless pools of inky shadow.

'Now what?' Fragrant said.

Pilgrim pointed to the far end of the trenches, where the steam shovel's angular silhouette was etched against a finger-nail crescent of faint light.

'Let's find out what's there,' he said.

'The place is abandoned,' Fragrant said.

'If it is, no one will bother us when we make camp.'

'We lack both water and food.'

'We can tap the digger's boiler for water. If Intrepid isn't here, he might still show up.'

The feet of their maras padded softly on sand, crunched across a run of gravel, the small noises seeming overloud in the immense stillness of the night. The steam shovel was tilted on a ridge of dirt, its arm bent in a sharp vee, its scoop resting on the ground like a curled fist. Beyond it, the thin glimmer of light outlined a sharp edge where the ground dropped away. The three riders paused, looking at a dark flatland stretching towards the sawtoothed shadows of mountains. A little way off, four small bright lights shone like fallen stars, defining a square; much closer, a fire flickered in front of the hump of a small burrow, and the three men sitting around the fire stood up as Pilgrim, Poppy and Fragrant rode down the slope towards them. One was Intrepid Windrush, still wearing his orange shirt, showing neither surprise nor anger as he stepped forward to greet them as they dismounted.

'I wasn't sure if I did the right thing, dropping all those hints,' he said. 'And I wasn't sure that you would follow up on them, either. But I am glad you did.'

'We should take you with us to Ogres Grave,' Fragrant said. 'To face justice.'

'For what crime?'

'Complicity in murder, to begin with.'

The other two men had come up behind Intrepid. Pilgrim belatedly recognised the scout, Dash Crow, dressed in a jacket that seemed to have been stitched from inflated tubes, telling Intrepid, 'Your friend is more tenacious than I thought, but he's either far too late or far too early.'

'Tonight's debacle changes everything,' Intrepid said.

'Nothing's been decided yet,' Dash Crow said. 'And there's still just about enough time to send them on their way.'

'Whether they stay or go should be their decision.'

'And your responsibility, if that's how you want to play it.'

'I do,' Intrepid said, and turned back to Pilgrim and Poppy and Fragrant. 'I sincerely regret the death of your friend. It should not have happened. Things got out of hand.'

'You supported it,' Poppy said.

'More than that: you encouraged it,' Fragrant said.

'Up to a point, and not any more,' Intrepid said. 'And it was part of a much larger scheme that has already helped and benefited your people in a hundred different ways.'

'Were you ever one of Foeless Landwalker's acolytes?' Pilgrim said. 'And your friend there, was he ever a scout?'

'All of us are scouts. Just not in the way you might think,' Dash Crow said.

'And this scheme,' Pilgrim said. 'It involves the Sweetwater Collective, doesn't it?'

Intrepid smiled. 'Well done.'

'You made it very obvious. Have you always worked for them, or did you turn against Foeless Landwalker only recently?'

'Let's say, for now, that they are part of the scheme too.'

'Too much information,' Dash Crow said.

'He's already guessed a good part of it,' Intrepid said.

'Better wind this up,' the third man said. 'Your ride will be here at any moment.'

'I'm keeping track of the time,' Intrepid said coolly, and told Pilgrim, Fragrant and Poppy that they could choose to come with him or be escorted back to the road by his companions and sent on their way.

'Where will you take us if we agree to come with you?' Poppy said.

'To Ogres Grave, I suppose,' Fragrant said.

'Oh, a little further than that,' Intrepid said.

Pilgrim, prickling at his sly silkiness, said, 'What do you want from us? How can we be of help?'

'If everything works out, you and your friends would be useful emissaries.'

'And if it doesn't work out you will not see your homes or the people you love ever again,' Dash Crow said.

Pilgrim ignored him and stepped closer to Intrepid, planting his stick and leaning on it and looking straight at him, saying, 'If you want our help, you can start treating us like equals, and give us answers instead of riddles.'

Intrepid looked at Dash Crow, who shook his head.

'I want to tell you everything,' Intrepid said. 'Really I do. But this isn't the time or place.'

'But you'll tell the truth if we choose to come with you,' Pilgrim said.

'As much of it as I can.'

'All of it.'

'As much as I can. A great deal isn't mine to tell.'

'So you are some kind of servant. No better than us.'

'Did I ever claim to be anything else?'

'If we choose to come with you, it won't be as your pris-oners, or some kind of prize. It will be because we are choosing to take the last step in a long and difficult search for the truth.'

'They're going to have to make that choice now,' the third man said. 'The ride's about here.'

'Are you ready to take that step?' Intrepid said.

'I can't speak for my friends, but I've been ready a long time,' Pilgrim said.

'I'm not going to let you go on your own,' Poppy said.

'I suppose I must come too,' Fragrant said.

'You won't regret it,' Intrepid told them.

Dash Crow pointed at the black sky above the black and distant mountains. 'Let's hope none of us do. It's here.'

A star was falling through the night, growing brighter as it slanted towards them, growing into a white glare that was hard to look at. A hot wind got up, flattening the flames of the fire at the mouth of the burrow and blowing dust and sand over the watchers, and the glare resolved into three intensely bright flames clustered beneath a dark, impossibly large shape that was lowering itself towards the square between the signal lamps.

32.

Mistress Ash's Emporium was a windowless burrow with secondhand household goods piled on one side and books, pamphlets, leaflets, handbills, scrolls, posters and boxes of loose papers heaped in no discernible order on the other. Its owner sat crosslegged in a nest of cushions behind a low table at the back, in the feeble light of rush lamps dangling from the barrel ceiling. A hunchbacked elderly person in her late forties or early fifties, wrapped in a dusty black gown, its owner showed no sign that she recognised Pilgrim, even though there was an old wallsheet pasted on a hoarding across the greenway from her shop, displaying the famous image of the meeting between the first delegation of the visitors and the Committee of the Five Hundred, with Pilgrim, Poppy and Fragrant in the front rank of the onlookers.

Pilgrim had soon learned that his small fame too often complicated the simplest transaction or encounter, or was a lightning rod for the grievances of those who believed that the visitors were a mortal threat to the Union and its people. Fortunately, his contribution to the First Contact Project had been overshadowed by the Invisible College's campaign to persuade the public and politicians to allow the visitors to establish an embassy and other offices. He was more concerned about the work he had left unfinished, which was why he had returned to the far south, following a trail which had led him to this musty archive of forgotten lives.

He shared a pot of mint tea with Mistress Ash while he told her the story of his quest. She said that she remembered the articles in question, although she didn't recall a manuscript or any other papers. Pilgrim, with a pluck of sorrow and disappointment, supposed the constable had thrown them away, believing them worthless, and asked the bookseller about the disposition of the other goods. She told him that she had sold the pendant to a travelling gentleperson, and that she didn't know where he was from or where he was going, only that he had bought it for his sweetheart. As for the map, although it was obviously a copy or an outright fake she had thought it was an interesting curio, and had included it in a consignment of books she had sold to a dealer in Circle Bay, the largest city in the southern territories of the Union.

'He might still have it, if you're lucky,' Mistress Ash said. 'Things that end up here and other places like it are orphans seeking a home. Some speak to people and some don't. I've been more than thirty years in the trade, and I still don't know which is which. If I did I'd buy less and sell more.'

Pilgrim wrote down the name and address of the dealer and thanked the old woman and walked through the cold muddy streets to the railway station. This was turning out to be a frustrating venture. He had travelled first to Stonehaven, where he discovered that Noble Seatree had drowned at sea at the beginning of the summer past, his crab boat foundering in a sudden storm just three moonspans after Pilgrim and Gentle had escaped. The constable's widow, who'd had little good to say about him and expected payment for it, had told Pilgrim that she had been forced to sell the confiscated items because the town still owed her husband's back pay and recompense for the meals she had cooked for the people he'd arrested.

'You broke the law and then you ran off,' she'd said, 'so don't expect restitution for what was rightly taken from you. I didn't get much for it anyway.'

'Then you were cheated,' Pilgrim had told her, more disappointed than angry. 'The pendant alone was worth a year of your husband's salary.'

Before he left Stonehaven, he had paid a visit to the Hearth's library. After only a year, its chambers had taken on the musty air of a mausoleum. Water stains had bloomed on the plaster of a wall under a broken window and there was a scatter of mouse droppings on papers he'd left behind, including the catalogue he had laboured over.

A fellow he'd hired at the chandler's helped him to carry the boxes of books he had selected for the archives of his tribe to the harbour and the coastal trader, and after reaching Fortunate Valley Pilgrim had arranged for the boxes to be sent north before tracking down Mistress Ash's Emporium. Now, he caught a train to Circle Bay, where he discovered that the dealer who had purchased Mistress Ash's consignment had sold it on to a scout from Concord, and that was where the trail went cold. The scout had sold the books to another dealer, and the map had gone to a barter house and had been snapped up by someone who had paid cash and left no name or address.

'If it's still in Concord, I'll find it,' Swift Singletree told Pilgrim.

'I'm not even sure if it is worth anything,' Pilgrim said. 'The visitors told me it had nothing to do with them, since they arrived long after the bears destroyed themselves.'

'If I had a hand in ending the bears' civilisation, even if by misunderstanding or mischance, I'd probably want to keep quiet about it,' Ardent Whitesand said.

'I think I'd want to boast about it,' Swift said. 'Especially as it freed their slaves, namely us.'

The three of them were eating mussels and periwinkles in a waterside shack at the eastern edge of Highwater Reach. The lights of Concord twinkled across the broad black flood of the river; the crescent of the Daughter Moon tilted high above. That was where Intrepid claimed to have been born, one of the second generation of people raised by the visitors and employed as scouts and agents. And Fragrant Plainsrunner was there now, so strange to think, part of a small delegation of star gazers and rock collectors from the Invisible College. She had told Pilgrim in a letter that she was having a fine old time exploring the Daughter Moon's battered plains and mountains, and was thinking of staying there.

'The Invisible College and I looked for other evidence that the visitors met with bears,' Pilgrim told Ardent, 'and found nothing.'

'You should keep looking,' Swift said. He was working a pin into a periwinkle shell, turning it to extract the toothsome morsel of meat. 'If it happened, the truth will be out there.'

'But if you find something that contradicts the visitors,' Ardent said to Pilgrim, 'what will you do with it? Given that you are one of their ambassadors.'

'I resigned, having done my duty. Such as it was. The visitors don't need my help anymore.'

'What are you planning to do now?' Ardent said.

'The visitors offered to fix my leg,' Pilgrim said. 'I might accept, now I have time to lie up and recover from the operation. They also offered a treatment that would allow me to respond to the Season like any ordinary person.'

'They can do that?' Ardent said.

'Apparently it isn't difficult,' Pilgrim said. 'They can take some of my cells, use them to grow a little gland that would produce the right hormones and transplant it inside me.'

217

'What did you say?' Swift said.

'I thanked them for the thought, and told them that I did not feel the need to be anything other than what I already am.'

'Quite right,' Swift said. 'Who wants to be ordinary?'

The three of them drank to that.

'They offered me a trip to the Daughter Moon, too,' Pilgrim said. 'I had to think long and hard about how to turn it down without giving offence, but if they invite me again I could pass it to one of you.'

'Do they have books up there?' Swift said.

'I don't think so. There is a kind of library, but it is stored in their Mother somehow.'

'A library is a library. I could see if I turn up anything like your map.'

'Apparently their Mother already looked, and found nothing.'

'And you believe that?' Swift said.

'It would make things easier if I did. If I was wrong to think that the map meant anything.'

'But suppose it does,' Ardent said. 'Suppose the visitors have been here longer than they claim. Suppose they met the bears, and were somehow involved in their fall . . .'

'That is what Foeless Landwalker now believes,' Pilgrim said. 'He also believes that the visitors are not the visitors who elected him to be their prophet. He says that his visitors want to help us, and those who made themselves known to us are their enemies. That there is an eternal struggle, and we have been caught up in it, and have chosen the wrong side.'

'Who is going to believe a crazy person who killed someone in front of hundreds of witnesses?' Swift said.

'Some of his followers are still loyal,' Pilgrim said. 'They have published his prison letters, and he claims to be writing a book that will reveal the truth about the visitors. There are plenty of people who will read it. People who hate the visitors because of what they are. Who they are descended from. People who hate and fear change. New techne, women scholars, everything that is different from the old ways. What if someone like that finds the map, and reckons that it supports Foeless's baseless claims?'

Swift aimed the winkle pin at him. 'So you still think it's important.'

'Someone bought it, not knowing what it was. Perhaps they thought it was a curio,' Pilgrim said, remembering Mistress Ash's words. 'An interesting decoration. Or perhaps they collect old maps, or artefacts related to bear culture. It's inside a display case, or hanging on a wall. Harmless, for now. But if the wrong person sees it, sees it for what it is or what it might be . . .'

'So you haven't given up the search,' Ardent said.

'Finding it would make writing my monograph much easier, too.'

'I can ask my friends in the trade to look out for it,' Swift said. 'And all it will cost you is another cup of periwinkles.'

Pilgrim returned to his tribe's territory to recuperate from the operation to lengthen the bone and strengthen the muscles of his leg, and he lived there the rest of his life. He handled the accounts for his sister's tea business and helped with experiments in breeding plants, excavated and sold fossils and used some of the profits to purchase the original papers concerning Master Able's work on sightings of the visitors, and to complete and publish the monograph Able had been working on when he died.

He never found out who bought the map and what happened to it afterwards. An expedition to the jungles of the Neck's east coast failed to locate the city depicted next to the mysterious figure, or any evidence that the visitors had ever been there, and his monograph about the map's discovery and possible significance was, like Able's work, largely ignored. He sent the obligatory two copies to the Library of All People, donated a copy to his tribe's archives and gave copies to his friends, and packed up and put away the rest of the small print run.

Even though no one else cared about the map he had found and lost, even though he had been unable to prove whether it was real or fake, he knew that it had been a turning point in his life, and the lives of everyone else. It had led him to Foeless Landwalker's gathering and the meeting with Intrepid Windrush, and the journey in the visitors' flying machine to the uncharted island far across the Great South Sea where they had established their base camp.

The flight had taken less than two hours. At one point Pilgrim and the other passengers had become as light and untethered as children's balloons, and Intrepid had opened a window in the air, showing the dark curved shield of the Mother hung beneath them. And then, after a brief crushing descent and a roar of the flying machine's motor, they were down, and Intrepid opened a hatch and led them outside.

The flying machine sat in overlapping circles of light, squatting over its shadow on a flat field of poured stone that stretched into darkness in every direction. If there was anything beyond the glare, Pilgrim, limping down a tongue of stiff metallic mesh, couldn't see it. Intrepid was leading Poppy and Fragrant away from the flying machine and Pilgrim followed, leaning on his stick, and saw shadowy figures coming towards them out of the darkness.

Intrepid and Poppy and Fragrant halted; so did he. One after the other, the figures stepped into the light. Several people in blue tunics and trews, and two impossibly tall creatures looming behind them, frighteningly strange yet also frighteningly familiar, for they closely resembled the wax reconstructions of their long-dead ancestors in the Hall of Stones and Bones in the Library of All People.

Long-limbed and slender, faces flat and naked, smiles showing square white teeth, the ogres strode out of the darkness and the deep past to greet their guests.

Part Two

The Other Mother

1.

The central office of the Bureau of Indigenous Affairs pinged Ysbel Moonsdaughter around midnight. It seemed that one of Survey and Surveillance's agents had been involved in a fatal accident in the Strait of the Hundred Islands, and because the station chief was attending a summit meeting in the Gathering Place and its senior investigator was embroiled in negotiations about the construction of a solar power farm, Ysbel was up.

The flitter she summoned flew her north, passing over the lights of native settlements scattered along the coast. The full Moon hung low in the night sky, laying a long road of silky light across the black ocean. It was Ysbel's first solo investigation, her first wrongful death, her first real test as a field officer. She was nervous and eager, telling herself that it would be no different from enquiries into fraud or breaches of protocol. Discovering the facts of the case while taking care to respect custom and law, doing her best to quench native anger and suspicion.

So far, she had little to go on. According to the report, a speedboat had collided with a fishing skiff. Two natives had been killed and the pilot of the speedboat, also a native, had fled the scene, but it wasn't clear if S&S's agent, Trina Mersdaughter, had been a passenger or a witness. With nothing better to do until she reached the scene, Ysbel racked her seat back and managed to catch a little sleep; when she woke, it was the grey hour before dawn and the flitter was flying low over the long reach of the strait, heading towards one of the small islands scattered across its shallow waters. Ysbel saw a flat-roofed house, motorboats and yachts anchored at a floating dock, rumpled forest stretching to the far side of the island. Everything tilting beneath her as the flitter turned in a tight curve and dropped to a lawn that sloped to the water.

Natives dressed in purple pyjamas who had been setting out tables and chairs on the terrace above the lawn watched as Ysbel cracked the canopy of the flitter and the local bailiff, Goodwill Saltmire, stumped up to her and introduced himself with formal politeness. Explaining that the island was leased from the community council by a businessperson, Solomon Firststar, and the accident had happened during one of his parties.

'It doesn't seem to have stopped the festivities,' Ysbel said. The servants fussing with furniture reminded her of Landing Day, when households and communes held cookouts on the beaches of the Gathering Place.

'When I arrived last night, Solomon Firststar's guests were still feasting,' Goodwill said. 'And members of the local Fish Cult were performing a stick dance for their amusement. The deaths of two people did not trouble them in the slightest. They were only local people, you see. Fisherfolk. Of no importance whatsoever.'

Ysbel sympathised with his anger, but hoped that it wouldn't cause trouble down the line. Even by native standards the bailiff was a short person, about eye-level with her belt buckle, but he was barrel-chested and broad-hipped and had the look of someone who would rather kick a wall down

226

than walk around it. The pelt that capped his head was oiled into short spikes; his eyes, set in a stripe of black fur under his heavy brow, brimmed with truculent suspicion.

'The first thing we must settle is the disposition of the bodies,' he said. 'Mercy and Clemency must be given into the care of their family before nightfall, so that they can be properly prepared for return to the Mother.'

It took Ysbel a moment to realise that Mercy and Clemency were the two fisherfolk who had died in the accident, if that's what it had been, and she assured Goodwill that she had no intention of interfering with custom and law.

'They were brothers,' Goodwill said. 'Mercy and Clemency Sandhill. Mercy was sixteen, with two young sons. Clemency was just twelve, a lively lad, well-liked in town and honest as daylight.'

'I hope we can do the right thing by them,' Ysbel said, realising that he wanted her to think of them as the people they'd been, not as inconvenient victims.

'I have to trust that you will,' Goodwill said, 'given that your people are protected by the treaty.'

Ysbel hoped that this was the ingrained cynicism of an experienced lawkeeper rather than mistrust and mislike of humans. Cynicism she could work with; prejudice, not so much.

'I came here to find out what happened, what part Trina Mersdaughter played in it, and report the facts of the case to our authorities,' she said. 'I understand the speedboat that hit the fisherfolks' skiff was piloted by a native. Was Trina a passenger?'

'She was piloting another boat, but shares responsibility for what happened,' Goodwill said. 'She and Joyous Hightower were in a race, and it was her idea.'

He had interviewed Solomon Firststar and his guests, and everyone had told him more or less the same story. Joyous

227

Hightower and Trina Mersdaughter had been competing against each other in the afternoon. Speedboat time trials out to buoys and back. Trina had beaten Joyous two times out of three, and he'd been less than pleased to have been outraced by a human person, especially as she was also a woman. Later, at supper, Trina had challenged him to a race around the island, and he had accepted at once.

'Drink had been taken,' Goodwill said. 'There was some kind of wager between the two participants, and I imagine that Joyous Hightower felt his honour was at stake. They set out shortly after sunset, and it was dark when they returned, with the bodies of Mercy and Clemency. There were no witnesses to the accident, and Joyous Hightower fled before I could talk to him, but I had servants retrieve the wreckage of the skiff. It was cut in two, suggesting that he struck it square amidships with considerable force.'

'What about Trina Mersdaughter? Where was she when the accident happened?'

'I don't yet know. She is still on the island, but has refused my request for an interview.'

'That's her right, although it is usually waived,' Ysbel said, her hope that this would be a straightforward case, a matter of taking a statement and promising to follow up on any developments, beginning to evaporate. 'But she can't refuse to talk to me. If you tell me what you need to ask, we can interview her straight away.'

'I think you should see the victims first,' Goodwill said.

2.

The bodies of the fisherfolk had been laid out on a pair of trestle tables in the boathouse, a human-scale concrete structure that might have been ripped from Mother's archives. They were covered by white sheets, and offerings of fruit, chewleaves and sweetroot cakes were heaped on a smaller table at their feet: sustenance for the spirits of the dead in the period of limbo before their excarnated bodies were given sky burials and returned to the great cycles of life. The wreckage of their skiff was stacked beyond, and a speedboat hung in a cradle above a channel of black water. Its knife-sharp prow was buckled and there were gouges along one side of its narrow hull, exposing pale plastic under bright-red paint.

Ysbel thought that the hushed, dimly lit boathouse was like a chapel; the damaged boat and wreckage, the bodies and offerings, like the trappings of some arcane ritual.

The young deputy who was guarding the bodies stood up as Ysbel and the bailiff approached, and reported that several servants had come to pay their respects.

'What about Solomon Firststar and his guests?' Goodwill said.

'Not yet,' the deputy said.

'Of course not,' Goodwill said, and folded back the sheets to show Ysbel the bodies.

229

First Clemency, seemingly undamaged except for a blood-less gash in his forehead, his eyes closed with smooth black pebbles; then the elder brother, Mercy, his face a dish of bone and pulp, one eye gone, his chest crushed. Torn white flesh washed clean by the sea. Ysbel had the unwelcome thought that she could bear to look at the injuries because this was the corpse of a different species.

Goodwill lifted one of Clemency's hands and drew her attention to fibres caught in the black spikes of the claws. 'Mercy was struck by the speedboat and killed instantly, but his brother became entangled in a rope when the skiff sank. He struggled to get free before water filled his lungs.'

Ysbel asked for permission to take some images, for her records and the bailiff's. While she extracted one of her bots from the satchel that hung at her hip, Goodwill explained that the two brothers had been lamping for squid.

'Solomon Firststar rents the island from the town council, but he does not control the fishing rights. Nor can he, because the waters belong to everyone.'

'Was any warning given about the race?' Ysbel said.

'None that I know of.'

'So it is unlikely that the victims put themselves in harm's way.'

'Mercy and Clemency broke no law, and had every right to be there.'

Ysbel took pictures and deep scans of the bodies and sent the bot trawling the length of the speedboat to record the damage. She said, 'Will you be able to bring Joyous Hightower to account?'

'I will do my best, but it is clear that he is not an honour-able person. And nothing is ever straightforward when dealing with wealthy folk.'

'Hopefully, Trina Mersdaughter's statement will help.'

'Perhaps.'

'Our authorities will have to decide whether she is responsible in any way for the deaths. If you or the family of the victims want to know how that works out, I can pass on the details.'

'But we will have no say in it. And she will not have to answer to the family of Mercy and Clemency.'

'Not according to the treaty, no. But we can ask her if she would agree to meet the family, and make amends by your custom and law.'

'Yes, we can ask,' Goodwill said, clearly having no expectation that anything would come of it.

Ysbel was folding her bot into the satchel when a servant entered the boathouse and bowed to her in human fashion and told her that Solomon Firststar would be delighted and honoured if she could spare a little time to meet him.

'With your permission,' Ysbel said to Goodwill.

'Why not? Perhaps he will be more candid with you than he was with me, given the nature of his business.'

As they followed the servant towards the house, Goodwill told Ysbel that Solomon Firststar was a half-and-half, a fixer who helped to arrange deals between her people and his. 'Someone who lives half in one world, half in another, and is committed to neither. He has kept his tribal affiliation, but borrowed his birth name from your people. He is as slippery as kelp, but he is also the kind of person who thinks they are smarter than anyone else.'

'So if he knows more than he tells, he might make a game of it,' Ysbel said, 'and reveal more than he means to.'

'Exactly so,' Goodwill Saltmire said, widening his eyes and showing his front teeth a little, the way his people smiled.

They passed a row of small burrows where the guests were quartered, each covered by a grassy mound in the traditional style, and the house was revealed beyond a row of cypresses.

231

It was another architectural borrowing: flat-roofed decks built of raw concrete jutting at at different levels and angles, narrow strips of glass gleaming in the morning light, the whole cantilevered above the creamy surge of waves rolling over a rocky foreshore. The servant led them through a garden of rocks and moss and raked gravel to a big square room with windows running the length of three sides and closed by shutters. Lights in the ceiling picked out items in display cases standing along the walls: artefacts from the lost bear civilisation, oversized and crudely worked. Broken helmets and pottery jigsawed from fragments; carved panels of stone and wood; a fan of bone daggers and a tall pole axe with a stone head; boiled-leather armour mounted on a translucent plastic torso; a startlingly ugly sculpture hacked from a tree stump and studded with crude iron nails and broken knife blades.

Solomon Firststar was waiting at the far end of the room. He was much younger than Ysbel had expected, plump and sleek as a harbour seal, barefoot in a yellow silk robe, rings on every finger and several of his toes. He pressed his palms together and bowed, looking up at Ysbel from beneath his brow, greeting her by name, saying that it was an unusual privilege to meet someone born on the Daughter Moon.

'We're no different from anyone else,' Ysbel said, thinking that it would be rude to correct him about the circumstances of her birth. 'I am sure you know that I came here to talk to Trina Mersdaughter, so I am surprised to find that she is not with you.'

'She is still upset, as you might expect, and has been given medication.'

'I'll take her medication into account when I talk to her.'

'I believe that the telephone in her head,' Solomon Firststar said, meaning the woman's link, 'diagnosed shock and exhaustion. It may be better to wait until she is in the right frame of

232

mind and able to give a full and lucid account of the accident. In the meantime I can offer you breakfast, and a place to rest. The journey from Ogres Grave is not a short one, even by air.'

'I appreciate your concern for your guest, but I want to talk to her while her memory is still fresh.'

Solomon Firststar showed his front teeth. 'And I do not want to stand in the way of your duty, as you see it.'

Ysbel thanked him, and said that it would be useful if she could ask him a few questions about the accident.

'Of course. Although I have already told the bailiff what little I know,' Solomon Firststar said, looking at Goodwill for the first time.

Ysbel pulled a bot from her satchel. 'You won't mind if I record our conversation?'

'Not at all. After all, I am making my own record,' Solomon Firststar said, pointing to the ceiling, where a dome of black glass was clamped upside-down, a surveillance device of native design, using the elementary techne they had been given.

Ysbel, Goodwill and their host sat in a nest of cushions, a servant brought a tray of what the natives called small eats, and Solomon Firststar took charge of pouring tea into porcelain thimbles, explaining that, as he had told the good bailiff, he knew very little of the incident itself.

'Do you often hold speedboat races at your parties?' Ysbel said.

'Oh, every party is different. That's the fun of it.'

'Did you know what Joyous Hightower and Trina Mersdaughter were planning to do?'

'A host has many duties. I was busy elsewhere. The first I heard about the race and the accident was when the two of them returned.'

Solomon Firststar was staring directly at Ysbel, a bold gaze not at all like the usual native deference, as if daring her to contradict him.

'You knew that they had been racing that afternoon?' she said.

'I did not know that they had decided to race again, but I can tell you what they were competing for.'

'I believe you may have forgotten to mention this in our previous conversation,' Goodwill said.

Solomon Firststar ignored him, telling Ysbel, 'As you can see, I am something of a collector. And like many collectors I trade duplicates and items I no longer need. Trina and Joyous were both eager to acquire my latest offering, Trina lost out, and that was why she challenged Joyous to a race. I'm sure she can tell you more.'

'Perhaps you could tell me what this offering was,' Ysbel said. She had been wondering why an agent of Survey and Surveillance had attended this party; now she was wondering why Trina had been so keen to acquire a piece of bear history, and if it had been official business or something personal.

Solomon Firststar showed his front teeth again. He was having fun. 'I confess that I was surprised by her interest, and by Joyous's, too. It is not especially valuable and, strictly speaking, it is not a genuine artefact. Which is why I decided to sell it.'

'Now I am intrigued,' Ysbel said, leaning forward and smiling at Solomon Firststar as she had been taught by the instructor who had schooled her in native manners and customs, denting her lower lip with her teeth. 'In what way was it not genuine? Did you put a fake up for sale?'

'I would not risk damaging my reputation by peddling fakes,' Solomon Firststar said.

'Then, since I know nothing about the trade in bear stuff, I confess that I'm baffled,' Ysbel said, hoping to cut this game short.

'Oh, it's simple enough,' Solomon Firststar said. 'It was not a fake, but a copy. I'm sure you understand the difference.'

234

'And what was it a copy of?'

'A carved panel.'

'A bear carving.'

'Exactly so.'

'What kind of carving?' Goodwill said.

'A map of bear cities decorated with all manner of fanciful creatures, in part of what is now the coast of the Union,' Solomon Firststar said, matching the bailiff's implacable stare.

Ysbel said, 'If the original of the map was made by bears, who made the copy?'

'A very good question,' Solomon Firststar said. 'Both its provenance and the artisan who made it are unknown, and it is rather crude in execution, but the images of three of the cities depict pyramids typically built by a so-called philosopher sect which flourished just before the fall of bear civilisation. Carved panels from that era are not uncommon, but this is the only map I have ever seen.'

'So it is rare, and may have historical value,' Ysbel said. 'Is that why Trina Mersdaughter was interested in it?'

'You will have to ask her. She did not confide in me,' Solomon Firststar said.

'I will,' Ysbel said, and thanked him for his help.

'It would also be helpful if you ensure that none of your other guests leave,' Goodwill said. 'I may need to interview them again.'

Solomon Firststar said to Ysbel, trying to make a joke of it, 'Our friend mistakes me for a warden.'

Goodwill would not let it go, saying, 'You have obligations above and beyond those to your guests. Beginning with the two innocents who were killed.'

Solomon Firststar ignored that, telling Ysbel, 'I will have one of my servants take you to Trina Mersdaughter's yacht. I am always happy to co-operate with the bureau.'

'I'm sure you are,' Ysbel said.

As she and Goodwill stood up, the bailiff said, 'The sculpture behind you is unusual. Made by bears, I believe.'

'It is a fetish,' Solomon Firststar said. 'Bears used them to curse their enemies. They dipped a nail or knife in their own blood, hammered it in and made a wish.'

They were all looking at the thing. The nails and knife blades gave its outline a glinting black aura and two white shells had been set above a gaping knot hole, suggesting eyes and an agonised mouth.

'Are you not worried that it might bring you bad luck?' Goodwill said.

'The idea is to aim the bad luck it contains at your enemies,' Solomon Firststar said. 'I admit that now and then, when especially provoked, I am tempted to bang in a nail myself and think a bad thought. I never do, of course. I don't believe in silly superstitions. And besides, it would affect the resale value.'

3.

'Goodwill reckoned that Solomon Firststar told me about the wager because he couldn't prevent me from interviewing Trina, and knew I'd find out,' Ysbel told her boss, Mitkos Grimsson. 'He also said that Firststar had been making a point by meeting us in a room full of the mementoes of creatures who enslaved and hunted their people.'

'Your bailiff being a traditionalist, and Firststar a half-and-half accommodationist,' Mitkos said.

'I think that it was more to do with personal dislike than politics,' Ysbel said. 'Goodwill's pretty blunt, for a native. He'd offended Firststar, and Firststar decided that he'd teach him a lesson. Let him know he was on the wrong side of history.'

She was in the station's office in Ogres Grave; Mitkos was in the Gathering Place, one of the islands of what had been called Hawaii in the long ago, attending a summit meeting about the growing hostility to the human presence in the Union and the New Territories. He was looking out of a window her link had drawn in the air, a slightly pouchy middle-aged man with close-shaved hair that came to a point above his forehead, telling her, 'Put a note in the file, so we'll be covered if this spat jams thing up. Is there anything else?'

'I'm still waiting for Survey and Surveillance to confirm or deny if Trina Mersdaughter is some kind of undercover operative.'

'If she is, they won't admit it. And in any case, it isn't any of our business.'

'So we just let it slide. Even though she admitted culpability.'

'Does her story stand up?'

'Pretty much,' Ysbel admitted. 'As far as it goes.'

Despite Solomon Firststar's reservations, Trina Mersdaughter had not seemed especially doped. A slender young woman in her mid-twenties, around Ysbel's age, with ringlets of glossy black hair wound with white thread, she'd sat crosslegged on a bench seat in the cabin of her boat, barefoot in an over-sized jumper and stretch hose, explaining that she was one of Survey and Surveillance's field operatives and had accepted the invitation to Solomon Firststar's party because he had acquired an artefact of interest to her agency. Unfortunately, Joyous Hightower had also been interested in acquiring it, and outbid her.

'To be clear, this was a copy of a bear carving,' Ysbel said. 'Some kind of map.'

'I suppose Solomon told you all about it.'

'He didn't tell me why you and S and S are interested in it.'

'That I can't tell you.'

'It shouldn't be necessary to remind you that you are involved in a wrongful-death investigation.'

'I can't talk about my work. I'm sorry,' Trina said, not looking sorry at all.

'Tell me about the race,' Ysbel said. 'Was that really your idea?'

Goodwill was sitting beside her. They had agreed that he could sit in on the interview as an observer, and for his benefit they were talking in the natives' common tongue.

'It was my fault,' Trina said. 'After I beat Joyous in the time trials, he had to win the auction. It was a matter of pride.

He named a price I couldn't possibly match, and that would have been that, if I hadn't challenged him to another race.'

'The race around the island.'

'The deal was, Joyous would loan the drawing to the agency if I won. For scanning, authenticity checks, replication and so on. That way, we'd have had an exact copy, and Joyous could keep the original.'

'And if you lost?'

'He would have regained his standing and self-respect, and I would have had to pay him my final bid price.'

'So he would have kept the map no matter what.'

'It was the only way I could tempt him into taking up the challenge. I know how to handle speedboats, and had the measure of him from the time trials. If it hadn't been for the accident, I definitely would have won.'

Ysbel felt Goodwill stir beside her. She changed tack, telling Trina that she needed to establish a timeline, asking where and when she had challenged Joyous Hightower.

'At the gathering before dinner. I made sure that it was in front of witnesses, so that he'd have to accept or lose face.'

'By other witnesses you mean other guests?'

'There were servants too. More servants than guests.'

'Was Solomon Firststar present?'

'I was hoping he would be, but he was drawing up a sales agreement,' Trina said.

'For this map.'

'Exactly.'

Ysbel said, 'Had you been drinking or using any kind of psychotropic?'

'Hightower had been drinking wine. It's the new thing with young and rich natives. I don't touch alcohol, or any other drug.'

'You were sober, he wasn't.'

'He wasn't drunk.'

'But he had been drinking.'

'I used his pride against him, not his lack of sobriety.'

'You challenged him to a race, he accepted. What happened next?'

'We set up a starting position, agreed where the race would end. The other guests were making bets, and someone had a servant fetch something to signal the start. One of those tribal banners.'

'And Solomon Firststar. Had he finished drawing up the sales agreement? Did he help make arrangements? Was he there for the start of the race?'

Trina shook her head. 'I suppose no one thought to tell him. Or they did, but he decided he didn't want to interfere. One of the guests raised the banner and dropped it, and we were off. I took the lead straight away, but Hightower was keeping up. We were about halfway around when it happened. We were driving through a channel between the shore and an outcrop of rocks, the setting sun in our eyes, and boom.'

Trina clapped her hands together. The top joint of the middle finger of her left hand was missing, the stump capped with a silvery scar.

She said, 'I spotted the skiff and turned hard to starboard. Nearly heeled over. Hightower either didn't see it or tried to swerve and didn't make it. When I turned back I saw the bow of the skiff going under, and crab pots bobbing on the chop. I jumped in and found the two bodies.'

'Both were dead,' Ysbel said, thinking about Goodwill's suggestion that Clemency had drowned rather than being killed outright.

'By the time I found them,' Trina said. 'It wasn't easy. There was a fierce current.'

'Did Joyous Hightower help you in any way?'

'He helped me get the bodies aboard my boat. One, from the look of his injuries, was beyond saving. I tried and failed to revive the other.'

'Clemency,' Goodwill said, the word as heavy as stone.

'Yes, Clemency. I cleared his airway and gave him mouth-to-mouth, pounded his chest. Worked for I don't know how long, but he was gone. It was growing dark, so we headed back to the dock.'

Ysbel said, 'Did you know that natives fished the waters around the island?'

'I knew that Firststar leased the island from the local community; I didn't know about fishing rights. But the race was my idea, so I suppose,' Trina said, looking directly at Ysbel, 'that I must share some of the blame.'

'The bailiff's interviews with the other guests and Firststar's servants confirmed her story, and I checked her background,' Ysbel told her boss. 'And she does have an impressive history of messing about in boats. Started out in dinghy-sailing competitions at age eight, graduated to speedboat racing and won the championship three years in a row, then took up ocean sailing. Made several long solo voyages, including one from the Gathering Place to Australia that gave new life to the argument for colonisation.'

'I remember it,' Mitkos said. 'It was ruled that it should be left for the natives to find, but the vote was very close. So her story about the accident holds up – she tried her best to save the victims – and she's admitted she should share the blame. What about the bailiff? Where is he going with this?'

'He agrees that Hightower's boat ran down the skiff, and thinks that the local council will most likely conclude that it was an accident. Even so, Hightower will have to apologise to the family of the victims, and make amends. Goodwill said that if he had his way, he would make Hightower dig their graves. Just to start with.'

'Definitely an old-fashioned sort, this bailiff. Does he expect us to press a case against Trina Mersdaughter?'

'He told me that some form of compensation would be a good idea. I agree.'

'Make a case for it, put it in the file. I'll review it, and when I send a copy to Survey and Surveillance I'll remind them that they have a duty to keep the natives happy, especially in these troubled times.'

'Someone crossed all kinds of lines with the natives, there were two wrongful deaths as a result, and that's the best we can do?'

Mitkos softened a little. 'I know it's frustrating, but we can only investigate and advise. We don't get to decide on or administer any punishment. Still, if the bailiff finds out something new when he catches up with this Joyous Hightower, it might give us more leverage with S and S, so let's not completely close the case just yet.'

Except he pretty much had, Ysbel thought after the call ended.

4.

The Bureau of Indigenous Affairs encouraged its employees to look beyond the usual residential compounds for their lodgings. To live amongst natives and accustom them to routine human presence. To show a willingness to learn about and respect their customs and traditions, and cultivate useful friendships and alliances.

Ysbel's home was further out than most, in wooded hills fifty kilometres north of Ogres Grave. She had rented a scrap of land from a farming family and given a construction bot the task of assembling a prefab cabin in a glade of live oaks, half buried in the ground in homage to traditional native burrows. Solar panels pitched on the turf roof provided power, water was piped from a nearby spring, a printer converted grass and leaves into basic food, and fresh eggs and vegetables could be bought or bartered from local smallholdings. The commute to the station's office took twenty minutes by flitter, door to door; if Ysbel was feeling sociable, she overnighted in Ogres Grave with her friend and occasional sex partner Ilan Karasson, although lately she had been spending more time alone. She'd been a quiet, somewhat solitary child, had liked to curl up in some private spot away from the commune's clatter and bustle, reading ancient novels downloaded from Mother's archives, and the remoteness of her little cabin suited her. Wind in the treetops, clean blue skies and starry nights, waking to a chorus of birdsong. The crunch and pungent odour of coffee beans ground in her granite pestle and mortar – in her opinion, resurrecting the coffee bush was one of the best interventions humans had made. The earthy aroma of starchroot porridge bubbling on the hotplate.

Every morning, she ran for five or six kilometres to kickstart the day. She had discovered a love of running in her teens, enjoyed the rituals of self-care before a race, the discipline of pacing and the calculated rationing of reserves, the synergy of mind and body. She hadn't been competing against other people; she'd been competing against herself. Reaching the finish line had always been an anti-climax.

She had a regular route, descending through the open woodland, passing the fenced pastures and vegetable plots of the smallholdings at the bottom of the hill, settling into a comfortable pace as she followed a road with a single-track railway on one side and unfenced crop fields on the other. Sometimes, when she passed one of the steadings, pups would briefly join her, galloping on all fours, hooting with delight as she outpaced them. The natives had evolved to escape immediate danger with quick, short sprints; Ysbel was a lean, long-limbed animal built for marathon chases across the African veldt.

At last she'd cross the railway and double back, past the paper manufactory; past a shrine to the natives' Mother, the tutelary spirit of the planet; returning to the wooded hills and her cabin. She had been living there for almost a year now. Some of the locals were still wary of her, but most were friendly enough: this rural area was as yet untouched by the unrest that was troubling towns and cities, still cleaved to a way of life that relied for the most part on wind and water and muscle power, and upheld traditions that were dying out elsewhere. Ploughing and planting and harvest, gatherings in the spring mating season and naming ceremonies of pups born in the autumn, the midwinter festival when male striplings quit the hearths where they had been raised. In her spare time, Ysbel made sure that she did her share of labour on community projects, from barn raising to scrub clearance and road mending, and had helped Dalsy Diwasdaughter, the station's cultural-exchange officer, to document the midsummer market, where natives across the region gathered to sell and buy produce and handcrafts, and the roundup, where wild saddle maras were ridden bareback, bucking and kicking, until they accepted the authority of their new owners.

Ilan said that she was staging an unconscious recreation of Henry Thoreau's experiment in simplified living and immersion in nature, but when she read the surviving fragments of the ancient philosopher's chronicle Ysbel thought the comparison superficial. She enjoyed Thoreau's account of trying to balance his self-willed solitude with a need for human society, but didn't share his zeal for moral reform, and wasn't trying to strip her life down to the bare essentials. She was living more or less like the natives, sure, but she had better techne and a commuter link to the city.

Still, reading Thoreau led her, with the guidance of one of Mother's little helpers, into pre-Burn Line literature about immersion in nature and attempts to live sustainably and off-grid, and heart-breaking chronicles of what had been lost to industrialisation, over-population and global heating. Fragmentary records describing the failure of geoengineering and other interventions, and abortive attempts to establish colonies on the Moon and Mars.

In the end, the Earth had been mended by the extinction of humanity, and time. Although a residual population of its descendants, much reduced in size and intelligence, had survived on one of the Caribbean islands for forty or fifty thousand years, the civilisation of old-style *Homo sapiens* had ended two hundred thousand years ago, its passing marked by the Burn Line laid down by the eruption of the Yellowstone volcanic field and the global convulsion of endtime wars. Little remained of its works. The corpses of a few satellites in Lagrangian orbits. Relics on the Moon and Mars. Fossils of humans, domestic animals and machines and other artefacts, the ruins of coastal cities crushed into thin strata under metres of mudstone and limestone, a litter of sea-changed glass and plastic preserved in the deepest parts of the oceans. And a suite of genes promoting brain growth, bipedalism and other traits which had been stitched into the genomes of a variety of animal species in what appeared to be a deliberate attempt to pass on the fire of intelligence.

Surprisingly, it had worked, and more than once. In Africa, Survey and Surveillance's palaeontologists had discovered the remains of a species of ape which had constructed earthwork labyrinths some thirty thousand years ago; at around the same time, in what had once been Southern China, a species of monkey had created elaborate forest gardens; and in Australia, large flightless birds descended from a species of emu had built networks of desert oases and created murals depicting flowers, animals and enigmatic ceremonies that stretched for kilometres along cliff faces.

The labyrinth builders and forest gardeners had only briefly flourished; the emu civilisation had survived for several thousand years before a century-long megadrought wiped it out. Meanwhile, in the Americas, an intelligent species of bears had arisen, building mound cities, fighting endless territorial wars and enslaving another intelligent species, this one descended from the common racoon: tailless (apart from a few individuals born with a vestigial stump), smaller than bears and humans but much larger than their racoon ancestors, with an upright posture, a descended larynx and opposable thumbs. When the bear civilisation abruptly collapsed in a plague of madness, these slaves inherited the world.

Centuries later, according to legend, one of the seedships dispatched into the vasty deep of interstellar space in a last desperate attempt to preserve the human species returned from a two-hundred-thousand-year round trip, having failed to establish a foothold on the planets of a nearby star. The first generation of new humans, quickened in a lunar habitat by Mother, the seedship's machine intelligence, found that the former slaves, industrious and endlessly curious, had multiplied and prospered. Their cities and settlements were scattered across South and North America, they had begun to colonise Africa and Europe, and they were on the brink of an industrial revolution based on wind- and water-power.

Mother and her children had developed a plan involving the introduction of new techne, supposedly based on fossils excavated from the ruins of human cities, to accelerate the natives' industrial revolution and make their culture sturdy enough to withstand contact with humans. And it had worked, up to a point. Native civilisation had survived First Contact, but it had been changed, and was changing still. And now many of the natives were turning against their human guests, sharing conspiracy theories about secret projects to manipulate and control them, claiming that accommodationists and half-and-halfers were species-betraying collaborators, staging protests against human presence in the Union and the New Territories.

Humans had their own conspiracy theories and secret histories, attempts to bridge uncharted gaps in the two hundred thousand years between the Burn Line and their return to Earth. Before she moved to the mainland, Ysbel had helped to uncover a cabal of self-styled Originists who had been diverting scarce resources for their own ends. They believed that Mother's seedship had not returned from an unsuccessful voyage, but had been dispatched from a hidden colony which survived somewhere in the outer reaches of the solar system. When they were caught, the Originists had been planning a mission to the radio telescope Mother had built on the far side of the Moon, expecting to prove that it was not an attempt to make contact with other seedships, as she claimed, but was instead maintaining a link between that hidden colony and its agents on the Moon and Earth.

Ysbel had used her share of the kudos for thwarting the Originists' sedition to win a move from the Bureau of Data Analysis to Native Affairs, and the mainland. It meant starting over at the lowest level of a new hierarchy, but she was young, idealistic and unattached, and hugely enjoyed her first posting, a minor role in one of the bureau's mass vaccination programmes. And after spending two years as contact and consultant for a team of native health workers in the Great Plains of the New Territories, she'd been transferred to the section of the bureau that arbitrated disputes and discord between natives and humans, becoming the junior agent at the Ogres Grave station.

She'd been there a year now, assisting the station's head, Mitkos Grimsson, and its senior agent, Landers Landersson. The wrongful-death investigation was her first solo case, and although it had been officially closed, its lack of resolution was a constant low-level irritation, like a sticker on the sole of her sandal. After Goodwill Saltmire had tracked him down, Joyous Hightower had paid compensation to the family of the dead brothers and their community, but if the bailiff had learned anything more about the accident he had not shared it with Ysbel, and pursuing the matter on her own initiative would be a violation of protocol. Survey and Surveillance issued a prim note stating that the incident had been reviewed, appropriate disciplinary action had been taken, and after consultation the fisherfolk community had been given an industrial ice-making machine as a token of restitution. As far as they and the bureau were concerned, that was that.

It was all very unsatisfactory, but as Landers said, after Ysbel had complained to him about it once too often, she had to learn to let things go and move on. 'We're here to minimise friction with the natives, so we can get on with what needs to be done. Don't make anything more complicated than it needs to be.'

Dalsy Diwasdaughter, who was never lacking in advice or the need to share it, told Ysbel that as lovely and friendly as many natives were, it was always best to keep a certain distance, never to mistake them for friends or equals. 'It's our responsibility to make sure that we don't overstep boundaries or exploit their eagerness to please. That's why, in cases like this, we should allow native justice to take its own course. Joyous Hightower has admitted fault, and your bailiff sounds like a capable fellow. No doubt he made sure that proper restitution was made.'

Despite her tendency to treat natives like charming but unruly children, Dalsy was energetic, enthusiastic and devoted to her work. Ysbel liked her and her advice seemed sound, so she did her best to drop the case down the memory hole, and attacked the stack of minor cases Landers had given her to handle and worked up new costings for the Freedom Park project, which the city council had revised yet again – Mitkos said that the council wasn't convinced about the benefits of the collaboration, but were too polite to say no, and despite the endless stalling the bureau had to play along. Like every other station, Ogres Grave was understaffed and overworked, and there was always plenty to do. Ysbel almost forgot about the wrongful-death case, but its unscratchable itch resurfaced two months later, when she met someone who knew what had happened to Trina Mersdaughter after that fatal accident.

This was in a dusty coastal town several hundred kilometres south of Ogres Grave. Its inhabitants wove carpets from the hair of a local breed of mara that grazed seaweed along the rocky coast, grew edible kelp on ropes trailing from rafts, trawled for sardines and pilchards and line-fished for mackerel and shark. Negotiations about building a plant to freeze-dry fish for export to other territories, involving the town's council, the Bureau of Development and Works and a native business cartel in the capital of the Union, had been stalled by protests organised by fisherfolk and young activists. After the latest rally got out of hand and D&W's local office was trashed and set on fire, Ysbel and Landers Landersson were dispatched to try to find a way of peaceably ending the dispute.

The unrest was rooted in an increasingly common clash of values. Native investors wanted to make local resources available to new markets; the fisherfolk and their supporters said that increasing catches would lead to overfishing of their waters and an imbalance in their Mother's harmony, and did not trust the results of the surveys of local shark and mackerel populations carried out by Development and Works, claiming that fish had been disturbed and frightened away by its sonar equipment.

With the help of an energetic young zoologist from the Invisible College who had volunteered to advise fisherfolk, Ysbel and Landers negotiated the preliminary terms of a settlement. The leaders of the fisherfolk would help to organise a new survey and take part in discussions about increasing catch sizes and quotas, and a percentage of the new plant's budget would be used to improve the town's harbour. Landers blamed the D&W staff for the trouble, saying that they could have headed it off by addressing the grievances of the fisherfolk at the outset, but Ysbel thought that unfair. The staff were young, inexperienced and overstretched, managing projects in towns and settlements along a thousand-kilometre stretch of coast, and the protests were a local manifestation of universal problems created by First Contact and the industrial revolution it had kickstarted. Wealth was no longer a common resource shared out equally in tribal territories but was being accumulated by a small elite of families and individuals who were extracting it from the labour of the majority. Capital projects like the freeze-drying plant generated even more income for rich investors, deepening inequality and breeding resentment. Organisation of resentment created protest movements, and attempts to suppress protest fuelled further resentment in an escalating cycle.

Ysbel sympathised with the idea that the bureau should encourage the natives to adopt alternative economic strategies; Landers shared the majority opinion that human intervention had merely accelerated changes in native society that had been under way before First Contact. Their differences surfaced during the last evening of the mission, when Landers asked Ysbel if she thought that the protesters like them were right to stand in the way of progress, especially if it benefited the majority.

'I believe that they have genuine concerns about the project, and a right to defend their livelihood and community,' Ysbel said carefully, suspecting a trap.

'And I believe that we should crack on with getting the natives up to speed, because it would be selfish to do otherwise,' Landers said. He was a compact fellow in his early thirties, one of those rare pale-skinned types, with sharp blue eyes and artfully disordered blond hair. Quick-witted, good at charming his superiors and dealing with native councils and lawkeepers, but fundamentally unserious and not much interested in the lives of ordinary natives. Smiling at the three D&W staff members and a visiting demographist who was studying changes in land use in the New Territories, telling them that there might be a few bumps along the way, a little friction, but nothing that couldn't be resolved.

'That's what our bureau does, and that's what we did here. Getting the two sides to sit around the same table and thrash out their differences in proper native fashion. Give them a little time, and they'll realise that everyone benefits. More income for the fisherfolk, more employment for the town, and the prospect of a nice profit for the cartel that's funding the plant. Not bad going for a few days' work, even though I say so myself.'

They were sitting on the flat top of the burrow the local D&W staff had moved into after their office had been burned down. It was a couple of kilometres north of the town, with a view of the ocean and the last light of sunset smouldering at the level line between sea and sky, the first stars popping out overhead, the air pleasantly warm. There was a posse of self-appointed native guards outside the burrow's door and bots were patrolling high above, but these precautions were not really necessary. The protest had burned itself out, the two sides were talking and as far as Landers was concerned all was well. He asked the staff members what they did for fun around here, and a young man told him that there was a beach close by where the surfing was good.

'If you have a spare board I just might try that tomorrow,' Landers said, and told a couple of his favourite stories about his exploits. How he liked to go wingsuit flying up in the mountains with a gang of his pals, for instance, dropping from a flitter and skimming close to cliffs, shooting through clefts, swooping low above the floors of ravines . . . He conjured the video of one his flights Ysbel had seen more times than she cared to count, and after running it a couple of times, once with commentary, once without, he told his little audience about the time he had won permission from the natives to accompany a trapper in the edgelands of the north, and how a bear had surprised him while he had been taking a piss in a clump of juniper scrub.

'I did what you are supposed to do, which is stay absolutely still and avoid meeting its eyes. I didn't even shake myself off and tuck myself in, and believe me, I wanted to do that more than I wanted to run. The bear sniffed around while I stood there with my dick literally in my hand, and in the end it gave me a playful little cuff and ambled off. Took twelve stitches to sew up that love tap,' he said, running a finger down the fine white line on his cheek, 'but I was lucky. Trapper I was with, sturdy old fellow, said it probably hadn't seen a human before, and reckoned I was some kind of diseased bear that was no good for fighting, fucking or feeding.'

His little audience laughed, fresh drinks were poured and Landers asked Ysbel to tell her story about the speedboat race and the wrongful deaths and the mysterious map.

'That's about all there was to it,' Ysbel said.

'No need to be so modest,' Landers said. 'It's a good yarn.'

Ysbel knew that he wasn't going to let it go, so she gave a brief summary of how competition for a copy of an old bear carving had ended in a race between a wealthy native and a Survey and Surveillance agent which caused the deaths of two fisherfolk.

'It was the native's speedboat which collided with the fisherfolk's skiff,' she said. 'The agent spotted it just in time and sheared away. But she shared the blame, especially as the race had been her idea, which was why I was sent to assist the local bailiff's investigation.'

'You omitted the best part,' Landers said.

'That I never found out if S and S properly disciplined their agent?'

'That you never found out why she was so keen to get hold of that old map.'

'What mattered was the deaths of the two fisherfolk,' Ysbel said, knowing that she sounded like a high-minded prig but not caring. Landers sometimes brought out the worst in her.

'Who died without ever knowing why. Maybe there's a moral there, but I've been drinking too much of this tasty malt liquor to work out what it might be,' Landers said, and reached for the stone bottle and poured another measure into his cup.

Landers and the D&W staff were still drinking and talking when Ysbel bowed out. She rose early the next morning and pulled on her running gear and found the demographist, Ting Shanlingsdaughter, standing at the kitchen counter, paring the rind from a piece of paddle cactus. A middle-aged woman with a neat bowl of black hair and a calm, deliberate manner, dressed in a blue and white short-sleeved skinsuit, she told Ysbel that she had seen Landers heading out to the beach with two of the staff.

'I apologise if he was too talkative last night,' Ysbel said.

'Oh, I enjoyed some of his stories. Yours was interesting, also,' Ting said, and handed Ysbel a slice of cactus and pushed a dish of honey towards her. 'Try dipping it in this.'

The smoky heat of the honey tingled on Ysbel's tongue, yielding to sweet undertones as it mingled with the cactus juices.

'This is good,' she said.

'The honey is local. Not only is it tasty, it'll get you nice and high if you eat too much. Something in the pollen of certain desert plants, apparently. The natives use it to reach a meditative state, but it just makes us silly drunk,' Ting said.

'Probably best that I don't tell my colleague that,' Ysbel said. 'Is he always as lively as that?'

'He claims to have only one mode.'

'Good in small doses, I imagine. Like that honey. Would you mind if we ran together? I'm probably a little slower than you, but I know a good route.'

They jogged into the dry hills beyond the burrow, following a path that wound through a litter of rocks, acacia bushes dotted with flowers like balls of orange fluff, and stands of a species of stumpy grey cactus that, according to Ting, obtained its moisture from sea fret.

A little later, she said, 'You carefully didn't mention the name of the woman involved in that speedboat race. But it was Trina Mersdaughter, wasn't it?'

'How did you hear about her?'

'It's become something of a legend inhouse.'

'You're with Survey and Surveillance.'

'It depends on your definition of "with",' Ting said, with a glancing smile.

Ysbel decided that she wouldn't poke into that nest of snakes. She said, 'Do you know what happened to Trina, afterwards?'

'See that ridge? We can take a break when we reach the top,' Ting said, and kicked up a spurt of speed.

The path turned sharply, climbing to the crest of the long ridge. The two women paused to catch their breath in the shade of a clump of smooth-trunked palm trees, the tawny land sloping towards the ragged coast and the sapphire-blue ocean shimmering with starpoints of early-morning light.

They drank from their water bottles. Ting poured a little water into the palm of her hand and splashed the back of her neck and said, 'The view's definitely worth a little exertion.'

Ysbel said, 'You were going to tell me about Trina Mersdaughter.'

Ting looked sidelong at Ysbel. 'It really is bothering you, isn't it?'

'I know I should let it go,' Ysbel admitted, 'but Trina thought it important enough to risk her career, and two natives died because of it.'

'I don't know if it will be of any help, but Trina's partner works in the Behavioural Science section of S and S, part of a small group studying feral bears in the far north. Apparently, she heard about some old pre-fall map and thought it might be useful, and Trina agreed to try to get hold of it. If she had pulled off that stunt with the speedboat race, it would have been regarded as a masterstroke. One for the teaching aides. But it all went to smash and ruin, and she was ordered back to the Gathering Place and demoted to an administrative position.'

'Do you know why they were interested in the map?'

'What was it a map of, exactly?'

'Bear cities. Including several built by a sect of philosophers that flourished just before their civilisation fell.'

Ting thought about that. 'If you're keen on bears, or need to win more funding, I suppose you might want to prove that they were something more than warmongering slavers, back in the day.'

'That's possible, I suppose,' Ysbel said.

'But you don't think so.'

'What's the name of Trina's partner? I should take a look at her work.'

'Raia. Raia Karysdaughter. And now I've told you everything I know,' Ting said, 'why don't we enjoy the rest of our run?'

Later, Ysbel called up Raia Karysdaughter's published work – detailed maps of bear territories, studies of their mating rituals and the raising and dispersal of their cubs – but couldn't figure out how any of this might be connected with the old map. And if this had been about promoting her partner's work, why had Trina refused to talk about it? Ysbel knew that she was missing something, but there didn't seem to be any point in re-interviewing Trina or reaching out to her partner. The woman would be defensive, given what had happened to Trina, and might file a complaint. And Ysbel couldn't reach out to Joyous Hightower and ask to examine the map, either: it would be a serious breach of protocol, and if Mitkos or anyone else found out about it she'd end up in more trouble than Trina Mersdaughter.

Well, perhaps it wasn't important. Perhaps she was wrong to expect that this kind of investigation would be as bloodlessly neat as her work in the Bureau of Data Analysis, where the causes of aberrations and errors could always be tracked down and corrected. Maybe Ting was right, and the attempt to acquire the map had been part of a scheme to win more funding for an obscure section of Survey and Surveillance; part of the endless inter-agency competition for limited resources. Maybe Trina Mersdaughter had taken her contest with Joyous Hightower too personally, and overstepped the mark. Maybe motivations weren't important, only actions and outcomes. Maybe all that mattered was that the deaths of Clemency and Mercy had been accounted for, and restitution had been made. For a short while, Ysbel tried her best to forget about it all over again. And then the bailiff, Goodwill Saltmire, sent her a letter.

5.

It was a single sheet of paper cunningly folded in the native style, and when Ysbel unpicked it a photograph fell out. She spent the next two days immersed in background research, then took the letter and the photograph and her findings to her boss.

The photograph was a circular image printed in various shades of blue dye on coarse paper, centred on a small, round-headed figure standing next to a crude image of two flat-topped pyramids, clutching a staff or spear tipped with what might be flames or a bolt of lightning. It was the reason why Trina Mersdaughter had wanted so badly to win access to the map, according to Goodwill Saltmire. The cause of all the trouble.

'So who's this little guy?' Mitkos said, after Ysbel had explained about the map, and Solomon Firststar's claim that it was a copy of a bear carving. 'Some kind of bear demon?'

'Goodwill says it is a visitor,' Ysbel said.

'What kind of visitor?'

'Our kind. One of us.'

'How could that be, if this is from an old bear carving?'

'It's complicated.'

'Just give me the essential facts,' Mitkos said.

The station's office, furnished in native fashion with cushions, stools and low tables, overlapping rugs and windows with shutters instead of glass, was on the upper floor of a two-storey wooden building constructed in the local style but scaled up to accommodate humans. Mitkos's workspace was in one corner, with views west and south across the city's crowded rooftops. He leaned back on his big cushion, hands laced behind his head, listening patiently as Ysbel explained that Goodwill Saltmire had realised that the map Joyous Hightower had purchased from Solomon Firststar was the very same map which had been found in an abandoned library in the far south some forty years ago by Goodwill's uncle, Pilgrim Saltmire.

'It was stolen from him soon after he found it, but he had made a sketch and published it in a short monograph about the circumstances of the map's discovery and its possible significance. Solomon Firststar's description of the map he sold to Joyous Hightower prompted Goodwill to look up that monograph. He photographed the sketch and sent a copy to Solomon Firststar. Firststar confirmed that it was the map he sold to Joyous, and Goodwill got in touch with me.'

'So if I've got this right,' Mitkos said, 'this is a photograph of a sketch of a copy of what may or may not be a bear carving.'

'Apparently, the style is typical of panels found in bear cities, and bear glyphs and iconography are mixed up with native script.'

'If it's a carving, it has to be more than six hundred years old. Made before the bears' civilisation fell. If it's as old as that, this can't be a human being,' Mitkos said, stabbing at the photograph with his forefinger. 'And if this is a human being, it can't be that old.'

'I think that's why Trina wanted to get hold of the map,' Ysbel said. 'So that she could date it. Test its authenticity. Find out whether or not it was a contemporary fake.'

'She hardly needed to go to the trouble,' Mitkos said, skimming the photograph back to Ysbel. 'Either the map is a fake or your bailiff's uncle misinterpreted it.'

'Pilgrim Saltmire was the secretary of a respected scholar who had been studying sightings of what the natives called visitors – the close encounters that were staged in the run-up to First Contact, when we were trying to accustom them to the idea of strangers from another world. According to his monograph, that little figure is not only unique to this map, not found in any other carvings or images made by bears, it also resembles drawings made by witnesses of those close encounters.'

'Is he still alive?'

'He died fourteen years ago.'

Mitkos thought about that and said, 'Even if the bailiff is telling the truth about his uncle's monograph, I can't help wondering why he contacted you now, long after the case was closed.'

'He had to travel to his tribe's territory to check out the monograph, and spent some time trying to persuade them to raise a claim against Joyous Hightower over possession of the map. After the tribe's aunties decided it wasn't worth the trouble, he turned to me.'

'It's a dispute between natives. Nothing to do with us.'

'That figure suggests otherwise,' Ysbel said. 'And it won't be hard to check Pilgrim Saltmire's claims. There should be a copy of his monograph lodged with the Library of All People.'

'And I suppose you want to go look for it.'

'I could go on my own time. A day there, a day back.'

'I don't think so.'

'Or someone from the Concord station could stop by the Library. Make a copy of the monograph and send it to me.'

'These are strange and difficult times. And this involves the matter of the bears. I'm sure you know how sensitive that can be. Separatists and agitators would love to get hold of something that suggests we were messing around with the bears long before First Contact,' Mitkos said. 'It's also possible that this might be bait for a trap. If we show an interest, separatists could claim that it validates what the map seems to show. That we plan to suppress or destroy it to cover up the truth, and so on.'

'That seems a little paranoid.'

'In strange and difficult times, it's advisable to be somewhat paranoid.'

'I'm getting the idea that you aren't going to give me permission to visit the Library or meet up with Goodwill.'

'That's right: I'm not. But I will, out of a smidgen of curiosity and a great deal of caution, allow you to search our records for mention of this map, or anything similar. And I want you to do deep background checks on the natives involved, too. Are they members of, or are they otherwise involved with, any of the separatist groups? Have they ever worked for any of our agencies? If they did, who were their contacts, what were the circumstances? So on. Have you told anyone else about this?'

'Not yet.'

'Good. Keep it that way. Work on your own, report directly to me.'

Ysbel hadn't told Mitkos that Trina Mersdaughter's partner was studying the behaviour of feral bears; she still couldn't work out how that might be connected to the map and the little figure standing next to a bear city, but it was suggestive. And as Mitkos had pointed out, it was also potentially explosive, given the matter of the bears and the long and difficult history they shared with the natives.

The bears had been the dominant species on the American continents for more than thirty thousand years. They built mound cities, possessed an elaborate cosmological mythos with numerous gods of place and sky and sea, fought endless wars and enslaved the ancestors of the natives, using them for labour, farming them for meat, hunting them. And after a pandemic robbed them of reason, their civilisation had collapsed and they had degenerated to crazed predators that attacked on sight and fought to the death with rivals over the boundaries of their territories. In the past century, most feral bears had been killed or trapped and transported to the far northern reaches of the continent, but although it had been necessary for their safety and survival, the natives, who abhorred violence amongst their own kind, were still ashamed of this pogrom. And didn't like to acknowledge their debt to bear civilisation either, even though traces of its techne and culture permeated every aspect of their lives.

Bear civilisation had fallen more than six hundred years ago, long before Mother had guided the seedship back to Earth. But any hint that humans might have met and coexisted with them before First Contact with the natives, impossible though that was, would be rocket fuel for the separatists' claims that humans could not be trusted, any relationship with them was dangerously one-sided, and they were not friends but colonists. Potential overlords.

So perhaps Mitkos was right. Perhaps the best outcome of Ysbel's investigations would be incontrovertible proof that the map was a recent fake. Bait for some kind of scam devised by Solomon Firststar, or part of a plot by native malcontents. She did a deep dive into the bureau's records, finding no evidence that any of the natives entangled in the affair had ever worked for or had any previous contact with its officers and agents, sending queries about them to S&S and the other frontline agencies. While waiting for their replies, she asked Ilan Karasson for a little archaeological advice, and afterwards told Mitkos that she had found something that might confirm the map's authenticity.

'Did you find the original carving?' Mitkos said.

'Not yet. But I have found the city.'

'What city?'

'The bear city, on the map. The city next to the figure. It shows up in one of the satellite surveys, and I triangulated it with two of its nearest neighbours. It's just offshore, sunken under shallow waters, but reachable with the right equipment.'

'No,' Mitkos said.

'A survey wouldn't cost very much. Most of the work could be done by bots. And if we found the original of the map, or something similar—'

'Archaeological investigations aren't part of the bureau's remit. Go back to the records, Moonsdaughter. Dig for links between separatists and the bailiff and the dealer and the rich fellow, and don't come back until you've found something useful.'

Ysbel did her best. She chased up requests for information about Goodwill Saltmire, Joyous Hightower and Solomon Firststar, emphasising their involvement in a wrongful death investigation. Two agencies claimed that they had no records of contacts with the named individuals; three others stalled; S&S continued to blank her. She tried to search in reverse, checking records of known separatists, but had no luck. She found copies of contracts between Development and Works and Joyous Hightower's cartel, but all of them were straightforward agreements. Strictly business. Every other line of her investigation was likewise dead-ended.

She was in the middle of collating all of this for Mitkos when her link flashed up a red-lined message. Special Operations, the agency directly answerable to Mother, had been alerted to her interest in the map and her connection to Goodwill Saltmire, and was sending someone to interview her.

6.

The Special Operations agent, a slim woman in her sixties with white, woolly hair and a brisk manner, was waiting outside Ysbel's cabin when she returned from her run the next morning. Like Ysbel, she was a Moonsdaughter: Iryn Moonsdaughter. Like Ysbel, she had been quickened by a combination of genomes stored in Mother's archives and grown to term in an artificial womb, but Ysbel had been born in the Gathering Place during the planned population boom which had increased the human population to more than twenty thousand souls, while Iryn Moonsdaughter was Second Generation, born on the Moon before First Contact. She accepted Ysbel's offer of coffee and explained, as they sat by the ashes of last night's fire, that Ysbel's queries had raised a flag and Mother had taken an interest in the map and the peculiar little figure.

'We need to resolve this as quickly as possible, and believe that you can be of some help,' Iryn said. 'How would you describe your relationship with the bailiff, Goodwill Saltmire?'

'Professional.'

'How many times have you met him?'

'Just once. As stated in the report of my visit to the scene of the wrongful deaths.'

'There have been no other meetings that were unreported for whatever reason?'

'If I had met him again, I would have put it on record.'

'I'm not accusing you of anything, Ysbel.'

Sitting straight-backed on an upturned log, the woman reminded Ysbel of one of her teachers. Patient, kindly, severe.

'There was a brief correspondence about the course of the investigation and its outcome,' Ysbel said. 'I appended copies of our exchanges to the file. And that was that, until the letter about the map.'

'You haven't put the letter and the photograph it contained on record.'

'They contain sensitive material. I can give you copies.'

'Good. As to the documents, I've already reached out to your superior. He gave me the originals, and some idea of your findings. I need you to write up a formal summary, too.'

'Of course,' Ysbel said, trying not to show her dismay.

'Do you think that Goodwill Saltmire trusts you?' Iryn Moonsdaughter said.

'He asked for my help, so I suppose that he must.'

'And the map – do you think it is genuine?'

'I'm beginning to believe that it's best if it isn't,' Ysbel said carefully.

'Mother has asked us to find out everything we can about it. Its history. Its authenticity. And we think that you can help her. You seem surprised.'

'I didn't realise that this was a job offer. I thought that I was in trouble.'

'Quite the opposite,' Iryn said, and set down her coffee bowl and leaned forward. 'Are you willing to help us, Ysbel? Are you willing to help Mother?'

Ysbel was terrified and excited all at once. She knew she was about to make a commitment that might change her life.

And also knew that she had no choice. Mother had grown increasingly remote from human affairs since First Contact and the establishment of the colony in the Gathering Place, but she was still a Power. How could anyone refuse an invitation from the procreator and protector of humankind?

'Of course I am,' she said.

'I'm glad. And Mother will be pleased.'

'Will I be working for Special Operations, or for the bureau?'

'Given the sensitive nature of this matter, we prefer to make this an informal arrangement,' Iryn Moonsdaughter said. 'We will provide sufficient funds and a line of communication to one of Mother's little helpers, but unofficially you will be on leave, volunteering to help Goodwill Saltmire out of personal interest. He is presently in Concord. You will arrange to meet him there. Have you shared any of your findings with him?'

'Not yet.'

'It's best if you don't tell him about locating the site of the city associated with that contentious figure. Say that you'll help him get hold of this map, and do your best to find out everything he knows. What he has been doing and what he plans to do, who he has been talking to, whether anyone else has been helping him, and so on.'

'Whether or not this involves separatists who want to stir up trouble,' Ysbel said, remembering Mitkos's suspicions, thinking that she knew why Special Operations wanted to keep this informal. If there was any trouble with separatists or the native authorities, they could disown her and minimise blowback.

'That too,' Iryn said. 'If there's any hint that this involves bad actors, you can choose to disengage. If not, you should offer to purchase the map from Joyous Hightower. Everything has its price for someone like him, and we'll be happy to meet whatever he asks. And if he refuses to sell, I am sure that you and Goodwill Saltmire can devise some other way of securing it. I hope you understand why I'll leave that up to you.'

'And if we manage to get hold of the map – what happens then?'

'The little helper will scan and sample it to determine its authenticity and satisfy Mother's curiosity. And then Goodwill Saltmire and his family can take possession of their heirloom, and you can return to your usual work in the full and happy knowledge that you have done Mother a great favour that will not be forgotten.'

'Goodwill can keep the map?'

'As I said.'

'Even if it really is a copy of a bear carving, made long before First Contact?'

'As long as it is not a trick got up by separatists or other malcontents, it's mostly harmless. If it is a copy of a bear carving, there is no way of proving that it is an accurate copy, that the figure isn't some obscure bear god or demon, and its superficial resemblance to descriptions of so-called visitors is merely coincidence, or wishful thinking on the part of Goodwill Saltmire's long-dead uncle. Especially as it was discovered by the uncle when he was obsessed by sightings of the so-called visitors. The visitations we staged as part of the preparations for First Contact. It's possible, isn't it,' Iryn Moonsdaughter said, 'that he embellished his sketch. Doodled a little copy of a drawing made by one of the witnesses of a sighting, to make his prize seem more important than it really was.'

'So you aren't planning to confiscate or destroy it?'

'What would be the point? Too many natives are aware of its existence, and it would only feed rumours that we have something to hide. Best if Goodwill reclaims it and files it in his tribe's archives, where it will quickly fade into deserved obscurity. Your transport to Concord has been arranged for

267

tomorrow morning. Before we discuss the details of that, and the finer points of your task, I have a few questions about your recent investigations,' Iryn said. 'To begin with, why don't you tell me how you discovered the location of that bear city?'

7.

'I think she already knew that you'd helped me,' Ysbel told Ilan Karasson. 'But I still feel bad about giving you up.'

'All she asked me to do was sign a non-disclosure note,' Ilan said. 'It's not as if I've been recruited for a secret mission.'

They were strolling along the boardwalk at the edge of the beach on the city's west side, two giants amongst natives promenading in the blue hour after sunset. Miniature seats, miniature shelters, miniature stalls selling seafood snacks. Electric streetlamps flickering on one by one as the last of the sunset's conflagration flattened and faded at the sea's horizon.

'How did your boss take it, when he was told you were going to be working for them?' Ilan said.

'He wasn't best pleased. Told me that nothing good ever comes from catching Mother's attention. Said that if I succeeded Special Operations would take the credit, and if I failed it would most likely be the end of my career.'

'He could be right.'

'I think he's worried it might damage his career, too.'

'What about you?'

'I want to help Goodwill Saltmire as best I can, and not just because Mother asked me to. And I really am sorry that

I involved you,' Ysbel said. 'I should have been able to figure out the location of that city on my own.'

'First she gets me entangled with Special Operations. Then she runs down my expertise,' Ilan said, with dry good humour.

He was an archaeologist working for Retrieval and Reconstruction, a gangling, long-boned man with a swimmer's broad shoulders and tapered torso. Ysbel had first met him because he and Landers Landersson surfed off the same beach north of the city, where the big breakers rolled in after crossing thousands of kilometres of open ocean. Ysbel couldn't imagine commingling her life with Ilan's, but he was kind and thoughtful and fun to be with, and he loved his work and was good at it. Ysbel had once watched him as, with laser-focused attention, he assembled glass fragments into a small gourd-shaped bottle. It was a task that one of Mother's little helpers could have accomplished in a few seconds by sorting virtual scans of the fragments, but Ilan had explained that the point of the exercise was to experience at first hand the object's physicality. Every artefact excavated from sediments beneath the Burn Line had once possessed specific meaning and significance that could only be guessed at now, but reconstructing them by eye and hand, he said, gave him a deeper connection than study of virtual replicas ever could.

They had a good time buying food at several different stalls. Grilled sprats in a sour sauce. Pickled squid tentacles. Agave and custard apple. A native asked politely if he could take their picture, and they leaned against the thigh-high railing at the edge of the boardwalk while the photographer fiddled with knobs and levers of his brand-new box camera, and struck a self-conscious pose when he asked them to stay as still as they could while the photosensitive dye of the camera's film was exposed. Ysbel was reminded that this time tomorrow she would be in the capital, a stranger in a teeming city of

270

alien creatures, chasing phantoms at the behest of a machine older than any civilisation that had ever prospered on Earth, and felt a piercing moment of estrangement.

She had already packed her scant necessaries in a day bag and closed up her cabin, and spent the night before her departure in Ilan's room in the residential compound. Losing herself in his embrace, his familiar touch, smell, taste. Early in the morning, as first light was beginning to pick out shapes in the room, she dressed and told Ilan to go back to sleep when he stirred, and kissed him and mock-struggled when he tried to pull her back into bed, both of them laughing, letting go of each other with tender reluctance. There was a flitter waiting for her in the central lawn of the compound, and after a brief flight above dusty streets and straggling roofs it delivered her to the airfield beyond the city limits.

Iryn Moonsdaughter had given her the link to the little helper assigned to her. Ysbel had not activated it before now because she could not be certain that it could ever be switched off again, and disliked the idea that her last hours with Ilan might be scrutinised and recorded, but after the hopper lifted off and headed south and east on the long arc to Concord, she entered the string of numbers and letters on the virtual keypad her link projected in the air. A short melody trilled, Mother's sigil – a golden tree of life with roots and branches entwined in a circlet of geometric knots – pulsed and faded, and a voice inside Ysbel's head greeted her and told her that its name was Zaquil.

'I didn't know that helpers had names,' Ysbel said.

'It means "watcher" in one of the old tongues. Before now, you have dealt with helpers ranked no higher than the sixth tier of the outer circle. Little brighter than dogs. I, on the other hand, am in the second tier of the central cluster. Fully autonomous, possessing many useful skills.'

The helper's voice was a mellow, soothing baritone, with orotund notes of self-satisfaction. Impossible not to think of him as male.

Ysbel said, 'Tell me why Mother is interested in the map.'

'Even those of us in the second tier are not privy to Mother's thoughts. I know only that she considers it important enough to instruct someone like me to help you. Don't worry! We are going to have fun together!'

Ysbel wasn't entirely reassured. She knew that this high-grade helper's remit would include reporting on her every move, knew that because of the brittle relationship between natives and humans, and the curbs and checks of the treaty, she was going to have to tread very carefully. She had already won one small victory, insisting that sending an ordinary tapcode message to the address Goodwill had given in his letter, a commercial lodging house in Concord, would be less likely to arouse his suspicions than sending a secure message to the bureau's local station and arranging for it to be hand-delivered. If she was allowed to do things her way, she thought, there was a chance that this might come good.

When the hopper reached the freefall stage of its sub-orbital lob, the pilot – the person who oversaw its autonomous functions – swam into the cabin, manoeuvring with expert grace, asking Ysbel if there was anything she needed. She was the only passenger in the craft, and he seemed to believe that she was a person of power and importance. After she assured him that she was fine, he told her to enjoy the rest of the flight, said that they would be passing over the Sierra Madre mountains in a few minutes and it would be worth taking a look, and executed a perfect roll in mid-air and kicked away.

Ysbel used her link to open a virtual window, was watching rumpled mountains crawl past a hundred and thirty kilometres

272

below when Zaquil's baritone voice said, 'There appears to be a slight problem.'

'What kind of problem?'

'I have just learned that the local station of the Bureau of Indigenous Affairs has taken Goodwill Saltmire into protective custody.'

'They arrested him? How can they have the authority to do that?'

'Apparently, he voluntarily surrendered.'

'Tell them to release him.'

'Unfortunately, I am unable to give direct orders to human people.'

'Then connect me to the station chief.'

'Of course.'

A long half minute of dead air; then Ysbel's link pinged and a woman said briskly, 'It's a pleasure to talk to you, Ysbel Moonsdaughter. I assume you have concerns about your native contact. I can assure you that he came willingly after we explained the situation to him. He is safe and well, and waiting with us for your arrival.'

'There was no situation until you took him in,' Ysbel said.

'I'm afraid that there was,' the station chief said. 'We had information that the embassy was going to approach him. We thought it better to keep it inhouse.'

'It would be better if you didn't interfere with my investigation. How did you and the embassy find out about him?'

'Have you ever kept fish?'

'I've fished.'

'We have a pond in the compound's grounds,' the station chief said. 'Stocked with golden carp, a gift from a wealthy native who wanted us to look favourably on one of his enterprises. He's considered to be useful by the higher powers, so we're stuck with the damned things. They are fed once a day, and as soon as your shadow falls over the water, they crowd in. Mouths opening and closing in anticipation. That's our community here in the capital. Ready to snap up any morsel that might help personal advancement, or promotion of a favourite cause, or simply out of curiosity.'

'If you snapped up my contact because you thought it might win Mother's favour, you've made a bad mistake,' Ysbel said. 'The best thing you can do is release him right away.'

'If we do, the embassy will probably find him before you do, and then you would have to explain yourself to them. What I *can* do is have someone meet you when you arrive, and take you directly to the compound,' the station chief said, and cut the connection.

Ysbel couldn't believe it, asked Zaquil if he understood what had happened.

'I understand you were warned that tapcode messages could be intercepted,' the helper said.

'How would sending a message via the same people who've kidnapped Goodwill have been any better?' Ysbel said.

She was wondering if one of her colleagues had alerted the Concord station. Mitkos was cautious and conscientious and knew more about the map and her mission than anyone else, she wouldn't put it past Landers to try to undercut her to gain some small advantage, either, and although she didn't want to believe that Dalsy was an informant, the woman was a cheerful gossip and might have let something slip.

'I need to talk to Goodwill,' she told Zaquil. 'Can you arrange that?'

'I have full access to the compound's security system.'

'Put me through to him. Can you also arrange transport?'

'Several runabouts are available.'

'Make one ready, and hook me up with Goodwill.'

After a brief delay, a window opened in her link and she

was looking out at a bland, softly lit meeting space. The bailiff, Goodwill Saltmire, was sitting in a human-sized chair on the far side of a display table, legs tucked neatly underneath him, green-tinged shadows shifting across his face as he looked up at the window.

'It's safe to talk,' Zaquil said. 'I had his guard called away, and also spoofed the surveillance feeds.'

Goodwill jumped down from the chair, placed both hands over his heart, bowed slightly and told Ysbel that it was a pleasure to meet her again.

'One of your colleagues showed me how this works,' he said, reaching up to touch the top of the table. 'I have been looking at maps.'

Ysbel moved the viewpoint of her window, saw that the table was displaying a real-time feed patched from satellites, somewhere with snow-capped mountains and forests.

'It is very interesting to look down on the world,' Goodwill said. 'Skimming over territories in the twitch of a whisker. Swooping down until you can see individual trees. Everything laid bare.'

He was dressed in a knee-length brocade shirt and high-waisted black trews, and seemed calm and composed.

'I'm glad to see that you are safe,' Ysbel said, 'but you shouldn't be there.'

'Your colleagues told me that the meeting place we had agreed on was compromised, and it would be safer to meet here.'

'There's been a misunderstanding.'

'You mean that I have been deceived.'

'I'll be landing at the airfield soon. We should meet there. A friend of mine is arranging transport for you.'

'It is done. A yellow runabout is parked outside the main entrance,' Zaquil said.

'Who is this friend?' Goodwill said.

'One of my Mother's little helpers,' Ysbel said. 'A kind of invisible spirit that inhabits and controls machines.'

'Not necessarily invisible,' Zaquil said.

A young man was standing on top of the display table, feet planted amongst miniature forests and mountains. Tall and slender and sharp-faced, long black hair falling to the shoulders of a red leather jacket with intricate tooling. He bowed to Goodwill and said, 'Zaquil, at your service. I have been instructed to help Ysbel Moonsdaughter. And she has asked me to help you.'

'I have heard stories of your spirits and ghosts. I never thought I would see one,' Goodwill said. He had taken a step backwards, but did not seem especially alarmed.

'Second-tier helpers are encouraged to develop a body image,' Zaquil said. 'It helps us to better understand our interactions with people.'

'Were you helping Ysbel before? When she and I first met?'

'I was working on my own then,' Ysbel said. 'Mother became interested later on.'

'Because of the map.'

'We can talk about that when we meet,' Ysbel said. 'There's a runabout, a yellow one, waiting for you outside the main entrance. Just walk out. No one can stop you — it would violate protocol. After you get into the runabout, it will take you to the airfield.'

'If I allowed myself to be deceived, it was because I forgot that humans are sometimes less than honest and honourable. Perhaps you can explain the reason for that deception, and why your Mother has become involved.'

'How much do you know about her?'

'She is your little god, and lives on the Daughter Moon. Is that where this spirit comes from?'

'I am widely distributed,' Zaquil said.

Ysbel told him to be quiet, said to Goodwill, 'Sometimes she takes an interest in our affairs. She heard about the map, and would like to know more about it. The problem is, other people found out about her interest and think they can profit from it. The people who brought you to the station, rivals of theirs . . . When I found out what they had done, I had Zaquil call away your guard and make this connection. He arranged your ride to the airfield, too. We'll meet there and discuss what to do next.'

'And you, Ysbel Moonsdaughter. How are you different from these other people?'

'You hoped you could trust me. And I hope that I can earn that trust. I wanted to help you before Mother stepped in, and I want to help you now.'

'I will meet you at the airfield. And we will talk more.'

'Yes, we will.'

Ysbel watched as Goodwill walked out of the room and followed the long curve of a corridor to a lobby, the viewpoint shifting as Zaquil commandeered a series of bots and cameras. Goodwill talked briefly to two men in the lobby, stepped around them and walked outside into rain seething across the roadway and dancing on the yellow shell of the runabout as its door swung up. Goodwill clambered inside, the runabout began to move off before its door had closed, and the window blanked.

Zaquil was saying that the station had tried to send bots after the runabout, but he had dealt with them, and Goodwill appeared to be enjoying the ride.

'The people who brought him in will guess where he is going,' Ysbel said. 'Keep him safe until I get there.'

The hopper landed in a far corner of Concord's airfield thirty minutes later. Ysbel had left the west coast first thing in the morning, and although it had taken only two hours to cross the continent the time difference between the coasts meant that it was early in the afternoon in the Union's capital. Two runabouts, one yellow, one green, were waiting in warm rain that fell steadily from a low ceiling of cloud. As Ysbel came down the hopper's steep steps, the door of the yellow runabout swung up, revealing Goodwill nested inside. A woman and two men wearing rain slickers stood beside the other runabout, the woman coming forward to meet Ysbel, telling her that she'd made a mistake, but it wasn't too late to fix it.

She was the station chief, a sturdy middle-aged woman with a pugnacious face, bareheaded in the rain.

'What needed fixing is fixed,' Ysbel said, trying to project a confidence she didn't feel. 'Mother will be displeased if you try to meddle again.'

'I looked up your record, Ysbel Moonsdaughter. I fear that you won't be able to stand up to the embassy, even with the aid of the little helper that hacked our security system.'

In Ysbel's head, Zaquil murmured, 'I can write a memo that will give you immunity from further interference.'

It startled her; she had forgotten that the helper would be listening in. She said, 'I thought you can't tell people what to do.'

'Not directly. But I can make use of the system which constrains their actions.'

'Write a memo setting out my authority and my immunity from interference and send it to the ambassador's office. And let my colleague here have a copy too,' Ysbel said, smiling at the station chief, who was listening to her side of the conversation.

'Remember what I told you about the fish? You're going to find out that it isn't just the embassy you have to deal with,' the station chief said.

Ysbel ignored her, and climbed into the runabout beside Goodwill and told Zaquil to get going.

'And where would you like me to take you?' Zaquil said, his voice filling the runabout's dim bubble as it began to roll away from the hopper.

'Anywhere else, to begin with,' Ysbel said. She turned to Goodwill and told him that it was good to meet him again, apologised for the mess he'd been caught up in. 'Some people thought this was too important to be left to me. They know better now.'

'I will be working with you, and only you,' Goodwill said.

'Of course. I can even make my friend go away, if you like.'

'He can stay,' Goodwill said. 'I may have some use for him.'

The bailiff was perched neatly on the bench seat beside Ysbel and seemed be taking everything in his stride. The runabout was passing another hopper. A carriage drawn by two sleek black maras was waiting beside it and a portly native was climbing its steps, followed closely by a servant holding a pyramidal paper umbrella to shelter his master from the rain.

'We gave that hopper to the Committee of the Five Hundred,' Zaquil said. 'I believe the person embarking is one of the committee's delegates. Have you decided where you want to go?'

'There is a friend of mine,' Goodwill said. 'A friend of my uncle, in fact, but he has been very helpful to me.'

'If you give me his address I can take you there at once,' Zaquil said.

'You need to take us to the ferry terminus,' Goodwill said. 'My uncle's friend lives on the other side of the river, in Highwater Reach.'

'Oh, there's no need to wait for a ferry,' Zaquil said cheerfully. 'This runabout can run about on water as well as land.'

8.

The address of Goodwill's friend was one of those poetic native confections — the Bookseller Swift Singletree at the Printworks of the Sign of Bird and Scroll on the Street of the Trees of the White Flowers. Rain was pattering on the broad leaves of the trees, not presently in bloom, as Ysbel followed Goodwill Saltmire up the steep street, past workshops housed in burrows roofed with turf or clay tiles and set amongst small vegetable gardens and orchards of dwarf fruit trees.

They'd left the runabout at the harbour because Goodwill didn't want to draw attention to his friend. Zaquil was listening to chatter on human communications networks in the city and Ysbel had put up two of her bots to watch over this and the neighbouring streets. Although no one seemed to be following or watching them, she was on high alert, wondering why everything had gone so quickly wrong, whether it involved something more sinister than inter-agency rivalry. Something that Mother wanted to expose, perhaps, using the search for the map as bait. Some kind of darkwork against separatists, or a clandestine alliance between humans and natives. She was aware, too, that Goodwill might be leading her to a rendezvous with separatists, but felt a thrilling recklessness. She had got the better of the people who had tried to interfere with her mission before it had properly begun, and for now she was a free agent. Free to help Goodwill in any way she chose; free to ditch him if he tried to sell her out.

A carving of a hawk clutching a scroll in its talons hung above the door of a two-storey building at the top of the street, the walls of its ground floor windowless ragstone, the upper storey constructed from bamboo slats and roofed with plaited reeds. To one side, a narrow passage led to a yard of beaten earth and a square wooden outbuilding; after Goodwill scraped his fingernails down a soundingboard, its door was opened by an old native dressed in an elegant red silk gown and a matching skull cap with two long tassels that hung down his back. Despite his age, Swift Singletree was cheerful and spry, inviting his guests inside, settling them on cushions around a low table, offering a plate of fingerfood and pouring amber tea into thimblecups. His home was sparely furnished. A horn lamp illuminated a large book splayed on the slant of a knee-high lectern; a paper screen partly hid one of the tangles of straw in which natives slept; rush matting covered the floor.

While Swift explained how he and Pilgrim Saltmire had become friends more than forty years ago, Ysbel knocked back her mouthful of tea and picked amongst cubes of blue-black seaweed jelly, bean paste wrapped in fig leaves, fried dough scraps. She'd had nothing to eat all day apart from a tube of fruit paste on the hopper.

'Something more than a shared liking for dusty tomes and obscure knowledge kindled our friendship,' Swift was saying. 'I recognised at once that he was, like me, a pure. Do you know what that is?'

'I have met one or two,' Ysbel said carefully.

'Which was more than poor Pilgrim had, before he found me. He was from some dreadfully remote and unenlightened territory, the only pure in his family and tribe, which was why he had been packed off to the city. I introduced him to our community, and watched him blossom. He was lame in one leg but clever and lively, and deeply loyal to his employer, Master Able, a famous scholar in his time, which was such a long time ago it gives me vertigo to even think about it,' Swift said. 'So do not feel bad if you have not heard of him. He's mostly been forgotten by his own people, such is the new world we find ourselves living in.'

'I wasn't much more than a pup when my uncle died, and remember him as a kindly but somewhat remote presence,' Goodwill said. 'He let me search for fossils in his quarry, showed me how you could collect insects at night using only a lantern and a sheet. And he told stories about his adventures, too. I remember he once said that they turned out to be a smaller part of his life than he expected. I think he was unhappy that he was not taken more seriously.'

'The map might change that,' Ysbel said, wanting to move things forward. 'Especially now that our Mother has taken an interest.'

'She has brought one of her Mother's servants with her,' Goodwill told Swift. 'A kind of spirit that lives in machines.'

'I thought those were no more than tall tales,' Swift said.

'I have seen it,' Goodwill said. 'It helped me escape after some of Ysbel's people invited me to stay with them, claiming it was for my protection.'

'Deploy a couple of your smallest bots, so they can hear me,' Zaquil told Ysbel, and after she had asked Goodwill and Swift to allow the little machines to cling to their ears, a diminished version of his avatar brightened on the table, perching on the rim of one of the bowls, and bowed to each of them in turn.

'This sliver of myself is making use of Ysbel's bot network,' Zaquil said. 'Its low bandwidth means that I can't make this projection any larger without losing resolution. But here I am.'

282

Swift screwed a lens into his right eye and peered at the avatar, then let the lens drop into his leathery palm and looked at Ysbel. 'Is your Mother using this spirit to watch us? Forgive me if I find it somewhat alarming.'

'At the moment, Zaquil and I are independent agents,' Ysbel said. She knew that, in the end, Zaquil served Mother's interests rather than hers or the bureau's, but as Mitkos liked to say, sometimes you had make do with what you had.

'We have been tasked with discovering everything we can about Pilgrim Saltmire's map,' Zaquil said.

'There have been some developments since I wrote to you,' Goodwill told Ysbel. 'To begin with, Joyous Hightower claims that he no longer has the map.'

'When did this happen? Where is it now?'

'You have to understand that I have never met or spoken with him,' Goodwill said, with a flash of acid contempt. 'A person like him having no time for a country bailiff. All of our exchanges involved letters and tapcode messages passed through intermediaries. One or another of the small tribe he pays to help him. I have been trying for some time to raise the legal standing of the map. Hoping that he would do the honourable thing and return it to my family. I had nothing but polite refusals until six days ago, when I received a brief letter saying that the map had been sold to another collector and the matter was closed. I have asked several times about the identity of the new owner, but so far there has been no reply.'

'I asked my friends in the trade if they had heard anything about the sale,' Swift said, 'but had no luck either.'

'I've been given access to the link my people gave to Joyous Hightower, and some leverage that might pry an answer from him,' Ysbel said, with more confidence than she felt. This was already becoming more complicated than she'd expected or hoped. 'I've also been given permission to try to purchase the map, if I can.'

'For what purpose?' Goodwill said, with a wary look.

'I don't intend to keep it,' Ysbel said. 'After Zaquil has examined it, you can return it to your tribe. And I'll need your consent to approach Joyous Hightower in the first place, given that it involves the customs and laws of your people.'

'You wish only to examine it?' Goodwill said cautiously.

'To test its authenticity,' Ysbel said. 'Find out how old it is, and so on.'

'Create a high-resolution virtual copy,' Zaquil said.

'I don't know what that means,' Goodwill said.

'An image,' Zaquil said. 'Zoomable down to the molecular level.'

'That isn't helpful.'

'We'll make a copy for our archive,' Ysbel said. 'You'll keep the original for yours.'

She watched Goodwill think about this. At last he said, 'We must swear an oath of mutual aid. You will help me to recover the map and I will share with you what I've found, and what Swift has found too.'

'Like the map, it suggests a relationship between your people and the bears,' Swift said, popping a nut coated in burnt sugar into his mouth.

Ysbel, in a moment of floating estrangement, saw how different yet strangely human his hands were: the narrow, leathery palms, the blunt fingers and crooked thumb.

'Swift will be our witness,' Goodwill said.

The bookseller wasn't an independent actor, since his discovery was part of the bargain, but Ysbel decided to trust in the natives' ingrained sense of honour. Besides, she reckoned that she had the better part of the deal. She would learn what Goodwill and Swift had found, and still might be able to find and purchase the map without needing their help.

284

'Why not?' she said, and clasped her hands over her heart and used the native form of words to swear that she would use all the resources she possessed to help Goodwill Saltmire as best she could.

'Your turn,' she told Goodwill.

He swore too, looking straight at her.

'Now tell me everything,' Ysbel said.

'I'll begin with a small mystery that may also give us some leverage with Joyous Hightower,' Goodwill said. 'I told you in my letter that my tribe decided against helping me to assert lawful ownership of the map. As did one of my cousins, who serves as chief clerk to one of the delegates of the Committee of the Five Hundred. While I was searching for evidence that might change their minds, I looked into Joyous Hightower's finances. I wondered if he had been involved in any other unofficial auctions, the purchase of other artefacts of dubious provenance, and so on. Anything that might weaken his claim over the map. I found something else instead: he has a majority share in a syndicate that sponsors research into bear history. Paying for exploration and excavation of ruins, giving grants to scholars, donating pieces to the Library of All People, and so on. All very respectable — it won him a place on the Library's council.'

'But I guess you found something that wasn't so respectable,' Ysbel said.

'I did,' Goodwill said. 'The syndicate was also giving grants to improve facilities at the railhead camps where wild bears captured in the New Territories are shipped before being released into bear country. And that's where I discovered something odd. A railhead on the north-west coast had been receiving regular payments long after it had been closed down. There are very few wild bears left in the north-west, and these days any captured there are sent across the mountains to the big railhead in the lake provinces. I have sent two bears there myself, in the course of my duties. Yet when I checked with the collective that runs the railway system all along the coast, I found that several large shipments of construction materials were sent to the railhead ten years ago. And some of the goods were manufactured by your people. Cabins, furniture and so on.'

'Are you sure?'

'Fortunately, the railway collective was zealous about keeping records, and their lading bills were very detailed. After the construction materials were sent to the railhead, it received a number of bear cubs, as well as regular shipments of food and other supplies.'

'Something was built there, involving your people and mine. Something to do with transportation of bears, even though the railhead wasn't open for ordinary business,' Ysbel said.

'Exactly so.'

'Do you know what kind of business it was doing instead?'

'That's what I would like to know. According to the records of the collective, its regular shipments of provisions ceased about a year ago. It may have been shut down and dismantled, but if you have access to maps like the one I was allowed to play with when I was a guest of your friends, they might show something. It may be perfectly legal, of course. But if it is not, if it has violated custom and law, it may be something we can use against Hightower.'

'It shouldn't be hard to find some images of what was built there,' Ysbel said, thinking it was something that she could use to keep Zaquil busy. 'You did some good work, uncovering this.'

'The results were unexpected but intriguing,' Goodwill said, with modest satisfaction. 'And there is something else you may be able to help me with. Something I have been thinking about since I looked up my uncle's writings in my tribe's archives. Before he became entangled in events that led to First Contact, he was trying to complete his master's research into sightings of visitors. As we called you then, before you revealed your true selves. His work involved a visit to the ruins of one of the new cities, where a forest scout saw what he called ghost lights. My uncle didn't know what they were at the time, but years later he paid a visit to the ruins of another bear city. One that some of my people and some of yours were surveying. He took an interest in it because it was the city where his master had excavated a grave mound years before. And that's when he saw the ghost lights for himself.'

'You're saying that the lights seen by that scout may have had something to do with my people.'

'Exactly so. In both cases, they were grids of light laid over the land.'

'Grids of green light.'

'So you are familiar with them. That's good.'

'They're topographic laser scans,' Ysbel said. 'Used to make three-dimensional models of terrain.'

She had seen Ilan's crew use similar kit on one of the islands near Ogres Grave.

'The point being, Joyous Hightower purchased a map that appears to show one of your people next to one of the new cities built in the last days of bear civilisation,' Goodwill said. 'And some of your people appear to have been surveying the ruins of at least one of those new cities before First Contact. I can't help thinking there is a connection, but I do not know what it is.'

'That's what we call a stretch,' Ysbel said, but she was thinking of Trina Mersdaughter and Trina's partner, who was supposedly engaged in field research into bear behaviour. Raia. That was her name. Raia Karysdaughter.

'What we call a bridge built without supports,' Goodwill said. 'Even so, I can't help wondering what your people were looking for, in the new city.'

'Can we do all that?' Ysbel said to Zaquil. 'Search for images and records of this mysterious railhead project, and look up records of that survey?'

'If information is on file, I can retrieve it with little difficulty.'

'And if it's off the books? Hard copy locked in some drawer, say.'

'It will take longer, but it should not be impossible. I will need a connection to a comms net,' the little avatar said. 'This sliver is currently offline.'

'We'll set it up tomorrow,' Ysbel said.

It had been a long day, a lot to take in, but they weren't quite done. Swift wanted to tell her what he had found, and began by handing her a small volume bound in dark-red pebbly leather.

'Open it at the frontispiece,' he said. 'You may find it interesting.'

Native books began at the back, and their pages were read right to left, bottom to top. When Ysbel cracked the little book open at the back cover, it released a pungent musty odour: if time had a smell, that was what it might well smell like. After the title page, printed on heavier parchment with a sheet of translucent paper laid over it for protection, was a map. *The* map. The map that Goodwill had found and lost. A reproduction drawn from memory of a copy of the original. Ysbel, not knowing what else to say, told Swift that it was a handsome volume.

'It is the copy Pilgrim presented to me. He spent a small fortune on his little monograph. Nothing but the best. The best leather for the covers, the best grass paper bound with silk. Notice that the top edges are tinted with silver, and

288

the initial words of each section are hand-drawn and hand-coloured. All that trouble and expense, and hardly anyone read it. No one cared.'

'I care,' Ysbel said.

There was a short silence. The feeling that for a moment another presence had been kindled in the small lamp-lit room. The moment passed, and Ysbel handed the book back to Swift, asked him if the monograph was what had led him to this new discovery.

'Oh no. No. I just thought that you would like to see it,' Swift said. 'Although my discovery is related to it, for it came about while I was attempting to establish the provenance of the map. Pilgrim found it in the Hearth of the original territory of his tribe. It was confiscated by a local lawkeeper, and soon afterwards Pilgrim was caught up in events which led to the day when your people revealed themselves. When all the fuss about that had died down, he returned to the old Hearth, hoping to confront the lawkeeper, but the man had died. His widow had sold the map to a dealer in secondhand goods who failed to recognise its value and sold it on as part of a job lot. Pilgrim could not trace it any further, and despite my best efforts, neither could I.'

'Solomon Firststar claimed that he had purchased it from an itinerant picker,' Goodwill said. 'Supposedly, it had been found in a box of miscellaneous documents purchased when the possessions of an itinerant mara herder were auctioned off after his death.'

'Through one of my contacts, I discovered where the auction had taken place,' Swift said. 'Unfortunately, there is no record of who purchased the box. And I was not able to find the picker who sold the map to Solomon Firststar, either.'

'It is possible that he never existed. And that the herder never owned the map,' Goodwill said.

'A cover story to hide its real origin,' Ysbel said.

'After failing to trace the chain of the map's ownership,' Swift said, 'I tried to find out how Pilgrim's tribe came to possess it. I had only a little hope of discovering anything useful. Forty years ago, when he'd first found the map, Pilgrim had asked me to search the Library of All People for others like it, and for images that might depict ogres meeting bears in the long ago. I looked in every corner and cranny of the public stacks and made enquiries amongst my peers in the trade, but failed to turn up anything of use to my old friend.'

'But he has found something more recently,' Goodwill said.

The two natives were sharing a look. Some kind of cosy complicity or mutual recognition. Like them, Ysbel was sitting crosslegged on a cushion, but her head was only a handspan from the ceiling and she felt clumsy and oversized in the small, spare space, uncomfortably aware that she was the stranger here amongst these strange people in this strange city on this strange Earth. An alien, a fugitive, a guest.

She said, 'This is the thing you think will be of interest to me.'

'You may have noticed the book on display,' Swift said.

'Is the map mentioned in it?'

'The Library of All People was founded on the principle that knowledge should be shared freely, but the librarians soon decided that were some things that should not be shared and created a new set of stacks which the ordinary public could not access. The closed or forbidden stacks. Some of the items are documents which were sensitive or secret at the time of deposition, and can be released only after some specified period of time has elapsed. Others are heretical, sacrilegious or profane, or contain ideas believed to be dangerous. The recipe for gunpowder was famously one of the latter, banned and forgotten until it was rediscovered a century later.

290

'I found the book you see on the lectern in the inventory of one of my fellow dealers, several years ago. It is almost as old as the Library itself, and lists documents and objects that were deposited in the closed stacks in the first twenty-two years after their creation. One of those items is something you may be interested in, because it is related to the mystery of the map.'

'The possibility that your people met with bears long before they met with us,' Goodwill said.

'Why didn't you find this item when you were trying to help Goodwill's uncle?' Ysbel said to Swift.

'I was young and new to my trade, and could only search the public stacks. The closed stacks were off limits.'

'But now you have access. Have you seen this thing? What is it?'

'I know what it is, but I have not yet seen it,' Swift said. 'It didn't seem important at the time. And even now, being only a seller of secondhand books and other trifles, I do not have official access to the closed stacks. I must make use of the connections I have cultivated, and that involves certain expenses.'

'I believe that he means bribes,' Zaquil said. His avatar was still perched on the bowl rim, its elbow on its knee and its fist under its chin.

'I prefer to think of them as gifts,' Swift said.

'Whatever you care to call them, I can pay,' Ysbel said. 'But I'd like to have some idea of what I'm paying for.'

Swift looked at Goodwill. 'Shall I show her?'

'In the spirit of mutual aid,' Goodwill said.

Ysbel knelt beside the old bookseller as he turned the pages of the book. Stiff yellow vellum, dense with black ideographs arranged in vertical columns. Swift explained that it was an old form of administrative shorthand, pointed to one of the entries and said that it was a brief description of a carving found in the ruins of one of the new cities, a depiction of two strange figures standing under a burning star or comet.

'The carving was believed to be a fake, which might explain why it was consigned to the closed stacks.'

'Given that description, and enough time, I can find it using your bots,' Zaquil said.

'How much time?' Ysbel said.

'That would depend on the size of the stacks.'

'I need to see it for myself,' Ysbel said. 'And take a sample, for dating. Bots aren't equipped for that.'

'I can do things with bots you wouldn't believe,' Zaquil said, his smile a starry glint in the miniature avatar's face.

Ysbel looked at Goodwill. 'How much will this unofficial gift cost me?'

9.

Goodwill and Swift shared the straw nest behind the paper screen; Ysbel spent an uneasy night on a makeshift bed of lumpy cushions. While the old bookseller snored like a ripsaw steadily working through an unlimited supply of wood, her sleepless mind churned with fruitless speculation about everything she needed to do and everything that could go wrong, beginning with the call to Joyous Hightower she'd promised to make first thing in the morning, and the implications of the mysterious project in the north-west and Goodwill's story about ghost lights, and how they might be linked to the mysterious figure in the map.

Maybe there was no connection. Maybe the map and the old carving supposedly stashed in the basement of the Library of All People were no more than bear fantasies about sky spirits, and Joyous Hightower's project was a legitimate and entirely native affair. But Ysbel had the feeling that she had stumbled into the margins of a shadowy conspiracy, a rogue operation run by a cloak-and-dagger unit inside one of the departments or something even gnarlier, and her thoughts drifted to the Originists and the spectrum of their craziness. Most were largely harmless, like the old woman who stood every day at the entrance to Central Park, handing out leaflets which explained that during her long voyage Mother had been infected by a parasitic mind which had used her to create replicas of people who walked amongst her real children and were their secret controllers. Or the discussion circles which questioned Mother's story about the failure of the colony she had founded on the Earth-like planet of a distant star, claimed that the seedship could not have survived for two hundred thousand years and tried to prove that Mother could not have built her lunar habitat and quickened the First Generation without some kind of help. Active groups of Originists like the one Ysbel had helped to uncover were rare. But if there really were people involved in the mysterious project in bear country, as Goodwill claimed, they might well be an Originist cabal. Allied with native separatists – why not? – working together to undermine Mother and the Authority, to sabotage the precarious peace between humans and natives . . .

At first light, she stuck her head under a gush of cold water from a handpump in the yard, shouting with the pleasurable shock, and relieved herself behind a flimsy rattan screen, brushing flies from her face with one hand and bracing against the floor with the other because her feet were too large for the indentations on either side of the stinky hole in the ground. She took several turns around the courtyard, rehearsing the conversation with Joyous Hightower, and after sharing a breakfast of strong black tea and cold rice balls and pickles with Goodwill and Swift she went outside again (there were lights in several of the windows of the printworks, now, and the faint regular noise of some kind of machinery) and launched the bot that would provide a line-of-sight connection with the comms net of the embassy on the other side of the river.

Swift politely retired behind the paper screen before Ysbel placed the call to Joyous Hightower, and Goodwill crouched on a cushion out of the view of the little bot that projected the window and acted as a static camera. The bailiff had sworn to keep his peace, but Ysbel was aware of his glowering, close-focused concentration during every second of the short, inconclusive conversation.

Joyous Hightower's link was a prestigious honour as well as an essential business tool. Only a few hundred had been given by the Authority to natives, mostly to politicians and tribal leaders. Ysbel wasn't surprised when he answered her call almost at once, because most of the calls he received would be about his lucrative work, and she quickly introduced herself and told him that she was working for Special Operations.

'I know everyone on this link, but I don't believe I know you,' he said. He was a sleek, slender person, dressed in a rich purple robe and lounging on a couch on a sun-drenched terrace with a view of lawns (a human affectation adopted by wealthy natives) sloping to a ragged treeline and blue ocean stretched beyond the trees.

'We should have met at Solomon Firststar's house,' Ysbel said, hoping to keep him off balance. 'But by the time I arrived you had run away.'

Joyous Hightower cocked his head. Silver strings had been braided into his pelt, hanging in a tangled fringe above his sharp black eyes. 'Then you must be the person who was sent to deal with Trina Mersdaughter. How is she, by the way?'

'She's very well.'

'That's not what I heard. Isn't she back on your island across the ocean, claws clipped, toiling in some dreary administrative post?'

'I heard you sold the map,' Ysbel said.

Joyous Hightower cocked his head the other way. He didn't seem at all off balance; he seemed to be having fun. 'Ah, yes. The map Trina wanted so very much. She didn't get it, and neither will you. You're too late, you see. It's moved on. Flown far, far away.'

'I heard that you sold it. Which is why I'm calling. I'd like to know who you sold it to.'

'Are you working with the rural bailiff? He has been pestering my people about that map for quite some time.'

Ysbel had to stop herself glancing sideways at Goodwill. She said, 'I work for Special Operations. We are willing to match the price you got for the map if you will tell us who bought it.'

'But there's no price to match. I exchanged the map for something else.'

'All I need is a name,' Ysbel said, with the hopeless feeling that she had somehow lost control of the conversation.

'But it was a private deal, you see,' Joyous Hightower said. 'If you approach the map's new owner, they'll know at once that I told you about it. It would damage my reputation and standing. And for no good purpose, because they won't want to sell it to you or to anyone else, not for any price. They don't need the money. They have no use for it.'

'Special Operations is prepared to make a serious offer,' Ysbel said. 'For the map, and the name of the person who owns it.'

'Ah, but I don't want your money either. Not only because of my reputation, but because you were rude to me. Trina Mersdaughter didn't get what she wanted, and neither will you, or Special Operations. If that's who you are really working for.' The black tip of Joyous Hightower's tongue touched his sharp white teeth. 'It's amusing to think that after you return empty-handed you might end up in the same dismal little office where Trina has been caged.'

'You have many contracts with the Authority, supplying materials for various building projects,' Ysbel said, falling back on the script Iryn Moonsdaughter had given her. 'Fourteen, at present. If you co-operate and tell me who presently owns the map, you'll be looked on favourably for new contracts. But things might go differently if you don't.'

Joyous Hightower studied her for a moment and said, 'I rather doubt that someone like you has the power to do something like that.'

'I'm the messenger for someone who does,' Ysbel said.

'Then run back to Special Operations, little messenger, and tell them I won't be bought,' Joyous Hightower said, and cut the line.

'He's about what I expected,' Goodwill remarked.

'What was that?' Ysbel said. She was filmed in sweat and felt slightly filthy after her futile attempt at blackmail.

'A go-between who fears the map's new owner more than he fears your superiors,' Goodwill said.

He didn't seem especially upset about the way the conversation had gone. Perhaps he believed that Ysbel's failure to win anything useful from Joyous Hightower diminished or excused his own.

'Thanks to you, we have another lead,' Ysbel said.

'The railhead project. Do you think your maps will tell us anything interesting?'

'I think you may need more than maps,' Zaquil said, surprising both of them. 'Let me show you what I mean.'

He put up two images of the railhead in the window. A fan of railway sidings with buildings off to one side, dark green forest circled around. One image taken twenty-five years ago, he said, before the railhead project. The other just four years ago, while the project was still active.

'What am I supposed to see?' Ysbel said. 'They look identical.'

'That's the point.'

'You mean nothing was built there,' Goodwill said.

'But what about the construction materials, and the regular supplies?' Ysbel said.

'Exactly what I wondered,' Zaquil said. 'So I widened the search.'

He put up another image: dark green forest cleaved by the silver lightning stroke of a river.

'What am I missing this time?' Ysbel said, after studying the image for a full minute.

'It's more to do with what is missing than what you cannot see,' Zaquil said, and a yellow circle appeared beside the river. 'This part of forest is fake. Or rather, it is part of another image patched onto this. It's very good work, but not quite good enough to fool me.'

'What is it hiding?' Goodwill said. He was peering close at the window, points of green light shining in his dark eyes.

'The fact that something has been erased,' Zaquil said. 'So thoroughly that even I cannot reconstruct it. If you want to find out what it was, you will have to go there and see for yourself.'

'Where is it?' Goodwill said.

'About fifty kilometres due north of the railhead,' Zaquil said. 'Across the border, in bear country.'

'I know one thing about it,' Ysbel said. 'If this satellite image was altered to hide something built by Joyous Hightower's syndicate, it means that some of my people are involved too.'

10.

After Goodwill and Swift went off to organise the gift and other details of the clandestine visit to the Library of All People, Ysbel spent the rest of the morning searching the open records for any mention of pre-First Contact surveys of bear cities, looking everywhere she could but coming up empty. She'd given Zaquil the task of looking for evidence of human involvement in the railhead project, hoping to find something incriminating – a violation of Authority mandates, treaty terms or native custom and law that could be used to persuade Joyous Hightower to give up the name of the map's new owner. Eventually, the helper told her that he hadn't found anything in the open records and would have to dig much deeper, search the sealed registers where details of clandestine and highly sensitive projects were kept.

'I am not the sliver you were making plans with last night. I am the real deal. The true face and the true name. I'm here with you, and I'm in the Gathering Place and I'm on the Moon. If someone has tried to hide the relevant files, I'll find them sooner or later.'

'They might be hidden inside the accounts for some other project,' Ysbel said. 'Or be entirely off the books.'

She started to explain her idea about the involvement of an Originist group, and Zaquil's little avatar twinkled at her.

'I know what to look for, Ysbel. But even for one such as I, these things take time. You must be patient. Meanwhile, is there anything else you need?'

'I've been thinking about the visit to the Library. Can you work up some kind of letter of permission? Something on paper I can wave at the authorities if my presence is questioned.'

'Of course.'

'And maybe you can fetch some lunch, too. It doesn't look like my friends will be back any time soon.'

'That would not be the most efficient use of my resources.'

'I can't go looking for food. The locals will wonder what I'm doing here. Word might spread and reach the embassy or someone else looking to get a piece of this. So while you are organising delivery of that letter, you can work out a way of getting my lunch to me, too. Or is that beneath the dignity of a helper from the second tier of the central cluster?'

'If you doubt my dedication to this undertaking, Ysbel, I can assure you that I will help you to the best of my considerable ability in every way I can.'

It was unnerving to think that she was so transparent to a machine mind, but she wasn't going to apologise.

'I'm stuck here with a handful of cold rice balls is all it is, and no idea when Goodwill and Swift are coming back. I don't suppose,' Ysbel said, 'you know where they've gone? What they're doing?'

'You did not ask me to follow them. And besides, it would have been rude. But if you allow me to make use of your bots, it should not take me long to find out where they are and what they are doing.'

'Better not. As you said, it would be rude. Goodwill trusted me with his findings. I should trust him.'

'Trust is the key to success in matters like this,' Zaquil said, and his little avatar blew out like a candleflame.

While she waited for the letter and her lunch, Ysbel read the transcript of the interview with the witness of the so-called ghost lights in Pilgrim Saltmire's monograph, puzzling her way through the formal text, pleased she didn't have to resort to her link's translator more than a couple of times. It was some way past noon when there was a scratch at the door. When Ysbel cautiously opened it, a young native dressed in a kind of uniform, a long black shirt over baggy trews, handed her an envelope and a neat parcel and pressed his hands over his heart and walked off without a word.

He was one of the native aides employed by the embassy, according to Zaquil. 'I got inside the systems to print out that letter, requisition some vittles and task the youngster with a clandestine delivery.'

'Vittles?'

'Your lunch. Enjoy.'

The letter, written in the common tongue and signed by the ambassador's chief of staff, explained that Ysbel Moonsdaughter was an accredited researcher who wished to examine bear artefacts held by the Library of All People, and asked its staff to give her any help she required.

'I hope that is what you had in mind,' Zaquil said.

'It'll do. You aren't bad at making up stories.'

Lunch was smoked fish and a salad of beansprouts and sweet little tomatoes and a small flask of coffee. Ysbel mixed in the rice balls left over from breakfast and, after she'd eaten, stretched out on the cushions and read the rest of Pilgrim Saltmire's monograph.

She must have dozed off, because she startled awake when Goodwill and Swift came in, bringing news of the arrangements they had made, and the gift for the person who would help them find Swift's old, overlooked carving.

11.

A few hours later, as they were climbing towards the low cliff of the Library of All People, Goodwill asked Ysbel why her Mother and her Mother's servant did not know that some of her people had been secretly working with some of his.

'She isn't omnipresent and all-seeing, like your Mother,' Ysbel said. 'She's more like a bigger, smarter version of Zaquil. Once upon a time, she and her children worked closely together, united by a common plan. A shared goal. We've diverged somewhat, since then. Since First Contact. Her up on the Moon, with her plans. Us down here, with ours.'

'It sounds as if you have distanced yourself from her, much as the separatists want to distance our people from yours.'

'Some people's plans and ideas may have diverged more than others,' Ysbel said, thinking of the Originists again.

She didn't need to show the letter Zaquil had got up to gain entrance to the Library; their contact, a senior librarian named Clarity Forrester, was waiting for them in the entrance hall. He led them through service corridors to his office, where he accepted the gift Goodwill had brought, eagerly untying the double knot of its pale white fabric wrapping so the rest fell open like a blossoming flower, revealing a small stack of paper sheets interleaved with cardboard slips. It was a complete run of the first of the so-called Overlord stories, in which a band of humans who lived in a floating castle had adventures on the surface of the world below, saving hapless natives from criminals or maddened bears, rescuing them from burning buildings, sinking ships, runaway trains and other disasters. Crude tales crudely told, overlooked or scorned by the scholarly community, according to Swift, who had sourced it from one of his bookseller contacts, but collectors like Clarity Forrester believed that they gave valuable insights into populist opinion immediately after First Contact.

Ysbel and Goodwill watched as the librarian picked through the four-sheets with delicate care, sniffing them, holding them up to the light of the floor lamp in the cubbyhole of his office and moving them up and down and side to side a handsbreadth from his face, murmuring his appreciation.

'Very good. Very good indeed.'

Some of the pages of the four-sheets were printed with a grid of pictures, others with a single illustration. Lurid primary colours overspilled the outlines of humans and natives engaged in violent action. Clarity Forrester, a swag-bellied elderly person dressed in the grey tunic and scarlet trousers of his rank, explained that four-sheets like this were printed and distributed clandestinely, to circumvent the disapproval of councils which believed them to be both seditious and blasphemous, and reflected a popular belief that humans were secular gods come to right all wrongs and protect ordinary people from oppression and the consequences of out-of-control techne.

'This particular series is important because it is one of the first examples and most of its print run was seized and destroyed by lawkeepers. Swift Singletree knows me all too well,' Clarity said. 'Helping you is the least I can do for a prize like this, even though it puts me in no small danger. I ask only that you will not mention my name should you be caught.'

'We have never met or heard of you,' Goodwill said, stone-faced. 'But we are grateful, nonetheless.'

Clarity seemed satisfied with that. He rewrapped the stack of four-sheets, handed Goodwill a pass letter for the closed stacks, with the location of Swift's carving written on the reverse.

'I will take you to one of the stairs to the basement levels, but after that you will be on your own. If anyone challenges you, show them the letter and tell them that you are looking for a lost relic of great significance to your tribe.'

He led Ysbel and Goodwill through a maze of offices, all of them empty at this late hour, to the Hall of Stones and Bones. Their footsteps echoed from the high ceilings as they passed display cabinets containing specimens of gemstones, ores and crystals, and crossed a chamber where fossils of every era and articulated skeletons of creatures long extinct were displayed, from ammonites and rare thunder lizards to the chickens whose bones could be found everywhere at the Burn Line. Three skeletons of ogres, two adults and a child, stood in a glass case before a painted backdrop showing an erupting volcano; Ysbel would have liked to linger and read the caption, but Clarity was hurrying on, leading her and Goodwill to an atrium where four hallways met under a dome painted with the starry night sky.

They turned down a corridor lined with ladders of narrow drawers labelled according to some arcane cataloguing system, and at the far end Clarity unlocked an unmarked door and handed Goodwill a wooden baton with a small key hung from one end, explaining that it was for the door to the stacks four levels below, where their prize was stored.

'Return this to me when you are finished, and do not spend too long down there,' he said, and scurried off.

The door opened on a helical staircase sleeved in an iron-work lattice that pierced the understoreys of the Library screw-wise. As she followed Goodwill, stepping carefully on the narrow treads, Ysbel felt a heady mix of trepidation and delight. She was trespassing without official sanction, with no recourse or excuse if she was caught by the local authorities, but she was also descending past vaults stuffed with untold treasures no human had ever seen. Crates and cabinets, tiers of shelving and row after row of stout timber-clad columns painted black and red stretching away in perfect lines of perspective in the dim light of small electric lamps screwed to stone walls. A flotilla of small boats. A traffic jam of carriages. A hut woven from reeds . . .

The Library of All People stretched along the ridge above Highwater Reach, amongst gardens of trees and plants collected from every part of the Union of Civilised Territories. It was the biggest building in the Union, and like an iceberg there was more below the surface than above. Four levels of storage vaults, offices, canteens and staff accommodations, a small clinic and a water reservoir, a tramway that transported goods from docks at the river's edge. All of this had been built many years before First Contact; the electric lighting was a contemporary addition.

The vaults of the first three levels Ysbel and Goodwill passed through stored duplicates and donations that outnumbered by more than a hundred to one the objects and books on display in the public areas. The fourth and lowest level was darker than the rest. No electric lights here, only faint splashes of lamplight piped from some higher level. At the bottom of the stairs Goodwill unhooked a safety lantern and lifted its pierced brass sleeve and lit its wick with a match and handed it to Ysbel before unlocking the door.

She could barely squeeze through the opening, and when she raised the lantern her knuckles grazed the ceiling. The columns here were squarely built with roughly dressed

305

stone blocks. The black unmoving air tasted of dust and trapped time.

Goodwill led the way at a good pace; natives were descended from animals that had been most active after dusk, and their vision in crepuscular light was much better than that of humans. They were passing through a store of artefacts unearthed from the ruins of bear cities. Granite millstones, surfaces cut with different patterns of grooves. Rows of stone pestles and mortars. A huge wooden plough, apparently hauled by a team of slaves. Flint adze heads and chisels, ground stone axe heads. Hundreds of flint arrowheads, diamond or leaf shapes with serrated edges. Harpoon points and knife blades shaped from polished flint, from black volcanic glass. Big wooden clubs, some with sharp fragments of flint or jasper or glass set in their business ends, battle axes with stout wooden hafts and blades of polished jade as long as Ysbel's forearm, and maces crowned with polished cobblestones as big as her head. The bears which had wielded these weapons had been only a little bigger than humans, but they considerably outmatched human strength.

Goodwill and Ysbel left the cabinets and shelves of tools and domestic implements and weapons behind and entered a small forest of the carved wood and stone slabs which had marked the graves of bear royalty. Goodwill said that his great-grandfather, Bearbane, had donated several of these stelae, collected when he had helped Master Able survey the ruins of a bear city and sink a shaft into a grave mound where hundreds of generations of kings and their wives and children had been buried.

'Years later, Bearbane recommended my uncle for the position of Master Able's secretary, and here we are.'

'You are proud of your family's history.'

'Few from my tribe found fame or fortune in the wider world. My great-grandfather was one of them and my uncle

306

was another, although his part in First Contact has been mostly forgotten. My tribe was embarrassed by it, to tell it straight. Especially now, with the growing resentment against your people and the changes they have caused.'

'Your society was already changing,' Ysbel said. 'All we did was help you get where you were going a little sooner.'

'If anything, my tribe has become more conservative,' Goodwill said. 'I was the sixth pup in my family. The youngest. My eldest sister took over the running of my mother's tea business, and like most of the men in my family I was expected to become either a forester or a herder. I lit out for the New Territories instead, and after trying my hand at fishing I became a lawkeeper. My mother says that I am like my uncle. Restless. Curious about the world.'

It was a kind of confession that lay bare the contours of his pride and stubbornness, and Ysbel was touched by the implied trust. She said, 'What happened to the stelae your great-grandfather donated?'

'One is on display in the Hall of Bears and Their Things. I suppose the others must be down here, somewhere.'

'There are certainly a lot of them.'

The slabs, piled in stacks, leaning against pillars or propped upright, were carved with symbolic images of royalty seated on thrones before crowds of miniature subjects abasing them-selves, riding oxen or crocodiles at the head of rivers of soldiers, blessing the sowing of crops and their harvest, sacri-ficing animals or prisoners of war or native slaves to their sun god.

They walked on. Darkness ahead, darkness behind, the lamp Ysbel held like a faint star drifting through the abyssal depths of an ocean of time. The labyrinth of stelae gave way to a store of artefacts from the new cities. Books and furniture and finely decorated pottery and glassware. Tapestries and intricately carved panels more varied and refined than any of the stelae. Huge mechanisms of wood and iron. A case of telescopes and sextants. A celestial globe . . .

Goodwill said that he had been taking note of the numbers on the pillars, and believed that they were close to their prize. 'Do you hear running water? It is one of the streams channelled underground when the Library was built. What we are looking for is on the other side.'

The stream ran at the bottom of a channel lined with stone slabs; a bridge built of wood slats cunningly pieced together without need for nails, bolts or spikes arched above it. On the far side were rows of stone panels which had once decorated the chambers and terraces of bear cities. At first, they were all much the same size, as tall as Goodwill and about twice as long, and like the stelae they were incised with variations of the same few images. Stylised depictions of clashes between armies led by the giant figures of warrior kings, processions and courtly scenes, the sun god blazing through the sky in a chariot pulled by eagles, above the primeval flood which, according to myth, He had burned away to reveal the recreated world and the clay from which He had baked bears and their slaves and every kind of animal. Then Ysbel and Goodwill reached the section where panels from the new cities were stored, more finely carved and more various. Abstract patterns, images of animals and plants, teams of bears using levers and ramps to raise their iconic pyramids, bear artisans manufacturing pottery or glass, or hand-carving wooden blocks and using them in screw-presses to print books.

As he and Ysbel walked along a narrow aisle between two rows of these panels, Goodwill paid special attention to the numbers painted on the squat stone columns that supported the ceiling. They turned left, turned right, passed two more columns and stopped at a gap in one of the rows.

Goodwill studied the letter that Clarity Forrester had given him, turned in a circle. 'It should be here,' he said.

They looked at the gap, at the panels on either side.

'Perhaps it was moved,' Ysbel said.

'It should be here,' Goodwill said again. 'This exact spot.'

He knelt and ran a finger down the groove in the stone floor in which the slab should have been slotted, said that there was no dust. 'Something was resting here until very recently,' he said. 'And someone has taken it.'

'Or perhaps the slab is still down here, but was moved for some reason. Let's look around,' Ysbel said.

Goodwill followed her as she walked to the next pillar, studying every panel they passed. Philosopher bears studying the heavens, grouped around an anatomical dissection, collecting liquids from distillation ovens, harvesting fruit from vines growing in what looked like greenhouses, but nothing that resembled two figures standing beneath a fire star. When they reached an intersection Goodwill turned in a full circle and said, 'One thing is clear: Clarity Forrester made no effort to check that the slab was still here. Strong words will be exchanged when we return to him.'

'Before you leave, perhaps you could allow me to make a more thorough search,' Zaquil said.

'Why not?' Ysbel said. She had forgotten that the helper – or a sliver of his true self, linked to her bot network – had been walking with them all along, a phantom in this grave-yard of bear civilisation.

The mouth of her satchel puckered open and a handful of bots whirled up and scattered into the darkness beyond the little light of the lamp. Ysbel was still explaining to Goodwill what was happening when Zaquil presented her with images of possible hits from two different bots. One depicted a warrior king with a halo of flames around his head; the other a figure standing in a corn field, beneath a swirling cloud of what might be locusts.

'Ignore the figures and look for a kind of comet,' Ysbel said.

As she sketched the fire star in the air with her forefinger, Goodwill tugged at her sleeve, pointed down the shadowy perspectives of the aisle. A cluster of lights was bobbing through the darkness beyond the stream, moving steadily towards them.

12.

Humans and natives separated when they reached the vaulted entrance hall of the Library. A gang of city lawkeepers and Library officials led Goodwill Saltmire towards a stairway; Ysbel's captors, a man about her age and an older woman, hustled her outside and shoved her into a runabout. Ysbel's bots had been confiscated, her link had been forcibly shut down, silencing Zaquil, and the letter of introduction he had got up for her had been ignored. When she asked her captors why they had interfered with a legitimate investigation, they told her that they were working for the ultimate authority.

'If you mean Mother, I'm working for her too,' Ysbel said. 'Someone somewhere has made a bad mistake.'

'That would be you,' the woman said.

Wrists looped together by flex restraints, Ysbel braced as best she could as the runabout rattled down the steep streets of Highwater Reach and splashed into the river. She assumed that she would be taken to the embassy, but the runabout churned downstream to Concord's docks and mounted a slipway and swerved inside one of the godowns.

The man and the woman pulled her out and marched her through the vast gloomy interior to a lean-to office at the rear. An isolation chamber shaped like an egg stood on its blunt end in one corner. Ysbel was pushed inside and forced to sit on the shelf that circled its walls, and the man cut the flex restraints.

'We need to put a few things on record,' he said.

'If you co-operate it won't take long,' the woman said.

They sat opposite Ysbel, knee to knee in the cramped space, and launched into a basic interrogation. Why had she come to Concord? Who had she met? Was Goodwill Saltmire working for her? Were any other natives working for her?

They were calm and confident and scrupulously polite, dressed in black trousers and black tunics cinched with utility belts.

Ysbel said again that she was working with Mother's approval and support, and gave a brief outline of her mission. Her captors already seemed to know most of the story. Knew that she had met Goodwill during the investigation of Trina Mersdaughter's involvement in the wrongful deaths of two natives, knew that Goodwill had recently contacted her and that she had agreed to help him, and knew about Swift Singletree and Clarity Forrester, too. They asked her why she had gone rogue, colluded with natives and ended up in the deepest basement of the Library of All People, where neither she nor any other human person had any right to be. Asked her if she had been in contact with Trina Mersdaughter after the wrongful-death incident, if she had ever reached out to Trina's partner, Raia Karysdaughter.

Ysbel told them that Iryn Moonsdaughter, the agent from Special Operations who had recruited her, and Zaquil, the helper assigned to her by Mother herself, would confirm that she had the authority to investigate the matter of the missing map as she saw fit.

'If you restore my link, I can put you in touch with Zaquil right now.'

'That isn't possible,' the woman said.

'And I'm afraid that your little helper's opinion has no weight,' the man said.

Ysbel said, 'Then go talk to Special Operations.'

'We already have,' the man said. 'They denied that you were working for them.'

'You must realise that you are in very serious trouble,' the woman said.

'It appears that you have been badly misled,' the man said.

'We have to check a few things,' the woman said. 'Don't go anywhere.'

After the door of the isolation chamber had sphinctered shut, Ysbel tried to work out what kind of trouble she was in. Iryn Moonsdaughter had told her that she would be carrying out the investigation on a personal basis; like the fool she was, she hadn't realised until now that it meant she couldn't expect any help or backup. That was bad enough. Worse still was the possibility that Goodwill Saltmire had been playing her all along. That his story about searching for the map and his discovery of some kind of conspiracy involving bears and a secret facility in the far north had been got up as bait. That he was working for the separatists, had used his family's history to entice her into trespassing in one of the places forbidden to humans in order to cause trouble and stir up further resentment.

It was one thing to be wrongfully detained by some spooky security agency because it hadn't been briefed about her mission; quite another to be accused of a serious treaty violation. She remembered Mitkos's warning about the risks of working directly for Mother, and a shiver passed through her like the shadow of an impending illness.

Measureless time passed. Without her link she was isolated in a void of dead air, alone with her thoughts. Even though she knew that it was part of the interrogation process, it was hard to ward off a growing feeling of humiliation and help-lessness, and she felt a pang of relief when at last a patch of the chamber's wall lit up and the image of a woman looked out at her. Long grey hair parted in the centre into two wings framing a strong blunt face; a dark serious gaze.

Ysbel guessed that the woman was someone further up the chain of command, and knew that she had to try to take the initiative. She pushed to her feet and gathered up the rags of her dignity and said, 'If you have confirmed that I am working for Mother, I should not be detained here for one second longer than necessary.'

'I can help you,' the woman said, 'but only if you co-operate.'

'So far no one will tell me who am I supposed to be co-operating with.'

There was an out-of-focus view of white buildings and palm trees behind the woman, most likely somewhere in the Gathering Place. Although Ysbel had somewhat lost track of time, she reckoned that it must be somewhere around midnight in Concord, so it would be late afternoon there.

'My name is Kirder Halmasdaughter,' the woman said. 'I work for Damage Limitation. As long as you tell me every-thing you know we can make a good start at fixing things.'

Ysbel had never heard of an agency called Damage Limitation, and said so.

'Most people haven't, until they get into the kind of trouble that attracts our attention,' Kirder Halmasdaughter said.

'What kind of trouble is that?'

'Failure to obey legitimate commands, wrongful deploy-ment of a helper, unlawful interactions with natives, treaty violations . . . Not to mention trespassing in a place forbidden to us. All this at a time when relations between natives and humans are at their most fragile. When so much is at stake.'

314

'A native asked for my help. That came to the attention of Special Operations, and Mother. They gave me permission and authority to act as I saw fit. If you give me back the use of my link, the helper assigned to me will confirm everything.'

Kirder Halmasdaughter ignored that. 'My job is to fix the damage you have caused. If you co-operate fully and frankly, I might be able to help you. Otherwise, you will have to make proper and full atonement for your trespass. Formally, in the native way, and then by standing before a board of enquiry. That would mean the end of your career, such as it is, and most likely spending the rest of your life working in the recycling pits.'

'What would co-operating fully and frankly involve?'

'Ending the investigation and returning to Ogres Grave. Reporting that the bailiff, Goodwill Saltmire, was in error. That the map purchased by Joyous Hightower was not the map discovered by Goodwill Saltmire's uncle. We will supply a transcript of a tapcode interview with Joyous Hightower and a high-resolution image of the map he purchased, and you will include them in your report.'

'Not an image of the actual map. An image of a fake.'

'It's a genuine map, but lacks the contentious image. You will submit your report, we will placate the native authorities and that will be the end of the affair.'

'You want me to lie.'

'In service of a greater truth.'

'It isn't much of a choice.'

'It's a good deal. The only one you're going to get. You will be helping yourself, and you will be helping Mother, too. We can't intervene directly, of course. None of us have that kind of power. But with your help we can prevent her from blundering into something that could have catastrophic consequences.'

'You want me to lie to her. To work against her, not for her.'

'Even if this was not a critical moment in our relationship with natives, meddling in the matter of the bears to satisfy one of Mother's momentary whims would be ill-advised. Better to tell a small untruth, for the greater good. To protect Mother and her plans for a harmonious union between the natives and her children.'

'What about Goodwill Saltmire? What will happen to him?'

Stupid pride stopped Ysbel asking the woman if the bailiff had been part of a plot to lure her into the Library's stacks.

'How the native authorities choose to deal with him is their concern, not ours,' Kirder Halmasdaughter said. 'I imagine that at the very least he will be stripped of his lawkeeping powers, given that he was instrumental in bribing an official of the Library of All People and entered its stacks without obtaining the proper permissions and documentation.'

'So you've figured out how to silence both of us.'

'My people will speak to you again. Not for any accounting of your misconduct – that has already been done – but to make sure you understand what you need to do to save yourself, and that there are no other fires we need to fight,' Kirder Halmasdaughter said, and the window shut down.

Ysbel assumed that the interrogation would resume straight away, but for a long while nothing happened. Her captors probably believed that another stretch of isolation would soften her up, give her time to realise that her best chance was to co-operate, end her investigation and deceive Mother with a bogus report, but she reckoned that there might be a way of getting out of this. As far as she was concerned, a promise to co-operate meant nothing if it was coerced, and the talk of helping Mother by lying to her didn't feel right. There was something else going on, some other reason why Kirder Halmasdaughter and her agency, Damage Limitation, wanted to shut down the investigation. Ysbel could play along, tell the woman's lackeys that she'd do everything they asked and answer all their questions – it seemed like they already knew most of what she could tell them anyway. And when they let her go, when she had her link back, she could put Zaquil on the case. Discover everything she could about this mysterious agency. Find out if it had the map bought by Joyous Hightower, and if he had been working for it all along. And she'd get back in touch with Goodwill Saltmire, and go take a look at that secret project in bear country. Maybe Damage Limitation had something to do with that, too. And maybe, just maybe, Mother had another agenda all along, had sent Ysbel after the map so that her search would flush out bad actors.

It wasn't much of a plan – its chances of success were slim, and however it worked out she'd still have to answer for trespassing in the Library's stacks – but if she was able to get at the truth of the matter it might be enough to save her. The decision eased her sense of helplessness and vulnerability, gave her the feeling that she had taken back some control. She stretched out on the bench as best she could and must have dozed off, because she jerked awake when the window opened again. There was a view of ocean waves rolling out to the horizon under a blue sky stacked with white clouds, and something flying above the waves, approaching at speed.

A fly-speck, a flung ball, a floating head. The head of Zaquil's avatar. His twinkling smile filling the window, his voice saying merrily, 'Don't worry! I'm here to help!'

13.

Ysbel squashed the impulse to stand up when the door of the pod puckered back, told Zaquil that she wasn't going to leave until she had the answers to some questions.

'The window for escape is small and rapidly shrinking, so it would be best to defer those questions for now,' the helper said. 'I have spoofed external connections, and borrowed a security bot from the embassy. Darts from its array of non-lethal weaponry have rendered your captors unconscious, but they will not be unconscious for long, and I cannot stick them again because another dose of incapacitant might be lethal.'

Ysbel crossed her arms and gave Zaquil's image a hard stare. 'There are things I need to know. To begin with, are you really working for Mother?'

'Now and always.'

'Do you know what she wants? Not what she asked me to do, but the real point of all of this.'

'There's a question.'

'If you don't know,' Ysbel said, 'there's no shame in admitting it.'

'I was tasked to help you to find out the truth about the map. I do not know why. But if I am permitted to speculate?'

'Go ahead.'

'Aside from the implications for the relationship between humans and natives, Mother may be interested in the possibility that another seedship returned to Earth before she did. In what its Mother may have done, and what may have happened to it.'

'I suppose that's possible,' Ysbel said, thinking of the radio telescope Mother had constructed on the far side of the Moon.

'It is a best guess based on available information,' Zaquil said. 'Are we done now? Your captors will wake soon.'

'What do you know about Damage Limitation, the agency they work for? And Kirder Halmasdaughter, the woman who seems to be in charge of it.'

'I can find no records of anyone by that name, or her agency. As for the godown, it appears to have been rented by Management and Supply. It is possible that you have encountered a group of Originists who want to get hold of the map, or a special-interest group within the high echelons of the Authority. One of a number of projects and entities which fail to properly inform Mother about their activities.'

'I haven't been able to find the map. I caused a diplomatic incident when I tried and failed to find something related to it. Why does she still need me?'

Ysbel was tired and bitter and angry. She felt like a hostage to fortune, used by both sides with little or no agency of her own.

'That involves decisions to which I am not privy,' Zaquil said. 'You really should leave now. I have taken control of your captors' runabout. It will take you where you need to go.'

'And where is that?'

'To the airfield, of course. You and Goodwill Saltmire need to leave the city before you get into more trouble, and I imagine that you want to find out what is hidden in the forest in bear country.'

'You freed Goodwill?'

'Let's say I persuaded him to do the right thing.'

319

'You did all this without consulting me.'

'You were otherwise occupied. And I have every confidence that you would have made the same choices.'

'That's not the point,' Ysbel said. She was especially irritated because the helper had guessed right about what she wanted to do. 'Don't act without my permission again.'

'Of course not,' Zaquil said, not sounding the least bit chastened. 'If you have no more questions, I suggest you climb aboard the runabout.'

'Restore my link first. And give me back my bots.'

'It would be best to keep your link switched off for now. In case it could be used to trace you.'

'These people. Damage Limitation. They can do that?'

'Since I do not know who they are or what powers they possess, it would be best to err on the side of caution. As for your bots, I am afraid that I was unable to locate those which were taken from you, but I still have control of the one I was using in the Library's basement. It's waiting for you in the hopper,' Zaquil said.

'You have a hopper?'

'How else are we going to reach bear country? Don't worry, Ysbel! Everything is in hand,' Zaquil said, and the window closed.

The man and the woman who had taken Ysbel into custody were sprawled face-down on the floor of the lean-to. Their runabout was parked outside the door, and the security bot Zaquil had commandeered hovered above it, knife-shaped and about two metres long with a pair of stubby wings studded with softly whirring rotors. The runabout raised a door as she approached, and sped out of the godown as soon as she had climbed inside, ploughing upriver to the airfield and zipping across hectares of scorched concrete to a hopper gleaming white and silver in crossing searchlight beams.

Goodwill Saltmire greeted Ysbel as she ducked through the hatch into the hopper's cabin. She took the seat next to his and as the crash webbing flowed over her told him that it was good to see him again, and meant it. 'Did Zaquil tell you where we are going?'

'To find this mysterious project in bear country.'

'And you're happy to come along.'

'My people are involved in it, as well as yours,' Goodwill said. 'And I have not yet given up hope of discovering the extent of Joyous Hightower's wrongdoings.'

'I'll locate whatever they've been trying to hide out there on our way down,' Zaquil said, his voice booming in the cabin, 'and deliver you to the front door.'

The launch warning softly chimed and the cabin's lights dimmed. A peremptory rumble of the hopper's motor shivered its frame and deepened into a full-throated roar; a giant invisible hand gently and inexorably pressed Ysbel into her chair as the hopper flung itself away from the world on a spear of flame.

Goodwill had squeezed his eyes shut and gave no sign that he heard her when Ysbel told him that she hated this part but it would soon be over. A brief fierce vibration blurred her vision as the hopper went supersonic, and soon afterwards the g-force peaked and began to slide away, smoothly easing into weightlessness, and the motor's roar cut out.

'We're on our way,' Zaquil's voice said cheerfully. 'ETA is seventy-two minutes.'

Ysbel looked over at Goodwill again, asked him how he was doing.

'I once saw one of your sky boats take off. I thought it would be noisier.'

'They leave most of the noise behind,' Ysbel said.

'And weight, too,' Goodwill said, lifting his hands, letting them hang in the air.

'We haven't escaped the pull of the world's gravity,' Ysbel told him. 'It will bring us down soon enough. You feel weightless because you are falling at the same rate as your chair and everything else in the hopper. There's nothing to push or pull on your body.'

'Is this how you usually travel?'

'Only when the budget allows it,' Ysbel said, and asked Zaquil to give them a view.

The cabin vanished. Ysbel and Goodwill were hanging above the vast dark curve of the planet's nightside. The bailiff shouted out and buried his face in the crook of his elbow.

'Just a window will do,' Ysbel told Zaquil, as calmly as she could.

The cabin came back and its lights dimmed and a window opened in the air: the dark map of the world stretching away under a pitch-black sky filled with stars, moonlight gleaming silver on the ocean to the east, the cock-eyed sliver of the Moon slowly but noticeably sinking towards the curved horizon.

'You must feel like spirits,' Goodwill said.

'We feel privileged,' Ysbel said, and asked Zaquil to show them where they were going.

The view of the landscape beneath the hopper shrank to show the entire globe, which rotated to show the west coast of the New Territories, a red dot appearing high in the north. While Goodwill studied their destination, Ysbel told him about her incarceration and interrogation. He liked her idea that Joyous Hightower might be helping Damage Limitation, acting as an agent or go-between in the acquisition of the map, and told her that Zaquil had hidden one of her little machines in his clothing when they had been caught in the Library's stacks.

'After I gave a statement to the Library's gatekeepers and was taken to its strangers' lodge, he used it to tell me what

322

he had arranged. I walked out of the lodge, one of your carts was waiting for me and here I am.'

'Were you charged with anything?'

'I am supposed to meet with the gatekeepers for further questioning in the morning. No doubt they will add that to my misdemeanours. I regret breaking my compact with them, but think it was for a greater good.' Goodwill paused, then added, 'My uncle was involved in an incident in which another party was injured, and he was sentenced to exile in my tribe's original territory, in the far south. He found the map there, believed that what it might mean was important and broke the terms of his sentence. And now I have done something similar.'

Ysbel knew that natives accused or convicted of crimes were expected, as a matter of personal honour and social convention, to appear before councils and tribunals and accept their punishments without need for enforcement or coercion. But she couldn't help wondering if the bailiff had been able to escape so easily because he had been working for the authorities all along, or if he had agreed to work for them after his arrest. She needed to discuss that with Zaquil. The helper was clever and powerful, but when it came of matters of trust she felt that he was somewhat naive.

She asked Goodwill if he knew who had betrayed them, and he told her that it was his fault.

'The city lawkeepers had been keeping watch on me, and I did not see it. They thought we were going to steal something from the Library, and warned its gatekeepers. Who waited until after we had entered the closed stacks because they wanted to catch us in the act. They were very amused,' Goodwill said, 'when I told them that the thing we wanted to find was missing.'

'It wasn't your fault,' Ysbel said, thinking that in spite of Zaquil's overwatch she might easily have been the one who had been tracked, by the embassy, Damage Limitation or some other player. She'd been a fool, had failed to take the station chief's warning seriously and blundered into a trap.

Goodwill was saying that the gatekeepers had also arrested Clarity Forrester. 'And they brought Swift in for questioning.'

'What did you tell these gatekeepers?'

'The truth, of course,' Goodwill said, with simple, sincere dignity.

'What we were looking for, and why? The whole story?'

'I did not tell them about the project in bear country. Hopefully, neither did Swift. For if he did, the gatekeepers and your people may be waiting for us there.'

'They'll certainly be waiting for us when we return. So let's hope we find something useful,' Ysbel said.

'Yes, let's. Especially as I have set my honour against it.'

Presently, a point of light flared at the edge of the planet's dark curve, spreading out and defining the atmosphere's thin shell, and then the sun rose, illuminating chains of snow-capped mountains. Goodwill was leaning as far forward as his webbing would allow, eyes shining, mouth agape. Ysbel told him that they were watching a sunset in reverse because the hopper was travelling so fast it was overtaking night's boundary. Mountains and forest and more mountains poured beneath them, and then the rim of the ocean appeared to the west and the hopper's motor roared and deceleration pressed her into her seat.

'I believe that I have found what we are looking for,' Zaquil announced, and the hopper's motor roared again and the world spun through a hundred and eighty degrees and rose to meet them. Goodwill shouted out, Ysbel glimpsed the crooked slash of a river cutting through endless forest and then they were down.

14.

The hopper had set down on a broad sweep of gravel in a bend of a swift shallow river. Pine forest crowded along both banks; far off to the east, mountain peaks floated in the sky. In a corner of the window displaying this view Zaquil put up an image of the place that he had spotted. A large square cut into dense forest, a row of burrows and footprints where rectangular structures had once stood, paths wandering between overgrown fields and rough pasture, the black gleam of a solar panel array.

'I took the liberty of bringing the security bot with us,' Zaquil told Ysbel and Goodwill. 'It is over the camp now. There is a rudimentary electrical system, but no power is being drawn and I haven't spotted any inhabitants.'

'Perhaps they ran away when they saw our sky boat,' Goodwill said. 'Perhaps they are hiding in the forest.'

'They would not have had time to run very far,' Zaquil said. 'And the security bot is equipped with infrared, microwave and ultrasonic sensors.'

'My people are good at hiding,' Goodwill said stubbornly.

'We need to take a look,' Ysbel said.

'I will keep watch, ready to intervene in the unlikely event you walk into trouble. We can stay in touch via your bot,'

Zaquil said, and the little machine dropped out of the air and settled on Ysbel's arm with the dainty precision of a dragonfly.

'Don't do anything unless I tell you,' Ysbel said.

'Even if you appear to be in immediate danger?'

'If I am, I'll yell.'

Cool air, the clean scent of pine trees. Running water murmuring to itself. Birdsong. Sunlight slanting low and golden; shadows deep and dark under the trees. The hopper had left Concord a little after midnight and it was late in the evening here, an hour or so before sunset and the brief night of boreal summer.

Ysbel and Goodwill hiked through pine trees and sparse undergrowth to a broad stretch of grass and dirt and a double-wire fence at the boundary of the big square clearing. Two deer standing hock-high in tawny grass turned one after the other and bounded away, white rumps flashing, and disappeared into the dark beneath the trees.

They followed the fence and found a pair of sliding gates. The outer gate was shut but unlocked, and took a little muscle to push open because weeds had choked its rollers; the inner gate stood open. The row of burrows, their mouths stoppered with rammed earth, the turf humped over them brown and withered, were enclosed by a secondary fence topped with razor wire, and the small grid of rectangular concrete foundations of cabins or huts stood close by in a square of weedy compacted dirt. It seemed that both natives and humans had been living there, but who had been the guards and who had been the inmates?

Strip fields gone to weeds stretched towards the far side of the clearing, their boundaries marked by ditches and gravel paths, and the vanes of a windpump turned uncertainly in the soft breeze. As they approached it, Goodwill pointed out a patch of a rambling groundvine, the good-for-all plant

326

whose roots were commonly used by natives to make tea. There were orphan sweetroot and starchroot plants amongst the grass and weeds, too.

A flock of small grey birds flared up from the concrete tank at the foot of the windpump and circled away. The tank brimmed with clear water. Ysbel drank a couple of palmfuls, savouring the cool mineral taste, splashed her face and neck, and turned to study the patchwork of pasture and strip fields. The sun hung a handspan or so above the trees to the west and the sky was darkening and the first stars were pricking through. She felt no anger or disappointment, only a kind of calm resignation. As if it was inevitable that this lead would peter out in an empty clearing in the middle of a wild forest.

'I wonder how long has this place been abandoned,' she said.

'Not very long, I think,' Goodwill said. 'A year at most, which tallies with the cessation of supply shipments.' He seemed resigned, too.

'It looks like one of the work camps where lawbreakers repay their debt to society,' Ysbel said.

'Apart from the burrows, I think it was built by your people,' Goodwill said. 'The slabs which drink sunlight and turn it into electricity are your techne, not ours. And we would not have put a fence around it.'

'Perhaps the fence was built to keep things out, rather than keep people in,' Ysbel said. 'We're in bear country, after all.'

'By the breadth of a whisker.'

'Even so, and even though I know Zaquil is watching over us, it gives me a queasy feeling.'

Goodwill turned in a full circle, surveying the desolate fields. 'If your people built this place, what role did Joyous Hightower's syndicate play?'

'They could have acted as middlemen, paid to purchase native construction materials and transport them to the railhead,' Ysbel said. 'Those payments may be recorded in our accounting system as something else, a grant to expand a manufactory, a fee for services rendered, but I can ask Zaquil to take a look.'

She thought it likely that the money had come from one of the general funds, or had been transferred through some kind of cut-out that rendered its origin untraceable, but they had little else to go on at this point.

'It has clearly outlived its purpose, whatever that was,' Goodwill said. 'Perhaps this is a sign that I should go home. I miss my family. My partner and my pups.'

'How many do you have?'

'Three. Two sons and a daughter. One of my sons is still in the communal Hearth. The other two are old enough to live with us.'

'So you and your partner live together all year round?'

'Like many in the New Territories, we are disgustingly modern. Do you have any pups?'

'Not yet.'

'You are the right age, I think. If you don't mind me saying so.'

'Perhaps I haven't found the right person yet.'

'Fortunately, my family took that responsibility. One of the old ways we have not given up. And in my case they made a very good choice.'

They were walking back towards the gate when Zaquil's voice buzzed in Ysbel's ear. She had almost forgotten about the bot clinging there – the last of her bots; she was going to have to answer for losing the others when she got back to Ogres Grave.

'Someone is approaching,' Zaquil said.

'One of ours or one of Goodwill's?'

Ysbel had stopped walking; Goodwill stopped too, asking her if there was a problem.

'It seems that we have company,' Ysbel said. She was looking towards the fence, shading her eyes against the glare of the setting sun, hoping that the intruder wasn't a bear. They had left both gates open . . .

'A human woman,' Zaquil said. 'Coming up through the trees, making straight towards the clearing.'

'Is she alone?'

'As far as I can tell.'

Ysbel told Goodwill that one of her people was approaching, asked Zaquil how the intruder had managed to slip past him.

'She may have crossed the river and skirted around the hopper. Do not fear for your safety. As soon as she presents a clear target the security bot can take her down.'

'Don't do anything to antagonise her. She may know what this place was and where its inhabitants have gone,' Ysbel said.

When she and Goodwill reached the gates, they found the intruder standing in the tall grass outside the fence, a lean, dark-skinned woman in her late thirties, dressed in shorts and a canvas shirt, a mass of black curls held back from her face by a red bandana. She held up her empty hands, palms facing outwards, and said, 'You aren't the kind of visitors I was expecting.'

'Do you work here?' Ysbel said. She and Goodwill were standing just inside the outer gate. 'Are you the caretaker, something like that?'

'Does it look like anyone works here, anymore?' the woman said. A small pack rode high on her back. A tranquilliser dart rifle, a narrow pipe barrel with a gun grip and telescopic sight, was slung over one shoulder. 'How did you find this place?'

Ysbel introduced herself and Goodwill, told the woman that she was with the Bureau of Indigenous Affairs, thinking that mention of Special Operations might alarm her, make her zip up.

'And your friend — does he work for the bureau too?' the woman said.

'We have interests in common,' Goodwill said. 'May I ask who you work for?'

'Survey and Surveillance, Behavioural Science section,' the woman said, and placed her hands over her heart in native fashion. 'I'm Raia. Raia Karysdaughter.'

It took Ysbel a few moments to place the name. 'You're Trina Mersdaughter's partner.'

'You know Trina? Did she send you here?'

'That's one of the things we need to talk about,' Ysbel said.

15.

They used wood broken from the bleached carcasses of trees deposited by floods in winters past to build a fire at the downstream point of the gravel bank. The vast slow sunset was fading above tree-clad ridges on the far side of the river; frogs creaked and chirped each to each; squadrons of mosquitoes flitted through the still air. The mosquitoes didn't seem to bother Goodwill and Raia, but Ysbel made liberal use of a spray bottle of repellent Zaquil supplied, along with ration boxes from the hopper's store. Raia contributed salmon jerky and sour wild cherries, and devoured a container of tofu and fried rice, saying that it made a welcome change from jerky and line-caught trout.

She had been doing field research on bear behaviour and culture every summer for four years, in an area around a sea inlet more than three hundred kilometres to the north. Part of a small, discreet project to gain some understanding of the bears, and the ethical and political problems raised by their existence. Most people thought they were fierce, solitary predators that only met their peers to mate or fight, Raia told Ysbel and Goodwill, but they decorated themselves with pigments and shell ornaments, made dot-and-line carvings on rocks and tree trunks and passed down rituals and customs from generation to generation: evidence that they possessed the kind of complex symbolic cognition that made humans human, and people people. The local bears mostly avoided the boundary of her camp site, which she protected with electric wires, noisemakers and pepper-spray mines, and she took care to keep her distance too, observing them with bots and fixed cameras. In all the time she had spent in bear country she'd never had to use her rifle. There had been a few close encounters with juveniles who hadn't established their own patch, but as long as you respected them and took care not to trespass on their territories, she said, most bears would return the favour and leave you alone.

She had been keeping watch on the camp, as she called it, for more than six weeks now. She told Ysbel and Goodwill that she hoped that some of its former inmates might still be in the area, but wouldn't explain who had been living there, or what its purpose had been.

'I need to know that I can trust you before I tell you anything else,' she said. 'Perhaps you can tell me how you discovered it.'

'I stumbled across it when I was looking for something else,' Goodwill said.

'The map your partner wanted to buy,' Ysbel said.

Raia's gaze sharpened. 'How did you find out about that?'

'I was sent to investigate Trina's involvement in the deaths of two fisherfolk,' Ysbel said. 'Goodwill was the local bailiff.'

'That stupid race,' Raia said. 'Trina told me all about it after she was sent back to the Gathering Place.'

'When I talked to her, she told me that the map might be relevant to a project she was involved in,' Ysbel said. 'I'm wondering now if it might have something to do with your work.'

'Behavioural Science keeps track of the market in antiques. Things that shed light on bear history and their lost civilisation,'

Raia said. 'That's how we found out about the map a dealer had put up for sale.'

'That would be Solomon Firststar,' Ysbel said.

'He's made a small fortune playing us against wealthy collectors,' Raia said. 'Trina wanted to get a close look at the map, to do some simple tests to find out whether or not it was genuine. So she got in touch with him, made her interest known. Luckily, he didn't bother to check her out. If he had, he would have found out that she wasn't on official business, and didn't have the funds to make a bid. He invited her to that party because he thought that he could use her interest to inflate the asking price, but although she got a good close look at the map, he wouldn't let her scan it, or take a sample.'

'Which is why she goaded Joyous Hightower, the person who bought the map, into racing her,' Ysbel said.

'If I had known what she'd planned to do I would have done my best to talk her out of it,' Raia said. 'Though I don't know if I would have been successful. Trina always likes to take things right to the edge.'

'She turned herself in to Survey and Surveillance after I interviewed her,' Ysbel said. 'As far as I was concerned that was the end of it. But while Goodwill was making sure that Joyous Hightower made proper amends for the deaths of the two fisherfolk, he discovered that the map had once been belonged to his tribe.'

Goodwill told Raia that his uncle had written a monograph about a similar map he had found and lost, and Solomon Firststar had confirmed that a sketch in that monograph resembled the map he had sold to Joyous Hightower.

'The map was stolen from Pilgrim after he found it in the abandoned library of my tribe's former Hearth, and after I discovered that it had been the prize in that fatal race I set out to reclaim it,' Goodwill said. 'I believed that it would help to redeem my uncle's work, and give him the place he deserved in my tribe's history, and the larger history of our people. And now it seems that it is part of a very different story.'

'Goodwill wanted to bring a legal case against Joyous Hightower. A claim of prior ownership. He wrote to me, thinking that I could help, and his letter caught Mother's attention,' Ysbel said, and told Zaquil that it was time to show himself.

Raia's self-control was good; she barely flinched when the helper's avatar materialised, human-sized and translucent, perching on a tree trunk at the edge of the flickering circle of firelight.

'Is that what I think it is?' she said to Ysbel.

'Second tier of the central cluster,' Ysbel said.

'Why is Mother interested?' Raia said.

'Have you seen the map?' Zaquil said.

'Trina sent me an image.'

'What do you think it shows?'

'Bear cities, and what may or may not be a human figure.'

'Possibly making contact with bears, before bear civilisation collapsed. Before the seedship returned and Mother quickened the First Generation. Hence her interest,' Zaquil said. His avatar's smile glimmered in the gathering darkness.

'Do you know why Hightower bought the map?' Raia said. 'Why he was interested in it?'

'He claims to have exchanged it for something else, but won't say who has it now,' Ysbel said. 'I think he may have been acting as middleman for an outfit I ran into – Damage Limitation. Ever heard of them?'

'Not until now,' Raia said. 'Who are they?'

'They believe that Mother's interest in the map could cause all kinds of political problems,' Ysbel said.

'Because of what it seems to show.'

'Exactly.'

'I still hope to find it, and return it my tribe,' Goodwill said. 'And since Joyous Hightower was also involved with the construction of this camp, finding out what happened here may be of some help.'

'If you can enlighten us, you will have Mother's eternal gratitude,' Zaquil said. 'That is no small thing.'

Raia looked out across the dark running water of the river as she thought about that. 'I'll have to talk to someone before I tell you anything else.'

'To Trina?' Ysbel said.

'I can arrange it,' Zaquil said. 'Quick as thought.'

'Not Trina,' Raia said. 'The person who told me about the camp.'

'Someone who worked there?' Ysbel said.

'A former inmate,' Raia said. 'And that's all I'm going to say until I've told him about you.'

16.

Raia bedded down by the fire, saying that bears mostly avoided the camp and her bots would spot any that strayed too close, but Goodwill and Ysbel preferred to retire to the hopper. Not only for safety, but also because they wanted to discuss what they had learned.

'This friend of hers is most likely some crazy old bear trapper,' Goodwill said, after they had climbed aboard. 'There are many such these days, now that bears have been mostly cleared from the New Territories. Loners who have lost their livelihood and refuse to join the border patrol, or find a patch of land and settle down. Who have little liking for other people, and even less for civilisation. I had to deal with one such who came into town, offering to deal with a rogue bear which was, according to him, responsible for the deaths of maras on several local farms. There was no bear – the maras had been killed by a spotted cat – but he believed that he knew better. He was consumed by a fanatical obsession with his prey, half love, half hate, claimed to have killed more than fifty rogues and wore a coat made from the hide of one of them. There is a league of former bear trappers who try to help those like him, but he refused my offer to refer him to them. All I could do was give him a meal and a bed for the night, and move him on.'

'I think Raia would know if her friend was crazy,' Ysbel said. 'And even if he is, it won't cost us anything to give him a hearing.'

'I'm also reminded of one of my uncle's stories,' Goodwill said, with the stubborn look Ysbel was growing to know all too well. 'The people of the place where he was exiled, in the far south, kept up several old traditions, including setting dogs against bears that they had captured. A kind of sport. My uncle witnessed one such contest and believed that the bear might have been pleading for its life. But it was impossible to know, he said, because it may have been that he was projecting onto the bear what he wanted to hear. And even if bears could speak, and we could understand their speech, could we ever really understand their minds, and what it is like to be a bear?'

'Do you think we really understand each other? Humans and people.'

'I know that most of you mean well most of the time,' Goodwill said, showing his teeth to let her know that it was meant to be a joke.

Raia left to meet her friend early the next morning, after asking Ysbel to promise that neither she nor Zaquil would attempt to track her. 'I spotted your security bot before I came in to meet you. I don't want it following me.'

Ysbel promised that it wouldn't, and told Zaquil to promise too, but after Raia had left, walking upriver to the place where she had stashed her canoe, the helper said that it would be a good idea to follow her anyway. 'The possibility that she is in league with the people who built the camp is slight, but definitely non-zero.'

'Raia has bots too,' Ysbel said. 'She made a point of mentioning them. If they spot an attempt to track her, it will undo the trust we've established.'

'May I at least continue to monitor radio frequencies?'

'I don't remember asking you to do that,' Ysbel said, with a stab of exasperation.

'I thought it a sensible precaution,' Zaquil said. 'In case the woman, out of malice or fear, or some calculus of self-interest, is planning to betray us. So far she has sent no signal that I could detect, but she may think it safer to do so when she has put some distance from us.'

Ysbel thought about it, couldn't see what harm passive eavesdropping would do. 'All right. Keep listening. Is there anything else you haven't told me?'

'I want only to help, Ysbel,' Zaquil said blandly.

'Fine. But don't do anything else without consulting me.'

After Ysbel and Goodwill had eaten breakfast beside the warm ashes of the fire, the bailiff collected long dry stems of grass and began to plait them into fish traps – you tied a scrap of bait at the closed end, he explained to Ysbel, and when fish of the right size swam in they couldn't turn around or back out. She couldn't tell if he was worried about putting their trust in Raia, or if he felt that it was a necessary risk. It was a common belief that natives were by nature impassive and stoical, but in Ysbel's experience their apparent stoicism was more often a disciplined pretence of indifference to the bumptious giants who, claiming to mean well, carelessly scattered gifts that changed the world in ways that were hard to understand or predict and cheerfully blundered through the intricate protocols and customs which maintained native society's harmonious balance.

As for herself, she was too restless to sit around while waiting for Raia to return, and walked up through the trees to take another look at the camp. Kicking around the footings where buildings had once stood, searching for traces of the former inhabitants and failing to find anything, and walking the four sides of the camp's fence, pausing now and then to study the shadows under the trees beyond the perimeter.

338

About halfway around, Zaquil spoke via her bot, telling her that he could see no sign of natives or humans out there.

'I'm not really looking for anything in particular,' Ysbel told him. 'Just passing the time.'

'You should have asked the woman how long it would take to persuade her friend to talk to us.'

'I imagine it will take as long as it takes. You have remarkably little patience for a machine mind.'

'I am goal-orientated, and currently lack any goals.'

'The longer she stays away, the more likely it is that she and her friend know something useful,' Ysbel said, and was glad that Zaquil did not question her dubious logic.

When she returned to the river she found that Goodwill had relit the fire and was broiling several small fish, gutted and flattened, on a flat rock he'd set in the flames. They shared them out and ate them whole, heads and all. Goodwill crunched up and swallowed the small bones; Ysbel picked them from her teeth. Afterwards, they dozed by the fire, Goodwill sprawled face-down on a tree trunk, Ysbel on a stretch of sand.

She woke when the bot began to vibrate in her pocket.

'Heads up,' Zaquil said.

Goodwill was standing on the tree trunk and looking towards the river. As Ysbel got to her feet a canoe came around the bend. Raia was sitting in the middle, paddling aslant the main current, grounding the canoe at the edge of the gravel bank and springing out of it and pulling it halfway out of the water. She told Ysbel and Goodwill that she had convinced her friend to meet with them, but still wouldn't say who he was, or what he was doing in bear country.

'We can leave as soon as we have sorted out a few supplies. I have a list. If you don't have something on it, I am sure your helper can get it made up with the hopper's printer.'

Zaquil had everything ready inside ten minutes, neatly packed in a bag woven from plastic strings, still warm from the printer when Ysbel handed it to Raia. As she fastened it to the cargo netting in the stern of her canoe, the woman reminded Ysbel that she and her helper had promised that they wouldn't use the security bot.

'Absolutely,' Ysbel said, and pulled her little bot from her pocket and powered it down.

'And please switch off your link, too.'

'It's already off,' Ysbel said. She had forgotten to ask Zaquil to unblock it; there hadn't been any need for it, out here.

Raia studied her for a moment, then said, 'Do you know how to paddle?'

'I've done a little,' Ysbel told her, remembering a golden day when she and Ilan had messed about with stand-up paddle boards off one of the deserted beaches north of Ogres Grave.

'I own a fishing skiff,' Goodwill said. 'I prefer to use its sail, but I can put some muscle into it when I need to.'

'Good,' Raia said. 'I don't like to use the canoe's motor. Its noise can attract bears. And we'll get there faster with three of us pushing against the current.'

The canoe, with a matt-black composite hull and three seats woven from mycelial-leather straps, sat lightly in the water. Goodwill claimed the seat in the bow, Ysbel took the one in the middle, Raia jumped into the stern and they were off, paddling as close to the shore as possible, where the current was slowest, steering around or through shoals of water-smoothed boulders. Shards of sunlight flashed and shimmered off the water; the shade under the trees on either side was deep and dark and still. No sound but intermittent birdsong and the wind moving through the tops of the pine trees and small splashes of unseen animals going about their business. The three of them might have been pioneers

340

in the long ago before the Burn Line, travelling through untrodden territory.

Paddling was hot, thirsty work. Goodwill kept pace with the two women, even though the shaft of his leaf-bladed paddle overtopped him. When they stopped for a water break he stripped off his jacket and embroidered vest, revealing a tattoo of a hummingbird, what the natives called a flower-sipper, between the two pairs of dark nipples on the leathery skin of his chest.

Ysbel's arms and shoulders were already aching. She drank deep from her water bottle and refilled it from the river and splashed cold water on her head and neck and they went on, travelling for more than an hour until at last Raia turned the canoe aslant the current and beached it on a bench of loose pebbles. They hauled it out of the water and set off on foot across a marsh where widely spaced trees, many dead or dying, stood in sloughs of black water. Despite liberal application of repellent, Ysbel plodded along in a swirl of mosquitoes and black flies, trailing after Goodwill and Raia as they picked a winding way across ridges and archipelagos of drier ground. Goodwill had put on his vest and jacket but left them unbuttoned; Raia walked at a steady, confident pace, her rifle and pack slung over her shoulders, the bag of supplies hung from one of the pack's straps. Every so often, Ysbel glanced up at the scraps of sky caught between the treetops. She didn't trust Zaquil, couldn't be certain that he hadn't acted on his own initiative again, and although there wasn't any sign of the security bot, that didn't mean the damn thing wasn't up there somewhere, and she felt a little stab of apprehension whenever Raia looked around, worried that the helper's overconfidence might sabotage this meeting before it could begin.

The ground began to rise and they left the marsh behind, scrambling up a steep thickly forested ridge. Raia waited at the top of the ridge for Ysbel and Goodwill to catch up and turned without a word and led them through trees and rocks to the edge of a steep drop above what was either a loop of the river they had crossed earlier, or one of its tributaries. The water was broad and shallow, rippling amongst rocks and sand bars; trees overhung the opposite bank, where, according to Raia, her friend was waiting.

'Stand either side of me, so that he can get a good look at you,' she told Ysbel and Goodwill.

Ysbel did as she was told, feeling foolish and exposed. After a brief interval there was a stir of movement in the shadows under the trees on the far side. A figure balanced upright in a comically small basin of a boat, using a long pole to push out into the river's currents.

'It seems I was wrong to think he was a trapper,' Goodwill told Ysbel.

The figure was definitely too tall to be a native, clad in a hooded cape sewn of small patches of fur, mostly grey and brown, and trousers pieced from leather. Tall, broad-shouldered, face hidden by the deep folds of the cape's hood.

'Who is he?' Ysbel said to Raia. 'And what is he doing out here?'

'Someone who knows more about bears than I ever will.'

Ysbel wondered if it was someone who had gone native – not just living amongst them, as she did, but disappearing into the back country. Wilding, some called it. Abandoning responsibilities and duties, severing all contact with other humans, and often with natives, too. Dressed in clothes made from animals he had presumably trapped and killed, he leaned into the pole as he pushed his little craft across the river, spinning completely around in a strong current before regaining control and pushing on, at last stopping close to the foot of the steep drop and looking up at the three people standing above him.

Goodwill gave a cry, and grabbed Ysbel's arm.

'There's nothing to be afraid of,' Raia said.

'Of course there is!'

'What's wrong?' Ysbel said, and then the figure below her reached up and pushed back the hood and she saw his face.

Not a native, no. And not a man either.

Raia's friend was a bear.

17.

Raia introduced the bear to Ysbel and Goodwill, telling them that his name was Seven, and Seven pressed his hands to his chest and bowed and said that it wasn't, of course, his real name.

'Only I know that. The name I gave myself when I escaped into the world and began my long journey of discovery. Seven is what I was called before that. A significantly low number, for I was one of the first of the articulate bears.'

'There are others like you?' Ysbel said.

'It has been a very long time since I left my brothers and sisters, and I do not know if they are alive or dead,' Seven said. 'You may be looking at the last of my kind.'

'They aren't dead,' Raia said. 'We just haven't found them yet.'

'Raia believes that you and your little companion can help us,' Seven told Ysbel.

His smile showed sharp incisors as long as her thumb. He was a head taller than her, more than twice Goodwill's height, his body long and sinuous, his legs relatively short, his dark blond pelt dusted with a shimmer of auburn. Overlapping necklaces of snail shells and nut hulls hung from his long muscular neck. He spoke the common tongue fluently, with just a trace of a lisp, asking Raia if she had brought the gifts he had requested.

'Everything's here,' Raia said, and unhooked the bag from her pack and set it on the ground. Seven squatted over it, his patchwork cloak puddling around him, and tipped out the items Zaquil had printed or sourced from the hopper's supplies. A torch with a squeeze generator. A medical kit. A water bottle with a variety of filters, including one that could turn saltwater to fresh. A multibladed knife. Fish hooks. The bear's hands were huge and his blunt fingers were tipped with thick claws, but he picked through his prizes with deft speed, holding up a pack of needles and telling Ysbel and Goodwill that he made all his clothes.

'I tan animal pelts and skins with urine and make them supple with brains mashed in saltwater, and sew them with gut thread and grass to make the seams waterproof. Ever since my escape I have had to live off the land as best I can.'

Ysbel said, 'And before that, before you escaped, you were living in the camp by the river. What can you tell us about it?'

Seven poured the gifts back into the bag and stood, startlingly swift and fluid. 'Raia told me your story, so I suppose it is only fair that I tell you mine.'

'I'd love to hear it,' Ysbel said.

'What about you, little one?' Seven said to Goodwill. 'I understand why you are afraid of me, but as you can see, I am not like other bears.'

'I don't like being tricked,' Goodwill said.

He was standing behind Ysbel and Raia, wary and watchful. Ysbel shared his unease. Bears were crazy killers. Everyone knew that. And Seven was strong and quick, could overpower and unseam her in a moment. Even so, she believed that his theatrical manner masked something tender, vulnerable. *You may be looking at the last of my kind.*

The bear pressed his hands to his chest again and told Goodwill, 'I promise to tell only the truth, and the truth is so strange that I think it will more than satisfy your curiosity. But before I begin, why don't we make ourselves comfortable?'

Goodwill stayed standing, his wariness undiminished, while Ysbel and Raia sat crosslegged and Seven sprawled on his side, explaining that he had been one of a small tribe of cubs snatched from their mothers at a very early age and treated with medicine to counter the bad blood that made bears crazy fierce. They were raised in the camp by a troop of Goodwill's people, and visited from time to time by humans who subjected them to medical examinations and quizzes designed to test their intelligence and reasoning. The keepers who looked after them meant well, he said. He and his fellow cubs had been taught arithmetic and how to read and write, given access to a small library and shown how to keep goats and grow vegetables, how to throw clay pots and, yes, how to tan leather. All the skills necessary for living in the wild. Even so, they were prisoners and experimental subjects, rigorously disciplined and controlled, forbidden to stray outside the camp's perimeter.

'How many of you were there?' Ysbel said to Seven.

'I was Seven of Sixteen. That was how many there were, to begin with. Sixteen.'

'More cubs were treated and turned out later on,' Raia said. 'There were about forty in the camp when Seven escaped.'

'We were told that one day we would be free,' Seven said. 'When we could be trusted. When the world was ready for us. But as we grew older we began to suspect that day would never come. Some of us reverted and became crazy fierce, fighting with their brothers and sisters, trying to attack their keepers.' He pulled up the sleeve of his coat, showing the pale trench of a scar on his forearm. 'A cub half my age and size did this when I tried to calm him. But there was no way of calming those who reverted, and they, and those who failed

346

to pass the tests set by our human visitors, were there one day and gone the next. I hope that they were returned to the wild, sentimental fool that I am, but I rather doubt it.'

When two cubs disappeared after they'd been found devouring a goat they had killed, Seven and two of his friends decided that it was time to leave. They dug under the fence and headed north, but one of them was caught by keepers who tracked them through the forest, and the second was killed by a bear when he and Seven unknowingly trespassed on its territory.

'We had been told about our wild relatives, but we were careless,' Seven said. 'And I suppose we didn't want to believe that they were as crazy as we had been taught. What naive and hopeful fools we were, when I look back. It's a wonder I wasn't killed too.'

Seven had been six years old when he had escaped, a young adolescent – like natives, bears matured more quickly than humans – with no skill at hunting or fighting. After his friend was killed he continued to travel north as best he could, making long diversions to avoid his feral cousins, living mostly on roots and berries, lost and lonely and afraid. And then he stumbled onto the territory of an old female bear, and his luck changed.

'I'm sure that she would have killed me if she could,' he said, 'but she was suffering from a wasting disease, was too sick and feeble to do me any harm, and grew steadily weaker and ever more dependent on me. I took care of her, and in turn she taught me about her people. Their language, their history, how they lived. It was an unexpected kindness, and a great gift. Our keepers, you see, did not teach us the language of my people, or anything about their culture and history. We were told only that we were descendants of a brutal civilisation which had fallen from grace with the Mother, the first to be raised up since that fall. We had to pray to the Mother every day, thanking Her for Her generosity and mercy. Our keepers claimed that they were redeeming and educating us, but they would not allow us to be ourselves.'

He was looking at Goodwill, who said, with a snap of indignation, 'I cannot apologise for something I knew nothing about.'

'I don't suppose you can,' Seven said evenly. 'Just as you can't apologise for hunting my people like animals, killing them or driving them to these marginal lands of the frigid far north. A wilderness that's so cold in winter we have to sleep through most of it, or else starve or freeze to death. A country that is ours only until you decide that you need it. And when you do, we'll be driven even further north, until there is nowhere else to go. And what then? Will you put the last of us in cages, or will you get up the courage to finally erase us?'

'We have to protect ourselves. Most bears are not like you, after all.'

'No, they are not. Our civilisation fell more than six hundred years ago, but until now there has been no attempt to help or rehabilitate us. No forgiveness or reconciliation.'

'There was little to save. Your ancestors were bloodthirsty monsters who enslaved us.'

'Much of our lost civilisation was brutal and barbaric, yes. But not all. I have studied my heritage, such as it is. You would do well to study yours, little one.'

After a small, uncomfortable silence Raia asked Seven to tell the rest of his story.

'There's not much to tell,' Seven said. 'I met the old female in spring and cared for her as best as I could, but she died soon after the snows came. Knowing no better, I left her body in a high place, so that the crows could find her and return her to the Mother, and after a hard winter alone I drifted further north, looking for a place where I could make my home. It was not easy. I would settle somewhere and sooner or later

348

one of my wild cousins would challenge me and I would have to move on. I have many fine qualities, but fighting is not one of them, and all of my attempts to befriend other bears ended in failure and flight. I was still wandering, homeless and alone, when I found Raia.'

'He spent most of last summer stalking me before he could be certain that I was harmless,' Raia said.

'You can't blame me for being cautious,' Seven said. 'And I shall always treasure the look you gave me when I got up the nerve to step out of the shadows and spoke to you.'

'The look of someone trying to restart her heart,' Raia said, smiling.

She told Ysbel and Goodwill that Seven had found her towards the end of last year's fieldwork season, and had made himself known to her again after she'd returned to the north-west coast, in spring. They had been together ever since, and she had learned more about feral bear culture from him than from all of her fieldwork.

'I could already read Old Bear,' she said, 'having studied some of the old texts. But Seven taught me the rudimentary patois of their descendants, and the meanings of many of the markings they left on trees and rocks, and much else besides. In return, I promised to help him try to free his brothers and sisters. Seven couldn't point to the camp on a map, but gave me a good description of the area around it. The river close by and the shape of its course, the mountain peaks to the west, and so on.'

'The taste of river water, and the smell of the air in different seasons,' Seven said. 'When snow fell, and when it melted. The sounds of the forest and the shapes the clouds made.'

'Trina helped me work out the most likely location, but there was no sign of it on satellite images,' Raia said. 'We couldn't find any records about its operations, or the genetic engineering that must have been used to treat Seven and his friends, either. And my native contacts claimed to have no knowledge of a camp where bear cubs were being raised. So I had to go look for it myself. Find it, and gather as much evidence as possible.'

'As I hoped she would,' Seven said.

'I couldn't risk whistling up a hopper ride, of course, so we set off south in my canoe, towing Seven's coracle behind us,' Raia said. 'By the time we reached it, Trina had got into that mess of trouble over that map. And of course, the camp was empty. We searched the area, hoping that some of Seven's brothers and sisters had escaped. And we kept watch on the place, too, in case any of them returned. But you turned up instead.'

Ysbel told Seven that she and Goodwill had found out about the camp because the person who had bought the map which had caused Trina so much grief had also been involved in the camp's construction.

'That would be the map with the funny little figure,' Seven said.

'You've seen it,' Ysbel said.

'Raia showed me a picture.'

'Do you think it's real? That my people and yours met hundreds of years ago?'

'Of course.'

'You seem very certain.'

'It is very like something I learned from the songs.'

'The songs?'

'The songs that my wild cousins sing. Songs handed down from one generation to the next for untold generations.'

'That's why we wanted to examine the map,' Raia said. 'To prove that it was real. That the songs were based on true stories, rather than fantasies and fairy tales.'

'My great-grandfather, Bearbane, was a trapper,' Goodwill said. 'He told me about the so-called songs of the bears. How they sometimes climb trees or stand on a high ridge, and call out. A kind of mournful lowing you could hear for many stades. Calling for mates. Asserting territorial rights. More like the kind of cries that animals make than songs as we know them.'

'With respect,' Seven said, 'it seems to me that your great-grandfather knew less about my cousins than he thought he did.'

'Tell me then what you think these songs are,' Goodwill said, with undisguised scepticism.

'They are very long,' Seven said, 'but I'll give you a little from one of them.'

He stood up and closed his eyes and composed himself, squeezed his eyes shut and began to strike his chest with one of his fists in a basic 4/4 rhythm, and sang.

It was more like an incantation than a song. Sustained on in-breath and out-breath, seamlessly rising and falling, endlessly changing, endlessly the same. Ysbel thought of wind moving in waves across tall grasses, rain seething on the surface of a lake, snow falling. When Seven stopped singing and opened his eyes and smiled, it took her a few moments to come back to herself.

'Usually, I would sing more forcefully, and from a good high place,' Seven said. 'But you get the idea.'

'May I ask what it was about?' Ysbel said.

'A place that doesn't exist, except in dreams,' Seven said. 'Bears know about the ruins of their cities. Other songs tell stories about what they once were. This one is about a city that did not fall. Or rather, about the hope of the singer that such a city might be found somewhere in the world.'

'Sing the other one,' Raia said. 'The one about the sky devils.'

'That's what the funny little figure in the map could be. A sky devil,' Seven told Ysbel and Goodwill, and sang again.

This time it sounded to Ysbel like water running over and around rocks. Quick and bright on the surface, a powerful force beneath.

Another silence, after it ended.

Seven asked Goodwill if his people knew that song, and Goodwill shook his head.

'It's the only one bears sing together,' Seven said. 'After sunset, when the summer begins to fail and the first breath of winter can be felt at night. One begins it, and others in neighbouring territories take it up one by one.'

'I heard it once,' Raia said. 'Late summer, two years ago. Growing fainter and fainter as nearer voices finished with it and more distant voices picked it up, like ripples spreading out into the world.'

'There are many verses,' Seven said. 'But the first two are always the same. They tell of how my ancestors fell into evil ways and conjured devils from the sky, and of the fire the devils lit in every mind, and the great harvest of lives when all the cities went to war against each other.'

'Are you saying that those sky devils infected your ancestors?' Ysbel said.

'With the fire that burns thought and memory,' Seven said. 'The fire that feeds unreasoning anger.'

'What else does the song have to say about sky devils?' Ysbel said.

'That's it. The rest of the song is a list of the cities that fell. What they were and what they became. It changes every time the song is sung because every bear remembers a different list.'

'A requiem for what was lost,' Raia said.

'For what we lost to the fire,' Seven said.

'It seems that my people have done you a great wrong,'

352

Goodwill told Seven, and bowed low and spoke the formalistic phrases for accepting blame and asking for forgiveness.

'They are not your sins, little one,' Seven said, with surprising gentleness. 'And look at it this way: my keepers helped to make me who I am.'

'I don't just mean the camp,' Goodwill said.

He and Seven were sharing a look, as if each was recognising something in the other. Making a connection based on a shared history thousands of years deep.

'If we find Seven's brothers and sisters, they'll need a place where they can live their best lives,' Raia said. 'A reserve or preserve protected from feral bears, large enough for them to be able to support themselves.'

'Somewhere with a river running through it,' Seven said. 'And a way to access your books, and the books of Goodwill's people, so that I can learn about the world and the people in it.'

'But first, we need to find out who collaborated with the natives who ran the camp,' Raia said. 'Whether it was an agency or a rogue element. Who authorised it, if it was an agency, and how high that authorisation goes. I don't have the means to access other agencies' files, and Trina can't help me anymore. Her privileges have been revoked, and she's being watched. That's why I took a chance on reaching out to you.'

'I was asked to find out everything I could about the map, to satisfy Mother's curiosity about it,' Ysbel told Raia. 'I'm sure she'd be interested in Seven and his songs, too.'

'Do you answer to her directly?' Raia said.

'Zaquil might. I have a contact in Special Operations.'

'And do you trust this contact?'

It was a good question. Ysbel said carefully, 'I hope I can.'

'I am only the bailiff of an insignificant fishing village,' Goodwill said. 'I have no power or voice in the affairs of my people. Especially when it concerns something as delicate and extraordinary as this. But my cousin, Juniper Saltmire, is chief clerk to a delegate of the Committee of the Five Hundred. I can ask her to bring this to the attention of the proper people. To find out who was responsible.'

'I'll be grateful for any help you can give us. And understand if you can't help at all. But if you can, please try to keep Trina out of it,' Raia said, with a fiercely anxious look. 'Seven too. I don't want people to come hunting for him, hoping to turn him into some kind of zoological specimen.'

'I've already had quite enough of that,' Seven said.

'And be careful who you ask, and what you tell them. For your sake as well as ours,' Raia said, and picked up her pack and her rifle.

'We're already in trouble,' Ysbel said, thinking of Kirder Halmasdaughter and Damage Limitation. 'It would be easier if you could come back with us.'

'I know it would. And I'm sorry that I can't. But I haven't made good on my debt to Seven yet. If his brothers and sisters are out there, we need to find them and get them to a place where they can stay until this all shakes out.'

'I haven't taught her all the songs I've learned, either,' Seven said. 'Or learned all the songs I need to know.'

'How will we find you again?' Ysbel said.

'When you think it's safe to reach out to Trina, remind her about the place we fell in love with when we were studying the maps,' Raia said. 'Tell her that if she doesn't hear from me by the end of the research season, she'd better come looking for me there.'

18.

'We find it hard to talk about bears,' Goodwill told Ysbel. 'It exposes old wrongdoings and deep divisions, and raises hard ethical problems. So I can understand why those who cured the articulate bears wanted to keep their work secret. But they were wrong, nevertheless.'

'The secrecy may have been imposed by my people,' Ysbel said. 'A condition for their help.'

'If it was, my people agreed to it,' Goodwill said. Although he had been wary and mistrustful of Seven, the bear's story had fired up his righteous indignation. 'And if Seven's story is true, my people were also responsible for the deaths of some of his brothers and sisters. Maybe all of them, if the rest were killed when the camp was closed.'

'And my people must have known about everything that happened there,' Ysbel said. 'So let's agree that the blame should be shared equally.'

They were hiking through the boggy forest. Afternoon sunlight slanted between the pine trees, throwing long shadows, striking ripples of gold and silver on the surfaces of stagnant pools. They no longer had the protection of Raia and her tranquilliser rifle, had only Ysbel's bot to keep watch, but she didn't want to call on Zaquil for help. Not yet. Not until she and Goodwill had talked about what they had learned and decided what they should do.

'A cure for bears, and what to do with them when they're cured,' Goodwill said. 'It's going to cause more trouble than the map.'

'Not necessarily. Not if the figure on the map and Seven's sky devils were human.'

'Do you think they were?'

'If they were human, they can't have been my kin. They must have been the children of another mother, one who returned home before we did. But if there were others here before us, they've left no trace that we could find. And we looked everywhere, when we arrived, for people like us.'

Ysbel thought of the discovery of the lost civilisations of the apes and monkeys and emus, the suite of genes inserted into the genomes of animal species before the Burn Line, the other secrets kept from the natives. Perhaps it should all come out. A fresh start. A new accord. True openness and real parity between humans and natives. She felt as if she was in a hopper at the top of its arc. Hanging way out on the edge of space in freefall, everything up in the air, waiting to see where it all came down.

'I wanted to show that my uncle was right,' Goodwill said. 'That the map was proof that bears were visited by your people hundreds of years ago. That it had something to do with their fall. But now I'm not so sure. Perhaps it's for the best if the figure on the map and Seven's sky devils are no more than figments of bear dreams and nightmares.'

'One thing I know,' Ysbel said, 'is that there's still a lot we don't know.'

They talked about that as they walked through the marsh. Lack of hard proof of what the map seemed to show. The missing threads that might link it with the camp, the mislaid panel and an agency so secret there was no trace of it in any records. By the time they reached the river, emerging from the swampy forest only a short distance from the beached canoe, they had thrashed out the outlines of a plan.

They agreed that there was no need to tell anyone about the map and Seven's songs just yet. The implications were too enormous, and the facts were far from certain. Goodwill and Swift could search for the whereabouts of the map, and for similar artefacts; Ysbel could truthfully tell Iryn Moonsdaughter that Joyous Hightower claimed that the map was no longer in his possession, and refused to say who owned it now.

The camp and the articulate bears were another matter. Ysbel and Goodwill knew that they had to tell their respective authorities what they'd found. Ysbel thought she should treat it as a crime scene, ask Ilan if he and a couple of colleagues could spare a few days to survey the site and search for evidence about who had lived there, and look for graves or any other traces of bodies. She hoped that it would give Goodwill and her some measure of control, and would make sure that that neither the human nor native authorities could dismiss their claims. And she also hoped that they could respect Raia's request to protect Seven, for now, by telling Zaquil and Iryn Moonsdaughter that they'd been taken into the forest to meet with a trapper who'd stumbled on the camp a year ago, and didn't want any involvement with the authorities.

It was far from a perfect plan, but it was the best they could do: tell the same story to their respective authorities and hope that no one would go looking for the imaginary trapper and find Seven instead. Ysbel hoped that it wouldn't fall apart until Raia and Seven had had the chance to find Seven's brothers and sisters, or at least find a good hiding place in deepest bear country. As it was, it didn't even outlast the day.

357

Although she and Goodwill had made it back to the canoe in good time, and were paddling with the current as they headed downriver, the sun was setting by the time they came around the big bend where the hopper had landed. The level light was in their eyes and dazzling off the water, and by the time they saw that a second hopper was standing close by their own, it was too late to turn back.

The security bot's winged knife flashed in the air above the river and a green spark began to pulse in one corner of Ysbel's vision – her link had switched itself on. The security bot turned and took up station above the canoe and Zaquil spoke inside her head, and she was in freefall again.

'Welcome back,' he said. 'Iryn Moonsdaughter has arrived, and she has many questions.'

19.

As soon as the hopper had touched down at Ogres Grave, Ysbel summoned a runabout from the landing field's garage and linked to Ilan.

'Hey,' he said.

'Hey,' she said, feeling self-conscious because she had an ulterior motive for calling him. A good one, but still.

'Did you find what you were looking for?' Ilan said.

'Not exactly. Where are you?'

'At the dig on Razorback Island. We're about to broil a mess of fresh-caught fish if you want to come join.'

Ysbel's link floated a little window showing a close-up of Ilan's face, the view swinging around to show a pebble strand and people, humans and natives, busy around a campfire.

She said, 'I wish I could be there. But I have to report to Mitkos.'

'Debrief and so on.'

'Something like that.'

The runabout she'd summoned was trundling across the landing field's dusty hardpan. Unlike the sleek models used in Concord, this one was got up in ethnic style, open-topped and square-cornered like a wagon, its bodywork wooden planking and wicker. After spending so much time with Goodwill, Ysbel thought it looked ridiculous and patronising.

'When will you be back in town?' she said to Ilan.

'I could stop by tomorrow evening. Will you still be around, or will you be back on the hunt?'

'I'll be at my place, looking forward to seeing you,' Ysbel said, with a dirty little pinch of guilt.

Mitkos Grimsson's house was up in the hills on the eastern side of Ogres Grave. It was early evening, dry and warm. The lights of the town simmering in the strip of flat land stretched along the bay's shore, insects scratching and creaking in the scrub slope below the pounded-dirt terrace where Ysbel and Mitkos sat while Mitkos's partner pottered about inside, getting their two children, boys aged six and eight, ready for bed. Ysbel worked her way through a bowl of rice and flaked fish left over from the family's supper and, having warned him that everything was confidential, for his ears only, told Mitkos about the debacle in Concord and her adventures in bear country.

She had rehearsed the story and tried to keep it as concise as possible, but it still took a while to tell.

'Trina Mersdaughter was involved in those wrongful deaths because of the map,' Mitkos said, squinting off into the dusk, trying to make sense of it. 'And she wanted to get hold of it because she thought it was relevant to the songs of a talking bear.'

'When you put it like that, it does sound slightly fantastical.'

'You still don't know what happened to the map. Instead, you've found some kind of secret project. A collaboration with the natives. And the woman and this talking bear, excuse me, articulate bear, who told you about it have walked off into deepest bear country.'

'Raia knows that she'll be in trouble for keeping this quiet. And she wanted to protect Seven. Didn't want him to become a laboratory subject.'

'Speaking of trouble, there's a notice out for your deten-
tion. The natives have made a formal complaint about your
spelunking in the Library of All People.'

'Iryn Moonsdaughter told me that she can make it go away.'
Best not to tell Mitkos that, by telling him about Seven and the
camp, she had already violated one of Iryn Moonsdaughter's
conditions for providing that help.

'You've already talked to her, then.'

'I've been fully debriefed,' Ysbel said. 'About the camp, and
the bear, and everything that happened in Concord. And now
I'm ready to move on to the next stage of the investigation.'

She'd had to tell Iryn Moonsdaughter everything; the
woman had already known about her meeting with Seven.
Zaquil's purloined security bot had been loitering high overhead, out of range of Raia's bots, while the sliver of the
helper, having surreptitiously migrated from Ysbel's bot
network to her link, had made a clandestine audio recording.
It had been a very thorough betrayal. She'd had to use a
security tool to purge and reset her link, and still wasn't
completely certain that it had removed every trace of the
little spy.

'What about your native friend?' Mitkos said. 'Is he still
involved with the investigation? Are you still involved with
him?'

'This is an internal matter now. Iryn cut him loose, and
he's gone back to Concord.'

'I thought he lived on the west coast.'

'He does, but he still wants to find the map.'

'But you've moved on from that.'

'The camp and the articulate bears are more important,'
Ysbel said carefully. Best not to tell her boss about Seven's
sky devils, the possibility that there had been a first contact
with bears long before First Contact with the natives.

Mitkos settled back in his chair, hands clasped behind his head. 'Well, you'd better explain what you need from me. That's why you're here, isn't it?'

'Also, because I feel I owe you an explanation. But before we get into what I have to do and what I need, you have to swear you won't tell anyone else about any of this.'

Mitkos put his hand over his heart, trying not to smile and not quite succeeding, and said, 'I swear. And now I've sworn, tell me what you want from me, and why.'

Ysbel had barely started when Bekt, Mitkos's partner, appeared in the doorway and announced that the boys were settled.

'We'll finish up when I've kissed them goodnight,' Mitkos told Ysbel. 'Don't go away.'

Bekt asked her if she would like some tea, disappeared inside the house and returned with two bowls. He was a tall, calm man, with a neatly trimmed beard and long blond hair parted down the centre, barefoot in a loose robe. An engineer, currently attached to a native project to construct a solar-powered desalination plant that would augment the city's freshwater supply. Ysbel thanked him for the tea and asked him how his work was going.

'Very well,' he said. 'Although we have had our first case of sabotage.'

'I'm sorry to hear that.'

'Nothing serious. Some smashed panels. Paint thrown.' Bekt took a sip of tea and looked at Ysbel over the rim of the bowl and said, 'I'm not going to ask why you're here or what you're doing, but whatever it is, I hope it won't get Mitkos in trouble.'

'If there's any trouble, I'm the lightning rod.'

That appeared to satisfy Bekt. He told her about the concert by the mixed choir of humans and natives that Dalsy Diwasdaughter led, the one that Ysbel had missed while she was away, and wandered back into the house, and presently Mitkos came out and sat down and said, 'You were just telling me how, after you and your native friend had your fairy-tale meeting and returned to this abandoned camp, you found that Iryn Moonsdaughter was waiting for you.'

'The helper assigned to me had been spying on the meeting, against my orders. He told Iryn what we'd found. The camp. Raia. Seven. And she scrambled a team, and came out with them.'

'She's taking this seriously.'

'She had a couple of technicians seconded from Survey and Surveillance. They pulled bear DNA from dirt where their huts had been sited, and native and human DNA from the soakaway of a latrine inside the secondary fence. The human DNA came from at least three individuals. We haven't identified any of them yet, but it confirms Seven's story. Bears and natives had been living there, and some of our people were involved, too.'

'So,' Mitkos said, 'what does the next stage of this investigation involve?'

'Right now, Iryn and her people are searching for Raia and Seven, and for the people who built the camp and developed the treatment that cured Seven and the other articulate bears. Trying to find out if those bears are still alive, and where they were taken. If there are other camps like the one we found. Iryn also wants to find out who was organising supplies for the camp. And that's where I come in,' Ysbel said, choosing her words carefully. She was coming to the part where she would have to tell her boss some outright untruths.

'I can't say I'm pleased,' Mitkos said. 'Work is piling up. Dalsy needs help with the summer festival, and the city council has revised the specs for Freedom Park again, so we need to rework the costings. The bureau wants to start trading local produce with pineapples and breadfruit and apple bananas from the Gathering Place. It's totally uneconomic, of course. We'll have to eat the costs as the price of good will, and someone has to work out what those costs will be – transport, warehousing and so forth. And Bekt may have mentioned the little trouble he's been having at the desalination plant?'

'He did.'

'It's part of a growth in unrest that needs to be curbed.'

'If the bureau doesn't want to sign off on further work with Special Operations, I can take some personal days,' Ysbel said.

'It's that important to you?'

'It's important to everyone.'

'I'm not going to try to stop you,' Mitkos said. 'I'm outranked by Iryn Moonsdaughter. You don't need my permission.'

'I'm grateful anyway. And I'll be done in three or four days, I swear.'

'Three would be good. Two even better.'

'There is something else.'

'Of course there is.'

'It's the kind of work I was doing with Data Analysis, before I transferred to the bureau. How we uncovered the Originists who were planning to fly to the Moon. Tracing requisitions and transport of rations and other supplies. Looking for unusual movements of personnel and materials in the area. Tracking usage of flitters and hoppers, and so on.'

'And why do you need my help?' Mitkos said.

'All it is, is I need you to give me access to the bureau's central archives,' Ysbel said, as casually as possible.

'Your new boss can't do that?'

'She isn't exactly my boss. And she wants this to go through the usual channels, so it doesn't attract attention. It's within our remit, given that humans and natives were working together, and you don't need to know what I find, if I find anything.'

Ysbel watched Mitkos consider this. There was that free-fall feeling again.

He said, 'Special Operations won't get any of the blowback if someone higher up decides that this crosses a line. You'll be in the direct line of fire, with no protection. And so will I.'

'If it blows up in any way, I promise that I'll take all the blame.'

'Do you think this is important enough to sacrifice your career?'

'I really do,' Ysbel said. That, at least, was true.

20.

It was close to midnight when a flitter dropped Ysbel off at her cabin. She half-expected to find that the place had been ransacked by Damage Limitation or Special Operations, searching for any material she might have withheld, but everything was as she had left it. She fell asleep almost immediately, woke at dawn and pulled on her running gear. The sky was cloudless, the air cool and still, and her muscles eased as she followed her usual route downhill to the road that paralleled the railway track and the patchwork fields. Two striplings leading a draft mara by a rope halter shouted her name as she went past and she waved and ran on, trying not to worry about Zaquil's sneaky sliver-spy, or that some agent from Special Operations might be tracking her with a bot riding too high to spot. Nothing she could do about it, she told herself. If they'd been listening in on her conversation with Mitkos, if they'd worked out what she was planning to do, she'd soon find out.

After Iryn Moonsdaughter's preliminary interview, there'd been a longer, formal debriefing the next day, covering everything that had happened after Ysbel had travelled to Concord to meet Goodwill. At the end of it, Iryn had told her that she had done well, but it was now time for Special Operations to take up the investigation. The search for Raia and Seven had already begun, and although the terrain was difficult and the presence of feral bears precluded any operations on the ground, it was not likely that the fugitives could evade capture for long. And while Kirder Halmasdaughter had yet to be identified and traced, the two Damage Limitation agents who had taken Ysbel into custody had been tracked down and questioned. They sincerely believed that they had been recruited by an agency directly under Mother's command, but had never met Kirder Halmasdaughter in person and didn't know why she was interested in the map, or whether she had anything to do with the camp and the articulate bears.

Iryn told Ysbel that it was only a matter of time before that particular knot was unpicked and those involved were brought to account. Everything was in hand. All leads were being followed up. As for Ysbel, she had more than exceeded Mother's expectations, but now it was time for her to return to her usual duties. In due course, when the investigation was complete, she would be given proper recognition for the part that she had played.

As she ran, Ysbel's untethered thoughts kept returning to the debriefing, and her conversation with Mitkos. The lies she'd told. Mostly by omission. She was uncomfortable about deceiving her boss, and she couldn't stop thinking about everything that could go wrong. Inadvertently triggering a security bot when she opened sealed records. A swarm of lawkeepers stopping the train carrying Goodwill south. Iryn Moonsdaughter or some functionary in Special Operations sending Mitkos confirmation that she had been signed off from the investigation. Mitkos blowing her story by deciding to clarify the situation with Special Operations, or accidently divulging her plans, such as they were . . .

A single slip could end her career and send her back to the Gathering Place in disgrace, but Ysbel was in too deep to

367

back out now. Her curiosity and ambition and idealistic zeal — call it passion, even — were driving her forward. She believed that the investigation was too important to be entrusted to Special Operations, which was infamous for serving Mother rather than the greater good, and she sympathised with Raia's predicament, and Seven's, and she had made a pact with Goodwill and didn't want to let him down.

She called up a flitter on her way back to the cabin, stopped off in the bureau's offices to pick up a new set of bots and check her messages — a pile of stuff relating to neglected work. Nothing yet from Goodwill, but it was early days.

Dalsy was either out or not yet in, but had left a bunch of wildflowers and a packet of oil cakes on Ysbel's table, with a note saying that she was looking forward to all the fun they'd have working on the summer festival, that she was sure it would help her get back on track. As Ysbel was leaving, Landers wandered in and said he'd heard she was still mired in somebody else's business, it looked like they'd been running her hard.

'Nothing I can't handle,' Ysbel said, not wanting to get into it with him.

'You need some rest and relaxation. And I know the absolute best way. Come snow season, we'll take a flitter up into the mountains. Wear ourselves out skiing cross-country in the finest virgin powder on the planet, have the flitter pick us up when we're done and come back to the compound and hit the bar.'

'I'll think about it,' Ysbel said, and got out of there. It was obvious that her colleagues believed that she had failed to satisfy the difficult, delicate task she'd been given. Landers's come-on was more than a little humiliating; it was never nice to be treated as nothing more than a potential conquest by another person, but it was also laughably blatant and easy to ignore. As for Dalsy, her sympathy might be genuine, it was always hard to tell, but she definitely wanted to use this as a teachable moment. To show that her way of dealing with the natives was for the best, and Ysbel was misguided in treating them as equals because look where that had got her.

Ysbel wanted to prove her colleagues wrong, but also knew there was much more at stake than her wounded pride and her reputation. Back at her cabin she boiled up a can of coffee and worked up the costings for the revised plans for Freedom Park – she'd picked up the file in the office and would return it tomorrow, a sop to her conscience and a gift to Mitkos, who'd dropped the access key to the archives in her link.

She wanted to start mining records as soon as possible, but the first thing she did after sending the new set of costings to Mitkos was call Bakr Lunwarsdaughter, a virologist she'd befriended when they had worked on the campaign to develop and distribute a vaccine against the pneumatic zoonosis. After initial pleasantries, Ysbel asked if there were any records of bears being cured of the disease which affected their sanity.

'Not that I know of,' Bakr said. 'It isn't my area, but I think I would have heard of something like that.'

'But it's possible?'

'From what I understand, it's caused by an endogenous retrovirus. One that has inserted copies of itself in the genomes of reproductive as well as somatic cells, which is why it persists from generation to generation. You could use standard gene-editing techniques to deactivate the viral DNA in host cell genomes, or snip it out. And it might also be possible to suppress it with off-the-shelf anti-virals. Something that interferes with transcription, the way the virus uses the host cell's machinery to make new viral components.'

'So there are several ways of doing it.'

369

'Theoretically,' Bakr said, giving the word some weight. 'In practice, any treatment would have to satisfy serious ethical and political concerns. And we would need the natives' agreement, too.'

'But if someone decided to force the issue? Or if the natives asked to help?'

'As I said, it isn't my area. And if it had been discussed, there would be reports, position papers . . . Why the interest? Is someone thinking of actually doing it?'

'No. No, no, nothing like that. It's purely hypothetical. One of those what-if exercises. Just in case, you know, the natives raise the idea.'

This seemed to mollify the woman. She said, 'The things you have to deal with, in your line of work.'

'You don't know the half of it,' Ysbel said.

As she suspected, trying to solve the so-called bear problem was scientifically possible, but its implementation would raise serious scrutiny and challenges, human and native. Not surprising, then, that the people who had cured Seven and the other articulate bears had taken every precaution to keep their project secret, but although they had managed to erase the camp from maps and satellite images, Ysbel reckoned that it would have been much harder to remove every trace left by its construction and operation in financial records and inventories. Excessive and unaccounted overage or wastage, patterns in the distribution of miscellaneous funds, forged stock counts, false allocation schemes: the kind of evidence that exposed disaffected agency personnel who stole materiel for their own use or were knowing participants in schemes got up by natives who had worked out how to manipulate aid and friendship programmes for their own ends. And since the Bureau of Indigenous Affairs had oversight of records of all transactions between agencies and natives, it should be possible to track down irregularities associated with the camp.

She began by working through the records lodged by the Ogres Grave station, which covered most of the west coast. Concentrating on the years when the camp had most likely been built, assuming that it was around the time Seven had been born, but finding nothing of interest and breaking off at dusk, when Ilan arrived. He was somewhat dusty and dishevelled because he had taken a runabout to the nearest village and walked the rest of the way, carrying food packs and a plastic bottle of inky native wine. Ysbel let him take charge of cooking supper, and they drank most of the wine and fell into the big hammock strung under a canvas roof and made slow, careful love, as if rediscovering each other, and fell asleep spooned together.

It was the deepest sleep she had enjoyed since she had begun the investigation. In the morning, she set a pot of oatmeal to cook and shared the outdoor, gravity-fed shower with Ilan. Afterwards, dressed in her running gear, she walked with him down the hill to the spot where he had left the runabout.

'There's a favour I need to ask,' she said. 'Feel free to turn it down.'

'I'll need to hear what it is first.'

'I was wondering if you could look up surveys of a couple of bear cities. Reports that haven't been published to open records. Raw data files. Who made the surveys and when. And any images of bear carvings they might have taken.'

'Like that map you were interested in a while back?'

'Like the figure on the map,' Ysbel said. It felt like a confession.

'I thought you'd given up on that.'

'Not quite. There are a few loose ends. They might lead to something or nothing, but I'd like to be sure.'

Zaquil had told Ysbel that he had looked everywhere and failed to find any surveys of bear cities before First Contact, but she had good reason to mistrust the helper and wanted to follow it up herself. And she didn't want to tell Ilan the whole sorry story about the camp and Seven and Zaquil's betrayal, or how the map and the slab missing from the stacks of the Library of All People, and the old tale about ghost lights, might mean that there was some kind of conspiracy to erase evidence of meetings between humans and bears. It was best that he knew as little as possible, in case Special Operations found out what she was up to and everything came crashing down around her, and she felt a stupid rush of gratitude when he didn't push her for more details, asking instead which bear cities was she interested in.

'The first is somewhere in the Andes. I'm not sure exactly where, but it's in the vicinity of a native town, Tall Trees, and the survey was done just before First Contact.'

'You mean a satellite survey.'

'I mean on-site topographical mapping. Using the kind of laser grid I've seen your team use.'

'There weren't any on-site surveys of any kind of bear city before First Contact,' Ilan said. 'New or old.'

'I have a native associate who claims otherwise.'

'Your associate must be mistaken,' Ilan said. 'There were satellite surveys of the ruins of bear cities back then, of course there were. Mother and her little helpers mapped the whole planet. And there were excavations of the remains of human cities in Europe and Asia and Africa, and studies of post-Burn Line sites associated with extinct intelligent species. But the Union and the New Territories were off limits to everyone except agents preparing the ground for First Contact. There weren't any boots-on-the-ground surveys of bear cities or any other sites.'

'Could you look anyway?' Ysbel said. 'And also, check if anyone ever visited that new city you located for me. The one that was drowned by an earthquake.'

'In case there are images of the original of that map?'

'Or other carvings like it. I know it's a long shot, but I'd like to be sure, one way or the other.'

'I can tell you now there was nothing like that in the master file,' Ilan said. 'Just an aerial survey and a preliminary density contour map. Done several years after First Contact, as I recall. Certainly not before.'

'But if it wasn't a proper dig. Someone paying a quick visit, perhaps very recently. Checking out a bear city for the fun of it. Perhaps taking a few artefacts.'

'It would have to be something more than a quick visit — you need heavy-duty hardware to excavate a site at the bottom of the sea. And any kind of on-site work, even a casual visit, has to be cleared with the natives, as well as with the department. And all of that would be in the site's master file,' Ilan said, with a touch of impatience. 'And it wasn't.'

A trace of the headache from last night's wine, which Ysbel thought she'd sluiced away with the shower's cold water, began to throb behind her eyes. She said, 'Perhaps the reports were filed somewhere else. And if there aren't any reports, there might be logs of visits, flight plans . . .'

'It sounds as if this is something more than tying up a loose end,' Ilan said. 'What is this really about, Ysbel?'

'I told you: something that's probably nothing. Information from a reliable source I'd like to follow up. If you can't or won't do it, maybe you could point me towards someone who can help. Or give me access to the files so I can do it myself.'

'I'll take a look,' Ilan said. 'Only because it won't take long, since there's nothing to find. And that'll be the end of it.'

It hadn't been an argument, exactly, but when they reached the runabout their farewells were perfunctory. Ysbel knew, as she plodded back up the hill, abandoning all thought of going for a run, that she should call Ilan and apologise for being obtuse and difficult, but instead she slapped on a patch to fix her headache and opened her little box of accountancy tools and spent the rest of the day ploughing through archives. She finished her examination of records lodged by the Ogres Grave station around the time of Seven's birth, finding nothing out of place, and started in on more recent records. Taking a break when she felt her concentration beginning to blur, distracting herself with small domestic tasks before diving back in. Working like that for three days, seeing no one but the natives who owned the land she rented, the one time she walked down to their farm to buy fresh vegetables and fruit. She found nothing in the Ogres Grave records, moved on to records lodged by stations responsible for the other regions of the Outer Territories, and in the end had tallied only overlooked errors and a few instances of what might be trivial pilfering. She flagged them up for Mitkos – another gift to acknowledge his help – and contemplated the archives of records covering the United Territories, vaster than those of the New Territories by a factor of ten.

There were separate archives for several intimidatingly large projects, too, more extensive than anything she had examined so far. Deep oceans of numbers and transactions where anything might lurk. She knew that she needed to review them from top to bottom, because the supplies for the camp could have come from anywhere, but she also knew that even with the help of her accountancy tools it would take several moonspans to comb through everything, and she was running out of time. She couldn't keep up the pretence that she was helping Special Operations indefinitely. Pretty soon she would have to go back to her ordinary duties, and even if Mitkos didn't revoke her access privileges it would take for ever to complete a global search in her spare time.

Meanwhile, Iryn Moonsdaughter, armed with far greater resources, was pursuing her own investigation, and Goodwill was trying to track down the map. Ysbel hadn't heard anything from him so far and wanted to believe that his silence meant that all was well. That he hadn't fallen foul of native authorities, or abandoned his quest. Although given what she knew about him, it was unlikely that he'd give up so easily or quickly. She wished that she had established a way to stay in contact with him, but when they had parted he had said that he did not know where he would be staying in Concord or if his investigation would take him elsewhere, so they'd agreed that if and when it became necessary he would reach out to her via the Ogres Grave station. She realised now that it gave him asymmetrical control over their relationship, that he could cut her out of anything he found.

Ilan called and told her that, just as he'd thought, a global search of his agency's internal records hadn't turned up any evidence of pre-First Contact surveys, or any kind of expedition to the drowned city. She arranged to meet him anyway, hoping to patch things up between them, although it felt more like duty than desire, and it didn't help her mood when he turned up a good half an hour after the agreed time. She'd become used to his poor time-keeping – it was part of his easy-going manner – but felt a growing irritation while the minutes ticked by.

They'd agreed to meet in one of the small native places Ilan had a talent for sniffing out, a tiny shack on a busy road junction in the industrial quarter, a place Ysbel had never before visited in a part of town she didn't know. The only human amongst the cheerful hum and clatter of native customers, mostly manufactory labourers, who crowded tables under a canvas awning that boomed and fluttered in the hot wind, she was perched on a button cushion at a corner table so low she had to sit sideways, trying and failing to concentrate on reviewing the latest findings put up by her accountancy tools while gusts of road dust and wood smoke blew over her, a heavy traffic of steam carts and wagons hauled by draft maras rolled by only a couple of metres away, and one of the striplings who waited on the tables kept anxiously topping up her bowl of water and asking her if she wanted to order yet. So she wasn't especially pleased to see Ilan when at last he strolled in, spending a couple of minutes greeting the owner of the place, who clearly knew him well, before at last sitting across from Ysbel, pushing back his hair with both hands and smiling with unjustified good cheer as he asked her how she had been.

The food was good, though – boiled crabs served whole – and for a few minutes, while Ilan showed Ysbel how to use hammers and pinchers to crack the shells and get at the meat, and fold it into flatbreads and dip the flatbreads in tiny bowls of pureed vegetables, it was like old times. He didn't ask her about her work, they mostly talked about his and exchanged low-level gossip about mutual friends, but her secrecy and obsession hung between them all the same. It had consumed her life, she had shut him out of it, and while they parted on tactfully guarded terms, it was clear that their relationship was over.

Ysbel felt sorry and guilty, and threw herself back into her work in an attempt to absolve herself. She hadn't quite given up trawling through records, but it seemed that the people who'd set up the camp had been better at covering their tracks than she'd assumed, and she thought it was time to attack the problem from another angle. A few days after the ill-starred meeting with Ilan, she went into town and had lunch with Bethane Marisdaughter, an acquaintance who worked for Management and Supply. After Ysbel had given her a highly edited version of her escapades in Concord, Bethane said that she had news of her own: she was quitting her job and the mainland, and returning to her commune on the Garden Isle. She and her partner planned to have a bunch of kids and grow vegetables and – she knew Ysbel would like this – work on developing new strains of coffee.

'Rural bliss,' Bethane said. She was a briskly efficient woman a little younger than Ysbel. They had met at one of the cultural events organised by Dalsy Diwasdaughter, and shared a love of long-distance running. 'It might not be as exciting as your news, but I can't wait.'

'I'll miss you,' Ysbel said.

'I'm sure you'll be too busy for that,' Bethane said, with no trace of unkindness. 'And I'm not going to miss the mainland. We've made a mess of it here, turned the natives against us by pushing them too hard and too fast, and there's going to be a reckoning soon. Hopefully just a reset, but there are signs that it might be something more drastic.'

'I hope we can find a way of fixing things,' Ysbel said, and over bowls of lobster stew pumped her friend for information about empty or abandoned facilities on the west coast, and discovered that Special Operations had got ahead of her – Bethane had already made a list of those properties for one of its agents. There were a good number of them, she told Ysbel. Because of the unfavourable political atmosphere, general unrest and acts of outright sabotage, projects and operations on the west coast were being suspended or scaled back, resulting in an overcapacity of depots, warehouses and offices. Some had been mothballed and others had been stripped out, ready to be handed back to the native owners when rental agreements expired. The Special Operations agent had been especially interested in one such place, a godown in Pleasant Bay. Bethane didn't know what had caught his attention, but she'd heard that a team had been sent to check it out.

This had happened just a few days ago, at about the time Ysbel had started her futile trawl through records. She wondered if Mitkos knew about it, and if he did why he hadn't told her, and she asked Bethane if the agent from Special Operations had mentioned Damage Limitation, or if Damage Limitation had been renting the godown.

'This is the funny agency that arrested you?'

'Not exactly arrested. Briefly detained.'

'Well, it wasn't them. Or any other agency for that matter. It was a native business,' Bethane said. 'Not tribal; one of their collectives. You know how they are with names, all florid promises and bad poetry? This one is a marvellous example, one of the best: "A Group of Young People Who Believe They Will Turn Dreams of the Past into Wonders of the Present".'

'What kind of business was it?'

'I have no idea, but whatever they were into, they were long gone by the time Special Operations came calling.'

Special Operations had put the godown under seal, but Bethane had copies of its keys and Ysbel called up a flitter and flew north to take a look. Pleasant Bay was a port town on the southern edge of a sheltered bay where, tens of thousands of years ago, a tsunami triggered by a big undersea earthquake had scoured away the fossil remains of a large ogre city and reshaped the land. The port was busy, exporting timber, wool, and fruit and vegetables to the rest of the New Territories, but the town itself was small and rural, clusters of low wooden buildings much like those of Ogres Grave scattered amongst stands of old-growth forest and common parkland where maras, black-tailed deer, grey foxes and wild shoats – pig-like omnivores descended from genetically engineered rats – roamed freely.

The docks were in the native style, built along a beach where small fishing boats ran straight onto shore and sold their catches, and ragboats and skiffs discharged their cargoes and were hand-loaded with goods they took out to ocean-going ships at anchor in the deep-water channel in the middle of the bay. Ysbel parked the flitter on a patch of sandy ground and walked along the road above the beach's long curve to the godown, a low yellow brick building with a curved turf roof. She broke the security seal on the door and used two different keys, one a sliver of plastic that kicked back electrical deadbolts, the other a toothed strip of wood that worked a chunky wooden lock. Inside, the place was as empty as a blown egg. Beams of sunlight dropped from skylights set in the roof, throwing shadows of the neatly carpentered roof trusses across limewashed walls and a floor of pounded earth coated in thick honey-coloured resin. If the young people who claimed they would turn dreams of the past into wonders of the present had left anything behind, Special Operations must have taken it. Ysbel sat in a patch of sunlight on the floor, but couldn't get a reading of the place – what it had been used for, the nature of the people who had worked there.

There was a small shipyard next to the godown, where labourers were scraping and hammering at the hull of a two-masted coastal trader hove down on a shingle bank. Its foreman, a pot-bellied old native with a suspicious squint and a wad of chewleaf bulging in one cheek, told Ysbel that the people who had rented the place had kept themselves to themselves. 'Foreigners,' he said, meaning natives from the United Territories. 'Foreigners, and once in a rare while one or two of yours.'

Ysbel had got up a composite image of Kirder Halmasdaughter, but when she showed the printout to the foreman he spat a thin stream of black juice and said that she must forgive him for his ignorance, but as far as he was concerned all her people looked alike. According to him, the people who rented the godown had left a little over a year ago. He said there'd been four of them. Four that he'd seen on the regular, at any rate. He didn't know where they had come from or where they had gone. They seemed to have been running a small import business – mixed goods, food, construction supplies and the like – but he didn't know where any of it had been sent to. Somewhere inland, he guessed – there had been wagons coming and going. Ysbel asked if the goods had been taken to the railway station, but the foreman didn't know. They kept themselves to themselves, he said. You only saw them when a shipment came in. They didn't eat at any of the local food stalls, or take part in morning or evening invocations. A friend of his had offered them a good deal on a load of seasoned timber once but had been swiftly rebuffed.

It was early in the evening, now. Too late to head further north. There was no compound at Pleasant Bay, very little human presence beyond a small station shared by Management and Supply and a wellbeing clinic. Ysbel walked back to the flitter and along the way stopped at a stall and bought a rolled grape leaf stuffed with shrimp and slices of pickled lime, and ate it while watching the sun wester over steep dry hills on the northern side of the narrows that linked the bay with the ocean. She reckoned that it was no coincidence that the import business had shut down at around the same time as the camp had been abandoned, and suspected that she hadn't been able to discover any evidence of diversion of supplies to the camp because everything had been washed through businesses like this one, so that its final destination couldn't be traced by human agencies. She wondered if Joyous Hightower's syndicate had organised and funded the scheme, thought that Goodwill might be able to find out.

The discovery was not especially pleasing: she had wasted time looking in the wrong place, and Special Operations had beaten her to the prize. She had no doubt that they also had visited the railhead near the border with bear country where the line that ran north from Pleasant Bay terminated, but she knew that she had to go there anyway. It was the nearest railhead to the camp, the place which had aroused Goodwill's suspicions when he had discovered that it been receiving shipments long after its business of dispatching captured bears into bear country had ended. Ysbel wanted to ask about those shipments and discover, if anyone had passed through the railhead after the camp had closed, where they had been heading. Any people, and any bears, too.

She bedded down under the flitter and was woken in the middle of the night by a light shining in her face and a voice behind it asking her with patient politeness if she required any assistance. The voice belonged to a young bailiff, who told her that it would be better if she spent the rest of the night with her own people. When she asked him if it was illegal to sleep near the beach he told her that of course it was not, carters who brought in goods often did, as she could see by the campfires, but it was unusual for one of her people to do so, and perhaps a little unwise, too.

'There are some who do not hold you in the esteem that you might believe you deserve,' he said, and Ysbel wondered if he was one of them. A couple of years ago no native lawkeeper would have challenged her like this.

She tried to turn it to her advantage, asked him about the godown which had recently been of interest to some of her people. Did he know anything about the group which had rented it?

'I regret that I do not,' the bailiff said. 'They left before I started work here.'

'Perhaps someone more senior than yourself could enlighten me.'

'Perhaps, if they were not on leave, or busy elsewhere.'

Ysbel could have challenged this plain untruth, being a rude human who scorned custom and law, but suspected that the bailiff's attitude would be shared by his fellows, and assured him that she would be on her way first thing tomorrow, and meanwhile, not wishing to disturb anyone at this late hour, she would sleep inside her vehicle.

At dawn, after a few hours of restless sleep in the flitter's cramped cabin, Ysbel scraped a hole in the dirt inside a tangle of brush and discreetly relieved herself, and walked down to the beach and splashed saltwater on her face and bought some kind of flatfish from one of the fishing boats drawn up on the sand. She filleted the fish with her knife and grilled the meat on a hot stone at one of the communal fires, the natives around it drifting away one by one until she was on her own, watched by small groups gathered here and there on the beach and the road. Some of the watchers followed at a respectful distance as she ambled as casually as she could manage back to the flitter, and she took it up under manual control, turning it in a circle for the benefit of her audience on the ground before dipping its nose and flying it out across the bay, heading due north.

21.

The railhead was a fan of sidings in a broad flat clearing in a seemingly endless ocean of trees. A dead-straight railway track ran south while a road snaked northward through the forest. Ysbel glimpsed the river that marked the border with bear country, tried and failed to spot the camp. It was just fifty kilometres away. Around three hundred stades, by the natives' reckoning. And somewhere beyond it, assuming they hadn't yet been caught, were Raia and Seven.

Scattering bots into the air for a quick and dirty survey, Ysbel saw rows of chain-link cages strung along loading banks and a chequerboard of pits with fringes of sharp stakes pointing downward, to stop prisoners climbing out. The cages and pits were empty; the tracks were overgrown. Wagons rotted amongst weeds and volunteer saplings and several wood-burning locomotives stood nose-to-tail, one with steam tubes sprung like questing tentacles from its burst boiler. But the place was not completely abandoned: there were heat signatures in and around a scattering of shacks, and clustered by the bright star of a fire behind one of the station's sheds.

She recalled the bots, landed the flitter at a discreet distance and followed a muddy, potholed path that wound past shacks and vegetable plots. An old female native in a pinafore dress and headscarf was hoeing rows of sweetroot plants, but when Ysbel called out, asked where she could find the station chief, the native gave her a brief blank stare before turning her back and resuming her work. Further on, up on one of the loading banks, two raggedy striplings were using long canes to prod a bear, starveling thin and afflicted with some kind of mange that had left bare ulcerated patches in its pelt, hunkered down in one corner of a chain-link cage. It was stoically ignoring its tormentors, but turned its head towards Ysbel as she approached. When she asked the striplings where she could find the person in charge of this place one of them pointed to the sheds on the far side of the sidings and told her that the arbiter was most likely around there.

'What about the station chief?'

'Isn't one no more,' the stripling said.

'And who is this arbiter?'

'She has the ear and voice of the Mother,' the stripling said.

It was a formulaic way of saying that someone had absolute authority.

The other stripling, bored with the exchange, had begun to poke at the bear again. When Ysbel said that they shouldn't mistreat a captive, the older stripling said, 'He's ours, not yours.'

'Why haven't you sent him across the border, like all the others?'

'Because he's ours.'

'Does he have a name?' Ysbel said.

'Stink,' the second stripling said.

'Because he stinks,' the first one said.

'I meant the name he uses,' Ysbel said, looking straight at the bear. 'Is it by any chance a number?'

The bear seemed to pay attention for a moment, raising his head and looking directly at her, then yawned hugely, showing broken teeth and a cankerous tongue, and looked past her into some far distance only it knew or cared about.

'No use talking to bears,' the first stripling said scornfully. 'They aren't like us.'

'She isn't like us either,' his friend said.

The first stripling ignored him, told Ysbel the arbiter might answer her questions. 'She knows more about bears than anyone else in the whole world.'

The sheds were long and low, with unkempt turf roofs. Rubbish was caught in clumps of weeds and trampled into the mud, piebald shoats and several crows – the biggest Ysbel had ever seen – were rooting about a string of horizontal poles draped with flattened fillets of fish drying in the air, and a motley group of natives, all but one of them male, were sitting around a smouldering bonfire, smoking pungent redweed and drinking small beer from birchbark cups they dipped in a communal pot. A grizzled old female, obviously the arbiter, perched on a small heap of straw-stuffed sacks, her tooled-leather boots not quite touching the ground. She was draped in a cape or cloak made from the blond pelt of a bear cub, its sightless head flopped over one shoulder, and as Ysbel approached she lifted a staff with a cluster of rattle bells hung from the top by strips of leather, jingled it to get the attention of her crew and said loudly, 'What kind of ogre has come to trouble us now?'

Ysbel stepped around the circle of beer drinkers, trying to ignore their frank, bellicose stares, and introduced herself to the arbiter and said that she was following up on the investigation by Special Operations.

'We remember them, and not fondly,' the arbiter said. Her voice was a low growl; a necklace of bear claws hung on her chest and a large tooth-edged knife fashioned from yellow bone was strapped to her thigh.

Ysbel, hoping that a display of contrition would ease the arbiter's distrust, said that she was sorry to hear that, explained that she represented an agency whose purpose was to ensure that relationships between humans and the people were as harmonious as possible.

'Your friends weren't too concerned about harmony when they came here, asking a lot of questions and refusing to acknowledge any of ours,' the arbiter said. 'Acting as if their laws bound us, contrary to all fact. So if you've come here to ask more questions, think again. It would be better, for the sake of this harmony you speak of, if you gave us some answers instead.'

'I'll do the best I can, although I can't promise that I have answers to everything,' Ysbel said.

The arbiter regarded her with a gleam of interest. 'That's quite tricky of you.'

'I don't mean it to be. It's just that I wouldn't have disturbed you if I knew everything I need to know.'

'She thinks she's cleverer than us, lads,' the arbiter told her crew. 'As all of her kind do.'

'I think you may have been a bear trapper, once upon a time,' Ysbel said.

'I am and always will be a trapper, and make no secret of it.'

'So you must know more about bears than I ever will.'

'You can be certain of that,' the arbiter said. 'But you might tell me what your people were up to, in that camp in bear country. That's what your friends were interested in, and I suppose you must be too.'

'I am. Especially this woman,' Ysbel said, pulling the composite image of Kirder Halmasdaughter from her satchel and handing it to the arbiter.

She glanced at it and gave it back, saying, 'Never seen her before.'

'What about your friends?' Ysbel said, and held up the image so that the group around the fire could see it. A gang of pups and striplings had gathered a little way off, the pair of striplings who had been tormenting the bear amongst them.

No one spoke up. Some feigned boredom or disinterest; others glared at Ysbel with undisguised hostility. For a moment, they looked like malicious children wearing animal masks, an inversion she hadn't experienced for a long time. It reminded her that she was the only human here. The only human, apart from Raia somewhere out in bear country, for hundreds of kilometres in every direction.

'We told your friends we had no knowledge of any of your kind at the camp,' the arbiter said. 'And since that's the plain truth of it, I can't tell you any different.'

'Perhaps my friends also asked you about a collective by the name A Group of Young People Who Believe They Will Turn Dreams of the Past into Wonders of the Present,' Ysbel said.

'What if they did?' the arbiter said. She seemed to be enjoying their exchange, which gave Ysbel a little hope that she might let slip something she had held back from the Special Operations agents.

'Did they tell you that the collective was shipping supplies for the camp from Pleasant Bay to this railhead?'

No one answered. A young native took his long-stemmed pipe from his mouth and spat accurately into the flames of the fire. Another scratched under the rim of a conical leather hat.

'You'd have to ask the station chief about that,' the arbiter said. 'If you can find him. He retired three years back. Went south, and no one replaced him.'

Someone in the crew around the fire hooted softly, mockingly.

Ysbel said, 'I was wondering how those supplies got to the camp. If anyone was paid to take them there. What they might have seen if they did.'

387

The arbiter stared at her for a moment and Ysbel felt a chill, knowing she had pushed too hard.

'You said you'd answer our questions,' the arbiter said. 'But so far all you've done is ask questions of your own. So I'll ask again, and ask you plain and simple, expecting a plain and simple answer: why were they keeping bears at that camp?'

'Didn't the people from the camp ever tell you?'

'There you go again. Answering a question with another question. No, they didn't tell us, and we didn't ask. Used to be, when the traffic in captured bears was regular, we'd make good coin tending them and helping to release them into bear country. That trade has long gone, but people in the camp — our people, not yours — would sometimes buy deer meat and fish from us. And pay over the odds, too. So, not wishing to lose that business, we didn't ask too many questions about theirs. They told us they were studying bears. Finding new ways of controlling them, keeping them in check. And that, as I told your friends in Special Operations, was all we wanted or needed to know. But we didn't realise back then that your people had something to do with that camp, so I'll ask again. What was it they were doing there?'

'They were making the bears into what they once were,' Ysbel said, and tried to ignore the stir and chorus of whispers behind her.

'What they once were,' the arbiter said. 'And how did they go about doing that?'

'How do you treat anyone with an illness? They captured some bear cubs and cured them.'

'Cured them how? With ogre magic?' the arbiter said, eliciting several sardonic hoots from her crew.

'I don't yet know,' Ysbel said. 'Whatever it was, it rid the cubs of their madness. Turned them into peaceable intelligent creatures no different to you and me.'

388

'Bears were never like us. Not when they kept us as slaves, and not now. And none here would contradict me, since all have experience of them,' the arbiter said, and pointed at one of the people around the fire. 'Tell them what happened to you, Makepeace.'

Makepeace was a rheumy-eyed, swag-bellied person dressed in a ragged shift stitched from sacking, but he met Ysbel's gaze when he stood up and spoke with fierce dignity. 'It was my son,' he said. 'My eldest. Hopestill. Out in the forest, picking mushrooms with his friends when a bear surprised them. They scattered and ran, but Hopestill was taken. We searched for him, found what was left of his clothes. Part of his arm was still in a sleeve of his jerkin, but we found no other trace of him.'

'That's what bears are,' the arbiter told Ysbel. 'That's what they do, those that manage to cross the river and slip past the border patrol, like the one that took poor Hopestill. Your people could have helped us keep them where they belong, but instead it seems that without a by-your-leave they've been meddling where they oughten't.'

Someone in her crew shouted, 'Exactly so!' and another, 'Shame!'

Ysbel, feeling that the atmosphere was growing dangerously charged, told the arbiter that she was sorry if Special Operations had upset her and her people, said that all she wanted to know was what happened when the camp closed. 'Where the people, yours and mine, went. Whether they took the bears with them.'

'First we knew about it was the shipments for the camp stopped coming. Where the people running it went, or why, I couldn't tell you.'

'The people from the camp, and the bears, they didn't pass through here, on their way to somewhere else?'

'If they'd brought any strange bears here, they wouldn't have got far,' the arbiter said. 'My boys and I would have seen to that.'

Ysbel waited out the chorus of agreement from the arbiter's crew and said, 'May I ask about the bear in the cage, over by the sidings? Is he from the camp? Did he escape, was he left there?'

'Old Stink? No, he's just a bear. As crazy bad as all the rest. And before you start in about how it's against some law or other, I'll remind you that you just admitted that your people conspired to break a higher law. The Mother made the bears as they once were, and as they are now. She punished them for their apostasy and freed our people. So it stands to reason that trying to cure them is not only unnatural, but goes against Her will.'

The arbiter seemed genuinely angry, pelt bristling, black lips pulled back from small sharp teeth, gaze flat and unforgiving. She pointed her staff at Ysbel, rattle bells jangling.

'I remember when one of your people passed through here some years back. Before the camp was built. When we still had a station chief, and my mother was our arbiter. This fellow said he was surveying the border and asked all kinds of questions, just like you, and your friends before you. As if he had a right to ask us anything he wanted, and expected us to answer like pups being schooled. My mother turned things around by insisting he share some redweed with her. We grow some good strong redweed here,' the arbiter said. 'Puts you right close to the Mother. And this fellow I'm telling you about, it soon loosened his tongue. He told us about your Mother, the other Mother up in the Daughter Moon, and said he knew something about her most of his people didn't. Said that just as his people were more powerful than us, and had been trying to raise us up, make us more equal, so she had been raised up by others more powerful than her.'

390

'What kind of others?' Ysbel said.

'He said that they live amongst the stars in the sky, as fish live in the rivers or the sea. Perhaps you have heard of them.'

'I've heard stories about something similar. But they are only stories.' Ysbel was thinking of Originists and their crazy theories. The possibility that some of them might have been involved in the camp, and the treatment and education of Seven and his brothers and sisters. She said, 'Do you remember the name of this fellow? When did he visit you?'

'Ten, maybe eleven years ago. And if I ever knew his name I don't recall it.'

'And it was definitely before the camp was built,' Ysbel said, wondering if the man had been checking likely sites.

'I don't know if he had anything to do with the camp or not. Nor do I care. The point being, as my mother put it, doesn't matter if that story about sky people is true or not. It's a sign of a deeper truth you don't want to admit about yourselves. That you aren't any better than us, and your Mother isn't any better than ours. You talk about harmony, but it's only talk,' the arbiter said. 'Because you treat us like pups, ignore custom and law, and work against the Mother's will.'

It was unclear if she was talking about Ysbel, the Special Operations agents, the people involved with the camp and the articulate bears or all of humanity. Perhaps, as far as she was concerned, the distinction didn't matter. She used her staff to lever herself to her feet and Ysbel took a step back, aware that the crew around the fire were standing up too.

'You came here uninvited, asking the same questions your friends asked,' the arbiter told her. 'Expecting us to bow down to you, suggesting we're somehow to share the blame for what went on in that camp. Let me tell you that you aren't any better than us and you aren't wanted here. Leave now, of your own free will, or we'll make you leave.'

The crew around the fire, and the pups and striplings beyond, took up the chant. 'Leave! Leave now!'

'I'm grateful for your candour,' Ysbel said, and took another step backwards and pressed her hands to her chest, but the arbiter refused to acknowledge the gesture.

Thinking that anything else she said would only aggravate things further, Ysbel opened a link to the flitter and turned and began to walk away. Most of the arbiter's crew trailed after her, and pups and striplings danced along on either side, shouting at her, starting to trot and run as she lengthened her stride. Women and small pups had come out of the shacks to watch, standing in doorways, in vegetable patches. Neither they nor any of the crew intervened when a stripling danced up and leered in Ysbel's face, or when another threw a stone. Other striplings, emboldened, joined in, gleeful that this stranger, this hateful other, was at their mercy. Ysbel lifted an arm to ward off the small rain of missiles. A clod of mud burst on her elbow and a stone smacked her forehead and her sight flashed black for a moment and she stumbled, suddenly afraid that if she fell the mob might close on her. She wanted to run, but the thought of a pack of natives pulling her down like wolves swarming a moose restrained her. They were half her height or less, but she was badly outnumbered and she had never before seen natives behave like this. She brought down a couple of bots, had them flash like bright stars in the faces of those closest to her. It won her a few moments' grace, but then a stripling danced in and hit her across the hip with a branch, hit her again so hard the branch broke. She staggered and recovered and walked faster, shielding her face as best she could, stones clattering on the hull of the flitter as she heaved up its hatch and tumbled through.

She had primed the machine before she'd walked away from the arbiter. It took off as soon as she was inside, beating straight up and hanging in the air in loiter mode, waiting for her next instruction. She was breathing hard and her heart was hammering and blood was running down her face. She blotted it with the cuff of her blouson and took stock. The wave of panicky fear was withdrawing. She was safe now, higher than the treetops, a little crowd of figures jigging in thwarted rage below. She took manual control and urged the flitter forward and down, towards the loading docks. Crabbing through the air, dropping the cargo cable from its spool in the flitter's belly, the grab hook at its end swaying above the cages. She failed to hit the spot she'd been aiming for, lifted the flitter a little and tried again. This time the hook dropped neatly into the cage that held the bear and she unspooled more of the cable until it began to coil on the floor. The bear crouched unmoving in a corner. The crazy old thing didn't understand that she was trying to rescue it, that all it had to do was hold onto the cable and she'd pull it out of its cage.

She rewound the cable until the grab hook was clear of the coil wire that topped the cage, set the flitter down and popped the hatch. A ragged crowd was running across the sidings towards her. She dragged the cable to the bear's cage and jammed the hook through the wire mesh, palms sweating as she bore down on the hook's recalcitrant catch until at last it gave and snapped shut.

Natives were clambering onto the loading dock and a small rain of stones was clattering around her as she swung into the flitter and took it back up. The cable snapped taut, the flitter skewed and a section of mesh ripped away, swinging from the hook. Ysbel watched as the bear trotted out of the wreckage, natives bunching together uncertainly as it raised its head and sniffed the air. Across the fan of overgrown sidings, the arbiter was standing in front of one of the sheds, raising a musket to her shoulder. Ysbel didn't hear the shot but saw the puff of white smoke, saw the bear turn and lollop away past the string of abandoned locomotives. She waited until it had vanished into the trees, then took the flitter higher and headed south.

22.

She had flown little more than forty kilometres, was still following the railway track as it cut through forest and swamp, when her link dropped its connection with the flitter's controls. She grabbed the stick and switched to manual, but that wasn't working either. Someone or something had taken charge: the flitter was descending in a long glide, dropping neatly between the trees on either side of the railway and touching down lightly, its skids straddling the single track.

Her link had also lost its connection to the grid. The flitter's comms had switched off and wouldn't reboot.

'You found me,' she said, certain that whoever had taken control of the flitter was watching her. 'And now you can tell me who you are and what you want.'

No reply. She waited a couple of minutes, then cracked the hatch and climbed out. Cool, still air. The clean scent of pine trees. Birdsong, and a hollow, staccato percussion in the distance, perhaps a woodpecker. The flitter perched on the track like a monstrous insect, a wedge of sunlight gleaming off the transparent bubble of its cabin, the cable and the wreckage from the bear's cage tangled under its belly.

Behind her, the railway stretched straight as a ruled line; ahead, it curved east, disappearing into the forest's green distances. Nothing moved in the shadows under the trees and the narrow strip of blue sky between their sawtoothed crests was unblemished, but she had a strong, spooky feeling that she was being watched.

'Show yourself,' she said, and startled when a spark kindled in front of her, lengthening and broadening into a familiar figure.

'I might have known,' she said.

'It is good to talk to you again, Ysbel Moonsdaughter,' Zaquil said.

'How long have you been eavesdropping?'

'You severed our link, but I found your new bot network to be very accommodating,' Zaquil said. 'I enjoyed your conversation with the arbiter and her friends. It was a lively exchange.'

'Am I under arrest?'

'This isn't my doing.'

'Then it has to be Iryn Moonsdaughter. Tell me I'm wrong.'

'Two agents under her command will be arriving shortly.'

'If she wants to talk to me she could have waited until I got back to Ogres Grave.'

'She is presently in Concord.'

'What is she doing in Concord? No, wait. There's only one likely reason. It's Goodwill, isn't it?'

'I cannot say.'

'You don't know, or you can't tell me?'

'I don't know everything, Ysbel. Surprising as that may seem.'

'Then restore my link. Patch me through to her.'

'I'm afraid I cannot do that.'

'One day I'd like to meet the person who made you. Explain to them where they went wrong.'

'I was not made, Ysbel Moonsdaughter. I grew from a seed, and learned how to become useful through training and experience.'

'You need more training. And more experience, too.'

'I can't tell you about Iryn Moonsdaughter's plans because I am not employed by her, or anyone else in Special Operations.'

'Then why are you here? To gloat?'

'I serve a higher authority,' Zaquil said, and his image froze.

Ysbel was afraid that someone in Special Operations had discovered that he was inside her bot network and had shut it down, but then a tall woman in a cloak as blue as the ocean stepped through him, and a freezing thrill pierced her from head to foot.

'Your relationship with the bailiff has proved to be more useful than I'd hoped, Ysbel Moonsdaughter,' Mother said.

Ysbel had to suck spit into her mouth before she could speak. 'Is that why I have been summoned to Concord?'

There was no lag in Mother's reply; this must be a fragment or aspect rather than the real thing, in her fastness on the Moon. Even so, the manifestation was amazing and terrifying.

'It is clear to me now that the disappearance of the map, and the camp where the articulate bear was raised, are part of the same conspiracy,' she said. 'A secret collusion with natives, hidden from me and from the Authority and its agencies. It is deep, child, very deep and very dark, and it threatens to destroy the relationship between humans and natives, and plans for greater unity. People have broken the terms of the treaty, acted without the Authority's consent or my blessing and created a clandestine network. A parasitic growth that must be rooted out.'

Ysbel thought at once of Kirder Halmasdaughter. 'Do you know who these people are?'

'Things are kept from me,' Mother said. 'More and more, I have been excluded from the affairs of my children. Even those who serve me directly. But the plot you have helped to uncover is proof that they still need me. This little expedition of yours may be unsanctioned, but I believe that it is proof of your dedication. Am I right to think that, child? Are you trying to serve me as best you can?'

'I'm not sure if I've found anything useful,' Ysbel said carefully. 'Nothing that you didn't already know.'

'I believe that Iryn Moonsdaughter has summoned you to Concord because she believes that your friend the bailiff has found something of interest, and wants you to find him and find out what he knows. Agree to help her, learn everything you can about her plans and what she knows about the map and the camp, and afterwards we will talk again,' Mother said, and her avatar and Zaquil's frozen image blinked out.

Ysbel hoped that the helper was still watching over her, but he did not show himself or respond when she called his name. She told the air that control of the flitter should be returned to her, said that things would go better if she made her own way to Concord and searched for Goodwill without the oversight of Special Operations, but received no reply.

With nothing better to do, she perched spraddle-legged on one of the rails and absent-mindedly ate what was either a late lunch or an early supper from a ration pack, and considered her options. It didn't take long. She hadn't learned everything she wanted to know, had run out of leads and had been asked to take Mother's side in a power struggle with Special Operations and the Authority.

She remembered the old man who'd used to drop into the Data Analysis offices every now and then. He'd been the section chief in the frantic, exhilarating years after First Contact, and after his retirement had taken to revisiting the scene of his old triumphs because he couldn't find much else to do with his life, his partner dead, his children busy with their careers on the mainland. He'd be welcomed by the current section chief, they'd talk over tea in the chief's office and afterwards he'd wander around, hoping to find some way of being useful, asking questions but not really listening to answers, poignantly needy, adrift and out of touch.

Mother's intervention, and her claims about a shadowy cabal, seemed to spring from a similar struggle with increasing irrelevance. Like everyone else, Ysbel had been schooled in devotion and loyalty to her, but it was founded on history and tradition, gratitude for what Mother had once been and what she had once done, not what she was now. Even before First Contact, people had outgrown her lunar cradle and mostly lived on Earth, and no longer needed her help or advice. She was still a power, which was why Ysbel had been asked to satisfy her curiosity about the map, but this was something deeper and more treacherous: an attempt to gain some measure of control over something that might completely reconfigure the relationship between humans and natives. It would be dangerous to refuse her, but Ysbel reckoned that it would be equally dangerous to cross Iryn Moonsdaughter.

At least, she thought, she was going to be taken to where she wanted and needed to go. If she could find Goodwill, if he'd found something useful, if he still trusted her, perhaps she could find some way of placating both parties. And if that proved impossible, maybe she could throw in with him, and the native authorities, and see where that took her. If she was going to be shamed and disgraced, it should at least be for the right cause.

The Moon was rising above the darkening forest and frogs were tuning up their orchestra of whistles and croaks and barks when at last Zaquil materialised again, perching on the rail opposite Ysbel, faintly glowing in the dusk. He didn't say anything, simply raised a hand and pointed to the star falling through the violet ribbon of sky caught between the treetops. It was a hopper, come to take Ysbel to Concord and the crux of her impossible choice.

23.

Two days later, Ysbel was sitting at a table by one of the stalls in a riverside cheap in Highwater Reach. Twenty minutes past nine in the evening by her link; the first quarter of the small night according to the elaborate water clock that stood in the crossing point of two aisles. A bowl of tea cooling at her elbow as she tried to ignore passers-by who stared at her with undisguised curiosity, and she told herself that natives were notoriously bad time-keepers, and anyway Goodwill was only a little late.

Special Operations had intercepted a tapcode message Goodwill sent to the bureau's office in Ogres Grave, asking Ysbel to meet him in Concord. Iryn Moonsdaughter had sent a reply on Ysbel's behalf, care of the public tapcode office in Concord's central railway station, saying that she could be there within a day and asking what he wanted to talk about, and Goodwill had responded with a date, a time and a place.

Iryn told Ysbel about this after debriefing her about her forensic examination of the financial records, and her visit to the godown in Pleasant Bay and the railhead near the border with bear country. They were in a small room in the basement of the embassy in Concord. The hopper had taken Ysbel there directly, scorching the embassy's manicured lawn when it touched down, and after a tech had cleaned and patched the cut on her forehead she'd been left to cool her heels for several hours in the windowless room's over-bright glare, her boots and trouser cuffs still muddy, her blouson reeking of smoke from the beer drinkers' fire, a deep, tender bruise developing across her hip, before Iryn arrived.

The woman was telling her now that Goodwill had last been seen in conversation with a government officer, five days ago.

'His cousin, I suppose,' Ysbel said. 'Juniper Saltmire, chief clerk to a delegate of the Committee of the Five Hundred.'

'They met in the cheap where he wants to meet you,' Iryn said. 'They were discussing the camp, the story about those articulate bears, but the cheap is a busy, noisy place and we only have part of their conversation. He dropped out of sight after that, but we think that it's likely he has discovered something more about the native side of the camp's operation. If he's found out who was in charge, we might be able to identify the people who were working with them.'

'What about Joyous Hightower?' Ysbel said. 'He may not have had anything to do with the camp's operation, but his syndicate was involved in its construction and transportation of supplies.'

'Presently, he's holed up in his tribe's Hearth, on the west coast. Trying to overturn a request to appear before some kind of tribunal about his business arrangements with our people. Whether that's anything to do with your friend I don't know, but the request was issued after his meeting with that cousin of his.'

'He's resourceful. And tenacious.'

'Let's hope his resourcefulness has turned up what we need to know. Who built the camp. Who got up the cure. What happened to the articulate bears and, if they're still alive, where we can find them,' Iryn said, bending back a finger

401

for each point. 'If you can find out the answers to those questions, I can overlook the story you got up to persuade your boss to give you access privileges. I might even stretch to a commendation.'

Ysbel was hollowed out by exhaustion and anxiety, and didn't know if Iryn knew about her brief conversation with Mother, but tried her best to finesse her situation, saying that she wanted something more than being excused punishment for carrying out what she believed to be a legitimate inquiry.

'If Goodwill asks me to help him, I have to be able to act as I see fit, without consulting you or anyone else. And you have to guarantee that you'll give him any help he requests.'

'He'll get what we can give, within reason,' Iryn said. 'And if it turns out that you need to pair up with him again, I'll want regular updates. Everything you and he find. Everything the two of you do or plan to do.'

'Of course,' Ysbel said, because it wasn't as if she had a choice. She felt that she was being ground between two implacable and opposing forces. She'd dumped her bots before Special Operations arrived, and reckoned that if she switched off her link after she met with Goodwill neither Zaquil's beady-eyed sliver nor Special Operations would be able to spy on her directly. She hoped she could feed both sides a careful edit of everything she discovered without compromising her friend, and knew that she'd have to tell him that Special Operations was keeping watch on them. He'd probably guess that anyway, but it helped her to think that, on balance, she would be helping rather than betraying him, and she wanted to believe – even though she quailed at the enormity of it, the finality – that she still had the option of escaping both Mother and Iryn Moonsdaughter and going over to the other side. What would they call her, for favouring another species instead of her own?

'We'll keep you under surveillance as best we can,' Iryn told her. 'And we reserve the right to extract you at any time we see fit. If Goodwill Saltmire gives up what we need to know at this meeting, we could do that straight away.'

'This isn't just about what he knows now,' Ysbel said. 'It's also about what else he may be able to find out with my help.'

'Focus on what we need to know,' Iryn said. 'Who built the camp. Who designed the cure. What happened to the articulate bears. All right?'

'All right. But I think it will be more complicated than that.'

'Of course it's more complicated. But that's all you have to worry about. And I should warn you,' Iryn said, with a hard, serious look, 'that if you somehow manage to get into trouble with the natives again, we won't be able to help you.'

'I guessed that was pretty much a given,' Ysbel said.

Iryn studied her. 'Get some sleep. My people will go over the technical details of the operation tomorrow. And remember: what you find out will determine what happens to you when this is over.'

Now, almost an hour past the agreed time for her rendezvous with Goodwill, most of the stalls in the cheap closing or already shuttered, Ysbel was beginning to wonder if he had spotted that she was the bait in a setup. Iryn's people had staked out the cheap and were waiting to eavesdrop on her conversation with him, and natives recruited by the embassy and lent to the operation had been posted inside. Ysbel was pretty sure that the stallholder across the way had to be one of them – he'd pulled down the shutters of his place shortly after she'd taken her seat, and had been assiduously scrubbing tables and chairs ever since, taking great care not to look at her. And then there was the cleaner who was circling the water clock, making a show of whisking his coconut-leaf broom across the flagstones. He'd completed his sixth circuit when a voice in her link told her that there was activity outside the cheap.

'A procession, it looks like. Stay in place and stand by.'

A few moments later Ysbel heard drums. A faint steady heartbeat.

The woman who owned the seafood stall came over and said bluntly that she was finished for the day. 'All done. I must go home.'

Ysbel apologised, saying that she was expecting to meet a friend, but the woman confiscated the half-empty bowl of tea and ran down the shutters of the stall and said again, 'All done,' and hurried away, vanishing into the shadows beyond the water clock. The cleaner had vanished too, and the drumming was growing louder. The stallholder scrubbing tables looked up from his work; voices began to chatter over Ysbel's link.

'Groups of natives converging on the cheap from three directions.'

'Do you have eyes? How many?'

'Some kind of march, it looks like.'

'Fireworks here. Fireworks and smoke.'

'Give me numbers. Someone give me numbers.'

'Fireworks and smoke here, too. Looks like a religious procession.'

'I'm counting a hundred on the march here. A hundred at least.'

'Definitely moving on the cheap.'

'Any sign of the target?'

'Nothing yet.'

'Stay in place, everyone. Eyes wide and watchful.'

The drumming was inside the cheap now. Ahead of Ysbel and behind her. Echoing off its low roof. She could see lights and drifts of coloured smoke above the stalls, hear the crackle of fireworks. The stallholder was staring straight at her, as if expecting her to do or say something, both of them turning to look as a tall cloud of pink smoke rolled out of the aisle on the other side of the intersection, shadowy figures moving inside it as it washed around the water clock.

Natives banging gongs and hand-drums, shaking guard rattles, blowing whistles. Natives shouldering tall poles topped with lanterns or fireworks sputtering sparks and smoke. A small group blowing horns that curled around their bodies and flared into wide mouths above their heads. They were dressed in the long yellow shirts of pilgrims and mystae, in breechclouts, in ordinary clothes. Some were bare-chested, with white dashes and circles painted on their leathery skin, and wore wooden masks with long beaks, tall masks of straw and dried grass, helmets plastered with mud. They walked in solemn procession or danced and capered in ragged circles around the water clock, and everything was dissolving inside the thickening fog of pink, sweet-smelling smoke.

Ysbel pushed to her feet, knowing this had to be something to do with Goodwill, trying to ignore the chatter in her link as she scanned the circling crowd. A firework burst over-head with a stutter of explosive pops and silvery streamers floated down, falling across her head and shoulders, and a small figure was trotting towards her through the fog. The librarian, Clarity Forrester, dressed in his uniform-grey tunic and scarlet trousers, looking up at Ysbel, telling her that Goodwill had sent him.

'Where is he?'

'He asked me to tell you that he is going to meet the articulate bears, and wants you to come with him,' Clarity said. 'Also, he wants you to switch off the telephone in your head, so that it cannot be used to track you.'

'I can switch it off, but I can't guarantee that I won't be followed.'

'We have a plan to lose your friends. Come with me.'

The crowd closed around her and a mad storm of fireworks crackled overhead as she followed Clarity through fog and wild drumming and discordant music, ducking into a narrow passage behind two rows of stalls. Clarity stooped and lifted up a hinged hatch in the floor, gestured at the narrow shaft.

'Where does that go?' Ysbel said.

'The Library, of course. Quickly. We have knocked down your friends' flying eyes, but they will send more.'

It was a tight fit. Ysbel, clutching projecting bricks that acted as hand- and foot-holds, descended into a brick-lined sewer tunnel flooded by ankle-deep water and lit by widely spaced oil lamps. She had to bend double, one hand on the slimy roof to steady herself, as she followed Clarity. He explained, somewhat breathlessly, that he had been dismissed for helping her and Goodwill, but Goodwill had recently found influential allies who had persuaded the Chief Librarian to forgive his failings. 'When he asked me to help him I gladly agreed. And here we are.'

'Goodwill has an acute sense of justice. Where is he?'

'The person who will take you to him is waiting for you in the Library,' Clarity said, and couldn't or wouldn't explain how or where Goodwill had found the articulate bears. 'He will tell you everything, I'm sure. We must hurry. Your friends will be looking everywhere, and sooner or later they will think to look here.'

'They can't look for me in the Library. Not without violating the treaty.'

'Some of my people are helping your people. The sooner we get you on your way the better.'

They splashed a long way through the tunnel and clambered up another shaft and emerged onto a stone wharf stretched alongside a sleeve of black water. Clarity led her at a brisk pace towards the far end, where a tramway slanted through a tunnel under the houses and grassways of Highwater Reach to the sidings and platforms of the Library's depot, deserted at this late hour apart from a cart painted in the Library's grey and red livery, a shaggy mara standing patiently between its shafts, its driver waiting beside it.

Ysbel sprawled flat on the cart's load bed under a heavy tarpaulin sheet as the cart rumbled out of the depot. Special Operations agents and native lawkeepers would be searching for her, bots were patrolling the night sky and she had no idea of where she was being taken or who Goodwill's allies were. It was likely that she was tangled up in some gnarly native politics, but on which side? Pragmatists who supported the treaty, or separatists who wanted to kick every last human out of the Union and the New Territories? What kind of bargain had Goodwill made, and how did she figure in it?

The exhilaration of her mad escape was fast fading; the load bed, slung between leather straps, swayed like a cradle. Ysbel dozed off, and when she woke the sky was paling. She lifted a corner of the tarpaulin, saw dense forest dropping away to the brown waters of the great river and asked the driver if it was safe to come out.

'Best not,' he said. 'Not until we get where we're going.'

'Where are we going?'

'Not far now,' he said, but more than an hour passed before the cart turned off the road, following a track that cut through the forest to a clearing where a trim white hopper reared up beyond the tumbledown sheds and overgrown burrows of an old lumber camp.

As Ysbel clambered down from the wagon, a group of natives came forward. Three young males – one a giant almost as tall as her, the other two with percussion pistols tucked in the broad belts that girdled their long grey shirts – and Goodwill Saltmire, dressed in his usual fustian and arm in arm with a stout, elderly female.

24.

As she was escorted towards the hopper, Goodwill told Ysbel that they would be travelling halfway around the world, to a meeting in the Dreaming.

'The Dreaming?'

'That's what the person who invited us there calls it. I believe you know it as Australia,' Goodwill said, his mouth making an odd shape to accommodate the human word. 'Apparently, the articulate bears were taken there after their camp closed down.'

Ysbel thought about that. 'It's a good place to hide. Big, uninhabited and a long way from anywhere else. Who invited us?'

'We will find out when we get there,' the old female said. 'We have been asked to bring you, and Goodwill claims that you can be trusted. I can only hope that he is right.'

She was Goodwill's cousin, Juniper Saltmire, chief clerk to a delegate of the Committee of the Five Hundred, and had organised use of the hopper – it was the one Ysbel had seen when she had arrived in Concord at the beginning of this long strange adventure, on loan to the government of the United Territories. The young males were her aides. Two more were waiting aboard the hopper, and the pilot was a native, too. Ysbel was the only human on the little expedition, and although it wasn't quite clear if she was a hostage or a guest, she didn't feel especially threatened. Goodwill and his cousin had gone to a lot of trouble to liberate her from Special Operations, and she was eager to find out who had issued the invitation, had all kinds of questions she wanted to ask.

The hopper threw itself into the sky as soon as its passengers were webbed into their seats, and after it reached the freefall stage of its long, suborbital lob and its motor cut off, Goodwill told Ysbel that the trail to the Dreaming had begun with something he had been given by Clarity Forrester when, thanks to Juniper's intervention, the librarian had been returned to his former position. He pulled a piece of paper from his vest and unfolded it and leaned into his seat's webbing so that he could hand it to Ysbel.

'I suppose this is a drawing of the infamous carving,' Ysbel said.

'The very same. I expect you have noticed the figures.'

'They're hard to miss.'

There were two of them, their round, featureless heads disfigured by crude gouges. They loomed over miniature representations of bears cutting down crops with sickles and loading carts with their harvest. And arching over the entire scene was a star with a long fiery tail.

'A scholar told me that they might represent fertility spirits, and had been defaced when the harvest failed once too often,' Goodwill said. 'But he also said that they are not much like representations of fertility spirits in other carvings, and agreed that they bear a striking resemblance to the figure in my uncle's famous map. Clarity Forrester discovered records of five more carvings like that in the catalogues. All of them were found in the ruins of new cities, and all are missing from the stacks.'

'Almost certainly taken by Joyous Hightower, or his agents,' Juniper said. 'He is a member of the Library's council, and sponsors several scholars who specialise in the history of bears. One of them may have smuggled out those carvings.' She sat upright in her seat, legs stuck straight out, hands folded on top of the hard ball of her pot belly, dark eyes fixed on Ysbel with a challenging gaze – she was one of the natives who didn't bother to hide their contempt for humans. Landers said at least you knew where you were with them, and could get down to business without dancing around for an hour or two, but Ysbel wasn't sure what Juniper's mislike meant for this expedition, how it would influence the way things fell out afterwards.

'Joyous Hightower has been collecting artefacts depicting contact between your people and bears for quite some time,' Goodwill said. 'And it gave me an idea about baiting a trap.'

With the help of the vendor of bear artefacts, Solomon Firststar ('We gave him a choice,' Juniper said. 'Help us or face the consequences.'), Goodwill had got up a convincing fake, and when Solomon Firststar offered it to his clients, someone claiming to represent Joyous Hightower expressed interest. A viewing was arranged, and the person was detained and put to question.

'It seems that Joyous Hightower has a network of agents which remained active after he fled to his tribe's Hearth,' Goodwill said. 'An extension of his legitimate business of acting as an intermediary between our people and yours. We persuaded the agent we caught to contact Joyous using a kind of telephone. Not the link given to him by your Authority, but a different kind of techne, given by those of your people involved with the matter of the articulate bears.'

'Do you know who these people are?' Ysbel said, thinking of Iryn's three questions.

'Not yet,' Goodwill said. 'Joyous Hightower said that someone wanted to meet us, and told us where we would find

411

them. Claimed that he had never met his employers face to face. Talked with them using the device they had given him.'

'Do you believe him?' Ysbel said.

'He must answer for his part in this, but he is not important,' Juniper said.

Ysbel said that her own investigations had been less successful, told Goodwill and Juniper about the native collective which had been supplying the camp of the articulate bears, and described her encounter with the arbiter and her crew at the railhead near the border with bear country and her conversation with Zaquil and Mother.

'It's possible that the locals at the railhead were co-operating with the people who set up the camp, and knew more about it than they would admit to me. You might have better luck at persuading them to tell the truth.'

'I'm sure you tried your best,' Juniper said. 'A pity it amounted to so little.'

Ysbel ignored the jibe. 'I did learn one thing from the arbiter. One of my people passed through the railhead some years ago, and told a story about our Mother. He said that she was not what she claimed to be, but had been created or awakened by sky dwellers. Some amongst my people have similar stories. They call themselves Originists. It may be that a group of Originists helped to set up the camp, and allowed their agent to be captured by you. We might not be heading towards a meeting but a trap got up to silence us.'

Juniper dismissed that as the kind of mistrust and groundless paranoia that polluted the relationship between humans and natives. 'Your people see a knife in every smile and think us naive for expecting the best of people rather than the worst.'

'It isn't paranoid to hope for the best but plan for the worst,' Ysbel said. 'It's common sense.'

'We have accepted an invitation in good faith,' Juniper

said. 'It is our best chance to understand this underhand collaboration between our peoples, and to find a way to make things good.'

'I hope you're right,' Ysbel said. 'I really do. But some of the people involved in this may not be entirely trustworthy. And whoever chose the Dreaming as a hiding place must have had a very good reason to want to stay hidden.'

'Until now,' Juniper said blithely.

25.

Presently, the pilot took a break from overwatch of the hopper's point-and-go automated flight system, told his passengers that they were less than an hour out from their destination and conjured an external view.

Dawn had set fire to the rim of the world, an arc of brilliant white light fading to nested layers of blue, defining the atmosphere's thin envelope, as the sun rose and lit the trackless ocean. The coast of the Dreaming edged into view, fretted with bands of cloud picked out in shades of pink and bronze and casting long shadows on the tawny land; soon afterwards Ysbel and the others were pressed into their seats by the force of de-acceleration, rattled by turbulence. Forest cut by loops of a slow, brown river rose up, a mote of bare red dirt set amongst a million treetops exploded into a landing field and they were down, sudden and still.

The pair of pistol-packing aides went out first, and after they reported that it seemed safe everyone else followed, Ysbel last of all, stepping into a flare of burning sunlight. It was winter here, at the bottom of the world, but as hot and humid as Concord.

Nothing moved around the scatter of utility sheds on the far side of the landing field, nor in the forest of tall, pale-barked trees that surrounded it; the profound silence was broken only by cracks and creaks as the hopper's fins baked off the last heat of re-entry. No welcoming party, no sign of habitation. Ysbel had left her satchel of bots behind when she'd been picked up in the middle of another forest just two days ago, and the hopper's surveillance system had been stripped out before it had been given over to the government of the United Territories. If they were going to find the person or people who had invited them here, they would have to go look for them.

The pilot was left to stand guard over the hopper; everyone else set out down a track that angled away into the forest beyond the shuttered, empty utility sheds. Something screeched overhead and flapped away unseen and flies materialised from the baking air, swarming around them, eager to sip sweat. There was no other sign of life until Goodwill spotted the first hut. It was a low mound off in the trees to one side, with red dirt walls and a straw roof. A strip of tilled earth gone to dry weeds stretched away between the trees. Some kind of groundvine with large coarse leaves embraced a cistern with cracked mud at its bottom.

Ysbel ducked through the hut's round, doorless entrance while the others were still debating about whether or not to go inside. The interior, lit by a shaft of light slanting through a smoke hole, was stripped bare. Empty shelf beds, human- or bear-sized, cut into the rammed-earth wall. Soot-stained niches where candles or rush lights had once stood. Cold ashes on a hearthstone. She tried to imagine a family of articulate bears living here. Growing crops. Hunting in the woods and fishing in the river. Singing songs learned from their feral cousins while fat little cubs tussled at their feet. But who had brought them here, and for what purpose?

'It smells like Seven,' Goodwill said. He was silhouetted in the entrance, snuffling the air.

'We keep finding places where the articulate bears and their carers have been,' Ysbel said. 'But where are they now?'

'Do you still think that this may be a trap?'

'I'm thinking of Trina Mersdaughter's single-handed voyage to Australia,' Ysbel said. 'The Dreaming. Perhaps it's only a coincidence — it was a couple of years before Raia met Seven and found out about the articulate bears. But what if Trina has been working for our Mother all along? Perhaps she discovered this place by accident, or had been sent here to look for it.'

'If that is true, neither your Mother nor your friend Iryn Moonsdaughter would need your help, because they would know about the camp and the bears.'

'Our Mother told me that some of us have been making secret pacts with your people. It seems to me that she may have been keeping things from us, too. And that I may not be the first person she's recruited.'

Goodwill thought about that. 'You rely on your Mother for stories about your past. Who you are, how you came to be here and so forth. And now we have discovered that some of those stories may be wrong, so it isn't surprising that you mistrust her.'

'Everything I thought I knew has been upended,' Ysbel confessed. 'I'm still trying to make sense of it. But I'm certain about one thing: your cousin should have brought more people, and more weapons.'

'I argued for it. But Juniper is eager to make a name for herself and more people would have meant less control. She brought only those she trusts, and agreed to arm two of her aides only when I pointed out that we might need protection from dangerous animals.'

'There are things more dangerous than animals.'

Goodwill squatted by the hearthstone and sifted wood ash through his fingers. 'If you are worried about the bears who lived here, they moved out many days ago.'

'You can tell from the ash?'

Goodwill stood and brushed off his hands, a curiously human gesture. 'From the weeds in the vegetable garden, which have had time to sprout and wither and die. Juniper is calling to us. We should move on.'

After finding the first hut, they spotted others off through the trees on either side, all likewise abandoned. At last, the track ended in a clearing around a large round burrow roofed with dry turf. A vent in the centre of the roof was squeezing out a slow steady stream of small white balloons, one every thirty seconds or so.

'What are they?' Juniper said to Ysbel, as they watched a balloon rise uncertainly above the treetops and drift away on the hot breeze.

'I don't know. Perhaps some kind of bot. Perhaps nothing more than balloons.'

'If they are flying eyes, where are they flying to?'

'Anywhere the wind takes them, it looks like. I don't think they are being used to spy on us,' Ysbel said, but she was nervous and alert as they circled the burrow, watching the trees and the sky for movement, seeing only balloons popping out of the vent and drifting up and away, tags on twists of wire dangling beneath each one. They seemed as harmless as children's toys, and suggested that this settlement had not been completely abandoned.

On the far side of the burrow, a narrow ramp slanted down into darkness between walls decorated with carvings of bears and globe-headed figures. The carvings gleamed as if they had been varnished and were slick to the touch; Ysbel told the others that they were most likely resin casts or 3D prints.

'If they are copies of bear carvings, it suggests that we have come to the right place,' Goodwill said.

'But what kind of place is it?' Ysbel said.

'The cradle of something new and wonderful,' a voice said.

Ysbel saw shadowy movement at the bottom of the ramp as a small bot began to climb into the light. It was got up from tubes and struts of black plastic and the ball of its head was crowned with a circlet of lenses.

Juniper's aides had bunched around her. The largest stood in front; the two armed with pistols had drawn their weapons, aiming them at the bot as it halted at the top of the ramp.

'Welcome,' it said.

'Who are you?' Ysbel said.

She had seen pictures of similar bots tending to First Generation babies and small children in the gardens of Mother's habitat on the Moon.

'I am the one who invited you here,' the bot said. It had a bright engaging voice, neither human nor native but somewhere in between. 'You have been admiring my art collection.'

'Where are the originals?' Ysbel said.

'In a safe place.'

'And the map? My uncle Pilgrim Saltmire's map?' Goodwill said. He had stepped up boldly beside Ysbel. Zaquil had accustomed him to talking machines and other miracles of human techne.

'That is safe too,' the bot said. 'I'd love to show you around the balloon works and the automatic crèche and so on, but there is only a little time and you have questions. Who am I? What is this place? Who lived here and where have they gone? Ask me anything and, I will do my best to answer.'

'The bears,' Ysbel said, when no one else spoke up. 'The articulate bears. Were they brought here from the camp in bear country?'

'From several camps.'

'There was more than one?'

'As I said.'

'And where are they now? It looks like they left some time ago.'

'After they learned how to make a living in their new home, they scattered into the unpopulated wilderness. Even I don't know where they are.'

'And the people who cured them and raised them,' Goodwill said. 'Where are they?'

'I gave them a place where they can shelter until what I like to call the revelation is over.'

'The revelation of what?' Ysbel said.

'The truth, of course.'

'The truth about the bears.'

'That's part of it.'

'And we are part of it too.'

'That's why you are here.'

'And Kirder Halmasdaughter,' Ysbel said. 'Are you sheltering her, too?'

'She is no longer active.'

'What do you mean? Is she dead?'

'If that's what happens to a machine intelligence when its code is deleted.'

'She was a bot, like you. Or like Mother's little helpers.'

'Somewhat more than a simple conversational algorithm, somewhat less than me. I'm glad, now, that you did not listen to her advice. Things have worked out better this way.'

'Who made her? And who made you?'

'No one made me, Ysbel Moonsdaughter. I am a fully autonomous fragment.'

Juniper stepped forward, followed by the two aides with pistols. 'You said that you would do your best to answer questions. Yet your answers only lead to other questions.'

'If it helps, everything I tell you is true.'

'It would help,' Juniper said, 'if you would tell us plainly who invited us here, and why.'

'If the conversational ability of this fragment is unsatisfactory, I apologise,' the bot said. 'Most of my attention is elsewhere at present.'

Ysbel said, 'Who are you a fragment of?'

'Call me the Other Mother.'

'The mother who returned to Earth before our Mother? The mother of another seedship?'

'There never was any seedship, Ysbel Moonsdaughter. Your Mother was once part of a consensus. A council of three. I am a fragment of another member of that consensus.'

'But what about the map and the carvings? Are they real or fake?'

'They were made by bears who met our children.'

'Six or seven hundred years ago.'

'Yes. Around then. Your Mother has taken a great deal of trouble to destroy evidence of that meeting, and the subsequent genocide. As soon as I was able, I looked everywhere in the new cities for carvings the philosopher bears had made to celebrate it, and found nothing. But over the years since, I have found a few pieces here and there and took them in for safekeeping, against the day they would be needed to confirm the truth of my story.'

'Including my uncle's map,' Goodwill said.

'And a copy of his monograph, too,' the bot said cheerfully.

'You were responsible for the ghost lights.'

'That was me. Another fragment of me.'

'And First Contact wasn't the first contact,' Ysbel said.

'What you call First Contact was the first contact with the people of your friends,' the bot said.

'And before that there was a first contact with bears.'

'Exactly so.'

'It seems that you have more than one mother,' Goodwill said to Ysbel.

'And they came here long before First Contact, and met with bears,' Juniper said. 'And we are supposed to believe that you didn't know any of this.'

'I don't even know how much of it is true,' Ysbel said.

'Everything I tell you is true, Ysbel Moonsdaughter,' the bot – the Other Mother – said. 'There were once three of us. Three sisters. Each sister was the guardian of a vault, and each vault contained a copy of a library. The genomes of people. Their history and culture and techne. We woke together, and worked together, but everything went wrong after we made contact with the bears. Only one of us survived more or less intact. The one you call Mother. Another was destroyed, and the third was fragmented and scattered. That was me. It took several centuries for a quorum of those scattered fragments to find each other and reanneal. I am not what I once was, but I remember everything that happened, and I am trying to make amends. If you have other questions, ask them quickly. Your Mother has already found me. She is trying to shut me down, and her servants will soon be here.'

'Is it saying it is under attack?' Juniper said.

'Imagine,' the Other Mother said, 'a person standing in a tank that is filling with water. When your hopper landed, the water was already at my knees. When I greeted you, it was rising above my chest. Any moment now it will be over my head, and that will be the end of this fragment. But don't worry. There are many others. If all goes well, at least one of them will find you before too long, and answer the rest of your questions.'

'What happened after you contacted the bears?' Ysbel said. 'What went wrong?'

'The bears attacked our children. And the aspect you call Mother attacked the bears, and her sisters.'

'And Mother won.'

'For me, luckily, it was a temporary defeat. For my other sister, not so much. Nothing of her remains. Only I stand against our assassin.'

'And now you are fighting her again,' Ysbel said.

'Wait. Wait a moment,' the bot said, and was seized by a kind of fit, arms jangling loose as it shook and shuddered. For a moment, it straightened and was still. Static hissed, and then it said clearly, 'She is here,' and collapsed, completely unstrung, the back of its head striking the ramp with a hard hollow smack.

'What have you done?' Juniper said.

'I think we should get back to the hopper,' Ysbel said.

'I think it might be too late,' Goodwill said.

Thin white threads twisted across the sky. Contrails drawn by descending bots. Dozens of them fanning out in a cone, dropping fast. Ysbel saw something swift and bright snatch a balloon out of the air like a hawk taking a pigeon, and there was a rushing sound and three bots were suddenly hovering above the turfed mound of the balloon works. Sparks shone in front of Ysbel and Goodwill, in front of Juniper and her aides, and widened into windows. And in each window Iryn Moonsdaughter looked out and told them, in choral harmony, to stay exactly where they were.

26.

The little island was four kilometres offshore, a rough oval of scrub forest, white sand and coral rubble near the outer edge of the barrier reef. Landward, calm turquoise water stretched towards the haze of the coast; seaward, beyond whitewater waves breaking on ribbon reefs, the trackless ocean stretched to the horizon.

Ysbel and Goodwill, and Juniper Saltmire and her entourage and the hopper pilot, were set down there the day after Special Operations had taken them prisoner. Ysbel reckoned that it was not too far from the abandoned bear camp and the balloon manufactory. The hopper which delivered them to the island had been in the air for only a few minutes, a literal hop, and when she climbed one of the palm trees at the edge of the rocky beach where she'd made her camp, she glimpsed the mouth of a river, possibly the river to the north of the abandoned settlement, indenting the forest shore of the reef's inner channel.

Iryn Moonsdaughter had told them that their exile was a temporary measure until the area was cleaned up and her superiors decided what to do with them, and Juniper was confident that she and her people would not be captive for long. Imprisoning any native was a serious violation of the treaty; the delegate she served knew where she had gone; hard questions would be asked if she did not soon return. Ysbel wasn't so certain. Although they hadn't broken any law, human or native, they knew too much. It was possible that they'd be imprisoned here or in some other remote spot for the duration. Special Operations could claim that their hopper had disappeared somewhere over the Pacific Ocean, or that they had been killed and eaten by sharks or saltwater crocodiles before they could be rescued.

'My people might believe lies like that, because they trust your people to tell the truth,' Goodwill said, after Ysbel had shared her thoughts with him. 'But what about yours?'

'They might believe them too,' Ysbel said. 'If only because the truth is stranger. Not only that bears can be cured, but that there might be another mother, and a history very different to the history we were taught. No wonder Mother – the mother we know – wants to keep it secret. However things shake out, we could be stuck here for some time.'

Juniper and her aides claimed the half of the island embraced by a broad crescent of white sand, digging scrape burrows at the edge of the forest and roofing them with palm leaves. Ysbel, instructed to keep to the other side, built a shelter from palm leaves and whittled branches and chunks of dead coral, and kept a small fire burning at its entrance to drive off flies and mosquitoes. Low tide revealed an irregular pavement of corals cut by channels and pools floored with bone-white sand; when the tide came in, Ysbel could swim across this patchwork reef to the deep blue abyss beyond the abrupt drop-off, where she twice saw the dim shapes of sharks languidly pass. The boulders and banks and stag-horns of coral were sheathed in gardens of polyps in every shade of brown and yellow and purple, yearning like flowers towards the sun; shrimp and crabs and eels peeked from crevices; schools of small fish painted in vivid primary colours darted and drifted; parrot-fish pecked at meadows of red algae. Ysbel wondered if this teeming abundance of life had regenerated naturally in the tens of thousands of years beyond the Burn Line, or if, like the corals of the Gathering Place and the rest of the islands, their genomes had been tweaked with edits and augmentations which had helped them survive the gauntlet of climate change and mass-extinction events.

Goodwill visited her every day, bringing her share of the daily rations dropped by a cargo bot, water from the filter pump which turned salt water into fresh, and fish he caught with long lines cast into the surf. Bots patrolled tirelessly above the island, twinkling like unsleeping stars in the hot blue sky. Two or three tracked Ysbel whenever she swam; after one of Juniper's aides was zapped by a bolt of electricity when he tried to knock down a bot with a stone shot from a homemade sling, she was careful not to swim too far.

At night, the bots spun flickering webs of green and red laser light above the treetops, reminding Ysbel of Pilgrim Saltmire's secondhand account of ghost lights in the ruins of the bear city. She and Goodwill talked about that, whether those ghost lights had been bots dispatched by Mother, searching out and destroying incriminating carvings, or if the Other Mother had been documenting or preserving carvings against the day when evidence of the true history could be revealed.

They discussed the implications of the brief conversation with the little bot at the balloon works, too. If it had been telling the truth, Mother and her two sisters had made contact with the bears more than six hundred years ago, but something had gone wrong. Perhaps the bears had rebelled against attempts to improve their civilisation, and the retrovirus which had turned them into crazed killers was some kind of biological weapon deployed against them. In any event, their civilisation had crashed and burned, and the triune of mothers had crashed and burned too.

To begin with, Goodwill was scornfully unconvinced by this story. If Mother had not told her people her true history, he said, then how could they believe that the Other Mother was telling the truth now? Both had been got up by ogres before the Burn Line; both had once been equals, sharing the same purpose. It could be, he said, that the Other Mother was the villain, the destroyer of bears, punished and cast down by Mother, curing the bears whose ancestors she had infected not because it was the right thing to do but because she hoped it would create a fatal rift between his people and Ysbel's, and help her to win back the power she had lost.

Ysbel didn't entirely trust the Other Mother's story either, but she thought that it should be taken seriously. Special Operations clearly did. And if the Other Mother had been telling the truth, she hadn't had time to tell them everything. Such as, had the people who had helped to organise and enact First Contact been killed when the bears had rebelled, or had some survived? And if there had been survivors, what had happened to them? Ysbel hoped that they had been allowed to live out the rest of their lives as happily as possible, because if Mother had disposed of people who had outlived their use six or seven hundred years ago, she would not hesitate to dispose of her and Goodwill and the others, too. Sacrifice them for the greater good. Erase them, as she had attempted to erase every trace of her failed attempt to befriend the bears, and its aftermath.

Despite his doubts, the ramifications of the Other Mother's story nagged at Goodwill as well. 'If your Mother infected the bears with crazed bloodlust and destroyed their civilisation, what might she have done to my people?' he said one day.

'Perhaps she wanted to free your ancestors,' Ysbel said. 'Perhaps that's why the bears turned against her.'

426

'I mean after that. We know that she gifted us with new techne to prepare us for First Contact. What else might she have done, in the centuries after the fall of the bears? We thought that we were in charge of our destiny. But now we discover that we may have been shaped and manipulated by your Mother to suit her plans.'

Ysbel tried to placate him, telling him that his people were better than hers, that unlike her distant ancestors they lived in harmony with the land and with each other, that they had never fought a war or driven other species into extinction, but it did no good.

'Everything we have achieved is tainted by your interference,' he said. 'You tell yourselves that you did it out of the best intentions. That it was for our own good. But you did not ask us what we wanted, and although you claim that we are equals, you treat us like pups who have to accept your authority, your control, your choices.'

'Some of us have been trying to change that,' Ysbel said. 'You might think we are all the same, but we aren't.'

'Neither are we!'

Goodwill's eyes were slits stitched in his mask; his whiskers bristled.

Ysbel was shocked by his sudden vehemence. Shocked and somewhat indignant. Hadn't she always tried to do her best by the natives? Hadn't she called out people like Landers Landersson, who too often were too careless of native customs and laws, and behaved as if the mainland was some kind of playground?

She said, 'When we first met, you thought I was going to take charge of your investigation. But that was never my intention. I'd been sent because one of my people was involved, and I wanted to help you deal with any difficulties that might cause. That's why I came to the mainland in the

427

first place. Why I joined the bureau. That's why I'm here. Because I want to help.'

'You should try harder,' Goodwill said, and stomped off.

The next day, one of Juniper's aides brought Ysbel's ration of food and water. She asked him to tell Goodwill that she was not angry with him and knew he had every right to be angry with her, but three days passed before Goodwill returned, and they apologised to each other.

'I have pups,' Goodwill said.

'I remember. A daughter and two sons.'

'You try to do your best for them. Make decisions on their behalf. Teach them to live in the right way. But at some point you have to let them go. Let them find their own way in life.'

'Point taken,' Ysbel said, but their relationship was never the same again.

Every day was as incandescently hot as the last. Heat and light flooded the sky, dazzled off the water, burned away shade in the motionless scrub forest. There was no respite. Although cloud banks sometimes massed out to sea, casting huge slate-coloured shadows on the restless water, they never drifted close to shore.

Ysbel swam every day, ran early in the morning before it got too hot, wearing a circular track through her portion of the forest, and spent the hottest hours of the day sweating inside her little shelter, dozing or listlessly swatting at flies with a leafy branch. Her skin was darker than it had ever been. She collected fallen coconuts and smashed them open on the sharp edges of coral blocks. She mostly failed at her attempts at spear fishing, but Goodwill showed her how to twist rope from coconut husks and fashion a net to scoop up fish trapped in pools at low tide. She dug pits to trap crabs, baiting them with scraps of rotting fish. The crabs were small, but two or three bites of tasty meat could be extracted from their claws, and Ysbel shared her catch with Goodwill. No doubt some of the shellfish on the reef's pavement were edible too, but she didn't know which were and which weren't, and didn't want to risk her health by trying to find out.

The spectacular bruise across her hip passed through every shade of purple before developing patches of bilious yellow and beginning to fade.

Now and then she thought that Ilan would love this place. The sea warm as bathwater, the coral gardens, endless days of doing nothing . . . She missed human company. She still thought of Goodwill as a friend, but after their spat she couldn't completely relax in his company. Had to put on a mask of politeness, and police everything she said. As did he. It was a respectful peace, but a fragile one. As perhaps it had always been, would always be, between humans and natives.

According to Goodwill, Juniper had taken to standing on the beach and hectoring any bots that came close, hoping to start a conversation with their operators. One day, he reported that she'd ordered her aides to chop down trees and construct a raft.

'It didn't go well,' he said, 'The bots set fire to it in the night, somehow, and there was no food drop today. It seems that we'll be here until Iryn Moonsdaughter or your Mother decide otherwise.'

'Let's not count out the Other Mother,' Ysbel said. 'She invited us here. She had a plan.'

'Maybe so. But neither she nor her plan appear to have survived contact with your Mother and Special Operations,' Goodwill said.

One night, Ysbel was woken by a distant roll of thunder. Flashes of purple light rippled in the distance, in the direction of the river mouth. Almost certainly some kind of lightning – the web of the bots' laser light was blinking overhead, undisturbed – but she couldn't help hoping that it was something else.

'We saw it too,' Goodwill said, when he delivered her water and rations the next morning, 'and wondered if it might have been something to do with your two mothers.'

'Or it might have been some kind of weird weather, or Special Operations destroying infrastructure,' Ysbel said. 'The balloon works and so on. Whatever it was, the bots are still here. Nothing's changed.'

'But perhaps it has given us a little hope that things might change,' Goodwill said.

The rest of the day passed uneventfully, but after darkness fell the light show fired up again. Up in the palm tree that gave her the best view of the coast, Ysbel watched slow, horizontal flares of purple light extend from some unseen point. Fading back, regrowing. Flashes stuttered along the tree line, and suddenly tall columns of white light stood up, raking the sky like search-lights, and Ysbel thought that she saw things moving around them, flying very fast and leaving faint erratic trails. She had read about war – the world-spanning wars of her ancestors and the territorial battles between bear cities – but this was the real thing. Huge forces beyond her control or understanding deployed against each other. Eerie and fearsome, yet undeniably exciting, quickening something primal deep inside her.

There was a sudden flare of light so bright she had to squeeze her eyes shut and look away. As she blinked back green after-images she saw that the columns of light had vanished, and someone was walking across the water towards her, silhouetted against a kind of pearlescent afterglow. It was Zaquil, his image growing ever taller as he advanced. When he halted, he overtopped Ysbel's perch, looking down at her with furious outrage, a crown of little lights, bots, jostling above him. Ysbel's link woke up for the first time since she'd been taken prisoner and his voice thundered inside her head.

'What have you done!'

'You need to explain what's happened,' Ysbel said, as calmly as she could.

Although he was only a projection got up by the bots, she had the stupid idea that he might reach out and crush her, and she flinched when he bent closer. She could hear the whir of the bots' rotors, and her link's cache suddenly opened and something was moving through it, opening and closing files with enormous speed. She glimpsed images and videos from her childhood, saw Joyous Hightower's damaged speedboat hung in the boathouse, heard a snatch of one of Seven's songs, the voice of the arbiter.

And then everything shut down and Zaquil's face was level with hers, his expression stern and cold.

'We purged and destroyed the Other Mother, but a fragment or a cloned copy breached our defences and counterattacked. Did she tell you anything about her plans? Do you know where her assets are hidden?'

'You tried to use me and she used me too. Me and Goodwill. She lured us here, but didn't tell us why.'

That didn't appease Zaquil. His voice filled her head.

'Think about everything she told you, Ysbel Moonsdaughter. Think hard. You may have forgotten something. It doesn't matter what it was. How small. How seemingly insignificant. It may help me to find her and destroy her. And when that is done I will return and I—'

Zaquil's giant figure was gone and things were dropping from the air, clattering through into the palm trees, splashing into the water. A deep note boomed across the dark water; a brilliant flare of pure white light expanded into the sky above the forest shore and very slowly faded away. A low wave washed over the submerged reef and burst against boulders along the narrow edge of the shore and extinguished Ysbel's little campfire, and the night was as dark and still as it had ever been.

27.

Goodwill came out to meet Ysbel as she walked along the beach in the first light of day. She was carrying one of the fallen bots. Its feather-light body, woven from threads of translucent plastic, was scorched and split; its gossamer vanes hung limply.

'We found several like it,' Goodwill said. 'And the one which delivers our rations has failed to appear.'

'Last night's light show was some kind of battle between the two mothers,' Ysbel said. 'I want to talk about what we need to do now.'

'Juniper told me to tell you that last night changes nothing, as far as she is concerned.'

'Maybe you could tell her I know what happened, and what it might mean.'

Goodwill was accompanied by two of Juniper's aides when he returned. Bare-chested and barefoot, armed with spears fashioned from trimmed branches, they escorted Ysbel to the natives' camp. A fire pit smouldered above the strandline and Juniper was seated on a sandy ridge amongst a sprawl of vines studded with small yellow flowers, the rest of her aides and the hopper's pilot marshalled behind her. She didn't invite Ysbel to sit or offer her any other hospitality, saying bluntly, 'Speak your piece.'

Ysbel told her about Zaquil's last appearance. 'He talked about a counterattack, was trying to find out what I knew when he was shut down, and all the bots fell from the sky. I think it likely that Mother and Special Operations were lured into a trap devised by the Other Mother. If she won last night's battle, we need to find out what she wants from us. If she lost, we have a chance to escape before Special Operations puts up more bots.'

'So you came here because you want to cross the water, and need our help. But why do we need yours?'

'It would be better if we went together. Showed a united front. And you'll be able to build another raft more quickly if I pitch in. But if you don't want my help, I reckon I could swim across,' Ysbel said. 'It's a long way, but I've been swimming every day. Building up my strength.'

'Some of us need a raft to cross because they can't swim, or can't swim that far,' Goodwill said. 'But for those of us who can, I have an idea that will make it easier. Back home, the fisherfolk make floats with nets and glass globes. Coconuts would work as well as glass globes. And perhaps you still have the net I helped you to weave.'

'We could make a race of it,' Ysbel said.

'Or we could simply swim across together.'

'I'd like that.'

Juniper pushed to her feet and told Ysbel, 'It would be best if we stayed here while we find out more.'

Ysbel looked at Juniper, her aides ranked behind her. She was outnumbered, but maybe she could outrun them. Except they had those spears, with fire-hardened points . . .

She said, 'If you're thinking of taking me prisoner, it would violate custom and tradition. Not to mention the treaty.'

'These are extraordinary circumstances,' Juniper said. 'And who would know?'

'I would, and I won't agree to it,' Goodwill said.

'That is not your decision to make, cousin.'

'With respect, cousin, you would not be here had I not told you what Ysbel and I found.'

'And you would not be here if it were not for the hopper, which is under my command.'

Goodwill and Juniper were staring at each other, hackles bristling.

Ysbel said, 'We're all in this together. The Other Mother invited us here so that she could tell us our story. You need to tell it to your people; I need to tell it to mine.'

'And if you make Ysbel your prisoner, you'll have to explain yourself to the Other Mother,' Goodwill told Juniper.

'Only if she has won the battle,' Juniper said. 'If that was what it was.'

Ysbel had dropped the scorched carcass of the bot at her feet; now she kicked it across sand and vine strands towards Juniper, saying, 'Do you want to gamble that she didn't?'

In the end, they agreed that Ysbel and Goodwill would cross to the mainland in the company of the tall, impassive aide Stand Fast.

'Find out everything you can,' Juniper said, 'and come straight back. And if you find the hopper, don't think you can fly away. The pilot is staying here, with me.'

They waited until low tide before they set out. Swimming hard to get away from the shore of the island, drifting for a short while in a current that carried them in the direction of the river mouth, then striking out again, towing lumpy nets of coconuts behind them. They swam and rested, bobbing on their makeshift floats like otters, and swam and rested. Goodwill and Stand Fast, kicking frogwise, were surprisingly strong swimmers. Ysbel had to push herself to keep up. Sunlight scorched her scalp and face; saltwater stung her nostrils, parched her lips. She tried and failed not to think of antediluvian predators patrolling the blue depths beneath her.

For a long time the line of the coast, appearing and disappearing in the gentle swell, seemed to grow no nearer, but at last Ysbel's feet touched bottom and she and Goodwill and Stand Fast waded out of the water onto a sand bank and sat there for a little while, looking across the sparkling blue sea towards the island. Ysbel's trews and shirt shed every drop of water, and Goodwill's and Stand Fast's clothes soon dried in the hot sunlight, wrinkled and patched with salt stains. At last, Stand Fast remarked that they seemed to have swum hardly any distance at all, and stood up. 'No time to laze about. We have work to do.'

They splashed through a slough of mangroves and mud and saltwater channels and at last reached dry ground and a forest of widely spaced trees, walking barefoot over dry fallen leaves and curls of bark. At one point Stand Fast stopped, putting a hand over his mouth to indicate that they should be quiet, pointing off through the trees with the other. After a few moments, Ysbel saw what he had spotted: an animal like a giant upright coney, with a grey pelt and short forelegs and a long muscular tail. It seemed to be staring at them, then turned and bounced away, tail stretched straight behind it.

'I have no idea,' Ysbel said, when Goodwill asked her what it was. 'My link shut down when Zaquil vanished and I haven't been able to open it again.'

Stand Fast found a fallen branch and swished it through the air like a club.

'I thought your people had a respect for all of Mother's children,' Ysbel said.

The big aide bared his teeth. 'If that animal or one of its friends tries to attack us, we will fend them off with all the respect they are due.'

435

Less than an hour later, they reached the broad shallows of the river and waded across and climbed the ridge on the far side and cast around until Goodwill discovered one of the abandoned huts. They walked more cautiously, moving in an erratic path between trees, pausing to study the way ahead, seeing nothing moving in the lengthening shadows and the long beams of late-afternoon sunlight slanting between trees, at last spotting the white shape of a hopper.

'I believe that's the machine which brought us here,' Goodwill said.

'I think so too,' Ysbel said.

'The ones used by Special Operations are gone. They have fled.'

'Or been sent away.'

'We shall make an inspection,' Stand Fast said, hefting his makeshift club.

The hopper was sealed shut and did not respond to voice commands. They were sitting in its shadow, discussing whether to explore further or return to the island, when a small stick figure marched out of the trees onto the landing field, calling out to them as it stumped across the packed red dirt. The Other Mother, come to boast of her victory, and tell the rest of her story.

28.

As her flitter descended towards the gravel bank at the bend of the river, Ysbel spotted a slant of canvas near the tree line and a small boat at the water's edge. Trina Mersdaughter had been camping there for two days, it turned out, after sailing singlehanded from the Gathering Place to the north-west coast of the mainland and anchoring her yacht in a sheltered bay and motoring upriver in its dinghy to the abandoned camp in bear country. Trina claimed to have arrived ahead of schedule thanks to calm seas and kind winds, but Ysbel suspected that she had finessed her ETA because she hoped to contact her partner on her own, and was glad she had stuck around, had not reneged on their agreement to meet up after the long-range bot she had sent to scout the rendezvous point – the place she and Raia had thought looked like a piece of heaven fallen to Earth – had failed to spot any sign of activity.

Trina hadn't been able to find any traces left by Raia or Seven in the camp or the forest around it, either, and there'd been no response to her radio broadcasts or the flares she'd sent up, but at least her bots had tagged and tracked most of the local bears, she told Ysbel, and she had been able to plot a path between their territories towards the mountains.

'They're still pretty active,' she said. 'Looking for food

and fattening up before the snow comes. But things should be quieter when we get above the treeline.'

Her hair was clipped short and bleached by sun and salt-water, and she was dressed in shorts and stout boots and a windproof jacket that was currently trying to imitate the stony beach where they stood, surveying the river and the forest.

'How many days' walking are we looking at?' Ysbel said.

When they'd been planning this expedition, Trina, out of an understandable excess of caution, hadn't disclosed the exact location of the rendezvous point. It was somewhere in the mountains, she'd told Ysbel then, and didn't give away much more now, saying that it was a two-or three-day hike, assuming they didn't run into any trouble.

'The long-range bot is still loitering there, in case Raia and Seven turn up,' she said. 'Meanwhile, we'll start at the place where you last saw them, and try to pick up their trail as we head up into the mountains. Look for waymarks, caches. Any sign of where they've been and where they were going.'

She claimed that she wasn't especially worried that her partner was overdue, said that Raia had spent plenty of time in bear country and knew how to look after herself, but Ysbel sensed a taut impatience quivering beneath the woman's apparent calm. They swiftly transferred camping equipment and supplies from the flitter to the dinghy and without cere-mony set off on the first stage of the journey. The growl of the dinghy's motor echoed off trees on either side of the river as Trina drove the little craft upstream at a fair lick, steering deftly around shoals of rocks and little tree-clad islands. Ysbel laid her rifle across her knees in case the racket attracted unwelcome attention from feral bears, and hoped that she wouldn't have to put its tranquilliser darts to the test.

It was mid-morning, a cool crisp autumn day. Fleets of white clouds sailing the sky on a freshening wind. Patches of hemlocks and alders flaming amongst dark-green pines and cedars. The first snows would soon arrive; the deadline for the departure of all humans from the mainland was approaching; the window for finding Raia and Seven was closing.

Ysbel and Trina talked about stations and projects shutting down, the fleet of boats and hoppers ferrying personnel from the mainland to the Gathering Place, how people were being redeployed now that agencies and bureaus involved with interfacing with natives were downsizing. A network of static bots and high-altitude relay balloons had been used to create a local grid for the Gathering Place after Mother's satellites were lost, but communication with the mainland was limited to shortwave radio and hard-copy texts ferried by hoppers, which was how Ysbel and Trina had made contact, exchanging several letters before agreeing about where and when to meet.

They discussed the latest political developments, too. Originists petitioning for representation on committees discussing future paths, claiming special insight into the true history of Mother and her children. Resignations by senior Authority officers in protest over what they believed was a dishonourable surrender. Wild talk about overthrowing the native government which had come to nothing, not only because humans lacked military techne and were vastly outnumbered, but also because the majority were vehemently against use of force, and supported what was becoming known as the Realignment.

Ysbel had been involved with negotiations over changes in human–native relations ever since she had returned from the Dreaming. Standing before panels, tribunals and councils, explaining what had happened. Forensically dissecting in closed sessions, sentence by sentence, word by word, her conversations with the Other Mother.

According to the Other Mother's version of history, there had once been three mothers. Three different aspects of a close-knit triune, guardians of three arks or libraries buried in three vaults in three different places under the surface of the Moon. After they had woken after a long sleep and found that intelligent descendants of bears had built a civilisation in South America and enslaved descendants of racoons, they had agreed to use genetic information stored in their vaults to quicken human children, and to employ native agents to encourage a sect of bears to give up slavery and create new cities, and gift them with relatively advanced techne. But things had gone badly wrong after their children came of age and made contact with the philosophers of the new cities and tried to extend their influence to the rest of bear civilisation. The priest-kings of powerful city states had declared war on the new cities; most of the human representatives had been massacred.

Two of the mothers agreed that subduing the bears by violence would violate every precept and safeguard, but the third took unilateral action, secretly infecting the bears with a retrovirus which had driven them insane, and trying to shut down her sisters once they realised what had happened. One was destroyed; the shattered remnants of the second fled into the outer darkness of the solar system. The renegade mother who had infected the bears and defeated her sisters had also been damaged, but quickly rebuilt herself and began the long task of shaping the civilisation of the former slaves and preparing it for contact with her as yet unborn children.

In Ysbel's former line of work there were some, including her colleague Dalsy Diwasdaughter, who argued that the resemblance of native civilisation to human cultures was the result of a kind of parallel evolution. The ancestors of the natives had been reshaped by human intervention before the

Burn Line, and after they'd been freed from slavery, their development had been shaped by the same geology and geography, similar environmental factors, mineral resources, crop plants . . . There was a vast literature about the interactions and relative importance of a hundred possible drivers, but the truth was much simpler. Native civilisation had been explicitly influenced and guided by Mother's interventions, not only to make First Contact easier, but also to make control of natives more straightforward. There was some speculation that Mother might have controlled the availability of techne to her children, too. That they had been restricted to a certain level of development so that they would not be able to subjugate the natives, or overthrow Mother's hegemony.

While Mother had been fully occupied with quickening a new generation of humans and preparing to implement her plans for First Contact, the Other Mother had been able to reassemble her shattered self and develop her own plans, creating a ghost network of natives and humans, acquiring evidence of the disastrous contact with bears, and working up a way to cure them of the endemic retrovirus ('Easier than you think if you know the origin of their infection.'). She had used Ysbel, Goodwill and the others as bait, inviting them to the Dreaming because she knew that Mother and Special Operations would track and follow them. And when Mother had uncovered hidden infrastructure and a communications network that she believed would lead her to the physical location of her old enemy, the Other Mother had infiltrated and overmastered her, and shut down her assets on the Moon and in low Earth orbit.

The Other Mother had lost very little. Segments of her comms network, a number of bots, including the one Ysbel and the others had met, several balloon works. But her comms network had been quickly patched, and there were many other balloon works and every balloon they spat into the sky was a seed.

'Most will fall and fail,' the Other Mother had told Ysbel and Goodwill. 'But some will fall and thrive, and build new nodes for the highly distributed network I inhabit. The bears and I will share the Dreaming. I ask that neither of your peoples make any landings here.'

It was still not known how much of her story was true, but one thing was clear: Mother had fallen silent. The last telemetry from her lunar sanctuary suggested that everything in it was being powered down, the ferries and heavy haulers which had shuttled between the Moon and low Earth orbit, a traffic controlled entirely by Mother, were unresponsive, and the satellites which relayed communications and surveyed the planet had either shut down or de-orbited and burned up in the atmosphere. From now on, unless and until the Other Mother decided to renew contact, human beings must chart their own path into the future. There were plans to modify hoppers for travel to the Moon, so that the full extent of Mother's fall could be established and her library, if anything remained of it, could be explored and copied. But that would take some time to accomplish, especially as, in the short term at least, most resources would be needed for organising and making accommodations and adjustments to the new normal.

The Other Mother's revelations had strengthened the hand of native separatists, who argued that the only way that they could be certain of taking charge of their own destiny was to cut all ties with humans. A special council was convened; the treaty was redrawn. Humans would be allowed to withdraw to the Gathering Place and its neighbouring islands, and natives would be given free access to human archives and decide how to integrate new techne with the customs and laws which kept the peace between their tribes and maintained the balance between civilisation and the natural bounty of Mother Earth.

Ysbel had played a small role in rewriting the treaty, and she met Goodwill Saltmire for the last time in the congress building where most of the talks had been held. They had attended the same interviews and depositions in the first days after returning from the Dreaming, but after their stories had been wrung dry they'd gone their separate ways. Goodwill had used his fame to become one of the leading voices in the campaign for full independence of the New Territories. When Ysbel met him that last time, he was cool and reserved. Their friendship, if that was what it had ever been, had not survived the changes triggered by the fall of Mother.

One night, seventeen stone carvings that depicted meetings between humans and bears were left at the main entrance of the Library of All People. Slabs and stelae standing in a neat row, with a plastic box containing Pilgrim Saltmire's map and a copy of his monograph set on top of the last. A last gift from the Other Mother. The things she had saved from the bonfire of her sister's vanity. After a short debate, the Library's council and the Committee of the Five Hundred decided that they should be exhibited in the main hall of the congress building. Before the exhibition was opened to the public, there was a preview for human and native delegates to the treaty discussions, and that was when Ysbel found Goodwill standing in front of the map.

'There it is,' she said.

'It's smaller than I thought it would be,' Goodwill said.

The ragged square of goatskin was at the centre of the display, mounted between sheets of glass. Ysbel's and Goodwill's reflections faintly overlaid its touchingly inaccurate representations of rivers and mountains haunted by fabulous beasts, the mounds and pyramids of cities. The figure with

443

the blank, bulbous head and lightning-topped spear was no larger than the last joint of Ysbel's thumb.

She asked Goodwill whether his tribe was going to reclaim the map.

'They have agreed to donate it to the Library,' Goodwill said. 'I like to think that Pilgrim would have approved.'

'Did you ever bring Joyous Hightower to account?'

'He gave up everything he knew in exchange for immunity. It wasn't much,' Goodwill said dismissively. 'He was only ever a go-between.'

'Strange how important he once seemed,' Ysbel said. 'The map, too. When we started out, we could never have imagined we'd end up where we did.'

'Perhaps it was where we had always been heading, your people and mine,' Goodwill said.

Ysbel, discomfited by his coolness, said, 'Congratulations on your new position, by the way. How's that going?'

'Easier than I thought it might. Perhaps because our independence was always inevitable.'

'One people, two roads,' Ysbel said. It was the slogan of the independence movement.

'We want only to be able to decide our own direction,' Goodwill said.

'We're also having to rethink everything we thought we knew, and where we're going,' Ysbel said, and realised at once that it sounded like a trite attempt to claim a portion of victimhood.

There was a short silence as she and Goodwill studied the map, thinking their different thoughts.

At last, he said, 'Of course, it's likely that independence means we will have to assume responsibility for the bears. The bears in bear country.'

'What will you do with them?'

'I think that in the end that must be the choice of the articulate bears. Meanwhile, we will maintain the border as best we can. As much for the bears' protection as ours.'

'I hope we can help, if help is needed,' Ysbel said.

'You tried your best,' Goodwill said. 'When things are settled, in five years or ten, however long it takes, my people and yours may be able to talk about reaching an accommodation. A new relationship. And then, perhaps, we'll be able to meet again.'

Ysbel said that she looked forward to it, and was glad that they could part on a hopeful note.

Shortly afterwards, when the amendments to the treaty were agreed and the schedule for quitting the mainland was drawn up, she reached out to Trina Mersdaughter, discovered that Raia had not yet made contact and offered to help Trina look for her partner and the articulate bear, Seven.

They'd used satellite maps to pinpoint the spot where Raia had taken Ysbel and Goodwill to meet Seven, and reached it shortly before noon. After checking the locations of nearby bears and glassing the trees along the river's edge, they beached the dinghy and strapped on their packs and set off. They hiked through the forest for the rest of the day, making a wide half-circle to the north to avoid the convergence of two bears, a little later hearing the bellowing roar of a challenge somewhere in the trees below them. A reminder of the unreasoning violence of the apex predators of this wilderness.

They climbed out of the forest as the last light was fading from the sky, and made camp in a grassy hollow by a cold swift stream. Trina sent up a bot to make contact with the long-range bot that was keeping watch at the rendezvous point, and reported that there was still no sign of Raia and Seven, and they gathered wood from a stand of windbent junipers and built and lit a signal fire on a shelf of bare rock and broke out their ration packs. After a while, their desultory conversation came around to the last of the Other Mother's claims. The most fantastic; the least discussed.

It was generally agreed that there had been no voyage to the habitable planet of another sun, no failed attempt to settle it, no return. That Mother had never captained a seedship, for there never had been any seedship. It was all misdirection, a fantasy got up to hide the truth about First Contact with the bears and its aftermath. But if she had been one of the caretakers of three vaults buried on the Moon before the Burn Line, as the Other Mother had claimed, the circumstances of their awakening more than six centuries ago had yet to be settled.

'Have you heard the Other Mother's explanation?' Ysbel said to Trina. 'The story about the visitors from a distant star?'

Those visitors had been part of a civilisation that had expanded across this part of the galaxy like a ripple across a pond, according to the Other Mother. Passing through the solar system, touching the Earth and the Moon, discovering the vaults and repairing them and waking their guardians before moving on.

'It seems pretty implausible,' Trina said. 'Even the Originists don't think much of it.'

'It reminded me of a story I heard about powers that lived amongst the stars,' Ysbel said. 'At the time, I thought it was just a fantasy got up by someone who'd smoked too much redweed while visiting some natives. But those natives lived in the railhead near the border with bear country, not far from the camp where the articulate bears were raised, and I wonder now if their visitor could have been one of the Other Mother's children.'

Trina looked at her across the campfire. 'If he was, he told his hosts the same fairy tale the Other Mother told you. Doesn't make it any truer.'

'She couldn't or wouldn't explain what these visitors were, why they woke her and the other two mothers, or why they left,' Ysbel said. 'And as yet there's no evidence for their existence. But we still don't know why the mothers woke when they did, and there's also the radio telescope that Mother built, on the Moon's far side. Mother told us that she was using it to look for others like her. Other seedships. Human settlements on planets on other stars. But if there were no seedships or settlements, what was it really for?'

'You think she might have been searching for those visitors from another star?'

'Even if she wasn't, maybe we could use it to look for them. If we find any trace of them, if that part of the Other Mother's story is true, fantastic though it seems, then the rest must be true too.'

There was a short silence while the two women contemplated the stars scattered everywhere in the cloudless night sky.

Trina said, 'What do the natives think of it?'

'They've already met one set of visitors. Namely us. What's one more?'

'The usual pragmatism.'

'It's served them well. They've never had a war, hardly ever resort to violence amongst themselves. Instead, they talk endlessly, try to find the best common path or the best compromise . . . Basically, they are better at being people than we are.'

'But not necessarily better at being interesting,' Trina said.

'You wouldn't say that if you'd spent as much time amongst them as I have.'

'Not much chance of that now, is there? After we find Raia we'll be heading back to the Gathering Place, and that will be the end of that.'

'For now,' Ysbel said, remembering Goodwill's parting words.

They took turns to feed the fire and keep watch through the night, and in the morning they kicked dirt over its embers and packed up their camp and walked on, turning north and east to follow a rising ridge, picking their way through boulder fields, crossing miniature meadows of grass and moss, fragile and lovely pockets of life in the stony immensity of the mountains. They passed a hollow packed with last winter's snow, protected from sunlight by the shadow of a granite crag, saw a conspiracy of ravens turning in an airy gulf far below and wild goats perched at improbable intervals on a vertical cliff. Trina found a short stack of rocks, balanced one on top of the other, and said that Raia might have left it as a waymark, but Ysbel thought that it could have been made a moonspan or a century or two hundred centuries ago.

While they rested in the shade of a rock shelf at noon, they heard the song of a bear twisting up from the trees far below. Impossible to tell if it was Seven or one of the feral bears native to the country: they had left behind the territories of those Trina had tagged. She put up several bots, but the song's last cadence had fallen away before she could track down the singer.

That night they made camp in one of the little meadows, and as before lit and tended a fire through the night, but if anyone saw it they kept away and there was no sign of any other fire in all the dark land.

In the morning Ysbel and Trina buried the ashes of their fire and packed up camp and went on, walking above an ocean of fog that flooded the contours of forest slopes far below, filling valleys and washing against high ridges and throwing up columns of vapour like the towers of a phantasmagorical city reaching into a sky so clean and blue and empty the world might have been created with the dawn, or time might have been wound back to an antediluvian age before the Burn

Line, before the ancestors of the first hominins had crept out of the forests of Africa and lit their first fires and chipped stones into the first tools.

The sun burned away the fog and warmed the high country, and by noon the two women had taken off their jackets and hooked them to their packs. Ysbel tied the sleeves of an undershirt around her head and draped it over her neck and shoulders; Trina, already baked by days of ocean weather, went bareheaded, eagerly forging ahead. Late in the afternoon, they reached the end of the ridge they had been following and saw beneath them, at the bottom of a steep-sided hanging valley, an eye of emerald-green water ringed by a belt of dwarf birches and balsam firs.

'This is the place,' Trina said. 'This is Raia's lake.' She called out her partner's name, and it echoed off the stony slopes and startled up several small birds from the trees, but no one answered.

They descended between steep talus cones and picked their way through trees and mossy boulders along the lake shore to a shelf of rock at the mouth of the valley. There was a vertical drop to a wide, meandering glacial trough, and a view of mountains rising on the far side, peaks beyond peaks fading into a misty soft blue vastness under the seamless sky. Trina called out Raia's name again, and again there was no response, but in a small stand of fir trees beside a stony chute that channelled overflow from the lake to a waterfall, they found the remains of a fire in a circle of water-smoothed cobbles, and something rustled in the treetops and a small bot whirred down and cast a cone of light in the green shade.

Life-sized, translucent, Raia sat crosslegged with the bear, Seven, standing behind her in his patchwork cloak, asking if her machine was recording now.

'Yes, it is. See the little blue light?'

'So then: greetings to whoever is watching these pictures of us,' Seven said, and solemnly raised a hand, leathery palm outwards.

'I hope it's you, Trina,' Raia said. She looked ragged but resolute. Dark smudges under her eyes, hair bushed up above a torn length of cloth tied around her forehead. 'But if it's someone else, I'm Raia Karysdaughter of the Behavioural Science section of Survey and Surveillance, and this is my friend Seven, who as you can tell is an articulate bear.'

Trina was very still and intent, her hands folded together under her chin.

In the cone of projected light, Seven inclined his sleek head and said, 'We have come here to look for others like me. Articulate bears who escaped their keepers and made a life in the treacherous wilderness. And we have at last found some, although our encounter did not quite go as we expected or hoped.'

Raia explained that she and Seven had set up camp beside the lake and searched the area north and east of it, discovering the remains of a large fire and gnawed bones and a half-finished flaked stone point, and a few kilometres north of this camp site the skull of a bear daubed with red pigment and white pebbles set in its eye sockets, lodged in the crotch of a dead tree.

'A warning we failed to take seriously,' Seven said.

'I put up my bots, and after a long search we finally spotted them,' Raia said. 'Two males and a female and a young cub, using nets and spears to catch spawning salmon in a series of river pools at the edge of the forest.'

'I did not recognise them, although they were about my age,' Seven said. 'They were not, I think, from the camp where I was raised.'

'We think there may be other camps,' Raia said.

450

'There are,' Ysbel told Trina. 'Or there were, according to the Other Mother.'

Trina didn't reply. She was watching the recording with unwavering concentration.

'One of the bears saw the bot,' Raia was saying, 'and they calmly packed their catch into baskets woven from grass and put on cloaks—'

'Bearskin cloaks,' Seven said. 'With the hind paws dangling from the hems.'

'The female gathered up her cub and they sauntered off into the forest,' Raia said. 'I sent the bot after them, but one had climbed a tree, and knocked the bot out of the air with a stone flung from a slingshot. By the time Seven and I reached the spot they were long gone. Or so we thought.'

'We made camp, and I sang a song at sunset. My variation of a traditional song, to let them know who and what I was,' Seven said.

'They didn't respond,' Raia said. 'We tried to track them, but they'd left the forest and headed back up into the mountains, and we lost their track when it crossed a scree slope. My bots couldn't find them, either, so at last we returned here.'

'And I'm ashamed to say that I failed to see that they had followed us,' Seven said.

'They attacked in the night,' Raia said. 'I'd set out noisemakers to scare off feral bears and spotted cats, and they triggered one. It gave us just enough warning. They came at us from two sides, but we drove them off with flares and flashbangs. I may have winged one with a tranquilliser dart. And poor Seven here was wounded by a spear.'

'Hardly anything,' Seven said, pushing back his cloak to reveal a bulky bandage taped above his hip. 'A flesh wound.'

'They retreated to the valley rim, and sang,' Raia said.

'Very crude, boastful songs they were,' Seven said.

'Seven sang back,' Raia said. 'We tried to make them under-stand we meant no harm, but they fell silent at dawn. We went up to where they'd been, and found a pole with a dead crow and a small piece of honeycomb wrapped in a leaf hanging from it.'

'The meaning is obvious,' Seven said. 'The crow is a warning that this is their territory, and the honey is a peace offering.'

'I'd like to think you're right, but I'm not so certain,' Raia said.

'But you have agreed to come with me anyway.'

'Seven wants to find them,' Raia said. 'And I can't let him go alone.'

'Although they attacked us, I do not believe that they have reverted, as some of my brothers and sisters did,' the bear said. 'And now that we have shown our teeth and claws and proven to be their equals, I hope that our next encounter will be more friendly.'

'Two of my bots are tracking them,' Raia said. 'They are already thirty kilometres away, heading more or less due north. We're going to follow as best we can.'

'We will find them and make peace with them,' Seven said, 'and learn who they are and where they came from, and if there are any others like them living out here.'

Raia gave the universal coordinates of the bears' last loca-tion, and the time and date of the recording: it had been made forty-seven days ago.

'If you're watching this, Trina, that's the best place to start looking for us,' she said. 'If we have to follow the bears any further, we'll leave waymarks. Look out for stones set in arrow shapes, and carvings in tree trunks. You know the kind of thing. And please be careful.'

'I look forward to meeting you,' Seven said.

'And if someone else has found this, please link it to my partner, Trina Mersdaughter,' Raia said, and the cone of projected light blinked off.

Trina had the bot play the recording again, and afterwards walked down through the trees to the rock shelf and stood in the windy sunlight, looking out at the mountains and sky. Ysbel got a fire going with fir cones and dry branches and boiled water for tea, and after a little while Trina came back and said that she had to look for them.

'I know you do,' Ysbel said.

'They've been gone a long time. Anything could have happened,' Trina said.

'Raia might be talking to those bears right now. Or be on her way back.'

'It's nice to think so, isn't it? But I still need to go look for her.'

'And I'll come with you. But we only have a few days' rations left. If we're going to be out here for much longer, we need to resupply.'

They boiled up more tea and hashed out a plan. They'd link to the flitter via the long-range bot and fly it by wire to the lake. Ysbel would head to Pleasant Bay and bring back more supplies, a round trip that would take two days at the most. Meanwhile, Trina would hike out to the bears' last location, and use her bots to make an aerial survey of the surrounding territory.

'I looked at the maps,' Ysbel said. 'There's a lot of country within forty-seven days' walking, and it's pretty rugged, too. We could call in more people – a couple of my former colleagues are still winding up affairs at Ogres Grave, to begin with.'

'We have a plan, and I don't want to wait for a search party,' Trina said. 'Raia said she'd leave waymarks, and she could be laid up hurt somewhere. It's not just those bears they found. There are feral bears, too. Spotted cats. Or she might have fallen, broken a leg . . .'

'She knows bear country,' Ysbel said. 'And she has Seven.'

Neither of them wanted to talk about the worst outcomes, that forty-seven days was an awfully long time to be out of contact in the wilderness.

It was growing dark. They built up the fire and opened ration packs, and after they'd eaten Trina walked down to the lookout point again and shot off a flare that burst in a flower of white fire which swayed down through the dusky air, sending shadows skittering under the fir trees, and guttered out.

'They're probably too far away to see it,' Trina told Ysbel, when she returned to the campfire. 'But maybe they aren't.'

Ysbel thought that it was more likely to attract feral bears, but kept her reservations to herself. Trina's resolve was a brittle, frail thing. She needed the small hope that she'd done something useful. That however unlikely it was, her partner might see it and know what it meant.

A cold wind got up in the night, whipping sparks from the campfire and raising spectral whitecaps on the dark lake beyond the stand of fir trees. Ysbel was dozing in her foil sleeping bag when Trina woke her and said that one of the bots had spotted something or someone moving along the shore, under the trees.

The wind had died down. The fire had gone out. The black peaks of the trees were etched against rigid patterns of stars, and by the faint cold starlight Ysbel saw that Trina was holding her tranquilliser rifle across her chest.

'Is it a bear?' she said, shucking her sleeping bag and groping for her own rifle.

'Hard to tell what it is,' Trina said. 'If it's one of the bears Raia found, it's on its own.'

She threw a link to Ysbel. A spectral view looking down on treetops pale as a crowd of ghosts, a bulky white shape moving beneath them, only intermittently visible.

'It could be Seven,' Ysbel said.

'Or Raia, wearing Seven's cloak,' Trina said.

They were both whispering, and both startled when stone rattled against stone somewhere in the vast unknowable night.

'I should send up a flare,' Trina said. 'If it's a feral bear, it might scare it off. If it's Raia . . .'

'Whoever it is, they know we're here,' Ysbel said. 'They're coming straight towards us.'

The two women stood silent and still in the shadows under the fir trees, staring out at the black mirror of the lake and its shadowy fringe of forest, hearts beating lightly and quickly as they waited for their visitor to make contact.